John Lewis is a writer of short stories, novels and screenplays. He presently lives in Sydney with his wife and three children.

SAVAGE EXILE

JOHN LEWIS

MACMILLAN

For Wendy Green

First published 1996 by Pan Macmillan Australia, Sydney

First published in Great Britain 2002 by Pan Books
an imprint of Pan Macmillan Ltd
Pan Macmillan, 20 New Wharf Road, London N1 9RR
Basingstoke and Oxford
Associated companies throughout the world
www.panmacmillan.com

ISBN 0 330 40063 0

1 3 5 7 9 8 6 4 2

A CIP catalogue record for this book is available from
the British Library.

Printed and bound in Great Britain by
Mackays of Chatham plc, Chatham, Kent

ONE

Will Noling moved his head carefully and reached with the side of his face for the cool brush of at least one smooth plank in the deck on which he lay. All to no avail. It annoyed him that his one mobile protuberance, or at least the only one that at that moment he was confident he could safely control, the blunt but sensitive finger that was his left cheek, was again probing blindly into a mix of coarse sand and curls of rough-cut wood shavings and sawdust. So he lifted his face and tentatively touched it down again a handspan away. More grit and shavings! God save us all!

He opened his eyes, and as his flickering eyelashes caught the light from somewhere, he lay for a time watching it bombard the deck immediately in front of his nose with dancing spectrums. His surrounds then gradually came into focus and he saw that he was lying amidst shattered timbers and tangled set-lines. And as he lifted his gaze he realised that the fitful shadows that beat across him were caused by men and boys dashing past, some leaping into or scrambling from the hatchway beside him; marines with their rifles raised; messengers crouching beneath a hail of metal; powder monkeys hauling loaded canisters with their mouths opening and closing in time with the pounding of their feet. Some passed so close they were forced to step or jump over him, but all of them had their attention elsewhere. Not one of them so much as cast him a glance.

He carefully rolled on to his back and immediately found himself fighting a grating pain that might have been the twist of a boning knife working its way deep into his left shoulder. The effort left him drained, and once again he lay with his eyes clamped tightly shut.

Eventually the pain ebbed, soothed, he believed, by the familiar slow roll of the ship; and by being able to square his shoulders and spread the entire length of his body back against the deck so that his very core picked up the powerful pulse of the vessel, hammered into the hull by the tremble of the masts. When he opened his eyes he saw that the topgallants were gone and half the rigging had been blown away. Shot to pieces by the French, he decided. They usually shoot high. Loaded with chain. Double-shot, treble-shot.

His gaze stayed for a while with the transparent veils of thin blue smoke that were draped over the confusion of broken spars, tangled rigging and torn sailcloth that swayed precariously high above him. Fragmented shafts of light poked holes in the canopy creating an eerie impression that he was lying in the nave of a ruined Gothic cathedral looking up at what remained of the rib-vaulted ceiling.

How he could have fallen asleep amidst this frantic activity surging around him, and somehow ignore the brain-bruising thunder of several hundred cannon blasting away so close, was bewildering. He lowered his gaze. Here where the veils of drifting smoke were of various weights and hues, they were billowing and pluming left and right—forward, aft and athwartships— pierced by batteries of hurtling shot, chain, scraps of what was probably human anatomy, shattered timber, splinters of oak, and flashes of fiery gases.

He turned his head and looked directly aft. A short distance away a group of people were gathered around someone lying on the deck. Red jackets. Blue. Some were stooping over the fallen man; others were kneeling beside him; one was behind him, moving to cradle him.

Will turned away quickly and closed his eyes again. Fragments of events that might have been the ones that placed him in this situation were beginning to emerge from the reaches of his memory and align themselves in some semblance of order.

What was that signal? He winced with the effort of recall. 'England expects—expects—that every man will do his duty.' And as it was communicated to the men, the rigging shook with their roars of approval. And then again as it was passed further down their own line, muffled waves of cheering drifted back across the water from the following ships. God knows why, he thought. If we knew anything, we knew our duty. But despite this the fine hairs on the back of his neck had risen and his shoulders had trembled in the grip of an involuntary shudder. God save us all!

And earlier: 'The admiral says you're something of a shot, Noling; that you could knock the balls off a bilge rat at thirty paces.' This was the skipper himself, the owl in a cocked hat. 'When we break the enemy's line you can help protect him from the marksmen in their rigging. I don't want some pantsless Frenchie shooting a hole in him on this day of all days. Draw three muskets from the quartermaster gunner and select a spare boy from the after boarding party to keep them loaded and primed for you.'

So it was with mounting trepidation that he returned his gaze to the scene immediately aft of him.

'We're taking you to the cockpit,' said the owl, his voice thick with grief. 'You'll be more comfortable there.'

'Help cover my gongs, will you, Hardy. No sense in telling my brave fellows that I'm down.'

And then, as they lifted him: 'And look after young Noling over there. Took a nasty blow when that yard came down on top of him.'

So that's it. Will closed his eyes once again and tested the credibility of what he had just heard, feeling from within himself for the extent and nature of his injuries. It's true, he decided finally. Will Noling, twenty-two years old, pressed able seaman in His Majesty's Navy, reluctant defender of his motherland, on this twenty-first day of October, eighteen hundred and five, while somewhere off the Spanish coast south of Cadiz not far from a cape called Trafalgar, in Farmer Georgie's good ship *Victory*, was poleaxed by the main's topgallant yard. Or maybe the mizzen's. To confirm the results of his internal inspection, he carefully tested his limbs by moving them slightly.

Able Seaman Noling has perhaps escaped serious injury, he decided. His wounds seem to consist of no more than a possible broken collarbone, a dented head and a gashed arm. All of these injuries suffered while protecting his admiral from sniper fire. Badly, it seems.

So what did the man expect, striding about as if he were watching a review at Spithead when he knew their riggings were crammed with marksmen?

Without any warning his chest rose and fell with a heavy, spontaneous sigh and his eyelids batted, to no avail, against the flood of tears that suddenly welled beneath them. God save us all! He bit his lip and quickly turned his face away from the men who approached and knelt beside him.

'Jasus, Noling, what did you do t' your scone? Stick it in a barrel of raspberries? Here, Dingy, give us a hand. Gentle now. Watch 'is arm. You're a lucky prick, Noling. You've scored y'self some shoretime. Where do you hail from?'

'Lowfoley,' Will replied, closing his eyes as a wave of pain surged through him.

'Well, wherever that is, it's where you'll soon be headin'.' The speaker cringed as a blast of hot gases and smoke from behind him whipped his long hair around the sides of his face. 'If we all don't get blowed to kingdom-fockin'-come aforehand.'

The village of Lowfoley nestled against the southernmost extremity of a broad spur that reached out towards the coast from the low undulations of Hampshire's South Downs. The farmland beneath the village swept away to the sea in a series of flat expanses, divided one from the other by shallow indentations that marked the courses of narrow reed-choked marshes and back-waterways that drained into tidal flats bordering Southampton Water and the Solent.

Some two and a half years before the events at Trafalgar, on the outskirts of Lowfoley, a young couple in an uncharacteristically sombre mood were approaching two men displaying equally uncharacteristic joviality. It was a fairish day in May, with the lift of spring and the heady scent of the blossoms tempered by irregular chill bursts of wind from the west. The young couple were on foot. The men were in a four-wheeled chaise-cart. They were approaching each other from opposite directions along a lane lined on both sides by hawthorn hedgerows. A low rise kept them from seeing each other, and at the speed they were travelling they would probably meet at the crest.

The hedges were spattered with bursts of white blooms and the sides and middle of the lane were strewn with a carpet of colour. Brushing the base of the hedges, dandelions and knapweed sprouted in yellow and purple clumps over irregular beds of wild violets; in the centre of the lane, primroses and woundwort pushed through the mix of grasses that formed a broad green strip between the wheel tracks. The undulating drum of the bees at times caused the travellers to raise their voices.

For Will Noling and Jessica Glider, their low spirits were a result of Will having broached the possibility that he might have to seek work in Southampton.

For Sir Rory Fitzparsons, who was driving the two horses that were pulling the carriage, and his cousin Garth Barlester seated beside him, their ebullience was very much related to the amount of brandy that had been drained from the leather-encased flask Barlester was nursing on his lap.

It was fitting that this day's more pleasant ambience was interlaced with the hint of bitter weather.

'How long will you be gone?' Jessica asked. Her eyes were on the ground, the despondency that had earlier crept into her voice assuming an even more hollow ring; what might have been an echo bouncing off iron-grey images from a blacker day.

'Three days. Maybe four.'

'And what if they do offer you a job? What if they want you to start right away?'

'I doubt they'll not let me take a couple of days to collect my things.'

'And then what?' A spark of her more normal zest flared momentarily somewhere within her. She bit her lip. 'Off you'll go ne'er to return. What about us?'

'I'm doin' it for us, Jessie. Do you think I want to leave you? Even for a moment? I have to earn some money of my own.'

They remained silent until they had passed an area of the hedge that was crammed with unseen birds and a level of noise rising from the prickly refuge that would have defied any attempt to compete.

'Jim will pay you.'

'He can't pay me.'

'He owes you, Will.'

'The farm's fed me. It's been a roof.'

'You deserve more than food and a roof.' She turned away. 'It's not right. You've worked all these years for nought, and now your dad's passed on, Jim gets everythin'. It's not fair.'

'It's fair enough. Jim left school early so I could stay longer.'

'And what would have been the good of him stayin', may I ask?'

'He's a good fellow and you know it. And you like him well enough.' He cast her a glance. 'If I weren't around you'd be chasin' after him f'sure and certain.'

She lifted her chin. 'If you take off for Southampton and decide you'll stay there, I might still do that. Him and anyone else around here I might take a fancy to.'

She was a head shorter than Will, but that head was crowned with the same golden-red thatch. Hers was long and plumed in tight springing ringlets about her ears and cascaded well down her back, whereas his was short and, on this day, as usual, sprang in all directions above his ears, as if he had dipped it in a tub of water and allowed the wind to dry it. Even so, the hue, the curl and the texture suggested a common ancestor.

'You're a fallen woman, Jessica Glider. Nobody around here would have you.'

She kept her chin in the air and her eyes away from him. 'You might be surprised who'd be keen t' have me. Judgin' by the heads that turn when I walk by.'

'Well, maybe you could land someone like Gaunty Farlie or one of the other half-blind scrumpy guzzlers he hangs about with down at the Drake.'

Despite her mood, she could not prevent her face from being briefly illuminated by the beam of a smile that escaped before she could check the lift in her cheeks.

'But I doubt your chances of landin' a man of some standin' in the community,' said he. 'Someone such as myself.' He lifted his own chin.

'And what standin' have you got?'

'I'm a highly respected personage. Last Saturday at the market, Malachi Butler himself asked me what I thought of the bull he'd just bought. And Malachi isn't a man who'd waste questions on someone whose reply he wouldn't respect. And who is it old man Pillington asks to help out at the school each time he comes down too heavily with the pleurisy?'

'The only reason old man Pillington asks you to help out at the school is because he knows you won't ask for any payment. And the only reason Malachi Butler would ask you what you think of his prize bull is because he's probably heard all about you and is hopin' that his bull has similar inclinations to your own.'

He released an enthusiastic howl of delight followed by infectious peals of laughter that had Jessica again fighting vainly to stifle her own beams of amusement.

When they had both recovered they walked on in silence until he turned to her and said, 'Come on, Jessie, give me some support. I have to get a job. I don't have any alternative.'

She did not reply immediately and when she did she turned away from him slightly so that he could not see her face.

'You don't have to go to Southampton.'

When she turned to face him, he was so taken by the attractiveness of her earnest expression, and in particular by the swollen curve of her bottom lip, that he toyed with the idea of grabbing hold of her and kissing her. Prudently, he curbed this impulse and instead asked, 'What else can I do?'

'You should call in some of what is owing to you. From your brother. From old man Pillington, or whoever he gets his funding from—the mayor, the shire, the parish—and from all of the Malachi Butlers you've ever helped out in a crisis, or who think you might be worth askin' a question of. Surely someone around here would offer you payin' work if they knew you were lookin' for it.'

'I love you, Jessie Glider.' He placed an arm around her shoulders and squeezed her in an exaggerated gesture of reassurance.

She tried to shrug him off. 'I've seen the work they're doin' on that pier at Southampton. Backbreakin' work that nobody in their right mind would want.' She raised a hand to her face and with a finger pushed away a tear that was threatening to spill from one eye. 'If you don't die of ague, you'll be crushed to death.'

'I need the money, Jess. I need it for us.'

'You don't need to go to Southampton. Where nobody knows you. Where nobody owes you.

Where you might as well be Gaunty Farlie or any one of his mates from the Francis bloody Drake.'

They walked on again in silence. 'So you don't believe I have anything to show for my time around here?' said he at last, and turned and looked at her.

She met his gaze. Now that they were nearing the crest of the rise, behind his shoulder the sweep of the land towards the coast was visible above the hedges. And beyond the land, close to the horizon, there was a sudden tiny flash of white against the slate-grey of the sea. It caught her attention and her gaze shifted.

'What is it?' he asked, and looked back. From that point they were looking far out past the eastern edge of the Solent.

'Something white on the sea. But now it's gone.'

'Probably a ship turning.' He looked back.

Not that it had a direct bearing on the events occurring near Lowfoley that day, what she had glimpsed was a first-rate 100-gun ship of the line as it turned into the wind; a 38-year-old veteran of the American Revolutionary War that was testing its new fittings and rigging after extensive refit at Chatham. It was HMS *Victory*, presently en route to Portsmouth, and preparing for war.

'What were you saying?'

'I was goin' to say that I do have somethin' to show for my time around here.'

'What do you have?'

He pressed his teeth down on his bottom lip to

try and bite off a smile, and then suddenly reached out and, before she could step away, scooped her into his arms. 'I have Jessica Glider. That's what I have.'

'What are you doing?' she lurched and squealed as his fingers dug into her ribs.

He turned and began to run towards the crest. 'I have Jessica Glider,' he called out loudly. 'And I'm going to keep her.' A flock of blackbirds erupted from the hedge ahead of them and scattered across the fields.

Jessica repeatedly cried out for him to put her down, punctuating her demands with a mix of shrill squeals and shrieks of laughter. His strength gave out before he had travelled fifty yards. Just below the crest he slowed suddenly and staggered to the side of the lane. He sank to his knees on the grassy verge and released his burden. They were both lying where they had fallen, gasping for breath, their limbs entangled, when Sir Rory Fitzparsons and Garth Barlester topped the rise.

'Well, what in the bright blue blazes have we got here?' said Sir Rory, drawing rein. 'Fornication or ambushment?'

Will and Jessica quickly scrambled to their feet and brushed themselves down as they eyed the newcomers, Jessica with embarrassment, and Will with any uneasiness he had felt when the men first appeared snuffed out by Fitzparsons' words.

'No, no, no,' said Fitzparsons. 'We've got the fiery-haired twins of Lowfoley. William Noling for sure and certain. And the lovely Jessica Glider, if I'm not mistaken. What happened to you, you sweet young things? Were you knocked over by some careless fool in a runaway cart?'

He drove his horses closer. The mare on the offside was reluctant to approach the two humans that had risen mysteriously from the earth in front of her, so Fitzparsons struck her on the rump with his whip. When this had no effect he placed the fall high up between her rear legs and switched it backwards and forwards cruelly. She jumped a couple of times and then, with eyes flashing frightened-white, stepped out tentatively with her head slewed to one side watching the strange humans warily as she approached.

'You're still covered in dust there, young William,' said Fitzparsons as he brought the horses to a halt beside the young couple. 'You look like a poacher tha's been stuck down a badger's hole wrestlin' the tenant. There, tha's right, Jessie, give him a good paddlin'.' Jessica was using the flat of her hand to sweep some dried leaves and assorted small debris from the back of Will's shirt. 'Slap him hard as you like, girl. He's probably earned it, eh, lass?'

Sir Rory Fitzparsons, when standing, was below average height, legacy of a pair of shorter than average legs—shorter, knobblier and hairier than average, not that this was often evident to the populace at large—but when seated on a horse, or in this instance when perched and leaning forward

14

from the driver's seat of a two-horse carriage, he had the appearance of a much bigger man. The width of his shoulders, the length of his torso and the spread of his girth were contributing factors, as were the size and shape of his head. But the main cause of the deception was his neck, a swollen expanse of white flesh that extended over and beyond his collar in much the same manner as the crown of a loaf of bread when baking will balloon from a pan that has been overfilled with dough. At the moment he was moving his head from side to side slowly, as if this would give him a better appraisal of the state of the two people standing before him.

First the quieter horse on the near side, a gelding with the same glistening black coat as the mare, and then the mare herself, stretched out their necks and, pressing their soft muzzles through a lush bed of crimson valerian buds, began to pick on the sweet grasses growing close to the base of the hedge.

'I know wha's happened to you,' said Fitzparsons. 'Seein' 'tis Sunday. You were knocked over by the backwash of the devil himself racin' by escapin' from one of the right upstandin' Reverend Smith-Whistle's fire and brimstone sermons.' He chuckled and cast a wink at the man beside him. 'Not from the fire or the brimstone.' He belched loudly and from then on continued to punctuate his words with repeated belches. 'Tha's old Nick's home territory. Fire and brimstone. No, he wouldn't even be runnin' from Smith-Whistle's expulsion cries. His eviction notices. Get out, you evil creature! You Be-hellze-bub! No, that wouldn't worry old Nick. Tha's what he eats for breakfast. What old Nick'd be runnin' from would be the sheer plaguey boredom of the man. The sheer, awful, mind-dissolvin', soul-destroyin', arse-aching boredom.' The smooth white dough ballooning from the pan rim of his collar quivered in sympathy with the tremble of his lips.

'His name's Smith-Wilson,' said Will.

'What?'

'His name's Smith-Wilson. Reverend Smith-Wilson. You called him Smith-Whistle.'

Fitzparsons glared down at Will for a moment and then chuckled and turned to look at the man beside him again. 'What did he say?'

Barlester said nothing. His mouth remained drawn in a tight straight line beneath the long, aquiline curl of his nose. The image that remained with Will later was of his eyebrows, dark mirrored wings of a hawk or an owl thrown high to arrest its plummet from the heavens to seize a victim.

Fitzparsons turned back. 'If any man on God's earth knows your Reverend's name, then I knows it, Will'm. I went to school with the little prickle. I used to try and twist off his ears so often 'tis one of the wonders of this world that they're still stuck to the side of his head. And my mother—God rest her soul!—my mother dragged me to that rotten little church of his every Sunday, sometimes twice on Sunday. When I left school I thought I was shot of the prickle. But what does he do? He becomes a plaguey minister of religion and he gets himself assigned to my plaguey parish. Mine. And now I've inherited the most borin' little prickle I've ever met in my whole ffff ... (belch) ... my whole plaguey life ... (belch, cough, cough, jiggle) ... my whole plaguey life.' He shook his head. 'He might be Smith-Wilson to you, sweet William, but I know him for who he is. And he's a boring little farter who'll be Smith-Whistle to me till the day he dies. What do you say, Garth? You were there.'

Barlester still said nothing. He made no sign that he had even heard. His eyes, for what could be seen of them beneath his low, drooping lids, appeared to be on Jessica.

There may have been some discrepancy between Sir Rory Fitzparsons' apparent and actual size, but there was no doubt about the true size of the man sitting beside him. Garth Barlester was a big man, whether standing or seated or perched as he was now, seemingly uncomfortably, beside Fitzparsons, with inadequate room for any of him, but in particular his legs. His left one was stretched out clear of the carriage so that most of his massive boot sat dangerously close to the spokes of the near-side front wheel. The knee of the other was bent at an acute angle and swivelled across his body to keep it clear of his companion.

'These are two of my favourite people from lacklustre Lowfoley, Garth,' said Fitzparsons. 'They give the place a much needed lift. A burst of warmth. Look at them. Look at that hair. They're a couple of beacons in the mist.' He chuckled and rippling waves passed backwards and forwards through the dough. 'Soon as young William Noling here manages to scratch up enough Georgies to put down a payment on his own patch of land, I'll daresay we'll be hearing wedding bells drifting across the downs.'

'Well, we musn't keep you from wherever it is you're headin',' said Will, placing a hand behind Jessica and beginning to usher her past the buggy.

'Before you go, young Will, when are you likely to be ready to make that first payment?'

Will paused and smiled. 'You've got a plot you're interested in selling, have you, Sir Rory?'

Fitzparsons smiled back. 'You know better than that, young William. You know I'm a land buyer not a land seller. Never was. Never will be. It's just that I heard you've been makin' enquiries about a job.' He lifted his hand, and with the palm uppermost and his fingers curled back against his thumb, shook it a number of times. 'So I'm assuming you might still be a few Georgies short of what you'll need.'

'Just a few.'

'I also heard that you were considerin' goin' across to Southampton to work on the pier.'

'I was considerin' it.'

'That'd be a bad mistake, boy. A bad mistake.'

'That's what I've been tellin' him,' said Jessica.

'Then you've been tellin' him right, lass.'

'This lad here, Garth, is a fair shake at figurin', and pretty handy with grammar. When the school master is feelin' poorly, he gets young Will to take over tryin' to cram some learnin' into the heads of the local brats.' He shook his head. 'But he can't afford to pay you, can he, Will'm my lad? Not so much as a bent French sou. The village pays him barely enough to feed himself. Which is fair enough. There's no value in what he does. As you're findin' out, there's no point in teachin' the kids around here any a-rith-matick, or even how to read and write. Not when all tha's offerin' in jobs for them is labourin' of one brand or another. You don't need much figurin' or grammar to muck out a barn or pull a cow from a bog, or even to dig a plaguey ditch.'

He glanced at Barlester. 'They came to me, you know. The mayor and other townee stalwarts— three little mincy shop owners and a brace of lum- berin' rawboned tradesmen—all done up in their Sunday best and fidgetin' like a pack of choir-boys with fleas. And of course our Reverend Smith- Whistle with his ears still stuck on was there with them. They wanted me to help pay old Pillington's wages. The cheek of the plaguey prickles. "Why in the bright blue blazes should I support teachin' the local brats to figure," says I. "I'm the only person who has any need of figurin' on my estate. If I hire someone who's smart at figurin', I'll be forever wonderin' how long he'll take to figure out how to rob me." '

He leant forward and for a moment it appeared he might topple from his seat, but then settled back with his gaze locked on Will. 'Figurin' and labourin' don't mix, sweet William. Which is why you'd be makin' a mistake workin' on the pier. Where you should be headin' for is Portsmouth. And at Portsmouth for the navy ... (belch) ... the navy. And at the navy for their pay office. If you're as smart as Pillington says, you'll have no trouble landin' yourself a decent clerical job.'

'No,' said Jessica. 'No, that would be worse. Then I'd never see him.'

'But the pay'll be much better than he'll get on the pier, lass. He won't take so long in accumulating those ... (belch) ... Georgies. And on that subject I may be able to ... (belch) ... help out.'

He straightened and turned his gaze squarely on Jessica. He clamped a hand to the back of his head and with bunched fingers scratched vigorously at the nape of his neck. 'I mightn't be in the market for a figurin' man, but I could be in the market for an extra kitchen maid.'

'Jessica is needed at home,' said Will.

Fitzparsons did not shift his gaze from the young woman. 'Is your mother still ailin', Will? I heard she was pickin' up.'

'She's still not the best.'

'I was sorry to hear about your father. I remember him as a fair man ... (belch) ... a fair man. Now don't take this the wrong way, boy, but I don't believe you're bein' a very fair man to this lass. Seems to me you might be takin' advantage of her. You certainly haven't got any money to pay for her services and I'll wager your brother wouldn't be rushin' to put his hand in his pocket. That's not in his nature as I remember him.'

Jessica's hand tightened on Will's wrist. 'I'd ne'er accept any money from Will's family.'

Fitzparsons threw another glance at Barlester. 'What did she say?' Barlester remained silent.

Fitzparsons turned back and leaned towards her. 'Must remind you of New South Wales, eh, Gartie.' He chuckled. 'Garth here doesn't have to pay much for the services of his workers either, do you, old son? In fact, not a bent penny. Not in Sydney Town. He returned his attention to Jessica. 'When young Jessica was aged about ... what?' He raised his eyebrows and looked from one to the other seeking assistance. When none was forthcoming he continued unaided, '... about nine or ten, her grandmother died ... (belch) ... her grandmother died; and havin' already lost both parents to the ague some years before, she was all bundled up and on her way to the parish orphanage when Ma Noling stepped in and practically kidnapped her. She's lived with the Nolings ever since.'

'We must be off,' said Will, directing Jessica past the buggy.

'Before you go,' Fitzparsons raised his hand, 'on Tuesday I'm sendin' Rubin Mactaggart to the dockyard at Portsmouth with three drays of turnips. For the price of helpin' him and the lads unload 'm when they get there, you can ride with him.'

'I'll give it some thought,' said Will.

Fitzparsons twisted in the seat as they moved past. 'If you have any sense you'll give it more than some thought, young fellah m'lad. And remember as well, 'tis unfair on the lass, sweet William, t' 'ave her workin' for nought when I'm offerin' fair wages.'

As he turned he inadvertently pulled on the reins and the skittish mare threw her head in the air and jumped forward jerking the buggy a few feet. 'Steady! Steady! You black bitch!' As the mare settled, he swung back around and called out, 'And you know you could do with the money. You'd have that down-payment in no time.'

His gaze stayed with Jessica's retreating form as he added quietly, 'I'd be willin' to give a sizeable down-payment to get my hands on some of that, begad!'

Barlester twisted his huge frame around in the seat so that he too could observe their departure. Finally he growled, 'You ought to come visit me in Sydney Town for a while, Rory. We have young slatterns like that one lined up for the choosin' every time a ship comes in.' His voice was unnaturally low, like the sound of rocks scraping against each other on the bed of a river, and as he spoke the wings that were his eyebrows beat slowly in time with his words.

'She's no slattern, Garth. She's a sweet and lovely young woman. The sweetest in these parts.'

'They're all slatterns, Rory. If livin' among them at the end of the earth has taught me anythin', it's taught me that.' He took off his wide-brimmed hat, revealing an unnaturally high forehead and a thick turban of white hair which he ran his fingers through a number of times. The contrast with his eyebrows was remarkable, giving him the appearance of a portrait artist's charcoal sketch. 'And I'll tell you somethin' else: if that cheeky whelp's not swivin' her, I'm a Dutchman.'

'Oh, he's swivin' her all right, Garth. And if I have my way, he won't be the only one.'

'You reckon he's off to Portsmouth?'

'I hope so. The navy's recruitin' for the Mediterranean with rare vigour at the moment. And woe betide any stray country boy caught out of his ground from Dover to Plymouth during the next few weeks.'

'You wouldn't be plannin' to have someone nudge him out of his ground while he was far from home, would you, Rory?'

Fitzparsons shook his head. 'This isn't Botany Bay, Gartie.'

'Don't give me any of your sheart. I know you too well. What are you plannin'? To have a trustworthy man see to it the young whelp was in the wrong place at the right time, and was maybe a bit worse for wear? That's what I'd do.' He turned and gave Fitzparsons a searching look.

Fitzparsons appeared to ignore him for a time and then he said, 'I didn't think you were very keen on her, Gartie. You reckon women like her are thick on the ground back in Sydney Town.'

Barlester turned his gaze back on the departing couple. 'That doesn't mean I wouldn't swive the daylights out of her if I had half a chance. Just havin' her movin' around so close in front of me has got me all randified. And I reckon the sluttish little mott knew it and was tryin' to raise my interest. But she's a bit too thin and a bit too short for my likin'.'

Fitzparsons shook his head. 'You have to be jestin', Gartie. You can't be that spoilt.'

'On my place I'm king. I can do anything I want. I can have anything I want.'

Fitzparsons nodded his head. 'It's not so much different for me around here. There's not much that I can't do for the wantin'. And there's not much I can't have for the askin'.'

'It seems to me there's one thing you want that's goin' to take more than just the askin'.' Barlester nodded down the lane. 'Yonder slattern with the red hair and the big green eyes.'

'Early days, Gartie,' said Fitzparsons. 'Early days. It's a pity you're goin' back so soon.'

'I don't want you workin' for him, Jessie. I don't

24

like him and I don't trust him. I ne'er did.'

'He'd be harmless enough. But that other one! Did you see his eyes? And the way he looked at me?' She shuddered. 'My flesh still creeps at the thought.'

Later she asked, 'Are you goin' to go to Portsmouth?'

'It mightn't hurt to find out if there are any jobs, and what they're payin'.'

'It won't do you much good findin' out, if you're not seriously considerin' workin' there.'

'If the pay's all right it mightn't have to be for very long.'

'Then you are goin'?'

'I'm thinkin' about it.'

'Seriously?'

'Pretty seriously.'

A hawk swooped over the hedge in front of them and shrieked as it skimmed low overhead before wheeling abruptly and disappearing behind a small copse bordering the opposite field.

They walked on in silence, the echo of the bird's harsh cry ringing as a gradually diminishing echo in the reaches of their memory until they were well out of sight of the two men who remained watching them from the rise.

TWO

The three drays came down through a shimmering knee-high mist that cloaked the southern skirts of the Ports Down. From a distance, with the body of the mist concealing the exact definition of the teams of horses and the vehicles in their tow, and the surface picking up distorted reflections around the entire convoy, they could have been barges drifting down a river. This impression was strengthened by the tall reeds and marsh grasses that poked through the soft white blanket at the border of the road, by the relays of gulls that swooped in to investigate, and by the maritime accompaniment from the harbour ahead of them: the irregular chiming of bells atop buoys, the urgent flap of luffing sails on the fishing skiffs manoeuvring in the shallows, and the deep-throated shouts and banter of the men on board.

They passed through the crossroads at Cosham and rolled straight on to Portsbridge. By the time they crossed over to Portsea Island and moved on to the village of Hilsea the mist had pulled back to the west. Remnants of it were caught in low bushes on Horsea Island.

They were into the second day of their journey, having camped outside Whickham the previous evening. Since leaving the Fitzparsons estate Will had travelled with Rubin Mactaggart on the lead dray, sitting beside him on the solid oak plank that served as the driver's seat.

The open road at times was as bumpy as many a private road would get in the vicinity of a barnyard, and for the same reason: too much traffic after prolonged spates of heavy rain followed by ground-baking dries. Will had trouble resisting the temptation to use his duffle bag and its soft contents as a pillow.

The contents of the bag, which he had presently stowed beneath his seat, were a clean shirt, a plain grey neckerchief once owned by his father, his brother Jim's Sunday-best coat and trousers, and a new smoky-grey floppy cap that had a stiffened band and brim. He had been coerced by threat of personal injury at the hands of Jessica to wear this apparel to any appointment he could secure and decided that it would not be wise to destroy the effect of her careful ironing.

His own best coat and trousers had either shrunk in the arms and legs about two inches apiece since he had last worn them—which did not seem all that long ago—or his limbs had suddenly sprung out by the same amount. When he donned them and paraded for the family, the spectacle caused even the dispirited Jessica to release one of her more startled squeals of delight.

Jim stepped in and offered his own Sunday-best clothes, and they fitted well enough. Jessica volunteered to iron them; she wanted him to look his best, despite misgivings that it would enhance his prospects, but she could not bear the thought of his appearance causing him to be disadvantaged in the eyes of some disdainful civil servant. The cap was at his mother's insistence in the hope that before doffing it at any meeting and keeping it secured firmly beneath his arm—a manoeuvre he practised a number of times to the further amusement of his observers—it would perhaps keep his wayward hair in check.

To relieve his suffering rump during the journey, at regular intervals when the drays were moving slowly he would get down and walk beside them, and when the horses were rested he would sometimes go on ahead and wait for them to catch up. So it was, when Mactaggart and the other drivers seemed to spend an inordinate amount of time in Hilsea resting the horses and resetting the harnesses, that he walked ahead and was past the village of Kingston before they caught up with him.

While he waited, resting on a low stone fence a short distance from the roadway, the low thump of a cannon sounded in the distance followed by a volley of musket fire. He stood up on the fence and looked about him. But his view was blocked by thin strips of mist that swathed distant high points—farm buildings, copses and windbreaks—in soft white ribbons.

It was impossible for him to tell if what he was hearing was the navy practising gunnery on the harbour, or perhaps further south somewhere out on the Solent. The cannon sounded again followed by another burst of musket fire and he turned and looked behind him to the east, unsure now if the sounds were not coming from that direction. Perhaps what he was hearing was the accompaniment to a breakout from one of the prison hulks anchored in the shallows of Langston Harbour.

The rattle of musket fire gradually subsided and, given no further indication of what was the cause, he finally jumped down from the fence and moved into the shade of a large elm tree that overlooked a nearby crossroad. There he picked himself out a comfortable seat, formed by a tangled swirl of the tree's exposed roots, and placed his back against the trunk.

From where he was sitting, partly concealed by overhanging branches, he had a clear view of other signs that the navy was nearby, and in strength. A continuous stream of sailors, many accompanied by wives and family, were moving past him. Although many wore blue vests and pale duck trousers, none was dressed in what could be described as a standard uniform. Their headgear ranged from soft, short-brimmed black hats perched jauntily on the back of their heads, to wide-brimmed straw boaters and, in between, an assortment of high hats, low hats, peaked hats, multicoloured bandannas and woollen skull-caps. Those who were bareheaded revealed what the headgear on the others partly concealed: sometimes one, often two, and occasionally more, jaunty pigtails, some tied with bows and coloured ribbons.

Some of the men were carrying duffle bags and a few cradled a chicken on the crook of an arm; not game hens as might have been expected, but an assortment of plump red, spotted, black, and speckled egg producers. Food, not sport, seemed to be the aspiration, as was evident by the sight of an occasional suckling pig suspended in a net or a sling and slung over a shoulder.

Most were older men, their faces masked by the indifferent expression he had noticed before on veteran regulars at the Sir Francis Drake, and he surmised that these were the ones who had been trusted with shore leave so close to the departure of the fleet: seasoned able seamen and petty officers, some on foot, some travelling in carriages, and one or two on horseback. Mainly they were heading in the same direction as himself.

Occasionally a two-horse chaise-cart passed by, carrying senior officers dressed in cocked hats and frock coats. At one stage, three troops of marines marched past in close succession. All had muskets on their shoulders, and their fixed bayonets and the buttons on their scarlet jackets caught the sunlight, causing the eyes of shaded observers to squint.

The flow of people was regularly interrupted by convoys of drays laden with fruit and vegetables, and by small flocks of sheep and herds of cattle, each usually controlled by a single adult aided by either a small pack of dogs or a similar group of barefoot children. Whether dogs or children, they shuttled backwards and forwards along the periphery of their charges at a constant trot.

The parade was accompanied by an undulating cacophony that drifted across the fields, releasing startled hares from clumps of hogweed and hawkweed and scattering flocks of starlings and sparrows from the hedgerows. Men exchanged greetings, bells clanged, harnesses jingled, hooves clip-clopped, babies cried, children laughed, dogs barked, sheep bleated, cattle bellowed, and somewhere out past the marshes and the sandbanks, unseen beyond the ribbons of mist, more cannons thundered. And in keeping with the excitement of the times, young horses shied, whinnied and kicked up their heels, and a number of cattle of both sexes climbed on to the backs of others.

When Mactaggart finally caught up he seemed unnecessarily vexed that Will should have left them so far behind. Because Will was unsure of where his job enquiries would lead, he had made no arrangements either to return with the others, or even to remain with them until they departed.

Other than a loose agreement to help them unload their turnips, he had made no commitments. So he found it curious that Mactaggart should be so concerned that he stay close at hand.

When Mactaggart arrived he directed his team to the side of the road and eased his heavy frame down from the dray. Then, after checking the lead horse's collar, he looked somewhere past Will's shoulder and growled, 'If ye knows what's good f' ye, and even if ye don't, ye should think twice afore ye go paradin' too far outta the way in these parts, young fellah.' His stubble-shadowed John Bull neck and jowls bounced as he spoke. 'I 'aven't the time t'worry about ye flamin' whereabouts. I've enough to worry me already.' With this, he hoisted his trousers higher up his chest by gripping the waistband with both hands and screwing it backwards and forwards enthusiastically beneath his wide belt.

He then hauled himself back into his seat. At no stage did he meet Will's eye. Will contemplated making a conciliatory reply, but unable to think of something appropriate, he decided to remain silent.

Because of the traffic it was mid-afternoon before they eventually passed on down through the Portsmouth common to the dockyard. Outside the main gate Mactaggart dismounted, and after showing some papers to a sentry was escorted inside. He emerged some time later accompanied by a tall thin man that Will

32

surmised was a purchasing officer. The turnips were the final delivery from the Fitzparsons estate of an eighteen dray-load consignment of fruit and vegetables, and probably as a result of this Mactaggart was given preferential treatment in being led past a line of other waiting drays to a battery of unloading docks. However, it still took some time to locate an appropriate unloading bay, and most of the remainder of the day to empty the drays. When they finally completed the operation the supply official, whose name was Jenkers, drew Will aside.

'Mr Mactaggart tells me that you be interested in applyin' for a job at the pay office?' He was taper-thin and taller than Will, and he stooped—perhaps through the habit of talking to shorter men, Will surmised—and he swayed from one leg to the other as he talked. Will wondered, somewhat facetiously, if perhaps his balance might have been affected by spending too much of his time on wharfs with his field of vision taken up by the sides of berthed ships that were continually in motion.

'Do you think there's time to see someone today?' Will asked.

'That's what I be just tellin' Mactaggart. You be way too late to see anyone who'll take any notice o'ye. They work regular hours at the pay office, them little men do. And on any day of the week, in the last one or two of them regular hours I doubt they e'en listen t' one another, leastways to any stranger who might come a'callin' lookin' for a job. All their attention would be taken up by how long it is t'go before they can go home to their little wivies and childers.'

He moved closer to Will and conspiratorially motioned with an extended arm curled in the air behind the other man's shoulders for him to turn and move away with him from where Mactaggart's men were securing the sides of the drays and preparing the horses for departure.

'Which means that if you still wish t'try your luck you'll have t'stay o'ernight. Which means findin' a place t'sleep. Which means makin' sure that place be not a place where the bully boys'll find you. For if they do, it won't be a clerk in the navy pay office ye'll be; it'll be an ordinary seaman in the wavey navy bloody proper ye'll be.

'Nelson's off t' fight the French. He arrived this mornin' all decked out for war an' achin' t'get at 'm. My guess is he'll sail Friday, and the fleet be still short of hands.' He glanced back at the others before moving closer and lowering his voice. 'If I be you I'd stay well clear of them lot. They be too countrified. They stick out worse 'n the balls on a coursing hound that has its head stuck in a rabbit burrah. And they're plannin' to spend the night close to the old Mill Pond. F' sure 'n' certain they'll be hauntin' the likes of White's Row, 'n' Battery Row, 'n' Blossom Alley. That area'll be crawlin' with the press an hour after dark. I'll be surprised if all but Mactaggart himself, and maybe him as well, don't find 'emselves on the high seas by the weekend.'

'Where do you suggest I stay?'

'A long way away from the dockside.' He again glanced back at the others. 'There be an inn near where I live outside of Kingston. I'll drive you there directly. Get your things and take your leave of them others while I close me office and collect Betsy.'

Betsy was the frail mare that pulled his chaise-cart, a shoddy equipage with most of the original green paint either missing or peeling away from the woodwork in tightly curled slivers.

As they passed up through the common Jenkers asked, 'Have y'ever had anythin' t'do with His Majesty's Navy before, Mister Noling?'

'No. Nothing.'

'They be a law unto 'emselves around here, y' know. They can do near on what they like t'ye. Them and any of their friends in high places. And there's nothin' ye can do about it. In fact, not only can ye do nothing, they can make it very dangerous f' ye t' try. Very dangerous.'

Will turned and looked at him. 'How do you mean?'

Jenkers met his gaze for a moment and watched him silently for longer than seemed appropriate, before turning back to the road. 'See them houses there.' He flicked his whip to one side. 'Dock workers. When they first built on the common to be close to the yard, the Portsmouth military garrison in cahoots with the navy turned their cannons on them houses and threatened to blow them all to kingdom come if'n them that owned them didn't tear them down. If Queen Anne hadn't stepped in and stopped 'm, they'd 'ave done it, too.' He nodded to himself a few times as if contemplating this. 'Anyways,' he continued, flipping his whip from side to side, 'tha's why they call this road Queen Anne Street, or Queen Street. 'Cos she saved them houses from bein' blown to smithereens with the fuckin' consent of the Royal fuckin' Navy, who can do anythin' they like t'ye, any time they fuckin' like.'

Will was so subdued by the man's outburst that he remained silent until they were back on the Kingston Road.

'How long have you been here?' Will asked when they were again heading north. 'At the dockyard?'

'A good few years. All my life if'n you count the fact my father was a sailmaker here. As a boy I saw them hang Jack the Painter just inside the main gate. They strung him up on the mizzen mast taken off the old *Arethusa*. Hauled him right to the very top so he could be seen above the walls.'

'You saw that?' Will's interest was genuine. 'The arsonist?'

'I don't know nothin' about his personal fancies. But I knows he liked lightin' fires.' He waved his whip back over his shoulder. 'After they pulled him down they hung his body in chains over at Fort Blockhouse as a reminder t'all n'sundry not to get too friendly with no damned Yankees.'

They reached the inn at dusk, turning westward off the road not far from where he had earlier watched the passing parade. It was called the Admiral Anson and sat among a ramshackle collection of fishermen's huts opposite a wide beach of coarse gravelly sand. The building was distinguishable from the huts that surrounded it only by its size.

'You can walk across to that island when the tide's out,' said Jenkers as Will stepped down from the cart.

'What was that?' said Will distractedly, his eyes on the inn and his mind on how such a place could be considered a safe haven from anything. Not only did he doubt that it would provide adequate protection from the elements should the weather take a turn for the worse, it had all the hallmarks of the type of place a press gang would call on as a matter of course. After dark, it would surely be crammed with a ready haul of the human flotsam and jetsam they would be seeking.

Even now there were a number of shady characters hanging about, some lounging against the side of the building, others either sitting or lying on the grassy bank that flanked the beach. Seamen or fishermen? Or perhaps pirates or smugglers. Experienced looking types. A good proportion of broad hats, earrings and pigtails. Some were obviously the worse for drink. Or at least recovering from its effects.

He returned his attention to the building. The core, consisting of little more than the single-storey area defined by two narrow windows that stood on either side of the front door and the room immediately behind, was fashioned from local stone, the same stone used in the fence that he had used as a seat earlier in the day. But the bulk of the structure, including the upper storey, consisted of an assortment of irregularly shaped timber additions, their size and shape seemingly determined by the original size and shape of the structure from which the timber had been obtained. The high tapered contours of the upper storey suggested the remains of a weatherworn windmill; the large battened-down door that formed most of the front wall on the left hand side had obviously once belonged to a barn; and the clinker-built and rotting panelling on the right hand side, part of a shattered hulk.

No attempt seemed to have been made to alter or otherwise compensate for the original shaping of the timbers. Within all of the assorted structures there were numerous gaps between the various sized planks, and large jagged holes within the planks themselves, as if the building had played host at some time to a swarm of giant wood-crunching rats.

'That's Whale Island just off the point. You can walk out to it when the tide's right. But you have to be extra careful with the tide, it can come in twos around here.'

Will turned and looked to where Jenkers was indicating. The breeze had dropped and the water was a slowly vibrating sheet of silver. The shadow that was the island stood to one side of a long, narrow and dilapidated jetty that reached across the beach and stretched far out on to the harbour; a slim wavering line that the shimmering surface of the water rendered indeterminate in both distance and continuity.

Will found himself wondering if the few boats that were moored alongside it were settling on to the sand, or were beginning to rise clear of it. Was the tide coming in or going out? He then checked himself. Why in Hades do I care anyway? I haven't the slightest intention of walkin' out to that damned island at high, low or in between the first, second or umpteenth tide. He turned his back on the harbour in dismissal. But what was difficult to dismiss was the stench of rotting fish wafting on what remained of the breeze.

'I'll come with you while you get y'self a room,' said Jenkers as he climbed down from the cart. 'Then I'll leave you for half an hour or so and come back and have supper with you if ye'd rather be not doin' somethin' else. We may even have a couple of jars of ale and a pipe or two if that's to ye likin'.' Deducing the cause of Will's expression, he added, 'The next tide'll clear that smell later tonight. The stream that you can see emptyin' into the harbour over there runs past the back of the fishermen's huts. They cleans their catch into it.'

Will's hand felt for the two gold guineas tied in the corner of the handkerchief in his trouser pocket, and then his fingers moved on to close over an assortment of loose change. 'How much do they charge for a night's lodgin'?'

'A shillin'. Maybe one 'n' six, if you want a room with a window.'

Will selected a room with a window but chose to keep it shut until he could determine that Jenkers was right about the smell. The sole furnishings in the room were the bed, a washstand and a large wooden chest. He opened his duffle bag and carefully laid out Jim's clothes and his own clean shirt, neckerchief and cap on the broad lid of the chest, and placed his towel and shaving gear on the side of the washbasin.

After he had washed, he elected not to change into his good clothes that evening, deciding that the setting was not appropriate. But he did elect to shave, even though the fuzz that collected along the periphery of his jawline usually only warranted attention once a fortnight, and his face was still tender from having shaved the morning he left home. Consequently, when he joined Jenkers at a table in a corner of the bar-room, his face was a network of scratches and spots of dried blood.

'What happened to you, Mr Noling?' Jenkers asked, leaning forward to examine him more closely and waving his head from side to side in his customary manner. 'They only declared war on Boney yesterday, yet you look like you've been o'er in France havin' it out with him already.'

A young woman walked from the kitchen and stood beside their table. 'What do you think, Pol?' Jenkers asked, bobbing his head towards Will's face.

She leant forward and looked at him closely, exposing a breathtaking expanse of cleavage that had him wondering how the unseen portions of her breasts were prevented from bursting from her bodice. 'What happened t' you, m' lovely?' she asked. 'Did you have soap in y' eyes, and grab 'old of the cat instead of the towel?'

'I think I might have,' said Will with a grin.

'Can I feel?' She raised a hand towards him.

'If you feel gently.'

'If you feel gently,' she mimicked, and glanced at Jenkers. 'Maybe this'n be not as green as he looks, eh, Mr Jenkers?'

She brushed his cheek with the tips of her fingers. 'How long have you been shavin'?'

'Long enough,' he replied defensively.

'You shouldn't have scraped skin like this with no razor, m' lovely. Y' should've rubbed cream on it and let that cat you dried y'self with lick it off.' She glanced at Jenkers. 'I'll wager he has more fluff on his bum than he's ever managed to grow on his chin.'

Will blushed, and taking hold of her fingers

lifted them away from his face, throwing her a smile in case she was offended.

'Are you familiar with the local brew, Mr Noling?' Jenkers asked.

'I don't believe I am.'

'Then we should remedy that, eh, Pol? Two jars of ale, if you please.'

'I'd like to eat soon,' said Will, trying to gauge how long it had been since he had finished the last of the bread and cheese that his mother had packed for him.

'And you will, and so will I.' Jenkers looked up at Pol. 'What are the rough offerin's from the kitchen tonight, lass?'

'We 'ave salted pork or salted beef, both with onion gravy.'

'Would the joints be fresh, lass?'

'Would you be jokin'? Fresh!'

'Eatable then?'

'Not the pork. The pork'd kill a black dog.'

'The beef?'

'Providin' you don't spare the gravy.'

'Vegetables? D'ye have any vegetables?'

'You might find a scrap or two of turnips in the gravy. If ye be lucky.'

'What kind of gravy d'ye say it is?'

'Onion gravy.'

'With bits of turnips in it?'

'If you be lucky, I said.'

'The onions'd be fresh then, wouldn't they?'

'You won't find any onions in't, ye silly bugger.

This be the Anson, not the ruddy George 'Otel.'

So they both consumed some salted beef with gravy, and they also consumed several jars of Jenkers's 'local ale'. At least Jenkers did. What Will consumed, unbeknown to him, was a combination of an ale of sorts mixed in each jar with a healthy portion of French brandy essence.

After the first two he stopped commenting on the peculiar sharpness of taste that Jenkers explained was caused by the flavour of the local hops when they were in flower. After the fourth, he could not sit squarely on his chair, and after the fifth he was leaning so far forward his face at times brushed the surface of the table.

Pol refused to serve him a sixth despite Jenkers's animated urgings above Will's shoulder. It was at this point that Will slowly came to his feet, knocking over his chair. He stood for a few moments swaying backwards and forwards and then in a sudden stumbling rush staggered across the room and burst through the back doorway into the open air.

Outside, he moved quickly across a broad strip of cobblestones on to a grassy waste that flanked the fishermen's huts. And then vomited with such force the first rush from his stomach speared way out ahead of him like the discharge from a broken downpipe. He sank to his knees and continued to vomit and retch with such ferocity that when the spasms subsided he was left trembling from the effort.

He felt someone place a hand on his shoulder. His head had cleared a little. 'Just give me a moment, Mr Jenkers. I'll be all right in a moment.' His tongue was leaden and he felt detached from the sound of his words, as if someone else had uttered them.

'No you won't, m' lovely,' a deep voice growled.

There were two of them. One large, one small. Broad hats and earrings. Smugglers or cut-throats. Probably both. He vaguely remembered seeing them among others at the end of the room. The bigger one hauled him to his feet and stood behind him. The sudden movement caused his vision to tumble and he fought to overcome more waves of nausea.

'Can he walk?' the smaller one asked. The light from the open door was on this one's face and Will saw that he had something wrong with one eye. The pupil was only slightly darker than its surrounds and it seemed to wander about independent of its neighbour.

'Don't matter,' growled the man behind him. 'We won't be takin' him far tonight.'

'Where's Jenkers?' Will asked, again with a sense of detachment from his own words. Takin' him? What do they mean, takin' him? A fine slither of concern stroked him between the shoulder blades, and he shuddered. 'Where's Jenkers?' he repeated, trying to gauge the distance to the back door of the inn.

'D'ye feel somethin' sharp stickin' into ye back,

sonny?' the tall man growled close to his ear. 'Well, if you don't do hexactly as y'told, you'll feel that same somethin' stickin' out through y' belly button with a piece of your liver stuck on't. D' y' understand what I'm sayin'?'

The area of cobblestones behind the inn served as a broad walkway to other structures. Probably the kitchen and toilet. And further back in the gloom, past where illuminated insects speared out from, and back into, the darkness, were the stables. Bordering one side of the paved area was a crumbling trellis over which the gnarled roping of an ancient flowering vine was entangled.

Despite his head beginning to pound with extra ferocity, Will's attention was caught by an object that was resting against one of the uprights of the trellis. It was a boathook, a curl of metal topped by a blunt spearhead mounted on a seven-foot pole.

When he first looked back at the inn his intent had been to gauge his chances of escape. But he found the door surprisingly distant, a good eight or nine strides away, even for an able man. The boathook, he judged, was no more than four strides away, even for an impaired strider. And it looked as if it could be a formidable weapon in the hands of anyone who was determined to defend himself, whether he be able or impaired.

Perhaps prompted by fear that a blow from behind could already be under way, he found himself in motion almost before he had made up his mind to act. He careered into the small man with his shoulder, striking him a glancing blow to the head that hurtled him to the ground. A moment later he had reached the trellis and was snatching up the boathook.

He spun around with the pole in both hands, his left high, his right low, and the metal hook describing a circle in front of his face. The tall man was closing in on him fast, the size of the knife he held out ahead of him indicating his warning had probably not been an idle threat. Will instinctively swung up the lower end of the pole in a sweeping arc. The man tried to duck beneath it but was caught high on the side of his head. He dropped as if his legs had been cut from beneath him.

Will was almost as surprised as his victim and wondered fleetingly if perhaps pole-fighting was a natural instinct of man. With both his adversaries down it looked for a moment as if it would be his day. But then the full fury of the effect of the alcohol descended on him again and he staggered beneath its weight. His head began to spin and a swarm of fiery bees spiralled before his eyes.

Someone called out from the door of the inn and was answered by the short man, who was coming to his feet. Will then saw that three others of rough appearance were converging on him, one from the open doorway and two from the shadows at the side of the building. Two seemed to be armed with long clubs, probably axe handles; the third was carrying a knife of similar size to the one that was lying at his feet; it caught the light as the man probed the air ahead of him with it. Where in Hades was Jenkers? He tried to call out but his throat refused to operate.

He backed away, trying to keep all his opponents in view, while at the same time fighting to keep his balance and stay on his feet. He held the pole high in front of his chest, as if he could and would strike out with either end if they came too close. At the edge of the cobblestones he stumbled and then recovered his footing and backed haltingly on to the grassy waste. The others began to spread out as if to encircle him. He saw that the man he had felled with the boathook was now sitting up.

Will's head began to sag once more as if a garland of chains had been slung around his neck, and his shoulders protested as he fought against the bias. He felt his boots crunch through a thin crust of sand. A few steps further and he was back on turf, and then a moment later on more sand. Something small struck his face. He had a fleeting impression of a rapid beating of wings. A bat.

The smell of rotting fish pervaded the air he breathed. He could taste it. Feel it. His stomach lurched. The men were closer. The tall one was on his feet and advancing again. A dog suddenly barked angrily somewhere behind him. Perhaps he could find sanctuary in one of the fishermen's huts.

He felt more sand beneath his boots. Softer.

Deeper. And then suddenly he had stepped into empty space. His gasp at the shock of tumbling backwards became a gasp at the shock of plunging into icy water, became a gasp at the shock of landing heavily on the sandbank beneath the water.

As he came to his feet, spluttering and choking, they were leaping at him from the bank of the stream.

'Jasus Christ, what 'ave you in the sack, a load of mackerel guts?' The voice came at Will from somewhere behind and above him.

He felt himself being hauled upright. Whatever it was that covered his head, it was not sufficient to prevent sunlight from entering the coarse weave and firing jagged barbs deep into his brain. His stomach lurched dryly. There was nothing left within it that could further soil the mix of fish refuse and vomit that clung to his clothes, nor worsen the smell that enveloped him like a second skin.

As the previous night had been the worst of his life up until then, it was fortuitous that he had only vague recollections of it; usually moments when he regained consciousness, coughing and vomiting and fighting for breath, gripped with real fear in the knowledge that he was in the process of drowning. At one point, the motion, the creak of oarlocks, the slap of oars and the shock of being partly immersed in a freezing bath told him he was lying trussed up like a pig on its way to market in the bottom of a boat.

Later he awoke to hear voices again, among them the growl of the tall man. At one stage the voices were raised in anger, and when they had quietened, he heard the clink of coins. Shortly afterwards he was hauled roughly out of what he later deduced was a small craft into a larger vessel. Each time he came to his senses he was racked by waves of nausea that forced him to retch and try to vomit, activity that usually attracted blows and kicks from out of the darkness.

It was shortly after he awoke to realise that the sun had risen that he felt himself suddenly being lifted high into the air. His thoughts went to Jenkers's story of Jack the Painter. He felt as if he were being hauled to the top of a mast of some description and braced himself in case the intent was to drop him and allow him to be killed by the fall. But he doubted this would be the case. Whatever it was that was happening to him, it seemed too elaborate to be simply a way of disposing of him after robbing him. And although what was happening also seemed far too elaborate to be simply the navy's way of impressing him into its service, this was what he guessed was the more likely explanation.

He did not have to wait long to find out. He was lowered on to a firm surface, the sack that was bound around his upper body was removed and the bindings were released from his hands and feet. Then he was grasped by the arms and hauled to his feet.

When the fluttering of his eyelids slowed enough for him to focus properly on his surroundings and determine his whereabouts, he saw that he was on the upper deck of a large warship. And that he and a number of others standing beside him—some of whom appeared to be in as frail a state of health as himself—were being watched closely by a number of burly sailors armed with batons and marines armed with muskets. God save us all!

A small man in a flat black hat, a blue vest and pale duck trousers was addressing them, but Will's attention was on the water, gauging the distance to the battlements at the harbour entrance.

'You there with the red hair. Pay attention when I'm talkin' to you.' The man walked across to Will and raised his baton beneath Will's chin. The baton was in fact a belaying pin used for securing set-lines to trim the sails.

'I shouldn't be here,' said Will. 'I have to . . .'

'Silence!' shouted the man. He suddenly stepped backwards. 'Jesus, what's that smell?'

'I shouldn't be here,' Will repeated.

'Silence!' The man shouted again and stepping forward struck Will a sharp blow on the side of his face with the belaying pin.

Will was so surprised he stood for a moment staring down at the man in disbelief before saying quietly, 'This is a mistake.'

The man raised the pin and slashed it at him again. But this time Will was waiting for him. He grabbed hold of the pin and in one swift motion wrenched it away from the man, who stumbled backwards cowering behind his raised forearms.

The sailors and marines who were standing guard were caught by surprise by such a blatant display of irreverence, but they recovered almost immediately and, as one, stepped towards Will, raising their weapons.

'Avast there!' a thickset man cried out in a voice that commanded attention. He strode on to centre stage pushing aside those who stood in his way.

'Give me the pin, son,' he demanded, walking straight across to Will and holding out his hand, palm uppermost.

Will's eyes narrowed and he lowered his head slightly to one side, transmitting an obvious query.

'The pin. The belayin' pin.'

Will looked at the column of wood in his hand as if he had seen it for the first time. After a moment's hesitation, during which he matched the man's gaze, he complied.

'I shouldn't be here,' he said. 'This is a mistake.'

'It's a mistake that you should be defendin' your country from invasion? Is that what you're sayin'?' The man was dressed in a similar manner to the small man, but he was much older and had a neatly trimmed set of grey whiskers bordering the periphery of his face.

'I'm not a sailor. I'm a farmer.'

'Well, how come you aren't on your farm?'

'I came to Portsmouth lookin' for a job.'

'Well, I'd say you've found one.'

The men around him laughed, including some of those Will assumed were in the same predicament as himself.

'What's your name?' the man asked.

'Will Noling.'

'Well for better or worse you're in His Majesty's Navy now, Will Noling. So best you get used to it.' He began to turn away.

'I have people at home expecting me. My mother. My ... my ...'

'Your wife?'

'No.'

'Many of us 'ave mothers waitin' for us, son. Mothers, wives and sweethearts. That's one of the reasons we're off to fight the French. To protect our dear women.'

'I can't leave now. Not like this.'

'You can and you will. And if I was you, son, I'd accept it.'

A slightly built man wearing a cocked hat and blue frock-coat looked down from the poop deck and said to the man beside him, 'Mr Scott, who are those men the bos'n is talking to?'

'They're new recruits, m'Lord. They came on board this morning.'

'Pressed?'

'Aye, m'Lord. I believe so.'

'Good God! Sutton's left it a bit late, hasn't he? I warned him that come hell or high water we're sailing tomorrow. What good will any of that motley lot be when we're crossing the Bay?'

'I don't believe he had any option, m'Lord. I hear he's lost forty over the side in the last week.'

'Has he now? Well, I'll tell you something, he's just lost another one. That red-headed youngster the bos'n was addressing has just leapt into the harbour.'

A short time later, after walking to the ship's side so that he could watch the events that then ensued, the man chuckled and said, 'Whoever that fellow is, he's leading them a merry chase.'

Will was a good two hundred yards away when the ship's pinnace drew alongside him. As the rowers on the side of the boat closest to him shipped their oars and a battery of outstretched arms reached for him, he ducked beneath the water, and in a splashing flurry of strokes, veered away at right-angles to his original course.

The pinnace was forced to come about. Again when it drew alongside him he ducked beneath the water and swung away, this time gaining momentum by pushing off from the hull with both feet. The coxswain then brought his craft around in a wide circle to approach him from ahead.

This time, as the bow bore down on him, the rowers on both sides shipped their oars, so that grappling hands would be available on both sides of the boat should he move to the left or to the right. He did not move to either. With the whistling slap of the bow-wave less than half a boat's length away, he dived deeply and swam beneath the keel. And as he resurfaced in the pinnace's wake, the cries of complaint from those in the boat were accompanied by resounding cries of encouragement from those watching from nearby ships.

But these sudden and repeated bursts of activity had taken their toll on him. The charge of adrenalin that had surged through him as he leapt overboard was all but spent. And the bone-crushing exhaustion he had experienced on waking returned with a vengeance. Suddenly he found it difficult to keep his head above water.

So it was that when he sensed the boat was close, he could hardly summon the strength to look behind. When he did it was to see the bow wallowing in the swell only a few feet away from him, with the solidly built man from the ship leaning out and stretching an open hand towards him.

He immediately ducked beneath the water but managed to swim only a few strokes. As he surfaced he felt the hand that had been reaching for him grasp the top of his head. And before he could take a breath his face was driven back beneath the surface. He ducked away and shot for the surface again. But again the hand was waiting, and again his face was driven back mercilessly beneath the surface. My God, he's goin' to drown me, his mind screamed. In desperation he kicked out violently and thrashed his arms about to get further away from his tormentor. And this time as he surfaced he did manage to get some air into his lungs. But it was air charged with water. As he coughed and spluttered he again felt the firm grip of the hand, and again it forced his head below the surface.

Back on the ship the man who had earlier taken an interest in the proceedings turned to the man beside him. 'Give me that glass, Mr Scott. I wouldn't be surprised if the bos'n's not trying to drown the blighter.'

'I doubt it, m'Lord. It's not in the nature of the man.' He handed a telescope he was carrying to the slightly built man, who took it with his left hand and placed it to his left eye, not that he had many sensible options in this regard for his right arm was missing and his right eye blind.

'Well, they've finally managed to drag him on board, and if he's not drowned he's not far from it.' He chuckled. 'He's as limp as a wet stocking. There's certainly no fight left in him.'

'That was probably the bos'n's intention, m'Lord.'

'Is he a good man, the bos'n? A fair man?'

'Yes, I've heard he's a good man. And fair.'

'Good. I wouldn't like to lose that red-headed son-of-a-gun. I liked the way of him.'

'How are you feelin', son?'

Will was lying on a bunk of sorts in a confined space he guessed was somewhere within the ship. His wrists and ankles were again bound tightly.

'I'll tell you one thing, you smell a hell of a lot better than when we first met.'

'You tried to drown me.'

'What I've done, son, is come out of my way t' give you some advice. And if y' 'ave any sense a'tall, you'll take it on board and keep it close by you.'

'You tried to kill me. Why should I listen to you?'

'I didn't try to kill you, sonny boy, I probably saved your life. If we'd hauled you on board when you still had any spirit left in you, and you'd so much's thrown a sideways glance at any of them flat-footed marines who knew they were in trouble for lettin' you go in the first place, they'd have run a spike through you before y' could blink an eye.'

'Where am I? Where is this?'

'You're in the good ship *Victory*, presently under the command of Captain Samuel Sutton, and as of yesterday flyin' the flag of the greatest man you're ever likely to clap y' eyes on in a dozen lifetimes. Vice-Admiral Horatio Viscount Nelson himself. You're a lucky man, son, to have been dumped where you have. Y' could've been dumped anywhere in the fleet.'

'You have no right to keep me here. I demand to be let go.'

'Son, I'm goin' to tell you how it is, and then I'm goin' to leave you to think about it. What you do with what I say is up to you.'

'I demand . . .'

'Shut up and listen, son. I won't warn you again.'

Something in the man's tone told Will not to press further at this stage.

'Not only have we every right to keep you, son, but if we wanted t'do it, we could hang you. We're at war with Johnny Crapaud, and what you did this mornin' we could call desertion. We'd have every right to string you up as an example t'others t'think twice about leavin' the fleet in a hurry durin' these dangerous times. As it is you're goin' to be let off lightly. All you're goin' to get is a taste of the cat. A dozen lashes. A slap on the wrist. And before you protest again, I'll give you the best advice you've probably ever had in your short life. There are some things in this life you can alter, and there are others that you can't do nothin' about. And you bein' in the navy right now is one of those. There's not a damned thing on this earth you can do to alter that fact. But how you choose to spend your time in the navy is somethin' you can do somethin' about. You can fight it. Or you can accept it and make the most of it.

'And I can tell you this, sonny. Them that's chosen the bumpy road often don't even see out their time. And if they do, they're often so crippled they'd probably wish they hadn't. Whereas them that've chosen the easier road have walked out of the navy with their heads held high. Proud men. Respected by others. The choice is yours.'

'How long will that be? When I can walk out?'

'When we've won this war. A month. A year. Two years. Whenever.'

Will closed his eyes and shook his head. 'You say I'm goin' to be flogged?'

'A dozen lashes. And to prove to you I harbour no grudges over your behaviour to me this mornin', I'm goin' to give them to you myself.'

'You're what?'

The man chuckled. 'I'm goin' to wield the cat, sonny. Which is about the best news you've heard today.'

'What are you sayin', that you're goin' to flog me gently?'

'No way. I'm goin' to cut a fine swathe across your back that'll have you thinkin' you've been flayed alive. The last thing I want you to do is to forget it. I want you to remember it as long as you live.'

'So why am I so lucky?'

'Because I won't be hurtin' you permanent. I won't be damagin' your kidneys, or strippin' the flesh off your shoulder blades down to the bare bone. In a fortnight you'll be healed. Long as you takes my advice and don't get yourself a taste of the same treatment again before then.'

'Can I send a message to my family?'

'Can you write?'

'Aye.'

The man stood up and spoke to someone on the other side of a heavy wooden grating. Will thought he caught a glimpse of a red jacket.

When the man turned back he said, 'I can't promise, but I may be able to get a letter ashore before we sail.'

'When do you sail?'

'Tomorrow.' He twirled one hand in a circular motion. 'Turn around and I'll untie your hands. Another word of advice,' he said as he slipped the bindings. 'You've won a few points from the crew already. If you can keep yourself from yellin' when you get your dozen, you'll earn a few more. It don't hurt your survival chances in this man's navy to earn yourself a few points from time to time.'

'Jesus Christ!'

'You're a religious man are you, son? That's good. To keep you quiet when you're lashed to that grating you'll need all the help you can get.'

THREE

It was a five-mile walk from the Noling farm to the Fitzparsons estate. The Fitzparsons had dithered in their allegiance during the Rebellion of 1642, and the fortified manor house had suffered in consequence. The east wing had been destroyed by fire and had never been rebuilt. It stood as a reminder of the folly of the attempts of the then incumbent, Sir Hugh Fitzparsons, to appease whoever was the conflict's ascendant of the moment. No one seemed very sure then, nor any wiser now, whether the arsonist had been a Royalist or a Roundhead.

The charred remains of the high vaulted roofing had long since disintegrated and blown away. But the crumbling walls remained. And the cold sweeps and contours of grey stone, punctured irregularly by the empty sockets of the windows, could project as stark an impression to an unsuspecting stranger approaching from the east on a bleak day as would a stack of giant skulls.

So it was for Jessica Glider. She had never been to the Fitzparsons estate before, and the day she chose to go was windy and overcast. It was not as black as the day before, the day Reverend Smith-Wilson braved the worst turn in the weather since the demise of winter to deliver Will's hastily prepared message. But anyone attempting to lift Jessica's spirits afterwards would have had trouble convincing her that this was not the darkest day of her life.

Her decision to seek Sir Rory Fitzparsons' help had been her own. She told neither Will's mother nor his brother Jim of her plans, for fear that Jim would either persuade her to try a different course or insist on accompanying her, perhaps to the detriment of her chances of success; a proposition that at this point she avoided examining too closely.

Will's message had struck the Noling household like a thunderbolt. When Smith-Wilson arrived the wind was howling and the rain was beating in broad horizontal sweeps across the fields. Jessica was returning from the barn with a bucket of milk and vainly attempting with her free hand to control Will's—for her—oversized oilskin coat as it billowed and flapped about her body with a force that at times almost lifted her into the air. She first caught sight of Smith-Wilson as he was dismounting at the front door.

It was not unusual for him to call in on the

Nolings when he was in the area. But this was hardly call-in weather. She froze, and stood as if paralysed while he eased his small, stooped frame with difficulty to the ground from the gaunt wild-eyed mount that the parish had saved for him from the knackery.

Beneath the weatherproof cape that flapped about his head he could have been the grim reaper himself, so effectively did the sight of him arrest her progress, and so sharp was the stab of concern that buried itself deep within her. Please, God, let him be safe, she cried out silently into the teeth of the wind.

By the time she reached the house the letter was lying where Will's mother had dropped it on the sitting-room floor, and Smith-Wilson was assisting her on to the sofa.

'He's not dead?' Jessica cried out from the doorway.

'No. He's not dead,' replied Smith-Wilson. 'Nor injured.'

She scooped up the letter from where it lay beside one of the pools of water that recorded his progress across the room.

Not dead. Not injured. Thank God! Thank God! Relief surged through her and her head began to swim. She moved quickly to the closest chair, and sinking on to it unfolded the letter with trembling fingers.

'The navy's taken him,' said Smith-Wilson. He was far less threatening up close. A small man with pince-nez glasses, which he was now taking the opportunity to clean with a torn, lace-trimmed handkerchief.

What? The navy? She tried to read all the words in one glance and then forced herself to scan them a line at a time. The navy!

Dearest Family,
I am safe and well in His Majesty's Ship *Victory*. The navy has demanded my services for the duration of the war. I cannot tell you more at this time. Jessica, I love you and I am so sorry. I love you, Mother. Look after them, Jim.
Affectionately,
Will

'He's at sea. The fleet sailed yesterday,' said Smith-Wilson.

Although he had the pinched elfin features of some small men, his voice was surprisingly low and resonant. Perhaps someone had once told him he had a good preaching voice and that was why he had become a minister, Will had once suggested, adding, 'I'll wager many people have ended up where they are for less reason.'

Smith-Wilson clipped his glasses back on his nose and, leaning towards Jessica, peered at her as if testing them. At another time she may have toyed with the idea that he wore pince-nez because he distrusted the security of his ears. Although the proposition was unlikely that these protuberances had suffered permanent damage as a result of Rory Fitzparsons' bullying, it was difficult to ignore the fact that they did droop somewhat precariously, as if their mountings were unstable.

'Sailed where?' she asked, recovering. 'Where is he?'

'He's with Nelson. He's headed for the Mediterranean.'

'It doesn't say that here.'

'The *Victory* is Nelson's flag, and that's where he's going. And I pray that God goes with him.'

The access road from the eastern side of the Fitzparsons estate passed through a belt of dense forest that clung to the parallel humps of two low ridges. In places the trees on either side were interlocked overhead, and the understorey was so dense that the road resembled a long winding cave. Jessica passed through the leafy cavern gripped by an increasing sense of unease. An observer may have noted that she seemed to be stooping slightly, as if she was avoiding striking her head, and her gaze more often swept the sides of the road and behind her than the way ahead.

When she finally emerged from the forest her sense of relief at escaping its claustrophobic confines was stifled by her first sight of the manor house. The wind returned to tug at her clothes as she moved away from the trees. Had she taken the wrong road, she wondered, as she stood with her hair whipping about her face and looked down on the shallow valley before her. She seemed to have stumbled upon a war- and weather-ravaged ruin, with its stepped skull-like countenances as grim and uninviting as any ancient structure she had ever seen.

Her reaction was mixed. If this was not the Fitzparsons estate, she could postpone her plans and return home; an option that invited immediate relief, albeit temporary. But if it was the place she sought, the damage to her resolve caused by its projected malevolence was probably irreparable. Her shoulders shook in the grip of an involuntary tremble. God help me!

Had the building not been surrounded by an untidy but extensive network of fields containing either grazing livestock or an assortment of crops in various stages of maturity, she may have turned away. But she was obviously observing a farming enterprise of some magnitude. And when she noticed that from behind the ruined building a number of spirals of smoke were rising briefly before being caught and dispelled by the wind, indicating that at least one, and possibly more, habitable buildings were being shielded from sight by the ruin, she decided to press on.

As she drew closer and the other structures came into view, she believed it was probable that she was approaching the place she sought, despite the absence of the trappings she had been expecting: a grand manor, expansive gardens, neatly trimmed lawns and hedges, and possibly a lake flanked by a Grecian summerhouse.

These expectations were based on other gardens she had observed from a distance, and on illustrations of the works of Inigo Jones and his contemporaries that she had seen at a fair in Southampton.

When the care of the estate had been in the hands of Rory Fitzparsons' mother, some of what Jessica had been expecting had been evident: the rose gardens, the neatly trimmed lawns, the hedges and the lake; actually more of a chain of duck-ponds than a lake, but attractive nonetheless, particularly when the willows that surrounded it were budding. There had been no Grecian summer-house, but Greek-like heroes and maidens had stood watch or cavorted at most twists and turns of the landscaping.

But Rory's tastes leaned more towards the functional than the decorative. Gardens and lawns took up space that could be used for livestock and crops. So one of his first acts when he became lord of the manor had been to dismiss the gardeners and tear out the roses. The Greek heroes and maidens he broke into coarse rubble to fill the channels he used to drain the duck ponds.

Not that his instincts were exclusively commercial. He did have an interest in sports, for instance. Particularly those that involved the letting of blood, or the terrorising of the local fauna. Hence a preoccupation with hunting, fowling, coursing and baiting. Activities that stripped the surrounding countryside of most of its foxes, hares, wildfowl and otters, and kept the few survivors in a state of almost perpetual terror. In support of his pursuits he kept a fine kennel of hounds.

It was the agitated barking of these hounds that brought Rory's housekeeper to the door before Jessica had time to knock.

She was a big woman. Jessica had seen her a few times in the village and each time had been struck by her mannish appearance. Her greying hair was cut so short that the top of her head resembled an upturned hairbrush. Her face was angular and her jaw protruded in every direction. A blacksmith would have been well served by the breadth of her shoulders, which were accentuated by arched cascading ruffles attached to the top of her sleeves. Her dress was high-necked and black, and swept to the floor in one smooth plunge from beneath the formidable bulwarks of her bust.

Jessica fleetingly speculated that if there was a female warden on any of the prison hulks on Langston Harbour, she probably wore such a dress. It had much about it that reminded her of a constable's greatcoat.

'Would you be expected?' the woman asked, loudly, possibly because of the hounds. Or possibly to convey annoyance at being interrupted from some activity in which she had been engaged in the deep gloom behind her, Jessica decided. The flogging of a subordinate, perhaps. Or the devouring of a child.

'No. But he . . .'

'Then you can't see him today. He's busy.'

'He told me to come. Any time.'

'When?'

'Any time.' He didn't actually say any time, she mused; but he implied as much.

'Not when you could come. When did he tell you?'

'Last Sunday.'

'Why do you want to see him?'

'That's business between m'self and Sir Rory.' Jessica had had enough. To reach this point she had had to overcome a succession of obstacles: the forlorn hope of success, the weather, the gloom of the forest, the broken building, the damaged landscape, the dogs. *If this perhaps-female thinks she's goin' to prevent me from seein' him, she can think on the other side of her square head.*

'Business, is it?' The woman had a pair of small spectacles perched on the tip of her nose. She threw back her head and used them now to observe the young upstart more closely.

'Yes, business.' There was no waver in Jessica's determination.

'Well, he's not here. So you can't see him.'

'Where is he?'

'He's out riding.'

'Then I'll wait.' She glanced past the woman, trying to pierce the gloom of the passageway behind her. *There's no way on earth that I'll risk entering that abyss,* she decided.

'He could be ages.'

'I'll wait at the stables.' She turned abruptly away from the door and walked back down the path, heading towards the row of buildings where she had seen a groom at work.

'If you must wait, you should wait in here,' the woman called after her.

As was the intent of her hasty retreat, Jessica pretended not to hear and kept going. If you think you can trap me into entering your dungeon so that you can lock me in chains, you can think again.

As she approached the stables the hounds, who seemed to be housed not far from the entrance, gave voice to their excitement with renewed enthusiasm.

'When did you get his letter?' Sir Rory asked. He strode around the room as he talked, his boots clumping heavily on the loose flooring. He was beginning to slow down from the pace he displayed when he first arrived. Although some time had passed since he had dismounted from the big lather-swathed bay charger that his groom was presently rubbing down, it was obvious to Jessica that much of him was still working as if he were travelling at a steady gallop.

His face was flushed, he was breathing heavily, rolling oscillations were passing through his ballooning neck, his chest and shoulders were rising and falling with each stride, and he was

69

punctuating his words by slapping the side of his boot with his riding crop. She, on the other hand, was sitting bolt upright, watching him warily, with her hands clasped on her lap and her knees pressed tightly together.

When she had arrived at the stables his groom had escorted her to the far end of the largest building where a right-angled extension containing two horse stalls had been converted from its original purpose. The wall between the stalls had been removed so that they now formed a combined storage and living area.

Sheaves of straw and large loosely woven sacks of chaff were stacked on either side of a small wooden hatchway in the far wall of what was originally the end stall. The contents of some of the sacks had spilled on to the earthen floor through holes that suggested mice had been at work. By design or default, the neat piles of finely chopped straw would undoubtedly be replenished each time the tiny thieves took their fill.

The side walls of this area were festooned with an assortment of odds and ends and harness bric-a-brac: branding irons, pincers, halters, bridles, bits, chinstraps, nosebands, breastplates, cruppers, girths and surcingles, stirrup irons and leathers, and a family of complete saddles mounted on short poles that jutted from every upright beam. The air was charged with pleasant aromas of beeswax and oiled leather.

Loose planks had been lain as flooring in what

had been the adjoining stall and was now serving as the living quarters, presumably for the groom. The furnishings consisted of a small table, two straight-backed wooden chairs—one of which Jessica now occupied—a large chest, a narrow bed covered by a dilapidated woollen blanket, and a brazier crammed with glowing coals mounted above a heavy metal dish partly filled with ash. Smoke from the coals streamed into the flared horn of a metal flue that passed up through the vaulted roof of the building. The room was lit by pale light streaming through a window mounted high on the outside wall, and from a metal-based lantern sitting in the middle of the table.

'Reverend Smith-Wilson brought it yesterday.'

'The *Victory*, y' say? Nelson's ship?'

'Aye.'

'I'll be roasted! Pressed, y' say? The lad's been pressed? Well, I never! Who'd've believed it? Nelson's ship, begad! Heading f'the Mediterranean?' He propped and threw her a searching look. 'Who told y' that?'

'Reverend Smith-Wilson.'

'Idle talk. Rumour. The man should know better. I'll wager Nelson won't sail any further than the western reaches of the channel and join up with Cornwallis blockadin' Brest. The ships'll then take turns in returnin' to their home bases to replenish supplies.'

Her mouth opened. Recovering immediately, she asked, 'Do you mean there's a chance he'll be home soon?' Her voice was little more than a whisper.

'No.'

Her face fell. 'Why not, if the ships return regularly?'

'The ships'll turn around too fast. And pressed men aren't allowed ashore when they're in a home port anyway. Not when there's a war on. Here, you're shiverin'. Move closer to the fire.' He helped her move her chair.

He walked to the door, opened it slightly and called out something that Jessica could not quite catch above the skirl of the wind.

The weather seemed to have worsened since she heard him arrive and had ventured to the door to watch him dismount. It was obvious then that he was in a state of good-humoured excitement. Between gulps for air he related something to the groom as the man took hold of the head of his heaving charger. And as soon as his feet touched the ground he turned to the man and, prancing around him in a parody of a prize fight, pretended to pummel him about the arms and shoulders.

Despite this, the groom apparently managed to tell him of her presence, for he straightened as if struck from behind and swung around to face her. Then immediately abandoned both horse and attendant to stride towards her and usher her back inside.

Now, when he closed the door again she said, 'It's his mother I'm worried about. She's had a relapse.'

'A relapse?'

'Another terrible attack of melancholy. Worse than after his father died.'

'Is that so? The poor dear lady.' He threw his riding crop on the table and sat down for the first time since arriving. He then leaned towards her with his face a mask of concern.

'It was all Jim and I could do to get her out of bed this mornin'. And she hasn't spoken a single word or eaten a scrap of food since we got the letter.'

'Is that right, lass? Dear, dear me! 'Tis a sad thing. For sure 'n' certain it is that.'

'That's why I came to see you.'

They were interrupted by a knock at the door.

'Come in! Come in!' he called out. The groom entered carrying a basket of wood on which was propped a leather flask and two metal cups. Fitzparsons slipped out of his chair and, retrieving these items, placed them on the table.

The groom put the basket down close to the brazier and pressed a number of short pieces of wood into the coals. Immediately odd puffs of smoke began to miss the flanged end of the flue and drift across the room.

Fitzparsons chuckled. 'You're bloody hopeless indoors, aren't y', Blakey? Now look what you've done, y'skinny ferret. Give me a go at it.' He snatched up a poker from the pan beneath the brazier and jabbed it about in the pile of wood and coals until most of the smoke was again being directed where it was meant to go. 'There y' are. Tha's better.'

He turned towards the man and then suddenly crouched and swept the poker backwards and forwards a number of times from close to the floor to high over his head. 'The Itchen gate, begad! And three times across the creek at the top of Long Common.'

Whether or not these cryptic utterances meant anything to the groom, Jessica could not determine. His gaze had returned to the brazier where thin spirals of smoke were again snaking around the lip of the flue and escaping into the room.

'You fool!' cried Fitzparsons, straightening and waving the poker in a spiral over his head. 'Y' 'aven't got the plaguey wind vane set right. Get y' skinny frame up on the roof and turn it about a bit while I give you directions.'

The groom stood for a moment looking at the brazier, probably weighing the risk of destroying his master's mood by daring to suggest that some further rearranging of the fire was all that was really required, against the risk of venturing on to the roof in the weather that prevailed.

He was a thin man whose most notable features were a sparsely thatched drooping moustache and a bowed back; so bowed that when viewed from the side he was the shape of a question mark. His name was not Blakey as Fitzparsons had called him, but Blakeney. Jessica had often seen him in the village and recalled hearing somewhere that he was a former professional jockey who had been forced to retire because of a succession of injuries. From his appearance it was difficult to dismiss the notion that a number of those injuries probably involved his mounts rolling on him.

'Out and up, Blakey.' Fitzparsons now waved the poker in a more threatening manner. 'Out and up. Before you have us gaspin' for air.'

At the point where Jessica was expecting Fitzparsons to actually strike the man, or do him some kind of injury with the poker, Blakeney turned and left, apparently deciding that the chance of being blown off the roof was the lighter risk.

'He's a hard man t'read, that one,' said Fitzparsons as the door closed behind Blakeney. 'I venture 'tis his weight stops him from showin' anythin'. His skin's so tight about his jaws he has trouble either frownin' or smilin'.' He spread his hand beneath the ballooning flesh of his own chin, and Jessica's attention was momentarily distracted by the remarkable colour and texture of that part of his anatomy. Where he protruded from the loose wrapping of his neckerchief, his flesh resembled the rump of a roasting pig, pink and crinkled with a sparse coating of fine white bristles poking through it.

He replaced the poker on the tray, flopped on to his chair, and picked up the leather-encased flask. 'The man's the best judge of horseflesh I've ever had.' He unscrewed the lid of the flask. 'Ever! That new bay o'mine has wings. Wings!

God! Jump! Run! The best ever.' He poured an ample helping of the contents of the flask into each of the metal cups and held one of them out to Jessica. 'Here, drink this before you catch your death.'

'No. I'm fine. Thank you. No.'

'Drink up, lass. It's medicinal. Heaven knows what you might come down with otherwise.' He thrust the cup into her hands. 'Drink.'

She sipped, and gagged.

'Not like that. It'll burn you. Down the hatch. Like this.' He drained the other cup in a gulp and leant forward so that he was leaning over her. 'Now you. Go on. Tip it up.'

He loomed around her. She was seized by a moment of claustrophobic panic and found herself doing as he demanded while she was still in the throes of refusing to. The liquid took her breath. She sat for a moment with her eyes smarting, wondering if she would ever again be able to breathe. After what seemed like an age, and besieged by continuing panic, her chest rose and fell heavily.

'Now, isn't that better? Surely that warmed the cockles o' your heart?' Before she could complain he asked, 'Now what is it exactly that you want me t' do? How can I help you?'

She waited until she was sure her breathing had returned to stay. 'I want you to use your influence to have Will released from the navy. His mother's life depends on it. I'm sure of that.'

'My influence? You think I might have that influence?'

'I believe you'd have more influence than anyone else in the area. Havin' once been in the navy, and havin' regular dealin's with Portsmouth. I've heard that men who have been pressed have been released after representation by someone such as yourself. When there was good reason. Farmers or men in business whose families depended on them for their survival, f'r instance. And men with other family problems.'

She waited, watching him. He had moved back slightly but was still too close. She had trouble looking at him without a sense of unease. As if she was leaning at an uncomfortable angle, or was standing too close to a precipice.

'Who told you these things?'

'Reverend Smith-Wilson.'

He shook his head sadly. 'That man again. Won't I ever be rid of 'm?' He turned away and picking up the flask refilled his cup. Then before she realised what he was doing, he reached out and refilled hers.

'He said that he would write to the navy himself,' she said. Her eyes were on the cup, as if she had missed seeing what he had just done and was wondering how the liquid had arrived there. 'But ... But he doubted his chances of success. Bein' only a village parson.'

'That little prickle'd have no more chance of success if he was the Archbishop of ruddy

Canterbury. He'd still be as useless as a flute to a pig.'

A heavy thump above them caused them both to look up.

Fitzparsons rose from his chair. 'Turn it out of the wind,' he called out loudly, and grabbing hold of the poker again began to jab it into the coals in a similar manner as before. 'More. Back a bit. Back a bit. Too far. Too far. Christ! Back a bit. Back a bit. That's it. That's it. Leave it. Leave it. Leave it, man. That's perfect. Don't dare touch it again. Come back down.' He put down the poker and dropped back into his chair. 'Strange skinny little man.'

Under different circumstances it would have amused Jessica to know that the thump they heard had been the sound of the top of a ladder striking the roof. Blakeney did have one foot on the bottom rung while Fitzparsons was yelling at him. But at no stage did he, or his other foot, leave the ground.

Fitzparsons sat staring at Jessica intently. Assuming he was trying to recall what was being said immediately before the interruption, she prompted, 'Can you help us?'

'Us?'

'Will's mother. Mainly.'

'And you?'

'Yes. And me.'

He glanced back at the roof. 'Funny man. Doesn't show an ounce of enthusiasm in anythin', but I'd miss the beggar now if he fell off and broke his plaguey neck.' He chuckled. 'But damned if I know how we'd tell he was dead.' He shook his head. 'That horse! I could've kissed him. If you hadn't been there when I got back I probably would've. Hugged him at least.' He sat staring at her.

She tried to match his gaze, but turned away abruptly when she felt sure that his eyes were locked, not on her eyes, but on her lips.

'Can you help us?' she repeated.

'Perhaps. Tell me what reason y'have that you think the navy would listen to?'

'I'm not sure. I thought you'd know how?' She watched him, waiting, concerned by his question, a possible change in his mood. 'Perhaps his mother's illness?' A question. Tentative.

He shook his head. 'I don't think so. Not alone. You'd need more. Most pressed men have mothers. And many of those mothers'd be in bad health. Bad.' He leant even closer, swamping her vision. His head, neck and chest seemed to expand as she watched.

'We need him at home?' She could taste the return of her panic. Her throat began to tighten.

'You're shiverin' again. Drink some more brandy. It'll do you good.'

She shook her head.

'Drink up, lass. I'll be wastin' my time tryin' to get him out for someone who'll be dead next week of plaguey p-monia.'

'You'll try, then? You think there's a chance?'

'Drink.'

She drank and winced, but more from the expectation of hurt than the reality. The fluid still bit her, but less severely. The bite was almost comforting.

Above them the shingles rattled, caught in a stronger than normal burst of wind. The contrast between their cosy surrounds and the weather outside was inducing within her a soothing sense of comfort. Her fingers tingled. Warmer than before.

'You'll try?'

'If I think it's worth the risk.'

'Risk? What risk?'

'Risk to me. Not to you. But more of that later. First tell me if you were lovers.'

'What?'

'A sick mother t'aint enough. Not by a long shot. But a sick mother, plus a wife endangered by hellfire, and maybe we're startin' to build an argument.'

'What are you talkin' about? Wife? Hellfire? We're not married. Not yet.'

'No. But silly little Smith-Whistle would swear on his good book that you were just about to be. And if you were to say that you were already livin' as man and wife . . .' He opened both hands and spread his arms as if he were about to clap them together. 'Man and wife in a house that you now have to share with a very sick mother-in-law to be, and a very healthy big brother-in-law to be . . . '. He fluttered his hands. 'Maybe we'd have an argument the navy would listen to.'

'What are you sayin'?' Her head was swimming.

'Jim the giant. He's a danger to your moral well-bein', lass. Specially with poor Mrs Noling unable to protect you.'

'But that's absurd. Jim's not a danger to anyone.'

'The navy don't know that. And who knows what danger he might become if Will doesn't get home for years.'

'Years?'

'As long as the war lasts. Years, for sure.'

Years! Her gaze was locked on the rim of her cup as he refilled it. She made no attempt to stop him. Years!

'Were you livin' as man and wife in that house?'

'No. Never.'

'Sailors don't often have legal wives. So as long as you shared his bed on a regular basis, they'd probably recognise you as his wife. Particularly if Smith-Whistle gives his blessing, and endorses the dangers of a healthy live-in brother-in-law.'

'We never shared a bed.'

'A hayloft?'

He tried to hold her gaze but she turned away.

'How many times?'

'What?'

'If the navy question us to determine if we're tellin' the truth, I'll have to know as much as you do about these matters. So how many times? Ten, twenty, thirty?'

'No.'

'How many.'

'Not often.'

'Ten?'

'I don't know.'

'We'll say ten.'

Now her eyes sought his. 'Do you think they'll let him go?'

'If I'm willin' to take the risk of representin' you they might.'

'What do you mean risk?'

'I mean risk risk. Like yon Blakeney riskin' breakin' his plaguey neck by climbin' on to a roof in this wind. Risk.'

'What would be the risk?'

'For you. None. For me, maybe all the trade I do with the plaguey navy.'

Her heart sank. 'Why would you be riskin' that?'

'Why indeed?'

'I mean. How would you be riskin' that?'

'By makin' waves. Strange as it may seem the navy don't like someone makin' waves. Do you know what a contract is?'

'An agreement.'

'Aye,' he watched her intently. 'An agreement.' Ripples began to surge through the gradually strengthening ache of concern that was forming in the pit of her stomach. He continued, 'An agreement. Usually between two parties where both of 'm will gain by it. Otherwise there's no reason t' enter into a contract. I guarantee t' supply the navy with good quality produce at an agreed price. They guarantee to buy my produce at that price. I have a guaranteed income regardless of what's happenin' with the produce markets, and they have guaranteed supply. We both gain.'

Although she did not perceive that he had moved, he suddenly seemed to be sitting even closer to her. Her throat continued to tighten. Panic. Swirling within her.

'You're shivering again. Drink up.'

'No.'

'The moment I write to the navy, I'll risk losin' that contract.'

'How?'

'Like I said, waves. I'll write to Porky Jamieson, deputy director of manning. Porky'll be all right. Porky's an old friend. He shoots at my place. But others who see my request may object to my inter-ferin'. Seein' it's war, Porky's decision might need endorsement. Who knows what jealous prickle at the Admiralty might take exception. If Jackie Jervis was to hear about it, for instance, or whatever he calls himself these days—Saint Vincent—I'd be chopped off cold from so much as thinkin' about doin' business with the fleet. They'd tear up my contract. I'd lose a lot of income.'

She could not even look at him now. He was far too close. The sense of panic was creeping into every part of her body, every limb, every blood vessel.

'Drink up, Jessica. Medicinal. Down the hatch.'

Panic. She was unsure if the words were real or remembered. She drank. No bite. Soothing. The panic began to subside. The glow from her fingers seemed to have spread along her arms and into her chest. She was being consumed by a curious mix of panic and comfort. Her head swam.

'So I ask myself if I were to agree to help you, how should I hedge against that possible loss of income? Loss of contract? Do you have any ideas, Jessica?'

She shook her head.

'I believe that you and I should enter into a contract. That way if I lose my contract with the navy, I'll still have my contract with you to salve my wounds.'

'How do you mean? I don't . . . don't have any money.'

'Contracts don't have to involve the exchange of money, sweet girl. This one would cover the exchange of services. My services for yours.' He waited.

She waited.

'On my part, my services will be representin' you in tryin' to get Will out of the navy.'

She continued to wait.

'Do you know Mrs McMarks?'

'What? Who?'

'Gretchen McMarks, the tailor's wife?'

'I see her at church. Why?'

'She and I have a contract of sorts.'

'What kind of contract?'

'Her husband makes m'suits. I used to have 'm
made in London. But he gets some decent cloth from
time to time, and he and his staff are fair hands with
needles, so I use'm. And I encourage quite a number
of my associates to use'm. They too could have them
made in London if they wanted. My contract with
his wife is quite a simple one: I agree to continue to
use his services and recommend him to my friends,
as long as each time he makes a suit for me, or for
my friends, she delivers them here to the house personal. Also, whenever I need to discuss orders or
payments or fittings, she's the one I deal with. Here.
At the house.'

'I don't understand.'

'The answer's quite simple. I'm a lover of
beauty, lass. Mrs McMarks is a beautiful woman.'

She watched him warily.

'I have a similar arrangement with Mrs Fletching, the saddler's wife. She too is a woman of rare
quality.'

'Mrs Fletching, the church organist?'

'On a regular basis she visits here as well. Very
regularly.'

'To deliver saddles.'

'No, no.' He chuckled. 'To play my mother's
violoncello.'

'You're interested in her music?'

'I'm interested in her beauty. Her music amuses
me as well. But, as with Gretchen, it's her beauty
tha's my real interest.'

'You've signed some kind of contract with these ladies?'

'Ladies?' He pursed his lips. 'We're talkin' about a tailor's wife and a saddler's wife, lass. No. I've signed nothin'. They've signed nothin'. The contracts we have are verbal. Same as the one I will make with you will be verbal. Verbal contracts between trustworthy people are as bindin' as written contracts.'

'I still don't understand. In return for helpin' me, do you want me to work for you?'

He shook his head. 'No.' He smiled. 'I just want you to come here. On a regular basis, same as those two. Not on the same days, of course. What's today? Monday. Let's say every Monday mornin'.'

'Why?'

'I want to see you.'

'That's all? Just see me? Like this? Like y'seein' me now?'

'Have y'ever seen any grand works of art, Jessica? Paintin's of gods and goddesses?' He swept his hand in an arc. 'I don't suppose you've ever had a chance to peek inside any of the big manors. But most of'm have paintin's of the type I'm talkin' about. I have one or two examples myself. We could go and see what I'm talkin' about later.'

She shook her head. 'No. I don't need to go and see. I know what y' talkin' about.'

'What am I talkin' about?'

'You're talkin about naked people.'

'You've seen such paintin's?'

'No. But I've heard about them.' A lie. A former school friend who was in service at Duckwick Hall near Hedge End, once showed her around the house when the owners and most of the staff were away on a picnic.

Suddenly she needed room. She gripped the sides of her chair with both hands, and taking all her weight on her feet for a moment, she manoeuvred the chair away from him. And when she could focus on most of him again she gave him a searching look.

'What?' he asked.

'You would be the last person I'd have picked for bein' an artist.'

'An artist?'

'That's what you get them to do, isn't it? Mrs McMarks and Mrs Fletching. Officially you have them comin' here to deliver suits of clothes and to play music. But that's not what they've agreed to do, is it? That's not what your contracts with them are about?'

'Officially?'

She described two mirrored circles with her hands. 'For show. To conceal the real reason.'

'The real reason?'

'You paint them.'

'Good God! Why would I want to do that?'

'But isn't that what you've been leadin' up to? Why you've been talkin' about paintin's of naked gods and goddesses. And you want me to pose for you as well?'

'No, I don't paint 'm.'

'You don't? What . . . what do you do?'

'I told you. I'm a lover of beauty. I like to look at 'm. I truly do. I love lookin' at beautiful women. I always have done. Sometimes I sit and watch'm for hours.'

She lowered her head. 'Naked?' Softly. A tentative footstep into the dark.

'Of course.'

'And that's all? Just look at them?'

'Sometimes. If it's in m' mood.'

'And at other times?'

'At other times I might feel inclined to touch 'm.' He chuckled. 'And of course, on the occasions when my mood is really up . . . ' He closed a fist and raised his forearm. 'I swive the livin' daylights out of the gorgeous creatures.'

Her mouth dropped open. When she regained some control of it, she said, 'You don't for a moment believe I'd be willin' to enter into such an arrangement with you?'

'You will if you want to see young Will'm before the shine's gone off 'im. Or maybe ever, if he gets into a decent battle with Johnny Crapaud. And with him sailin' around with Nelson that's more'n likely.'

'I don't believe this. What kind of person do you think I am? Do you think I'm a whore?'

'What kind of person do you think Gretchen

McMarks is, or Sybil Fletching, for God's sake? Do y' think they're whores?'

'How can you live with yourself? Those poor women!'

'Poor women, balderdash! I gain, they gain.'

'Gain!' She shook her head. 'You gain, that's for sure. And I suppose their husbands' businesses gain. But please don't offend my senses by claiming that those poor women gain.'

'Jessica, Jessica. Sweet little innocent Jessica.' He shook his head.

'How do they gain? By exposing themselves to your leering gaze? By letting themselves be mauled by you? You can't believe that.'

'Would you be surprised, Jessica, if I told you that Gretchen's husband hasn't swived her in five years? Apparently his interests in that regard lie elsewhere. And Sybil's husband has never seen her naked. Ever. Whenever he's had the opportunity, he turns away. Quickly. As if the sight of her would offend him. Offend him! One of the most gorgeous bodies that God ever put on this earth. Oh, he does swive her from time to time. But he does it in the dark, and under cover. Gets it over and done with as fast as he can, like it's some disagreeable duty he has to perform. Can you believe that? He's never seen her.'

'She'd tell you somethin' like that?'

'Of course she'd tell me somethin' like that. She trusts me. She likes me. It's the main reason why she comes, for pity's sake. T' talk. T' let me admire her beauty. She knows me for what I am. A true lover of beauty.

'Smith-Whistle's the culprit, y' know. The silly little prickle. Brow-beatin' his mindless brethren into believin' they should be ashamed of their own bodies. Ashamed t' look at their own loved ones. I tell you what the prickle's done, he's killed the lovin' relationships that once existed in many homes of Lowfoley. Killed 'm. Killed 'm dead. I could tell you of others. A host of 'm. Lowfoley's a sadder place for that prickle's comin', I can tell you.'

He waved a hand in the general direction of the house. 'Here Sybil's free to roam as naked as the day she was born. And she does just that. Proudly. And I watch her. And my eyes are filled with awe at the very sight of the beautiful creature she is. Not disgust. I gain. And she gains. Truly gains. I don't need to lie to you.

'Sometimes she plays the violoncello without a stitch of clothin' on her body. Not a stitch, from the top of her head to the tips of her long toes. Now that's a wonderful sight t' behold. Her legs spread wide and the inside of her knees caressin' the polished wood of that lovely instrument. Her head down. Her hair out and wavin' gently.' He swept his hand slowly from side to side. 'Back and forth as she strokes the bow. Paradise would not have many sights as breathtakin' as that one.'

'I can hardly believe we're havin' this conversation. Why are you tellin' me these things?'

'You know why I'm tellin' you. Gretchen McMarks and Sybil Fletching are highly respected members of the Lowfoley community. I respect 'm. You respect 'm. I can see by your surprise at what I've been telling you how much you respect them. And the whole damned parish respects 'm. And now that y' know they've entered into a similar contract with me as the one I'm offerin' you, what I'm offerin' probably doesn't seem as terrifyin'. And if you believe me when I tell you that they revel in our agreement—and I think you do—then also what I'm offerin' must seem less threatenin'.'

'Whether or not I believe what you say about these women doesn't alter the fact that you're demandin' that I become your whore or you'll refuse to help me. And by tellin' me that Will could be killed if I don't agree is nothin' less than cruel blackmail. So please don't insult me by makin' out that you're some kind of benefactor, and that I'll be advantaged by your attentions. What you're demandin' makes me sick to the pit of my stomach. If I knew that by killin' myself Will would be released, then I'd gladly kill myself rather than accept your offer.'

'Jessica, Jessica!' He chuckled and shook his head. 'You're so young. Only someone so young could make a statement like that. Kill yourself, indeed! There might be some fates worse than death, lass, but I can assure you that what I'm askin' of you isn't one of'm. It's not even as if you're a virgin. You've admitted to me you've been lettin' young Will'm swive you. You won't lose anythin' by this experience. You'll gain. I promise you, you will. You can look upon it as an extension to your education.'

She shuddered.

'Come closer to the fire, girl.'

She lowered her head and closed her eyes. 'I suppose you'll tell them about me? The others?'

He smiled triumphantly and nodded, his eyes focused intently where strands of hair on the top of her head glowed crimson in the light from the lamp. 'Of course. I'll even boast to them about you. I'll tease them. Try and make them jealous. But don't be afraid they'll be indiscreet. Talk of this to outsiders. They are both truly married, and would stand to lose more than you would in the eyes of the community.'

She raised her head and gripped him with her gaze. 'How do I know you'll do as you say and try and get Will released?'

'You don't. You must trust me. As I must trust you to come when I say, and do as I ask. Contracts of this type depend on trust. For instance, I'm not even goin' to demand that we consummate our relationship before I send off my letter to Porky Jamieson. I'll write the letter tonight and send it off to him tomorrow.'

'What do you mean "consummate"?'

He smiled and watched her for a moment before replying. 'We can blame Gretchen McMarks for that one. Consummate. Consummate doesn't do justice to the activity I'm referrin' to. I'll wager young Will'm never referred to what you two got up to in the hayloft as consummatin' your relationship. What I should have said was that as a mark of my trust, I won't even demand that you let me roger you before I send the letter.'

Again, her mouth fell open.

He showed her his teeth in an exaggerated smile. 'And as it'll be a full week before I see you again, you can appreciate the level of my trust that you'll honour our agreement.'

'I haven't ... ' Her voice wavered and failed. With an effort she continued. 'I haven't agreed to anythin'.'

'Oh yes you have, m' lass. Perhaps not in so many words. But you couldn't be more definite in your intentions if you'd had what you've decided to do drawn up by a lawyer.'

'I didn't say I'd do it.' She knew her words sounded hollow. The repeat of a revealed and acknowledged lie.

'Seein' you place so much importance on the words, just to be on the safe side, best I spell out what we're exchanging, and receive your verbal agreement. On my part I agree to use all the influence I can bring to bear on havin' young Will'm released from the navy, startin' by sendin' a letter to Porky Jamieson tomorrow, and further letters and affidavits if required to senior officers later. On your part you must agree to any demands I make of you of a personal nature, and to that end you must agree to come here every Monday mornin' until I release you of that obligation.'

'Every Monday?'

'Every Monday.'

'What about when Will returns?'

'The same. Every Monday. And when you have him back you'll be under a stronger obligation t' honour our agreement, won't you?'

'I couldn't do that to him. I couldn't.'

'Oh yes you could. If you want him released.'

'But what excuse could I use for comin'?'

'The same one you can use before we get him out. You can say that you're havin' violoncello lessons.'

'My God!' She lowered her head.

'Do you agree to the conditions, Jessica?'

She did not move for some time, and then she nodded. Once. Firmly.

'Say it then. Seein' you place so much importance on the words. Say "I agree".'

'I agree.' A whisper.

He leant forward. 'I didn't quite catch that.'

She lifted her head and faced him squarely. 'I agree. I agree. And may you rot in hell!'

His face broke into a beaming smile. 'Now that's more like it. That's the spirit I like to see.'

She stood up. 'I'm going now. But I'll be back tomorrow.'

'You don't have to come tomorrow, lass. Next Monday is when I'll expect you. About nine o'clock.'

'I'll be here tomorrow. I want to collect the letter you say you'll write tonight. I'll give it to Reverend Smith-Wilson. He's travellin' to London on Wednesday. He can deliver it to the Admiralty personally.'

He continued to smile. 'Jessica, I'm not sure that you trust me. If you come I'll show you the letter, but there's no way on this earth that I'll let you pass it on to Smith-Whistle to deliver. That incompetent prickle will have his work cut out findin' London, let alone the Admiralty Building. I'll post it myself. With my seal on it and directed to the right quarters it'll have a much better chance of arrivin' where it's meant to go.'

'I'd prefer you gave me the letter.'

'I know what's best, Jessica. Trust me.'

She made as if to reply but was as someone caught in a churning current. The events that swirled about her were transporting her towards some elusive destination at bewildering speed. She lost the thread of the reply that had been forming on her lips, and muttered instead, 'I'll be here at nine.' For a long moment she could not remember why she would be. Panic seized her and she trembled. Her eyes sought the doorway, and escape.

'I'll be expectin' you. But before you go . . .' He reversed his riding crop and placed the end of the thickened grip against her waist. The grip had a large silver knob attached to the end. A stylised leopard's head. Mouth agape. Snarling. The prow of a Viking ship in miniature.

He twisted the crop slightly so that the jaws of the leopard for a moment were caught in folds of material where her dress was bunched above the broad scarf she was using as a belt. 'As a gesture of good faith ... or at least as an indication of your sincerity ... would you disrobe for me, lass?'

'What?'

'Would you take your clothes off? I want to see you naked.'

'Here? Now?'

'I need a memory of you that'll last me a week.'

'But ...' She looked about her. Trapped.

'Please, Jessica. No buts. We have an agreement.'

'But you said ... You wouldn't. Not for a week.'

'I said I wouldn't roger you. And I won't. But I do want to see you. Here ...' He stood up. 'I'll give you room.' He lifted his chair away from her and sat down again. Then with his free elbow resting on the table and the other one tucked into his waist, he aimed the doubled thong of the riding crop at her and waved it up and down. 'Stand closer to the fire so you don't catch cold. And put your things over the back of the chair.'

She matched his gaze for a time, and then her shoulders rose and fell, and she turned away.

She did not look at him again until she was naked, and then only to cast him a contemptuous glare before picking out a spot over his head just below the window, and gazing at it steadily. Her mind was still juggling with their discussion about the letter. Something was not right. It worried her. A deep-seated itch her fingers could not quite reach.

'Turn this way, lass. A little more. Now take your hands away. Both of them.' He made a sound that may have been a chuckle, but when she glanced at him for a moment his expression seemed more strained than amused. 'You'll fall over if you try and stand like that, girl. Spread your feet. Further. Further still. Do as I say, lass. That's better. That's much better. My goodness, Jessica. Pardon me if I stay quiet for a while. I am a lover of beauty, lass. Whether you believe that or not. And what I'm lookin' at now leaves me speechless.'

She returned her attention to the spot below the window, with part of her mind still grinding away at the concern that eluded her. *What is it? What on earth could be more troubling than this? My God! What's happened to me that I can endure such indignity without fainting completely away? It must be the brandy!* Her fingers were still tingling. *But how is it that I can be less troubled by what I'm doing now, and what he'll be doing to me next week, than by some worry that I'm not even sure exists? Something I can't even identify?* Finally, she said, 'I've done what you said. Now I'm goin' to get dressed.'

'Before you do, lass, would you turn around

slowly. Yes. Now stop. Stay like that for a moment.'

Her back was to him. She waited. Suddenly she was aware that he was close. She began to turn, but his hands clasped her shoulders tightly. He pressed against her. She could smell the brandy on his breath. Feel its heat.

'What are you doin'?'

He turned her towards the bed and began to edge her forward.

'No,' she whispered. 'You promised.' You promised, she repeated somewhere deep inside her. And then again, *you promised!*

Suddenly her head cleared as if she had been struck by a blast of cold air. The letter! Of course! That's why he won't let anyone else take it, post it. He has no intention of delivering it. He never did. He's a liar! This is a trap!

'The sight of you has overwhelmed me, girl. I can't wait a week. I can't wait a moment.'

'No,' she whispered. He was almost lifting her now. 'No. Not here. Someone might come.'

'No one will come.'

She looked about her frantically. 'What's that? What's in there?' She pointed to the hatch on the end wall.

'The chaff store.'

'We can go in there?' she whispered.

'The chaff store? It's half full of chaff.'

'We'll be out of sight.'

'We're out of sight here.'

'Not if someone comes.'

He chuckled. 'I think you've had too many tumbles in the hay, lass. But if that's your choice, and it'll make you feel better, the chaff store it is. Providin' of course that I can fit through that hatchway.'

He could. Remarkably easily as it turned out, holding Jessica's hand for balance as he climbed through. And he went through first at her insistence to show her that there were no rats or mice waiting in ambush.

It wasn't until he was completely inside that he realised his mistake. But he was able to react a moment before she tried to wrench her hand from his. His anticipation caught her by surprise. His grip crushed down on her hand.

So she bit him, deeply, sinking her teeth into the back of his hand with all the force she could muster into her jaws. He gasped and released her, and fell back into the chaff. Before he could recover she slammed the hatch cover closed and drove home the bolt.

'You lied to me,' she cried, leaning against the wall, her chest heaving. 'You lied to me about the letter, as you lied you would not touch me today. You're an evil man.'

He flung himself against the inside of the hatch as she turned away and snatched up her clothes. She dragged them on, whimpering fearfully as resounding thumps and muffled cries sounded from the locker.

She was deep within the forest when she heard the pounding of hooves behind her. Immediately she turned and dashed to one side. She plunged through the dense undergrowth determined to put as much distance as she could between herself and the road before the rider came abreast of her. Wet foliage slapped at her. Dead twigs stabbed into her clothing, and vines twirled cords around her ankles threatening to bring her down. As the rumble of pursuit grew closer she threw herself to the ground and lay clinging to the shrubs that surrounded her.

She had run most of the way from the stables and her chest was heaving in protest. She almost choked trying to stifle the harsh rasping of her breath as a lone rider galloped past.

For many minutes the forest lay silent in the horse's wake. She waited. When some sounds began to return, a whisper of leaves here, a rustle there, and in the distance the cry of a bird, she rose from her hiding place and made her way back to the road. She was almost clear of the forest when she realised she was in danger. A horse whinnied close by. She froze. The sound came from behind, and from the low side of the road. She turned back and kept moving, angling off the road to the high side.

Fitzparsons stepped from behind a tree immediately ahead of her. He stood facing her with his legs spread wide and holding his riding crop in front of his crotch with both hands. She saw that his right hand was roughly bandaged.

'You disappoint me, Jessica. We had an agreement.'

'We don't any more.' Despite attempting to project an image of fearless resolve, she was unable to overcome the tremor in her voice.

'You deceived me, lass. You're not to be trusted.'

'You lied to me. You never intended to send that letter.'

'You don't know that.'

'I know it. The moment you touched me I knew you for what you were.'

'Would you have come back in a week, Jessica?'

'Perhaps. If you hadn't lied to me.'

'I somehow doubt it, lass. Not when you had a chance to think about it in slower time. And I'm not sure I did lie to you. I admit I wasn't seriously considerin' sendin' the letter at first. But when you agreed to come each Monday without too much complaint, even should Will'm be released, I contemplated takin' the risk.'

His words confused her. She wanted no truck with them. 'Would you please step aside. You're in my way.'

She moved towards him and he did step aside. But only for a moment.

Although she was half expecting him to make a move, his speed for a big man again caught her by surprise. He threw both arms around her and crushed her against him. She could feel the bulbous handle of his riding crop pressed into the pit of her back. She tried to drive her knee into his crotch but lost her footing and fell backwards. He fell on top of her, knocking the breath out of her. She lay gasping, desperately trying to inhale.

One of his hands worked its way beneath her dress. His other hand clutched her throat, cruelly driving back her jaw. For pity's sake, let me breathe, her mind screamed. You can do what you want but please let me breathe. By the time she regained her breath, he had forced her legs apart and had manoeuvred his huge frame between them. Her dress was bunched around her waist. She could still feel the handle of the riding crop pressed into her back.

When he lifted his weight away from her and began to open the flap at the front of his trousers, she managed to raise herself slightly and grasp the riding crop halfway along its length. Then, before he lowered himself on top of her again, she pulled the crop from beneath her and held it at her side.

'Raise your legs, lass,' he muttered amidst gasps for air close to her ear. 'I'll hurt you otherwise.'

She carefully lifted the crop away from her side and fully extended her arm, grasping it as she would a hammer. And then with a wild shout she pivoted her elbow and brought the weighted grip down onto the back of his head. It struck with a dull thud. He gasped and tried to scramble out of reach. She struck again. And again. And fought her way out from underneath him, kicking wildly and threshing with her legs. He clawed up at her face as she came to her knees. But now she had room to swing her weapon with more vigour and brought it down squarely on to the centre of his forehead.

He fell back, clutching at the wound. 'My God, girl. I'll skin you alive for that,' he shouted.

She lurched to her feet and, whimpering like a wounded animal, plunged into the forest in head-long flight. She ran as fast as her legs would operate, heedless of obstructions that would surely cripple her. More than once she was startled by loud and frightened whimpering, only to discover that it was her own.

Finally she began to stagger and then sank to her knees. She used her remaining energy to crawl into a patch of tall ferns.

She was uncertain how long she lay there. But when she sat up, she found the night had already grasped the understorey of the forest. A diffused gloom pressed in on her from all sides. A bird shrieked suddenly close by and she heard a scuffle in the undergrowth. She froze. And then instinctively she reached for the rough stone she could feel pressed against her thigh. Only it was not a stone, as she discovered when her fingers closed over it. It was Fitzparsons' riding crop. She had no memory of carrying it during her flight. But as she rose to her feet and looked about her warily, she clung to the shaft as she had clung to it earlier, ready to defend herself. It could have been a hammer. Or a battleaxe.

Something was wrong at the Noling farm. Jessica quickened her pace. The front door was open. Light spilled into the garden. People were moving about. Distorted shadows speared past her.

Black uniforms. Constables. One was carrying a lantern. My God! There's been an accident. She began to run. There's Jim. It must be Mrs Noling. No! Please, no!

'You there!' The shout assailed her from somewhere near the barn. 'Stop! Stay where you are.'

She stopped and peered into the dark.

'Sir. Jamie. Quick. She's over here. Stay where you are, miss. Don't you dare try and run.'

She could see him now. He was climbing over the railings beside the barn.

Suddenly she felt trapped. Instinctively she raised the riding crop. And then without fully realising why, quickly lowered it again and flicked it into the base of the closest hedge. She then stood as if bracing herself against an imminent collision as they converged on her.

'Jessica Glider?' the first one to reach her demanded, holding up a lantern and directing light on to her. He was a thickset man, with a moonshaped face and bristling grey tussocks beneath his eyes. As the others gathered around her she could see he was older than his companions.

'What's happened?' she asked.

'That's what we'd like you to tell us.'

'What do you mean?'

'Sir Rory Fitzparsons says that you attacked him and robbed him.'

'What? That's a lie.'

She turned towards Jim as he approached from the house.

'I told them it was a mistake, Jess.'

'Is your mother all right?'

'As right as when you left.'

'Thank God!'

'You'll have to come with us, miss. You can collect some clothes you might need.'

'But I didn't do anything wrong.'

'Others will be the judge of that.'

The man who had been in the barnyard stepped closer.

'She was carryin' this, sir.' He passed over Fitzparsons' riding crop. 'When she saw us, she threw it into that hedge.'

'Interestin' situation, this,' said the older man, holding up the crop and directing light from his lantern on to it. 'You claimin' you didn't do nothin' wrong, yet us catchin' you tryin' to hide this highly expensive item Sir Rory tells us you stole from him. And him lyin' in bed with his head banged up like he'd just done forty rounds with Jack Broughton, and you bein' in possession of this here handy head-banger that is still smeared with dried blood. Wouldn't you say that was interestin'?'

'I'm tellin' you, I didn't do anythin' wrong.'

'If I were you, missy, I wouldn't go insultin' my intelligence any further by persistin' with that ridiculous claim.'

FOUR

Earlier, on the same day that HMS *Victory* joined up with the Mediterranean fleet off Cap Sicie southwest of Toulon, Sir Rory Fitzparsons wrote a letter to his cousin Garth Barlester.

Making allowance for the original atrocious spelling and punctuation, the letter read, in part:

You will remember the young people we met outside of Lowfoley, the ones with the hair. The most amazing thing! The boy got himself pressed into the navy. Who would believe it, after what we talked about? He is somewhere with Nelson. But the big news that I am writing to you about is the girl. She was sentenced to death at the Portsmouth sessions. Yes, to death! Can you believe that? For highway robbery! I was there when the judge put on his cap and sentenced her, and you will never guess why in a thousand years. I was the one she robbed. Can you believe it? The judge said, 'Take her back to gaol, and thence to a place of execution, and there be hanged until she is dead, for felonious assault on one, Sir Rory Fitzparsons, on the King's highway, and violently taking from him against his will one riding crop with a crafted silver handle of the value eighteen pounds.' You know, the one with the animal's head. As I told the court, she came to see me on the same morning and asked that I use my influence to have Will Noling, a sailor she had an illicit relationship with, released from the navy. In return she offered me favours I could not bring my lips to repeat in front of the ladies present. When I refused her demands she became abusive and left. Later, on the Durley road, she struck me with a stone, knocking me off my horse, and then struck me a number of times with my riding crop, which she then stole from my person. Her face was covered but I recognised her red hair and clothes. I told the local constables and they went to the Noling farm. She tried to hide the riding crop and they arrested her. I approached the judges after the sessions to plead for leniency. I told them she always had been a good girl and may have been out of her mind because of Will Noling leaving her. As a result of my representation she was one of those the judges reprieved. She had her sentence commuted to transportation for seven years to New South Wales, which of course was what I intended. She is now on a hulk in Langston Harbour waiting to join the ship that has been chartered to transport them. It probably will be the *Weymouth Bay*, being outfitted at Plymouth. This letter might arrive on the same ship. Who would have thought you would be the one to gain? The best laid plans and all of that. I think I will have to visit you in Sydney some day like you suggested. Some fools think I must have forgiven her for acting as I did, but hanging her would have been too good for her after what she did. I was in bed for a week, and I will carry a great scar on my forehead for life, and one on my hand where she bit me through to the bone. I still cannot close my hand. The bitch! Her full name is Jessica Caroline Glider. I know you will make sure she pays. But never turn your back on her.

When the *Victory* joined the Mediterranean fleet off Cap Sicie, Nelson was not on board. He had already joined the fleet earlier, having transferred his flag to the *Amphion* commanded by his friend Captain Thomas Hardy. He departed from the *Victory* three days out of Portsmouth.

On the day Nelson left, the gunports were closed against the weather on the starboard side of the lower gun deck. Most of those on the port side were also closed, and the few that were not had their lids only partly ajar. Spikes of light from the openings speared backwards and forwards across the deck in harmony with the roll of the ship, highlighting here and there among the original timbers the more varied shades of the newer beams and planking of elm and oak that had been recently fitted at Chatham.

A seemingly endless row of 32-pounder guns stretched away into the gloom. Guns' crews were working on those at the for'ard end; treating the metal on some with vinegar and applying a liberal coating of hot oil from steaming pots to those that had been previously treated. Some of the guns were secured by jury rigs while the men spliced and attached new breeching ropes to the barrels. Men were also rigging the heavy wooden blocks with new rope, while others were greasing the runners and sheaves. Gunners' mates were servicing new gunlocks that had been fitted at Chatham, while others were checking the gun-loading and cleaning equipment used during action: the rammers and sponges used for servicing the barrel, and the rimmers and worms used to clear the firing vent.

Towards the after end of the deck on the starboard side, where all daylight was blocked from the opposite side, were two men whose bare-chested forms were caught in the regular sweep of a matrix of interlaced light and shadow thrown from a number of swinging lanthorns attached to the low deckhead. One of the men was sitting on a low stool facing a gun and bracing himself against the ship's roll with a forearm locked against the carriage. The other man was standing behind him, applying a thin ointment to the bare back of the man in front of him with a padded applicator that he was dipping regularly into a ceramic pot.

Only by getting close to them could their conversation be heard above the groaning of the timbers, the regular clump-thump of the gun carriages and the sympathetic creaking of the breeching ropes.

'I think you'll live. They be still weepin' but not so much.'

Will Noling risked unclenching his teeth. 'How can you people stand this?'

'A floggin'? You stand it by avoidin' it, matey. Keepin' well away from trouble, and by that, well clear o'the man with the cat.'

'Not the floggin'.' He waited out a trembling lurch of his stomach. The air was thick with a rich mix of tar-impregnated oakum, vinegar and oil, fresh paint, and vomit. 'This never-endin' movement. This forever pitchin' and rollin'. Is it always so rough?'

The other man chuckled dryly. 'This ain't rough, matey. This 'ere be a gentle swell. And it ain't pitchin' and rollin' neither. This only be rollin'. Ye're lucky ye don't have t' bed down up for'ard. Tha's where you'd find out what pitchin' be. You'll find out 'ere as well when we cross the Bay. If we cross the Bay.'

'What do you mean?'

'Nelson left us this mornin'. Maybe we won't be goin' to the Med after all.'

'What d'you mean? Nelson left us? This is his ship.'

'Not any more. He transferred to a frigate and sailed for Gibraltar without us.'

111

'Why?'

'We be off the Ile d'Ouessant. D'ye like m'French? Comes from runnin' brandy from Cherbourg to Weymouth in the days before the one when I ran clean out o' wind off Portland Bill.' He contemplated this for a moment. 'Anyways, the Grand Fleet was s'posed to be 'ere blockadin' Brest. Nelson weren't sure that Cornwallis didn't want t' keep the *Victory* for 'imself. Seein' what good nick she be in. So, he's told Sutton t' try and find him. That's what we be doin' now. If Cornwallis don't want us, we're t' sail on to the Med. In the meantime Nelson be off ahead of us in case someone tells him not t' go. Which shows you how keen the bastard is to get us into a fight. 'Tis a good thing he be gone if y' ask me. I'm not keen to get into a fight with any Frenchies. I'd rather be tradin' with 'm than fightin' 'm. Any day o' the week. If I hadn't run clean out of wind off Portland Bill that's what I'd still be doin'.'

'If we don't go to the Med, does that mean we'll be returnin' home regularly?'

'Maybe. But the likes of you and me and more'n half the crew won't be gettin' any shoretime.' He chuckled. 'And they'll have an extra special close eye on you. Knowin' you be a keen swimmer.'

'You were pressed too?'

'I were given a choice. The navy or Botany Bay. With the promise that next time it'll be Botany Bay f'sure 'n'certain. Just m' luck for 'm to declare war the moment I opted for the navy. If Nelson gets his way, I reckon there won't be the thickness of a whore's smile betwixt the two: havin' the sheart shot out of you by the Frenchies, or havin' ye back broke carryin' stone somewhere out past Chiney.'

'Was it you treated my back before?'

'Aye. Twice. Not that ye'd know much about the first time. Or much more about the second. Then you be greener than that paint on the bulk-head. But you've picked up a bit since. If ye hadn't, we might've been given ye the deep six b' now.'

Will fought off another threatened lurch of his stomach. 'What's your name?' he managed when his confidence returned.

'Alley Gable. What be your'n?'

'Will. Will Noling.'

Two days later, Will was again having his back treated by Alley Gable at the after end of the lower gun deck. The weather had eased and what sea was running was coming from astern, so all the gunports were open. Shafts of light and clean salt air swept in from both sides.

'You look like you be gettin' ye sea legs, matey. Y' ain't as green around the gills.'

'How's my back look?'

'It's startin' to dry out. Though most of it's still the colour of y' head. How's it feel?'

'Awful itchy.'

'Well don't scratch it whatever ye do. Let it scab right over. And then when it do, let the scabs dry an' fall off by 'mselves. If you scratch'm, the welts could fill up with pus and some mightn't heal ever.'

'The bos'n said he wouldn't hit me where it'd damage me permanent.'

Gable chuckled. 'I don't know about the places where he hasn't hit ye, but the prick hasn't spared ye where he has.'

Now that he could see Gable more clearly, Will was surprised at his age. He guessed that it could range anywhere between forty and sixty. In the previous gloom, judging him more by the way he moved than by his indistinct features, he had believed him to be not much older than himself. But now he could see that his hair was thin and greying, and his skin was wrinkled and weather-beaten. He had a strong jawline and broad open features that when he was younger, women would probably have judged handsome. But these were now marred by a ridged scar that skewed at an angle across his right cheek and terminated in his right eyebrow, pulling it down over his right eye like an awning.

'From tryin' to duck beneath an excise man's blade, when I should've been backin' away from it,' he explained one day when Will knew him well enough to ask.

'Is that the fleet we've been lookin' for out there?' Will asked.

'Aye. But it won't be out there for long.'

Will's mouth opened. 'What do you mean? Surely Sutton hasn't seen Cornwallis already?'

'He has. He's been over and back.'

'But we're only just approachin' them now.'

'That's the main van we're approachin'. We're headin' straight through them on the way to the Bay. We met up with Cornwallis's flag two hours ago.'

'So that's it, we're leavin'?'

'Aye.'

Will shook his head. 'So there's no chance of us returnin' to England?'

'Not for a while.'

'God save us all!'

'Amen.'

Both men were silent for a time.

'You know,' Gable said at last, 'when I heard that Nelson had left us, I was wanderin' around afterwards wonderin' why I was feelin' so bad when I should've been feelin' better. Knowin' how anxious the little prick was to get us into a fight. And then I realised what was wrong. I felt he'd let me down. Personal like. It's one thing bein' in this fockin' navy against m' will. But it kind of soothed the hurt a bit, knowin' that I was in the same ship as Horatio bloody Nelson, himself. Warmed m' blood. Stupid, I know. I must be gettin' soft in the head.'

'Aye,' said Will quietly.

'Stupid, eh?'

'Aye. Stupid.'

Will's head was lowered. The seasickness and the hurt were on the wane. But his teeth-grinding anger remained. Along with added aggravations, including a cold, seductive sense of excitement and a corresponding sense of guilt.

It took more than two months for the *Victory* to join up with the Mediterranean fleet. And within hours of joining them Nelson was back on board.

At the after end of the lower gun deck a group of men were sitting at a mess table set up between two of the 32-pounders. They were mainly occupied in enjoying their second rum issue of the day, but some were also making the most of the last light of the day to mend their clothes, or to re-read—or in many cases simply look at—mail from home that they had received before departing from Portsmouth.

A newcomer approached them and sat down. He was an idler, so-called because he was excused normal watches, his duties requiring him to work throughout the day.

'I see we have a new captain,' said he, glancing around at the others.

He was a carpenter's mate, a gaunt-faced Cornishman who had worked as an apprentice shipwright at a small dockyard in Falmouth. As with most of the impressed men on board, he had been taken early in March, when the navy belatedly started reacting seriously to the knowledge that the peace of Amiens was shot, and that war was again converging on them rapidly.

'What name?'

'Thomas Masterman Hardy.'

'Nelson's mate.'

'What's happened to Sutton?'

'He's swapped commands with Hardy. He's taken over the *Amphion*.'

''E won't like that. 'Avin' to swap a first rate ship o'the line for a fuckin' frigate.'

''Twas only a matter of time. Nelson never did take to Sutton. Blamed 'im for the delays in gettin' under way.'

'What's he like, Hardy?'

'If he's Nelson's mate, means he's another bloody hero.'

'That's all we need. Another bloody hero.'

'Bloody hell!'

'Bloody right, mate. Bloody hell!'

Will Noling was seated at the end of the table. His left forearm was stretched alongside a sheet of paper and his left hand was curled around a small pot of ink. With his free hand he dipped a pen in the ink and held it poised above the paper.

'Read the last bit again,' said a small man sitting beside him, screwing around on the bench and leaning forward to peer at the paper as if he were reading Will's handwriting himself and thereby countering the need for the request.

'"Keep a close watch on young Nellie,"' read Will. '"She is too young to know the dangers of horses and carts. Specially so many passing by so close to the front door, which is nothing like we had at home. Tell Ben to watch her close. And

Billy. Tell them I love them all, and God willing I'll be home to watch over them myself soon." '

'Did I say that?' He glanced at Will.

'Pretty close to that.'

'I suppose I did.' He thought about this for a while, turning away and locking his gaze somewhere in the gloom further aft. 'Doesn't sound like me, though. More like you.'

'They were your words, Moth. I just wrote them down.'

'It's all those "ings" on the end of them. And hisses on the front.'

'Hisses?' someone queried, looking up from his tot of rum.

'Hhhh's, then.' He made a noise like heavy breathing.

'That's how it is when you write the words down,' said Will. 'You put i-n-g on the end of some of them and aitches in front of others. If I spelt the words exactly as you said them, no one could read it.'

'Why not?'

'Because there's set ways of writin' down words. You do it the same way each time. That way the people who read them know what they mean. If you wrote them down exactly as they sounded a Londoner wouldn't know what someone from Newcastle had written.'

'Any self-respectin' Geordie would cut his throat before he'd write to a fockin' Londoner. So where's the problem?' someone offered with a chuckle from the other end of the table.

'What if the Londoner was a woman?' someone else proposed.

'There'd be no way on earth that any London mott who had anythin' to do with a Geordie would be able to read, for Christ's sake. He'd have to draw her pictures. And then she'd have to have someone explain them to her.'

'If Betty read them words to the kids I suppose they'll sound like they was mine,' said Moth.

'That's right,' Will agreed. 'Now if you don't hurry up and finish, I'm not goin' to be able to see to write anythin'. The light's failin' fast, so get a move on. What else do you want to say?'

'The only problem is that Betty can't read either. She'll have to get Mrs Bathgate from next door to read them for her, and she talks worse'n you. It'll sound like she wrote them.'

'Jesus, Moth!' someone exclaimed. 'I'll bet your Betty's glad you're at fockin' sea.'

Two men stood on the poop deck watching the crew working the sails against the clock. They were the same two men who had stood on the same deck watching Will Noling's attempted escape in Portsmouth.

The smaller of the two was Vice-Admiral Horatio Viscount Nelson, the other was a Mr Scott. There were two Scotts on Nelson's staff. This one was John Scott, his secretary. The other one was Nelson's chaplain, the Reverend

Alexander Scott, who, because of his linguistic skills, Nelson also used as a secretary when dealing with foreign correspondence and with the translation of foreign journals. To avoid confusion on board, John Scott was known simply as Secretary Scott, and the Reverend Alexander Scott was known as Chaplain Scott.

'See we still have that red-haired youngster on board, Mr Scott. Appears we didn't lose him in Gibraltar or Valletta. Top yard man no less. Seems he's done some seatime before.'

'Believe he's simply a fast learner, my Lord. Bos'n tells me he was a farmer.'

'Farmer!' Nelson raised his gaze and lifted the thin gauze patch that he used to protect his left eye from direct sunlight, a practice that caused some to believe it was that eye that was blind. 'If he's a farmer, he's a farmer that can run along the top of a yard and leap down on to a foot line as nimble as any jack m'hearty tar I've ever clapped eyes on. When you see the bos'n, tell him if I see him do it again, he'll wish I hadn't. We don't have enough skilled topmen to waste one through foolishness. Farmer indeed!'

'Did you hear from y'own girl?'

Alley Gable knew the answer before he asked the question. It had ridden the edge of Will Noling's voice as he read aloud Betty Pentridge's letter to her husband, Moth. Twice. It dulled his smile. And it remained now as a tightening of the flesh around the corners of the young man's eyes when he fished from a pocket in his vest a crumpled sheet of paper and placed it on the table beside his cup of wine.

The substituting of wine for rum at the two daily issues of alcohol had been at Nelson's insistence, along with ensuring that his ships carried an ample supply of fresh fruit and vegetables. 'Rough liquor rots good men, Hardy. Worse'n harbourtime. Wine, fruit and vegetables will help keep'm alive.' It was to this end that the fleet was now replenishing stores while anchored in quiet waters within the startling rocky outcrops of the Maddalena Islands off the north-eastern tip of Sardinia.

Realising that Alley was addressing him, Will raised an eyebrow in query.

'Is that from your girl?' Alley asked.

Will shook his head. 'My brother.'

The mail had arrived that morning with the storeships from Gibraltar. Most of those at the mess-deck table at the after end of the lower gun deck sat as they usually sat for their supper, some of them leaning back against the long barrels of the 32-pounders. Most of those who had received mail were nursing their letters along with their issue of wine.

In the fading light Will's gaze retraced Jim's painful script. There was no message from Jessica, nor would there be. Because, as Jim explained, she did not believe that Will had joined the navy unwillingly. She believed that he knew exactly what he was doing even though it would mean he would probably be away for years. She felt certain that he had deserted her. As a result she has left the Noling farm and gone to live with an aunt somewhere in Devon, leaving instructions that she wished never to see him or hear from him again.

Although the Reverend Smith-Wilson did not give Jim explicit instructions to lie to his brother about Jessica's fate, he implied that it would be dangerous to explain the absence of any mail from the girl by telling him the truth. As he pointed out, any hint of the real cause would almost certainly result in Will taking matters into his own hands, possibly at the risk of his life.

'By the time he finds out what has really happened, God willing, the circumstances may have changed. Will may have changed.' Remote possibilities, Smith-Wilson conceded privately to himself, even as he was uttering the words. Adding—still privately—that this depended on the lad being among the living at the end of the war. And then with some troubling of conscience contemplated that there was every possibility that he wouldn't be, which would mean of course that Fitzparsons and Lowfoley could rest in peace. Amen.

'Could you read m' letter?'

Will turned to see a boy he guessed was no more than thirteen years old standing at his elbow. The youth was rosy cheeked and had fair hair that fell about his ears in ringlets. Will had seen him before on the upper deck and had been struck by his similarity to a young woman. He belonged to that portion of the crew who worked as either cabin boys or servants in the officers' cabins at the ship's stern.

'Sit down,' said Will, moving to make room for him. Some of the others exchanged glances as the boy complied and handed Will a sheet of paper.

'What's y' name?' Will asked as he scanned the letter.

'Tom Clapham.'

'Where y' from, Tom?'

'Dover. It's about the baby, isn't it?'

'Is the baby Little Annie?'

'Aye. She be awful sick with the croup when I left.'

'Is this from your mother?'

'Aye. Is Annie all right?'

'I'm afraid she's not, Tom.'

'Jesus.' The boy bit his lip.

'Do you want me to read it here, or somewhere quieter?'

'Read it here.' He glanced around at the others, most of whom seemed preoccupied. 'It's all right.'

On a ship that was less than 300 feet long and 50 feet wide, carrying a crew of about 870, there was little point in being overly concerned with matters of privacy.

All other noise at the table died away as Will turned towards Tom, lowered his voice, and using some licence to accommodate the imaginative spelling and the absence of punctuation, read:

Each night I pray to the Lord that you are safe, Thomas. Your sisters send you their love and want you to know they pray for you also. It grieves me to have to tell you that little Annie passed away. The coughing was hurting her awful and I am sure she is resting more peaceful now in the arms of Jesus. The girls cry a lot when they think of her, but they will get over it. Your Uncle Caliph has come to look after us. I know you do not like him. But he is a better provider than most. And he is not drinking as bad as before. He has not hurt me or the girls since he arrived. I would not lie to you, my darling boy. Your friend Susan sends her greetings. Have someone write a letter for you and tell us how you are faring. Caliph says the war will be over before Christmas. God be praised that he be right. Keep safe, my darling. We all love you dearly.

Your loving mother,

Jill Clapham.

'Jesus!' said Tom. 'Little Annie.'
'I'm sorry, Tom. Was she your sister?'
The boy nodded.
'Do you want me to write a letter for you?'
The boy nodded again.
'I'll write it now if you like.'
'Tomorrow. Can I do it tomorrow?' Tom placed

the palm of a hand against each eye in turn.

'Whenever you're ready. But don't leave it until after the storeships leave. Otherwise you won't know when it'll get back to England.'

'What you be doin' there, Tom?'

All eyes turned to a man standing back from the end of the table. He was broad, bare-chested, and tall. Where he was standing he was forced to stoop beneath one of the crossbeams, and had a forearm resting against it for support. Will had seen him several times, and learned later that he was a servant from the wardroom.

Tom cast a frightened glance at the man and quickly rose to his feet. 'Just havin' a letter read.'

'You can do that any time. Right now you an' I have work to do in the bread room. Come on, get y'self movin'.'

'What work would that be?' Will asked. 'The lad's off watch.'

'It be all right,' said Tom, stepping over the bench and moving towards the man.

'Aye,' said the man, with his eyes locked on Will. 'It be all right, all right.' He ducked beneath the beam and stepped closer to the table. 'And what business be it of your'n to stick y'nose in?' Beads of sweat that had gathered beneath the bulging muscles that flanked the man's neck were tracking down into the matted hair on his chest. 'Y'jealous or somethin', sonny boy? D'you want 'im f' y'self?'

'Ease up, Bradley,' said Alley Gable. 'No one around here is lookin' for trouble.'

'Good thing that,' said Bradley, ''cos trouble's somethin' I be a fair shake at. Just make sure ye pretty farm boy 'ere keeps his nose out. Otherwise I might flatten it for him. Or better still, take a fancy t' 'im and come visitin' from time to time.'

'You don't have to go, Tom,' said Will turning and looking across at the boy. 'Sit down again and I'll write that letter for you now.'

Bradley reached out and taking Tom by the shoulder pulled him roughly so that he was propelled into the gloom behind him. 'I'll see you in the bread room.'

Alley Gable reached across the table and gripped Will's wrist, preventing him from rising. As Will's gaze locked with his, Alley shook his head and, leaning forward, whispered urgently, 'Leave it, Will. 'Tis better for the kid t'have one keeper than a pack o'hopefuls houndin' him. He keeps t'others at bay.'

'I'll be back to visit y' later, farm boy,' said Bradley, addressing the back of Will's head.

'I'll tell you somethin', Bradley, or whatever y' name is,' Will replied without turning. 'On that farm o' mine one of the jobs I was extra good at was geldin' horses.' He detached his hand from Alley's and picked up an apple and a knife from the table. 'I was so good at it other farmers brought their horses t' me.' He began to core the apple. 'I had a special way of trussin' them up.

126

Fast. So they couldn't hurt themselves. Even the biggest of the draught animals. And then castratin' them. Again fast. So they didn't suffer too much.' With a deft movement of the blade he divided the apple in two and held up the pieces on the palm of his hand. 'If you come near me uninvited, or if I hear you've been mistreatin' that boy, I'll relieve you of your balls so fast you'll think they've fallen off of their own accord.'

'Tell your boy he don't frighten me,' said Bradley to Alley Gable, gripping him in his gaze across Will's shoulder.

'Be that as it may, Bradley, he means what he says,' said Alley. 'And if ye do come around 'ere again lookin' f' trouble, it would please me no end t' give him a hand in removin' your crown jewels. You may not know him too well, but you know me. And I've never made an idle threat in m' life. So piss off while you can still walk without lookin' like you shit y'self.'

Bradley stood glaring down at the others for a moment before turning and beginning to stride away. But at his first step, his head collided with a crossbeam. The impact knocked him to the deck. In an instant Will leapt from the bench and, grabbing hold of the waistband of the man's trousers with one hand, pressed the point of his apple-coring knife into his crotch.

'Jesus, what are you doin'?'

'Don't move an inch or I'll cut y' deep. That's better. Just in case you think I was makin' idle threats, how would you like me to relieve you of one of your prize plums right now?'

'Jesus, ease back. You're hurtin' me.'

'I could, you know. In fact I could remove both of them as simple as shellin' peas. So remember what I said. Don't even think about comin' close to me uninvited. And don't even think about mistreatin' that boy. Tell me you understand what I'm sayin'.'

'I understand. Jesus, ease back.'

Will released him and stood up. The man scrambled away on his buttocks, and then rose carefully to his feet. Pressing the palm of one hand against his forehead and curling his other hand into his crotch to detach his trousers away from the flesh beneath, he turned away and moved off quickly into the gloom.

Will sat down again and placed the knife on the table. No one spoke for a while and when conversation did break out again it was guarded and subdued.

'Each night I pray to the Lord that you are safe, Thomas,' Will said softly.

'What?' Alley looked across at him.

'His mother's words.' Will picked up the paper in front of him. 'He left his letter behind.' He carefully folded it and placed it in his pocket. 'She prays for him every night.'

'Aye,' Alley nodded. 'Won't do him no harm.'

'Won't do him much fuckin' good either,' said Will softly. 'Not while he's out here.' He sat staring into space for a moment and then rose from the bench and turned away from the table.

'Where are you goin'?' Alley was watching him closely.

'I need some air.'

Alley continued to watch him intently until he saw him mount the companionway that led to the deck above, and only then did he relax.

'I'm worried about Chaplain Scott,' said Nelson.

'Why's that, m' lord?' responded Secretary Scott.

'He's workin' mornin', noon and night. I'm not sure he's getting any sleep at all.'

The two men were standing on the quarterdeck facing the west. Their conversation was punctuated by frequent and lengthy pauses. The sun was sinking through thin ribbons of cloud stretched across the horizon. The sea was a vibrating sheet of copper strewn with purple reflections that wriggled towards them from the neighbouring ships and from the ring of rocky outcrops that flanked the bay.

'I doubt there's anyone on board that can help him with translating every item that concerns us in the foreign journals. And I certainly wouldn't trust anyone else to transcribe my outward mail into whatever language is appropriate, but perhaps we could find someone to help him with his collating and filing.'

'I'd help him myself if I had the time.'

'No. You have little enough to spare for my dictation.' He chuckled. 'And sorting out your transcripts. Deciding which version of my diatribes and persuasions you should pass on to our esteemed colleague to translate. Ideally we need someone to reduce his workload and yours as well. Someone to do the lifting and carrying and keep all the documentation in order. A clerk. No, not a clerk,' he waved his hand seeking a suitable term, 'a sorter. A filter.' His face beamed triumphantly. 'A secretary's mate.'

Scott winced inwardly but managed to nod his agreement. 'Perhaps one of the midshipmen, m' lord?'

'Possibly, but I don't want a midshipman. Every man jack o' them has enough distractions already to keep him away from what he should be concentrating on—his seamanship.'

'You weren't thinking of someone from the lower deck, m' lord?'

'I'm not particularly worried where he comes from, as long as he can do his job and doesn't rub me the wrong way.'

'Yon Noling could be a candidate.'

'Who?'

'The red-headed swimmer from Portsmouth down there in the waist. His name's Noling.'

Nelson moved closer to the break. 'I thought you said he was a farm boy.'

'He was. But the bos'n tells me he's a farm boy that's been teaching a few of the lower gun-deck men the rudiments of reading and writing.'

'Hellespont! Why would he be doing that?'

'I believe some of them asked him to, m' lord.'

'My God, Mr Scott. Seems we don't have to wait for Bonaparte's invasion flotilla to bring about the end of civilisation as we know it. When we have farm boys taking it upon themselves to teach sailors how to read and write, we're already witnessing the beginning of the end of much of what is held dear in jolly old England. God save us all!'

'Will I have a talk to him, m' lord? See if he's suitable?'

'If he has decent writing skills, and he doesn't smell too bad, put him on probation.'

'And if he does smell too bad, m' lord?'

'See that he has a bath. And if you do decide to take him on, you'd better make him an Able Seaman. That should give him some protection against any of the cabin staff who might object to his presence.' He walked to the ship's side and turned his gaze back on the sunset. 'And you better check him out soon. I don't like the way he's watching the shoreline.'

'Who's that?' The question was fired from the starboard side of the Admiral's dining cabin.

Will Noling's head jolted upright. When he saw who it was that was addressing him beyond the journals and newspapers that were stacked on the dining table in front of him, he leapt to his feet.

'Will Noling, sir.'

'What are you doing?' The questioner was dressed in a nightshirt and was wearing a blue cap of soft cloth that had a red tassel attached.

'I'm sorting and cataloguing reading material for Chaplain Scott, sir.'

'What reading material?' The man moved into the light, and turning one of the journals towards himself, he leant back and squinted down at it. If Will had any doubts before, he had none now that he was addressing Horatio Lord Nelson himself. God save us all!

'Foreign journals and newspapers, sir.'

'My lord.'

Will looked at him blankly.

'When you address me call me "my lord".'

'Aye, aye, sir. Eh ... my lord.'

'What do you mean "sorting and cataloguing"?'

'I stack them in chronological order and note the titles, dates and page numbers of items that I believe he should read, my lord.'

'Chronological?' Nelson said softly, perhaps to himself, and moving closer peered down at the sheet of paper where Will had listed the information. 'You speak these languages, do you, son? French, Italian, Spanish?'

'No, m'lord.'

'Austrian?'

'No, m'lord.'

'Then how in the bright blue blazes can you determine what items he should read?'

'I note down any item that mentions the name

132

of a city or state we might be interested in. I know the foreign words for those.'

'Such as?'

'Well, most places, m'lord. England, France, Spain and Turkey of course; and Austria; and in particular Toulon and Malta and Sicily and Naples. I also include any articles that mention the name of a person that we might be interested in reading about.'

'Like who?'

'Like yourself, m'lord. Or Talleyrand, or Bonaparte, or any senior English or French official or commander such as Admiral La Touche-Tréville.'

'Talleyrand? Why do you name Talleyrand ahead of Bonaparte?'

'No particular reason. But I wouldn't be surprised if he's still around long after Bonaparte, m'lord.'

'Wouldn't you just.' Nelson turned and gave him a searching look. 'Where do y'get all of this, son? Who's been tutoring you?'

'Chaplain Scott, I suppose, m'lord. But most of it I get from readin'. I like to read.'

'You're not a spy are you, son? If you are I'll hang you high and handsome.'

'No, m'lord.'

'What's your home town?'

'Lowfoley, m'lord. It's a village.'

'Where is it a village?'

'In Hampshire, m'lord. On the edge of the downs.'

'Who's your local squire?'

'That'd be Sir Rory Fitzparsons, m'lord.'

'He knows you, does he?'

'Yes, m'lord.'

'What about your local minister?'

'Reverend Smith-Wilson, m'lord.'

'He knows you too?'

'Yes, m'lord.'

'So if I had Mr Scott enquire of them of your looks and your character, they'd describe you to a tee, and give you a glowing reference?'

Will smiled. 'I'd hope so, m'lord.'

'Well I might just do that. To make sure I don't have to hang you. Where were you pressed?'

'In Portsmouth, m'lord.'

'The day you tried to swim ashore? You were pressed that day?'

'The night before, m'lord.'

'What were you doin' in Portsmouth?'

'I was there to try and get myself a job at the pay office.'

'How come you ended up bein' pressed? I was told that at that late stage they were only pressing merchant seamen, and watermen and fishermen and the like.'

'I was kidnapped by a gang of ruffians who sold me to the navy, m'lord.'

'What do you mean, sold you to the navy?'

'I heard money change hands. Gold coin. Several pieces.'

'When they brought you on board?'

'Earlier in the night, m'lord. I assume when they handed me over to the press gang.'

'You're joking, lad. Several gold pieces! Even a scallywag gang working some mischief with the official bounties wouldn't exchange gold for you. Are you sure what you heard wasn't someone paying to have you impressed? An enemy? Have you any enemies who wanted you out of the way?'

'I don't know what you mean, m'lord.'

'Have you a girl?'

'Yes, m'lord.'

'Is she pretty?'

'The prettiest girl in the county, m'lord.'

'Have you any rival suitors who'd pay to have you taken out of the way?'

'No, m'lord. There's no one in Lowfoley who'd be that cunning.'

'Well, I can tell you, I know a few people who'd be that cunning to get close to the prettiest girl in the county. And from what I hear it wouldn't be the first time something like that has happened in this man's navy.' He moved away from the table and stood looking directly aft into his day cabin.

'I don't suppose Secretary Scott is still up?'

'Ah ... No, m'lord. No,' replied Will distractedly, his gaze on the gloom of the sleeping cabin from where Nelson had emerged. 'He went to bed some time ago.'

'Damn!' Nelson cast a glance at the lamp suspended over the table. 'I want him to take down some notes. It's a pity to wake the poor blighter, but this damned light is too dim for my sight, and if I leave what I want to say until morning I could lose the thrust. Would you call him for me?'

'I could take them down for you, if you'd prefer not to wake him, m'lord.'

Nelson turned and looked at him closely for a moment, and then turned and walked to a cabinet where he opened a drawer and extracted a magnifying glass. He returned to the table and picked up the sheet of paper on which Will had been working. 'Is this your writing?'

'Yes, m'lord.'

Nelson turned it into the light and peered at it though the magnifying glass.

'All right,' he said at last, 'sit down and write exactly what I say. Use a new sheet of paper.'

Will sat down and placed a fresh sheet of paper on the table in front of him. He then selected a pen from one of a number lying at the front of a shallow wooden writing case, dipped the pen in an inkwell mounted at the rear of the case, wiped off the excess ink, and waited with the pen poised above the paper.

Nelson stood, carefully watching every part of this preparation, and then turned and began to walk about the cabin. 'I'll say only the words, you affix the punctuation marks. Write: "I am distressed for frigates. From Cape Saint Vincent to the Adriatic I have only eight." No, make that, "to the head of the Adriatic I have only eight; which with the service of watching Toulon, and the necessary frigates with the fleet, are absolutely not half enough." No, make that "not one half enough."' He stood looking across the cabin without moving for a few moments and then swung back and locked his gaze on Will who was looking up at him.

'What are you doing?'

'Is that all, m'lord?'

'What do you mean, is that all?'

'I'm waiting for you to go on, m'lord.'

'You've already finished writing what I've said?'

'Aye, m'lord. I'll tidy up your two alterations when you've finished.'

'Let me see.' Nelson walked around the table and held out his hand.

Will passed him the paper and he examined the writing using the magnifying glass.

'Where'd you say you come from, Noling?'

'Lowfoley in Hampshire, m'lord.'

'I wouldn't be surprised if I didn't end up hanging you, son. I think you must be a spy.'

The following afternoon Alley Gable came upon Will standing in the waist watching the sunset.

'What be the matter with you, matey? Ye've got a look on ye says ye've got an ache somewhere.'

'I have a terrible bad feelin' about my girl, Jessie.'

'Terrible bad?'

'Terrible bad.'

FIVE

Deep inside the western arm of Langston Harbour, halfway along the Portsea Bridge Channel abreast of Lady Carrington's, was a prison hulk; not that it could be seen on this day from anywhere on the shore or the harbour. The fog was so thick that even someone standing on the landing platform beneath the steep gangway that led to the upper deck would have to take on trust that she was there. Or at least reach out and place a hand against the dim cliff-face that was the coarse planking of her hull, an indistinct shadow that soared into invisibility with the gloom.

Nor was the knee-weakening shock of the smell proof of her existence. At low tide, most man-made structures that protruded from the harbour smelt as bad, encrusted as they all were with a myriad sea-creatures—some living, some dead, some dying—and the refuse from a flotilla of vessels packed with human refuse.

Her sounds and those of the forces around her were probably the best indicator of her size and circumstance: the incessant moaning of more than a thousand tons of decaying timbers, and the spray-charged slapping and sloshing of the sea in which she lay dying. Chopped-up waves rose and fell about her sides and tugged at the flexible tree-trunks of weed that heaved about her waterline and trailed from the great rusting links of her mooring cables; and churning cauldrons of broken water sucked and hissed with the effort of escaping from beneath the curve of her bows and from under her stern and gangway platform. But her keel could have been planted firmly in the coarse sandy bottom of the harbour for all the effect these external disturbances seemed to have on her great bulk.

She was one of the oldest of the prison ships in the harbour—older even than the *Portland*—but she had not been there as long as most of the others and was therefore in better condition. Like many of them she was a former warrior that had fought under many flags and names.

Launched in La Coruna in 1759, she began her career as a speedy Spanish 64-gun ship of the line. In 1779 she was still carrying a Spanish flag and her maiden name when she was taken as a prize by Admiral George Rodney off Cape Finisterre along with a healthy catch of less impressive compatriots.

She carried a British flag and name three years

later when Rodney took her with him to the Caribbean, and south of Guadeloupe broke the back of a French fleet at the Battle of the Saintes. Later that same year she was captured by a French squadron off Toulon after losing most of her main and part of her mizzen masts in a gale that separated her from her British travelling companions en route to Malta.

In 1794 she was carrying a French flag and name when she was badly damaged and again taken as a prize by a British fleet; this time under the command of Admiral Lord Howe at the Glorious First of June.

She was then largely rebuilt, and in 1797 carried a British flag and name when Admiral Sir John Jervis all but destroyed a Spanish fleet at the Battle of St Vincent. And she was at the Battle of the Nile the following year under the same flag and name when Nelson dealt a similar blow to the French.

After the Nile she no longer had her speed and was awkward to manoeuvre. The accumulated repairs to the wounds she had sustained over the years had taken their toll on her seaworthiness, and she was condemned to eke out her final days anchored in Langston Harbour. It was a sorry end for a gallant old lady. Her guns had been removed, her gunports were either battened shut or barred, her rigging had been stripped away, her masts had been chopped off, and her upper deck was festooned with lines of ragged washing, and was further disfigured by putrid eruptions of ill-shaped ramshackle structures from which smoking chimneys protruded. Perhaps fittingly, the only name visible beneath the battened and shuttered remains of the cabins on her once ornately galleried stern was a faint imprint of the one she had been christened with: *Santa Ana*.

Towards the midships section of the port side of what had been her main gun deck was a partitioned sleeping compartment that poorly housed twenty female prisoners. On this foggy day, two of the women were engaged in an activity that—because of the poor light filtering through the partly open ports, a number of untidy hammocks slung fore-and-aft from hooks attached to the crossbeams, and the occasional coming and going of onlookers—could be observed only from close range.

One of the women had her back to the other and was sitting flat on the deck with her legs thrust out in front of her. The other woman was squatting at a slightly higher elevation behind her with her legs spread and the inside of her knees braced to steady herself against the seated woman's back. She was carefully shaving her companion's head with what appeared to be a shortened piece of razor, or perhaps a broken knife blade.

From time to time she would interrupt this activity to dampen what remained of the other woman's hair with a sponge that she dipped into one of two buckets that sat beside them, and occasionally she would sit back and stroke the blade a number of times across the flat surface of a small whetstone which she kept in a cloth bag tucked beneath one ankle.

At regular intervals she would also interrupt proceedings to observe the result of her endeavours more closely in the pool of pale light that surrounded a small oil lamp that she would lift from the deck beside her and move slowly in a circle above the crown of the other woman's head.

This head-shaving activity was accompanied by quiet exchanges between the two, and by infrequent and mainly subdued comment from the occasional onlookers as they shuffled past or paused to watch.

The activities that then followed were also accompanied by quiet exchanges between the two women, but sparked more animated responses from the passers-by than before, and at times even attracted heckling from one or two of those in the hammocks.

The woman who had performed the work with the razor, after carefully examining the now completely shaved dome of the other woman's head, extracted a small ceramic bottle from the cloth bag that she kept protected beneath her ankle.

'This will sting, Jessie, but not f'long.'

So saying, she poured a small amount of liquid from the bottle on to a piece of cloth that she bunched between the tips of her fingers and began to dab the dampened cloth on to the other woman's head.

'Sorry,' she murmured as she felt her companion push back suddenly against the spread of her thighs.

'It's all right,' replied Jessica Glider. 'I just wasn't expectin' it to be so cold.'

'Be that rum I smell?' A crumpled face appeared over the side of the closest hammock. 'Yer not wastin' good Jamaicy rum on that baggage, are you, woman? Jasus, Joseph and Mary, if y'are, ye should be flogged.' The cheeks were hollow, the hair ghost-white, the nose was hooked, and when the mouth opened, gaps and teeth were evenly proportioned. 'Hey, girls, look what be goin' on 'ere. Our red-headed motts are wastin' good Jamaicy rum.'

Mutters of discontent rippled backwards and forwards across the compartment, competing for a time with the groan of the timbers and the creak of the hammocks.

'What do you think ye're doin', woman?' another hammock occupant demanded, sitting up and leaning over dangerously to get a better view. 'Y'know damned well what a pint of that stuff costs us, for Christ Almighty's sake.'

Elizabeth Crowling turned her head slightly but kept her gaze locked on what she was doing. 'This 'ere ain't no pint. Ain't so much as a tot. Ain't even a wet. So aim y'noses somewhere else.'

She leant forward and murmured close to Jessica's ear: 'Poxy cows.'

When she had finished she replaced the stopper

in the bottle and returned it to her bag. 'All right, turn around and I'll do under your arms.'

'D'you think that's needed?' Jessica raised one arm and, twisting towards the light, tried to peer beneath it.

'There be no point in doin' half a job, girl.' Elizabeth lifted the lamp and leant closer. 'And as I were expectin', you have the makin's of a rash there. Can you see?'

'Aye, but there's no need f'you to shave me, Liz. I can do it m'self.'

'Oh aye, and probably nick yourself an' all. That be one way of takin y'mind off the mites. Havin' great weepin' sores under both y'arms t' worry about. Just leave that one raised and keep very still.'

They remained silent as Elizabeth went to work again, and for a time the other women were also quieter. Several times during this period the sound of brief scuffles accompanied by squeaks of threat or complaint could be heard from within the shadows of the crossbeams, reminding those who were still receptive to such portent that their times and circumstance were not propitious.

When she had finished with both of Jessica's armpits Elizabeth again prepared to dab on the liquid from her bottle.

'This'll sting worse'n before, lass,' she warned, ''cos o' the rash. Brace y'self now.'

Jessica flinched and sucked in air through her clenched teeth with each touch of the cloth.

'Sorry,' Elizabeth whispered, her lips pulling away repeatedly from her own teeth in sympathetic winces with each application. 'But you can't afford t' be breakin' out in sores in this place.'

'That be fockin' rum all right, yer stupid mott,' accused the woman in the closest hammock. 'Here, pass up the bottle. I'll show ye what ye should be doin' with it.'

'Go t' sleep, Mavis. Be a good girl now.'

'Don't you good girl me, yer young sow. I've a mind to come down there an teach y'some manners.'

Elizabeth turned and looked at her. 'Now, you know what happened the last time you tried to teach me some manners, Mavis. So just keep your mind on y'own business and your noisy trap shut. Otherwise I might have to give your nose another tweak.'

'Don't you threaten me, you mad bitch.' Even in the prevailing light it was apparent that the woman's face had turned a darker shade. 'You don't frighten me. You or your fancy little girlfriend. If you ever come near me again you'll regret it . . . ' As she was talking, the woman's face gradually slipped from view beneath the side of the hammock and her voice faded and was replaced by a volley of soft but deep-seated coughs.

Elizabeth waited, watching the hammock. When the woman's face did not reappear, she turned back to Jessica. 'Serve's her right if she's choked 'erself.'

'I wouldn't press her too hard,' Jessica whispered. 'I think she's a little mad.'

'I think she's a big mad. But I don't think she'll bother us, not after her last lesson.'

That lesson occurred the first evening that Elizabeth and Jessica spent on board.

The day that Jessica first saw Elizabeth Crowling was when they were mustered on the upper deck of the former *Santa Ana*, shortly after being ferried out to the hulk along with about twenty other women prisoners in two longboats.

A squat prison orderly dressed in a high-necked black jacket and carrying a long leather-encased truncheon was shouting orders at them in a northern accent that had Jessica straining at times to understand what he was saying.

So, as she clutched the chain that linked her ankles and shuffled along behind the woman ahead of her, she split her concentration between trying to decipher the man's utterances and watching what the other women around her were doing.

Her problems were compounded by the jarring clamour of a flock of gulls that were swirling around two women dressed in what appeared to be little more than the shredded remains of undergarments as they emptied what were obviously large buckets of human waste and other refuse over the ship's side.

Both of the women were covered in filth and had wild unkempt hair. One of them was calling out to the newcomers as they shuffled past. Jessica had no idea what the woman was saying, her attention being arrested by the terrible stench that emanated from them and from the containers in their charge.

A few moments later Jessica became aware that the orderly who had been addressing them seemed to have his gaze locked tenaciously on her and was striding across the deck towards her. His face was ugly with rage. She glanced quickly about her to see if something or somebody nearby had attracted his attention. To her dismay she could see nothing amiss. Dear God!

He began to shout at her while he was several strides away. 'What d'ye think ye're doin', ye cloth-eared mott?'

'What?' she stammered. My God! When will this ever end?

'What are those?' He pointed his truncheon at her feet.

'Irons, sir.' This is the stuff of children's games. Childish, ridiculous games!

'Not the fockin' irons. Them there what's on y' feet.'

'On my feet, sir?'

'On your filthy stinkin' feet. What be them?'

'You mean my shoes, sir?'

'Aye, ye shoes.' He waved the truncheon to either side of her. 'And what 'ave them others around you got on their feet?'

She glanced about her.

'Nothin', sir.'

'Aye. Because thems that 'ad shoes on, did what I told 'm to do. They stowed them away, didn't they?' He reached out with his free hand. 'Give 'm to me, smartish.'

She bent down and with some difficulty because of her irons slipped off both her shoes and passed them to him.

He strode across to where the women who were emptying the buckets had interrupted their work and were standing watching these events. Turning back to watch Jessica he then made much of dropping first one then her other shoe into one of the containers that had not yet been emptied.

As each shoe struck the oily surface of the mainly liquid contents of the container it kicked out a slimy green backwash on to the deck before sinking out of sight in a gurgle of slow bubbles. After the second shoe disappeared the companion of the woman who had called out to the newcomers opened her mouth wide to reveal a toothless chasm and released a battery of sharp, barking shrieks not unlike the cries of the gulls.

'Now come over 'ere and do as you was told t' do before. Stow yer shoes away.'

Jessica stayed where she was. 'Not in your lifetime, you ignorant brute,' she mumbled. The woman standing at her side turned towards her slightly and appraised her as best she could out of the corner of her eye.

'What were that?' the brute demanded, turning

his head sideways, perhaps to duck beneath the clamour of the gulls, and aiming one ear and one eye at her.

'Sir, most of these others were barefoot anyway. They didn't have any shoes to stow away.'

'What?' He strode back to confront her, his eyes crazy-wild, bulging as if they were at the point of popping out of his head. 'What are you comin' at?'

Despite the circumstances, she found herself wondering how he could stand the coarse material of his high-necked collar rubbing against his neck, particularly at times like this.

'I didn't hear what you said before, sir. And I was keepin' a close eye on what the others were doin', so I'd know what to do m'self.'

'What are you talkin' about, you stupid mott?'

'I didn't see any of them stow their shoes away, so I didn't know I had to.'

He reached out and grabbed her by the shoulder. 'I don't give a damn what you saw. I'm tellin' you now.' He raised his free hand and fired a finger back at the bucket. 'Go over there and get them shoes and stow 'm away.'

'But I don't have them any more. And I don't want them. I'm the same now as these others were when you told them to stow their shoes.'

'She's right,' a woman called out from the other end of the line. And then others nearby the speaker voiced similar agreement, some of them calling out to leave her alone.

'Silence!' The man shouted swinging around and

striding back towards them. 'Silence or I'll iron the lot of you.' The murmurs of rebellion abated.

He stood glaring at the probable seat of the clamour, his head and neck twitching from side to side. He then turned on his heel and marched back to confront Jessica.

'What be your name?' he demanded.

'Jessica Glider, sir.'

'Well, Jessica Glider, I'll give you one more chance.' He aimed his finger-pistol back behind him in the general direction of the containers. 'Get them shoes and stow them away.'

'I can't do that, sir. The bucket's been emptied.'

'What?' He hovered over her for a moment rocking between the heels and toes of his broad boots, and then he swung around and glared at the women who had been emptying the containers.

The one who had called out earlier shrugged her shoulders and raised both hands palm uppermost. 'Sylvie done it before I could stop 'er, y'worship. She be mad as a meat axe. Y'know she be. Madder even. But you can't blame 'er. She's been fucked by a demon.'

He stood as if transfixed, glaring at the delinquent Sylvie, who matched his gaze for a time. Finally she turned away and, opening her toothless chasm again, gave a repeat rendition of her bird calls.

The man turned back and gripped Jessica with his gaze. 'You'll pay for this, you filthy slattern.' He raised his truncheon.

'You shouldn't hit her just because she be deaf, sir.' The speaker was standing beside Jessica, the same woman who had watched her closely earlier.

'What do you mean?'

'She be deaf, sir. Partly deaf, leastwise. That be why she didn't do like you told her.'

He leant forward, peering at the woman. 'What be your name, may I ask?'

'Elizabeth Crowling, sir.'

'You look like 'er. Are you 'er sister or somethin'?'

'No, sir.'

'Well mind y'own fockin' business. If I want to hit 'er I will hit 'er. And as 'ard as I damned well please. If I want to lock 'er in chains and beat the livin' sheart out of her I will.'

'The surgeon wouldn't like that, sir. Just because she be deaf.'

'What do you know about the surgeon? You just came on board, for fock's sake.'

'I heard he be a fair man, that be all.'

'I don't give a hoot what y'heard, y'slut. If any of you step out of line I'll have you flayed alive, surgeon or no surgeon.' He turned to face Jessica squarely, and raising his truncheon drove the end up cruelly under her chin. 'And that goes for you even if ye be as deaf as a post. Do y' hear me?' he shouted.

'Aye, sir.' Dear God, how much more of this?

'Good.' He lowered the truncheon and stood glaring at her for a few moments longer. Then he turned and walked back to the front of the line where he involved himself in some activity that she could not clearly see.

When the heaving of her chest subsided she turned to the woman beside her. 'Thank you for that.'

'Don't thank me, y'stupid bint,' replied Elizabeth Crowling. 'I didn't do it for you. I did it for me. I've seen the likes of that bastard before.'

She was interrupted by a cry from the head of the gangway which was answered by the orderly. A few moments later he strode back past them, firing angry glances at both of them before moving on to where another group of women were beginning to file on to the deck. Elizabeth waited until he was well out of earshot, before continuing. 'Once his type hands out one thrashin', likely as not they start lookin' around for an excuse t' hand out another. And then another. I didn't want to be on the receivin' end of any of 'm. That be the only reason I opened m'silly trap.'

'Well, thank you anyway.'

Elizabeth stood looking at her for a moment. 'Where y'from?' she asked.

'Hampshire.'

'Well, stay away from me, Hampshire. You've got too much dumb innocence in your eye f'my likin'. One thing I don't need around here is t'be lookin' after anyone's interests but m' own.'

The activity at the front of the line that had attracted the attention of the man before he returned to the gangway was the removal of the women's irons.

As they moved closer another black-jacketed orderly imparted the message, 'This'll be a temporary measure if there be any trouble from any one of you.' This one was also a truncheon-wielder, but was older than the first man and had a way about him that suggested he would have better control of his temper.

He stood beside a blacksmith who was seated on a low stool with his knees astride a small anvil. A pile of manacles, fetters and their chains was stacked on the deck behind him.

When it was Jessica's turn, the smith directed her by example with his own wrists how to place her manacles on the anvil.

'And remove those rags,' the orderly demanded.

She quickly unwrapped the strips of cloth she had wrapped around her wrists and ankles to try and prevent the irons from chafing her flesh. She then squatted in front of the smith and placed each wrist in turn hard up against the cold steel of the anvil so that the riveted junction of each manacle lay on top of it with the rivet uppermost. The smith then placed a punch against the rivet and knocked it out with a firm blow from his hammer.

The ringing clang of metal on metal elicited a simultaneous blink and gasp from Jessica as each manacle fell apart. She then sat on the deck and positioned her ankles in a similar manner to her wrists, while the smith repeated the process.

When she first noticed where the man's eyes were focused she made a point of keeping her own gaze away from his, hoping that at the moment he swung his hammer he had it aimed at what he was doing. Not where it was aimed when she was positioning her wrists. Then it was definitely probing her cleavage, and when she was positioning her ankles it was aimed high between her legs. Adding to these distractions he had a fly crawling on his face. Without a free hand to brush it away his lips were pursed and were working backwards and forwards in concert with his nose in an effort to dislodge the insect.

When she was free of her irons—miraculously uninjured, she believed—she stood up and glanced back down to where the woman she had spoken to was sitting on the deck unravelling the strips of cloth from her ankles. Jessica was about to turn away again when a sudden movement caught her eye. The pale sunlight glinted for a moment on an object that arced through the air and fell close to her own feet with a distinctive ring of metal.

The orderly who had his back to them at that moment spun around. 'What were that?' he demanded. 'Everyone stand still.' He looked down at the smith. 'Did you see what that were?'

The man shook his head. Jessica had no doubts that he indicated honestly.

She reached down beside her foot. 'Stand still,' the orderly barked again.

As she straightened he stepped in front of her. 'What have you got there?'

She opened her hand, revealing a small comb.

He plucked it from her hand. 'What be this?'

'It's a comb, sir. I dropped it.'

'It be a metal comb, m'darlin'. You know the orders about weapons.'

'It's not a weapon, sir. It's a comb.'

He raised his truncheon and struck her on the side of the face. The blow knocked her head to one side.

'Don't argue with me. It be a weapon. It be made of metal.'

'I'm sorry, sir. I didn't know.' My God! My God! Tears of pain had sprung to her eyes.

'Well, you know now.' He placed it in his pocket. 'I'll let you off this time, seein' it be y'first day on board. But if I ever catch y'with a weapon again I'll have y'flogged, and I'll have you back in chains. Do y'understand me?'

'Aye, sir.'

'Now be off.'

'Aye, sir.' As she turned to leave she dropped one of the strips of cloth she had been using and bent down hurriedly to retrieve it. She then moved quickly away to join up with the women ahead of her.

'Come on, I ain't got all day,' growled the smith to Elizabeth Crowling who was still sitting on the deck and had been watching these events closely.

Elizabeth turned her gaze away from Jessica's

retreating back and moved forward on her haunches to place an ankle against the anvil.

When she joined up with the others she sought Jessica out and signalled for her to make her way to the back of the group. Sheltered from general observation by the junction of two of the shanty-like structures that clung to the upper deck—in this case a kitchen and a laundry, both of which had chimneys that were belching coal-black smoke that was coating the upper deck in a thin layer of soot—she leant close to Jessica and asked, 'Are you all right?'

Jessica raised a hand and tentatively touched the welt that was already beginning to etch a dark line into the side of her face. 'I'll live.'

'Why did you do that?'

Jessica gave her the makings of a smile. 'Like you didn't open your silly trap for me before, I didn't do what I did for you. I did it for me. I've seen the likes of that bastard before. Once his kind finds a real weapon on one of us, he starts actin' like he's found a real weapon on all of us. That be the only reason I did it.'

'Ye be a cheeky bint. I'll say that for you.' Elizabeth looked at her closely. 'At the time you stuck your foot on it you wouldn't know what it be.'

'You've got quick eyes.'

'You've got a quick foot.'

'I know what it is now.' Jessica opened her hand revealing part of a knife blade.

'You took a risk, m'love. If he'd caught you with

that he'd have made you pay dearly.'

'No less than if he'd caught you with it.'

'But it were mine. You didn't have to stick y' nose in.'

'Maybe I wouldn't have, if I'd known what it was.' She passed it to her. 'You better keep it.'

Elizabeth glanced about her to see that no one was watching, then hoisting up her skirts and tying a strip of cloth around one thigh just above her knee, she slipped the blade between the folds. Now that she had a chance to observe the other woman closely, Jessica noted that she did have a distinct resemblance to herself.

Her hair was only a shade darker than her own and although her eyes were more hazel than green her face was a similar shape. Older looking, she hoped. A little harder, perhaps. But then it was a while since she had seen herself. Perhaps her own looks had deteriorated. Hardened. There had been plenty of excuse for them to have altered for the worse.

She looked quickly away, out past where a group of half-naked women were hauling clothes from corroded metal tubs of steaming water, and out beyond the lines that supported row upon row of yellow-stained soot-topped bedding. On the other side of the wide sheet of grey water that separated them from the land—too wide for her to cross unaided, she'd decided earlier—the fields were a pastel mosaic of greens and golds and russet brown; and the downs on the skyline were a low, rolling expanse of purple wash.

Elizabeth turned and watched her. 'That be Hampshire out there, am I right?'

'Aye.'

'Well I'm afraid, my pretty, you can say goodbye to Hampshire for a while. Same as you can say goodbye to that comb. By rights I should let you keep this.' She patted the wrapping of cloth and pulled her dress down over her leg as Jessica turned back.

She could have done without the message, but the 'my pretty' eased the pain a little.

'What? Oh that. No, you'd be better at handlin' it.' She placed the palms of both hands gently against her eyes for a moment before letting them drop to her sides. 'I haven't had much experience with weapons. I'd probably end up cuttin' m'self.'

'This ain't no weapon, m'love. This be a leg shaver. I like to keep m'legs smooth as a baby's bum. Always have. I doubt I'll ever have to use it as a weapon. There bein' mainly other women t'worry about on board.'

She doubted wrong. When they were ushered to the quarters they would occupy along with a handful of other newcomers, they had hardly enough time to check their bearings before they were all set upon by a large gang of the established inmates and relieved of their possessions, including most of the clothes they were wearing. Both Jessica and Elizabeth gave some resistance and were left bruised and bleeding for their efforts, whereas most of the others offered little opposition and escaped relatively unscathed.

'There were somethin' else besides dumb-innocence that I noticed in your eye that worried me at the time, Hampshire.' The two of them were crouching with their backs against one of the bulkheads of their quarters, shuddering occasionally when caught by a breath of cold air from a nearby barred gun port. Elizabeth's gaze for the moment was on the other woman's face, glowing palely in what afternoon light managed to breach the compartment's defences. But at other times that gaze would stray and rest for a while on one or other of her almost bare breasts.

'What was that?' Jessica pulled up the top of her undershirt and dabbed it against her lip, the action causing a nipple to slip into view through one of several tears in the fabric. 'And m'names not Hampshire. It's Jessica. Call me Jessica.'

'Jessica,' Elizabeth repeated, momentarily distracted. But she recovered quickly. 'A flicker of fire. That's what I noticed. At the time I be thinkin' that's a bad combination, dumb-innocence and a flicker of fire. Now I'm not so sure. Now I'm startin' to think it might not be so much a failin' as a blessin'. Now I'm startin' to think that if you and me don't want to end up like those two hags we saw emptyin' shit over the ship's side when we arrived, then we're goin' to have to make a statement to them bitches who robbed us.'

She reached into the folds of the piece of cloth that was bound to her thigh and extracted the knife blade. 'And I reckon that this bit of steel and your bit of fire might be the makin's of a statement they'll sit up and take notice of. Or in this case, lie very still and take notice of.'

That same evening the two women ambushed their attackers one at a time and retrieved most of what had been taken from them.

Despite Elizabeth's reference to the value of Jessica's fire, she took the leading role herself, possibly because she was three years older than her newly acquired companion, but more likely because she was a touch taller. Their tactics were simple but effective. All of their attackers slept with their possessions, some of them in hammocks and others on makeshift bunks in locations where some protection was offered by the corners of the compartment, or by the proximity of pillars or the sides of the companionway.

Approaching each in turn when they were bedded down for the night, Elizabeth simply placed a hand over her victim's mouth and pressed the sharpest point of her knife hard up against the woman's throat. The words she chose to immobilise them would probably have been effective on any selected victim, regardless of size, sex, or physical inclination.

'My name be Elizabeth Crowling and I cut the throats of four grown men who raped me. If you so much as let your eyelid flicker I'll slit you from ear to ear and hold you while you drown in your own blood.'

Jessica would then rummage about in the woman's belongings and collect as much of what had been taken from the two of them as she could find.

From then on they moved about together, watched each other's belongings and kept their most prized possessions close to them at all times.

The others made many threats of retaliation but were either unable or unwilling to mount the combined assault that would be necessary to give them any chance of exacting retribution. Their enthusiasm for revenge probably diminished when their enquiries confirmed that Elizabeth had indeed been convicted of murder, and Jessica had been convicted of highway robbery. As most of them had been imprisoned for nothing more noteworthy than robbing their clients while working as prostitutes, they probably decided that it would be wiser to wait for less dangerous prey to come their way.

When Elizabeth had finished shaving beneath Jessica's arms she sat back on her haunches and smiled as she observed her handiwork. 'Jessica, you should see y'self. You look like a cute little bald elf or a pixie or somethin' in a play at the theatre.'

Jessica held both hands over her head. 'I've never been to a real play, or a theatre. All I know is my head feels very cold and very clean.'

'You'll soon be feelin' cleaner, m' lass. Hoist up your skirts and lie flat on your back.'

'No, Liz,' Jessica leaned forward and whispered her refusal close to Elizabeth's ear. 'That's one bit of shavin' I can do for m'self.'

'You can't lie flat on your back an' do it,' Elizabeth murmured. 'Nor can ye get your head close enough to see what you be doin'. An' that be what you'd be needin' to do, to do it right in this light. Come on. Don't be so bloody princessy.' She smiled. 'With a head like the one you've got now, y'ain't got nothin' to be princessy about. An' remember, I ain't doin' this for love alone, little darlin'. When I'm finished you're goin' to be doin' the same to me. That be the arrangement.'

Jessica groaned and shook her head despairingly. 'Bloody lice!'

'An' bloody crabs, m'lovely,' said Elizabeth. 'But not for much bloody longer.'

Some time later, after all traces of hair had been removed from both their bodies, they bundled their clothes into a burlap sack and sponged themselves down with water from the second bucket.

'Yer mad, both of you,' a passer-by offered as they dried themselves. 'You'll both catch p-monia for sure.'

'That be why we got ourselves these woollen caps, Susie,' said Elizabeth, pulling a skull-cap down over her ears to prove the point.

'Well even if you live, you'll be lousy again

within a week, an' know you've wasted your silly time,' the woman persisted.

'No we won't, Susie,' said Elizabeth holding up a pair of men's trousers and a flannel shirt. 'Because we also got ourselves fresh togs. Straight out of Government stores, and just to be on the safe side, ones we've already boiled the livin' daylights out of. So where the likes of you and this lot will be wallowin' around in the crappy old rags you came on board in, complaining an' scratchin' like dogs at a flea festival, Jessie and me will be paradin' around with our noses in the air as fresh as a couple of daisies.'

'You cunning bitch. You've been fuckin' the slops bos'n.'

'Move on, Susie.'

'The surgeon then?'

'Move on. The fish ain't bitin' today.'

Elizabeth turned her back on the woman. 'Roll up the bottoms, Jess. Aye, like that. Has your belt got enough holes in it? Be it tight enough?'

Jessica tested the security of her trousers. 'I think so. How do I look?'

'If ye weren't so clean you'd look like a Battersea mudlark.'

'Male or female?'

'Male.'

This seemed to please her. She turned and picked up the burlap sack. 'We should ditch these over the side.'

'No. That'd be too hasty by a long shot. Who

knows what we'll have left to wear by the time we get to Botany Bay. But before we even think about puttin' them on again, we'll give them a few good boilin's and a few good soakin's in piss; and then a few more good boilin's just to be on the safe side.' She bent down and peered at the closest port. 'Now might be as good a time as any to give them their first boilin', if it ain't rainin'.'

As they made their way aft after gathering up all their paraphernalia, a familiar face reappeared over the side of one of the hammocks.

'Did you rub some of that rum on her cunt, m'love? If y'did I'll be down later to help you lick it off.'

'You'll be down sooner than that, Mavis,' said Elizabeth, grasping the side of the hammock and jerking it downwards. The hammock flipped over as if it was secured to swivels, and its occupant crashed to the deck with a resounding thump before she had a chance to voice any hint of complaint or alarm. Whether as a result of Mavis being knocked out, winded, or simply stunned, the two women heard no more from her as they made their way up the companionway that led to the deck above.

SIX

The *Weymouth Bay* was one of three ships that was making the trip to New South Wales. Originally there was to be a bigger fleet, but because of the war, delays had occurred in obtaining the materials needed to bring the other ships up to the necessary level of seaworthiness. As the colony was still short of food, a decision was made to send the three ships that were already fit to sail, packed mainly with stores, but also with a consignment of female convicts, as women were also in short supply.

The other two were storeships, and although the *Weymouth Bay* had begun its career as a storeship it had recently been fitted out as a transport. But now, as there was a more urgent need for stores than for women, the authorities halved the number of convicts and marines that she was originally commissioned to take and stacked the extra space with stores, mainly sacks of grain. To facilitate the change of role, many bulkheads that had been fitted to accommodate manageable groups of convicts were removed from the lower decks and from the for'ard section of the ship.

A transportation official explained some of these matters to the assembled female convicts, including Jessica Glider, Elizabeth Crowling and an assortment of other women from the *Santa Ana*, as they were mustered on the Portsmouth dockside in preparation for embarkation. He went on to explain that the changes would provide more space and freedom of movement than was usually the case, and for this they should be thankful.

When he had gone one of the women claiming knowledge of such matters voiced a different opinion. 'If yer think any of that will make life easier on the voyage ye can think again. All it'll do is make it easier for the crew t'get at ya. That be the deal they demand before they'll sign on. One woman each. And the women they choose are the lucky ones. 'Cos the marines get the pick of what's left.'

'Stay close,' Elizabeth whispered near Jessica's ear when she felt her companion stiffen.

Most of the women were dressed in the best attire they had managed to retain during their incarceration, or had been able to scrounge or steal from others. The state of their clothing, most of it recently mined from the bottom of duffle bags, depended on how long they had been imprisoned, and in particular on how long they had spent on the hulks.

Many of the women were wearing their former working clothes, jaunty bonnets and gowns with plunging necklines chosen for night duty in London's Whitechapel and Portsmouth's Battery Row. Others were more soberly garbed in plain frocks and sensible woollen coats and cloaks.

But a surprisingly large number, who had obviously fared badly at the hands of others, were barely covered at all; they stood shivering in the tattered, and in some cases shredded and torn, remnants of undergarments or damaged items that their more fortunate neighbours had discarded. It was this lot who reflected the more acute discomfort each time the breeze from Gosport ruffled the calm surface of the harbour. Despite the poor condition of their garb most of the garments appeared to be clean, probably as a consequence of the hulks having a permanent supply of water readily available at the doorstep.

But regardless of how many times the clothing and those who owned it had been scrubbed, both the worn and the wearer were stamped with the odorous brand of the hulks. A general musty smell resembling the close proximity of a brewery, or the presence of decaying grain, or dusty burlap bagging, or a mix of all of these, hung on the morning air.

The women themselves were an assortment of different ages, heights and shapes, but had common denominators in the bleached pallor of their flesh and the resigned hollowness of their expressions. The younger ones were little more than children, most with faces worn by experiences beyond their years; and the older ones were not old by normal measure, despite their frail and trembling gait.

'Jesus!' breathed Elizabeth. 'I'd hate to see the others if we be the healthy ones.'

The *Weymouth Bay* was anchored off the motherbank. When longboats arrived to ferry the convicts out to her, the marines began to herd the women towards the edge of the wharf where a flight of steps led to the waterline.

As Jessica reached down and lifted the chains that linked her ankles, she cast an anxious glance back towards the dockside buildings. Beyond the heavy wagons that had transported the women across Portsea Island from the village of Milton, a number of onlookers were being held at bay by another cordon of marines. Most seemed to be sailors and dock workers, but there was also a scattering of others, possibly townspeople or visitors from afar: men in suits and women dressed in their Sunday finery.

'Can you see anyone y'know?' Elizabeth asked.

Jessica shook her head. 'I don't think I want to.'

'Aye,' Elizabeth agreed. 'When they shipped me around from Woolwich, I found myself lookin' for faces I was afraid I'd find.'

From time to time as they shuffled towards the steps they both cast furtive glances back at the crowd.

'I didn't sight any,' said Elizabeth as they moved down the steps. 'Then or now.'

'What?' asked Jessica distractedly.

'Familiar faces. None.' She glanced at Jessica. 'Did you tell anyone when we was leavin'?'

'No.'

'Then it wouldn't be likely they'd be there.'

'I don't suppose so. D'ye ever hear of anyone comin' back? From Botany Bay?'

'Not that I can recall,' Elizabeth replied, 'but then I never took much notice of talk of Botany Bay. Never knew I should've been payin' attention.'

'I'm goin' to come back. Or die tryin'.'

'You and me both, lass. I don't plan to spend the rest of m'days on no desert island.'

'D'ye think it's true about the crew?'

'What that noisy mott said? Never! What would she know? Just stay close when we get on board. We'll be all right, lass. We beat that filthy hulk di'n't we? Even beat the mites. We be survivors, you an' me.'

The attack on Jessica occurred late in the third week of the voyage. The sea had risen during the day and she was beginning to feel more queasy than at any other time since leaving Portsmouth. But knowing that they were due to anchor at Tenerife the following morning she believed that by bedding down early she could avoid becoming too incapacitated. So she slung her hammock and climbed into it before the sun had set, and without even attempting to eat any supper.

When the man dragged her out of her hammock her first reaction was to believe that he had mistaken her for one of the others. Neither her own nor Elizabeth's hair had grown much at all since they had last shaved themselves, and their almost bald scalps had the appearance of having been coated with a fine layer of nutmeg. Consequently both of them had been openly ridiculed by both the crew and the marines since the day they sailed. And whereas the situation that developed between most of the men and many of the younger convicts confirmed the prediction of the woman on the dockside, it appeared that she and Elizabeth would be spared unwanted attention.

So now as she was being hauled through the darkened sleeping quarters with a hand clamped firmly over her mouth, she believed that if only she could be allowed to identify herself she would be released.

She felt herself being partly dragged, partly carried down a companionway to the orlop deck. She could see bags of grain stacked in layers on either side of her and realised that someone had hung a lamp from a beam. Despite her predicament she recalled the first officer's warning shortly after they embarked that having an unauthorised flame at this level was a flogging offence.

Her abductor hauled her upright so that she was able to regain her feet. Then, with a cruel grip on one shoulder, he swung her around to face him.

He was not a tall man but was thickset, with a bull neck and broad shoulders. He had a low brow and a protruding mantle of scar-tissue shading a pair of small, deep-set eyes. She noticed with some surprise that he was young. Probably not much older than herself. She could not recall having seen him before.

All the women had been issued with sleeping attire in the form of men's nightshirts. Hers was loose-fitting, and following his gaze she became suddenly aware that both of her breasts had slipped free.

'Lie down,' he ordered, as she tried to cover herself.

'Let me go.' She made to move past him.

He slapped her so fast she was not sure where the blow had come from. It knocked her on to her back and she lay gasping from the shock. Although she was aware of pain from the blow somewhere in the vicinity of her head and shoulders, she found herself unable to identify either its nature or exact location.

He removed his broad belt and allowed his trousers to drop. As he stepped out of them and kicked them behind him his penis swayed obscenely from side to side.

'Please let me go,' she whispered as he stooped and took hold of the bottom of her nightshirt. She was vaguely aware of faces behind him.

He dragged the nightshirt up to her waist and

171

lowered himself on top of her. And as if he was the manifestation of her despair, a suffocating sense of complete helplessness crushed down upon her. She braced herself as she felt him at the point of entering her, and her mouth opened wide releasing a fearful silent scream.

The events that followed happened so quickly she was unable at the time to determine their significance; and only later, in recall, could she reconstruct what must have been their sequence.

The faces she had been aware of behind him had grown larger and were now at his shoulder. His eyes suddenly grew wide and an instant later his weight disappeared as he was hurtled backwards away from her.

She sat up. There were three of them. Older men, their bodies more seasoned. Two of them were holding her attacker by his shoulders. The third, a tall man, was standing directly in front of him and leaning towards him so that his face was only inches from him.

'You've been a naughty boy, Grapey. You've stepped way out of line. You didn't ask permission.' With this the speaker slammed his knee into the younger man's chest. The others then released him and he fell to the deck as a dead man might.

Jessica stood up and immediately staggered as her vision faltered. She raised a trembling hand to her face.

'Are you all right, m'lovely?' The big man moved towards her.

'I think so.' The sense of relief that flooded through her was overwhelming. Her knees began to tremble violently and for a few moments she believed she was going to faint.

'That's good,' said the man. He took her hand. She looked into his eyes. In that instant she realised her danger. But before she could react he swung her around so that her back was to him and, twisting her arms behind her, he forced her down on to the pile of grain sacks. He then hoisted her nightshirt high up her back and while the others gripped an arm each and held her immobile, he took her brutally, pounding himself into her, with one hand grasping the top of her near-bald crown and forcing her face against the rough weave of the uppermost sack of grain.

The second man then took his turn, and then the third. And as with the first man, they raped her where she had first fallen, with her face pressed out of shape against the sacking. She could have been suffocating. She could have been dead. But none of them showed any concern for her condition. To the contrary, with their lips pulled back from their teeth and bursts of saliva flying from their mouths, they spurred each other on, grunting in sympathy with the rider of the moment and assailing her with foul taunts and rebukes.

When the third man climbed away from Jessica, the first man chose to prolong her suffering. He was holding one of her arms and motioned for the second man, who was holding her other arm, to help turn her over and place her on her back.

When they had done this, and he noticed that her eyes were open and were on him, he said, 'I enjoyed that so much, m'little bald piglet, I've decided to take a second helpin'. To go around the buoy, so t' speak. But this time from where I can see your plump titties, and watch your cute little face so I can tell that ye be enjoyin' it too.' He then lowered himself on top of her.

What he was unaware of was that while Jessica had her face pressed into the burlap sacking, the mind-numbing terror that had first descended on her had gradually dissolved and was replaced by a strengthening sense of outrage. With each slap of foreign flesh against her flesh, with each invading thrust of foreign body into her body, escalating surges of teeth-grinding anger were building up within her.

This latest violation began to assume a single embodiment of all the wrongs that had assailed her over the preceding months; and her inability to do anything whatsoever to stop what was now happening became a condensation of her helplessness to redress those wrongs.

So it was, as this man hauled her on to her back, taunted her and then entered her for the second time, with his leering face hovering close to hers, that she decided to exact terrible retribution.

As he began to move within her—more gently than before, perhaps to prolong the encounter—she raised both her legs and entwined them around

174

his. He was surprised by this and muttered something she did not quite catch. The others also made some comment. One of them laughed.

She then raised both her arms and, wrapping them around his back, locked her wrists behind his waist. This had the effect of causing him to increase his tempo, gasping aloud in time with his extra exertions. She looked into his eyes and raised her head towards him as if perhaps to kiss him. He in turn lowered his face towards hers.

It was at that moment she struck. Like a leopard. Mouth wide, teeth extended. She moved so fast, the smirk was still on his face at the moment of impact. Her jaws latched on to his nose and she bit down upon it with a force that drove her teeth through skin, flesh, cartilage and bone, tearing, crunching, severing. And she held on to him. With her teeth. With her legs. With her arms.

He tried to scream but his throat refused to respond. He tried to pull away from her; scramble away; detach from her. But every way he went so did she, locked to him as if they were part of the same tormented creature that was bucking and writhing in the throes of some terrible silent torment.

When the others recovered they tried to assist, but to no avail. Her legs and arms were locked so tightly around him that in the poor light his companions could not see where to grip them. And her face was locked so close to his that for a time it was almost impossible to determine where one finished and the other began. Also, as he was on top of her, he prevented them from being able to direct unobstructed blows at her body. Finally, the man did manage to get his throat to work and he began to scream horribly, like a pig might if it was being butchered alive. The others finally managed to get a grip on Jessica and began to prise the two of them apart. But by then the damage had been done.

Jessica released her jaws, mainly because she had begun to choke from his blood. But as she detached so did much of his nose. Those parts of it that she did not spit out, or drag from her teeth with her fingers, hung by slivers of flesh from a gaping wound in the centre of his face.

Neither the man nor his companions tried to retaliate. He lay on his back screaming with diminishing vigour while the others hovered over him, using neckerchiefs or bandannas to try and stem the flow of blood. This allowed her to draw away from them; to place her breasts back inside her blood-soaked nightshirt and pull the hem back down to her knees and to move backwards up the pile of sacks until she was close to the deckhead.

When she could go no further she continued to clean blood and debris from her mouth. A number of times she interrupted this activity to lower her head and retch, spit repeatedly, and retch again.

When one of the men did turn away from attending his companion and moved towards her with the probable intention of dragging her down from her perch, his intentions were arrested by the thumping of boots on the companionway. A moment later a contingent of marines appeared accompanied by the first officer.

'Avast there!' he called out. 'What in the hell be goin' on down here?'

They locked her in a set of irons in the waist of the ship, adjacent to the boats. The irons were mounted flush with the deck and resembled large thumbscrews, but unlike thumbscrews, these were used to secure her ankles and thighs rather than crush any of her smaller protuberances.

The first officer had ordered her to be so secured until the ship anchored the next day in Tenerife, where he, or the captain if he was sober enough for long enough, would decide what should be done with her. His assumption when he came upon the scene in the orlop was that Jessica had been entertaining the men when a dispute had flared up over some matter, probably the payment she was demanding. This was more or less confirmed by the others. She offered no explanation, acting as if she had been struck dumb.

All were in serious breach of regulations. So as soon as the injured man was hauled off to the sick bay, he ordered the others to be confined to the brig and Jessica to be ironed. Her attack on the man warranted no less at this stage, he decided, regardless of the circumstances. Eventually she probably would be hanged, undoubtedly so if her victim were to die from his injuries.

When it was apparent to the first officer that all was now quiet and that the remaining convicts were secure, he allowed the duty watch of marines to return to whatever they were doing before. He then retired to his cabin, one of three located directly below the captain's, the others being occupied by the surgeon and the captain of marines.

He had roused the surgeon to attend to the wounded man. But he had left the captain of marines undisturbed to pursue whatever activity was occupying him at that moment; probably sleep, seeing that the commotion of booted feet running up and down the after companionway had not disturbed him; or possibly the attentions of the young corporal that he always kept in close attendance, if both of them were hard of hearing.

Whether or not Jessica would eventually be hanged counted for little at that time. Secured as she was on the upper deck, fully exposed to the unrelenting lash of freezing spray curling around the bows from the still-rising sea, it was doubtful she would survive the night, despite a young man from the watch on the upper deck risking being swept over the side by bringing her an oilskin cape and draping it around her.

Beneath the oilskin she was still garbed only in her blood-soaked nightshirt. After half an hour she was shivering so violently she had trouble clinging to the cape and keeping it from slipping from her head and exposing her near-bald scalp to the elements. At the point where she could no longer feel her fingers and began to drift into a state of resignation in which her will to survive was all but extinguished, she felt someone grasp her from behind.

'Jessie, it be me, Liz. I've brought you dry clothes.'

Elizabeth hugged her companion for a moment and then, with difficulty, because she had secured herself with a line to the skid-beams that supported the closest boat, she removed Jessica's cape, preventing it from blowing away by trapping it beneath her thigh. She then pulled off and discarded Jessica's soaked nightshirt and quickly covered her naked body with a heavy serge dress which she pulled down over her head and shoulders, tugging the hem beneath her buttocks and tucking it tightly around her legs. She pulled a heavy woollen jumper over the top of the dress, extracting each of these items from a duffle bag she had secured to her own waist beneath a bulky oilskin coat. Finally she pulled a woollen skull-cap over Jessica's head, tucking it under her chin, pulled her oilskin cape back on, and wrapped a length of sailcloth around her legs.

Throughout these exertions Jessica made no sound. The only sign that she was aware of what was happening was the way she compliantly positioned her arms, or ducked her head, as required to assist the other woman.

But when Elizabeth was finally satisfied and had drawn up as close as she could beside her friend, wrapping her arms around her and hugging her tightly, Jessica lowered her head on to Elizabeth's shoulder and cried. Her grief was pitiful and exhausting and her whole body shook and trembled. At times her mouth was locked open wide, screaming silently from the prolonged gasping effort of the release.

When she had recovered she told Elizabeth what had happened, reconstructing the events as best she could. Elizabeth in turn told her how she had bribed a sentry to allow her on to the upper deck, and then with the assistance of the upper-deck crew had made her way to where Jessica was secured. Elizabeth explained that the man Jessica had attacked was disliked by many on board and that as soon as she was able she would relate Jessie's story to the first officer.

His name was Angus Donwald. Elizabeth guessed that he was in his mid-thirties. He was of average height, athletically proportioned and had the makings of a beard. His forehead was high, his nose was straight and his eyes were a startling blue, bluer than any she could remember looking into.

'What proof have you that any of this be true?' he asked. He was sitting at a small desk secured to the inboard bulkhead of his cabin, with his chair turned so that he could face her. She was standing in front of him with a marine escort at her elbow.

'She be a farm girl. She ain't no whore. The only reason she be here was because she fought the local squire for her honour.'

'And lost?'

'And won. Otherwise she wouldn't be here, would she?'

'Just because she's a farm girl isn't proof that they were rapin' her.'

'You have two of them in the brig. I'm sure someone as clever as you could get the truth out of at least one of them. Especially if each of them thought the other was betrayin' him.'

'What's your name?'

'Elizabeth Crowling.'

'You have the same hair as her. Are you related?'

'No, sir. I have the same hair because we kept it shaved to get rid of the mites. They was awful bad on the hulk.'

'Do you have them now? Mites?'

'No, sir. Me nor her. We keep ourselves extra clean.'

He looked at her without speaking for a time, and then turned to the marine. 'You can leave us now, corporal. I'm sure this lady doesn't plan to attack me.'

'She ain't no lady, sir. She be a whore what killed her husband.'

'Regardless. I'm sure I'm perfectly safe. On your way, son.'

'Is it true what he said?' Donwald asked when the marine had gone. 'Did you kill your husband?'

'Aye, sir. But I ain't no whore. I might have taken a present from an admirer from time to time, but I was never no practisin' whore.'

'Why did you kill your husband?'

'He used to beat me somethin' terrible. One day I killed him for it.'

'How?'

'With a knife. I cut his throat.'

'How come you didn't hang?'

'I was sentenced to hang. But some of my friends petitioned the court. They said I was defendin' myself. If I hadn't killed him, he'd have killed me.'

'You must have lenient courts in London. They'd have hanged you f'sure if you'd been in Edinburgh.'

'Be that where you're from, sir? Scotland?'

'Aye.'

She smiled. 'I'd have never guessed from the way y'talk.'

'Don't you get cheeky with me, y'Sassenach bint, or I'll have you in irons beside your friend.'

'That'd be a shame, sir. I'd wager you'd have an easier job keepin' your eye on me down here, than way up there on the upper deck.'

'Who says I want to keep my eye on you?'

'Why else lock me in irons?'

They watched each other.

'Where are you from?' he asked.

'Devon by way of London.'

'By way of London. How come?'

'I took the short road.'

He laughed abruptly. 'Seems to me you got yourself lost, lass.'

'Aye, that too.' She waited for a reply. And then, 'What are you lookin' at, sir?'

'I'm thinkin' if it wasn't for your stupid bald head, you'd be a reasonable lookin' woman. Not beautiful, mind you. But reasonable.'

'You can't see much of me at the moment, sir. 'Ceptin' my head, of course. Would you like to see more of me? Though now I come to think of it, some of the rest of me be bald as well.'

'Is that so?'

'Aye. Or at least, near bald.'

'Would you like to show me?'

'Aye. I would.'

'Why?'

'Because I think you be interested. And because you have a trusty face. I'm sure I can trust that you will do the right thing by my friend Jessica.'

She then bent down and, taking hold of the hem of her dress with both hands, began to raise it towards her knees.

They unloaded the injured man in Tenerife. His name was George Lambton, a former Thames waterman from Tilbury. Angus Donwald convinced the captain that it was in the best interests of all officers on board that the ship's log state that Lambton had been injured when a cable had parted and whipped him across the face.

His two companions were each condemned to twenty-five lashes for having an unauthorised lamp on the orlop deck and for being in a food store without permission. As the sailor known as Grapey who had first abducted Jessica was long gone when Angus Donwald and the marines arrived, no charges were laid against him.

Jessica in the meantime was released from irons and all charges against her were dropped. Elizabeth took up semi-permanent residence in Angus Donwald's cabin.

All might have been well had George Lambton not been a thief as well as a rapist. When his sea chest was opened by Donwald with a view to sending ashore any possessions he might need, it was found to contain a number of expensive items that had been stolen from the cabins. Consequent investigation of the sail locker that was Lambton's part of ship revealed other stolen items secreted away, including a number of bottles of the captain's French brandy.

As these revelations came to light after the ship had completed provisioning and was due to sail, there was insufficient time to take up these matters with Lambton, so that as far as he was concerned, the discoveries were of no consequence—then or ever, for he died from complications from his injuries some six weeks later. They merely confirmed for some of those on board, including the captain, that the ship was well rid of him and that it was fitting no action be taken against the woman who had laid him low. But as far as some of his acquaintances on board were concerned, Jessica's attack on him, combined with the discovery of his loot, did have a marked effect. The men in question were a loose collection of undesirables who had looked upon Lambton as their leader, and whom he in turn had looked upon as his crew.

Lambton's cohorts were mainly from the Thames, east of London, some of them ex-watermen such as himself, others part-time fishermen and coastal boatmen. All were the refuse of the waterside hovels and back alleys, the product of the mudflats—long-legged waders surviving on the pickings from the tideline, with a weather-eye out for that elusive bauble among the flotsam and jetsam.

Lambton, with his bilge-rat cunning, his contacts and his cruel bravado, had improved the quality of the slough, increased their chances of success. Now that he was gone they were leaderless, and they were angry. Jessica had not only taken away their opportunity to gain some just recompense for having to endure the agonies of this long cruise, she had done it in a manner that warranted retaliation.

Originally there was an inner group of six in the gang, Lambton's longer-term, older, tougher confederates, but with him gone and the two men who had been flogged being too sick to participate, it was left to the three remaining to exact retribution.

Three of them may have been enough, but their opportunity to find out was severely compromised when their entry to the quarters where Jessica was sleeping was reported to Angus Donwald. The man who reported them was the same young sailor who had risked injury bringing Jessica the oilskin cape when she was secured in irons on the upper deck.

Angus and a hastily organised quintet of marines arrived before the trio of brigands had managed to locate where Jessica was sleeping. Since the attack on her, she had not been securing her hammock to the deckhead beams but had been spreading it together with her bedding within the narrow confines of the hammock stowage area adjacent to the companionway.

But even when afforded this extra protection she had not been able to sleep soundly. Consequently when the men entered the quarters she awoke, and suspecting that she may have had something to do with their presence, she drew herself into a niche between two of the upright supports where she could not be seen from anywhere other than from within the hammock stowage area itself.

This may have saved her life. Or at least her teeth. As Donwald was to discover when he later induced the least courageous of the undesirables to disclose the purpose of the iron bar one of them was carrying. He revealed, after some light persuasion and the threat of more robust continuation of it, that they had intended to smash her teeth with the bar, thereby preventing her from ever repeating the performance that robbed them of their leader, as well as sending a clear message to any woman on board who might have been tempted to follow her example.

For the remainder of the voyage, Jessica, in a similar manner to Elizabeth, took up semi-permanent residence in the first officer's cabin, except that whereas her companion spent most of her evenings in close attendance to Donwald, Jessica spent hers in a small alcove at the rear of his chart table.

'For my fockin' peace of mind,' as he explained to the captain, who was not particularly interested anyway. But Donwald believed the presence of a second woman in his keep warranted some explanation. 'We don't know who might want to have a go at her. And on her account I don't want to be floggin' any more of the hands. Or for that matter tryin' to stick any fockin' noses back on'm.'

There was a remarkable coincidence related to these matters. The young sailor who had come to Jessica's aid twice—mainly as a result of his developing a fascination for her from the moment he first saw her without her cap one day on the upper deck—was known as 'Clappers' on account of his name: Alfred Clapham.

Alfred's younger brother, Tom, was presently serving on the *Victory* and was the same Tom Clapham with the fair hair and rosy cheeks that Will Noling assisted from time to time with his mail, and later with learning to read and write.

None of the participants in these dramas was ever made aware of this. Had they been, and had any of them believed that extraordinary circumstances of this kind were brought about by intercedence from a higher authority, or by any phenomena beyond the understanding of man, they would probably have taken heart in the knowledge.

SEVEN

Gunroi stood like a pillar of stone, watching the sun climb above the dark feathery line of the horizon, moving fast, with quivering waves of fire rolling around its perimeter. Behind him colour began to flow back into the objects of the earth.

When he finally moved, it was to dip his head slightly and press one ear towards the ascending ball of fire and to hold his breath and try to filter out the stumbling chorus of the birds in the valley below him. Nothing. Not even a whisper. Either there was a heavy wind beyond the skyline that was pushing the sun's thunder away from him, he decided, or the sun itself was further off even than old Gaidimi had said. A long, long, long way further off.

He had tried to catch the sound of the rising sun before, of course. But always without success. Many times he had tried. But certainly more often of late. Such matters as the sun's thunder were of growing interest to him these days. This morning he thought there was a chance to hear it. There was no wind in the nearby trees. No rumbling from a nearby stream. No crackling of a nearby fire. No chattering of nearby women. There was only the sporadic song of the birds.

He sighed deeply, his shoulder brushing lightly up and down against the smooth shafts of the two spears he held clamped in the curl of the fingers of his right hand, with their butts planted firmly beside his feet on the expanse of cool stone on which he stood, the carved fire-hardened hunting blades nudging the morning air half his height again above him. When he glanced back he saw that Nunderri was watching him.

As their eyes met, his brother pressed the tips of three fingers to his nose and then pointed into the gully ahead. Gunroi turned back, and despite the distance—about three hundred paces—and the glare, he spotted the animal immediately. Furry nosed and grey. A female wallaroo, tender and juicy, her colour distinguishing her from her near-black tougher male counterpart and her nose rather than her size distinguishing her from her lankier drier cousin, the grey kangaroo. She was grazing on a patch of sweet grass in a slight depression that tracked the course of a stream that sometimes appeared during periods of wet weather.

Each man latched the butt of one of his spears against the barbed hook of his woomera, the spear-launching strip of wood that effectively doubled the length of his throwing arm.

The Wallaroo was in the open and so were they, so they approached her as she might have approached them: cautiously. Seemingly independently, first one and then the other man would move a few paces forward at a crouch, straighten, turn his head to one side, pause, turn his head to the other side, pause for a longer, or a shorter, time, crouch, move a few paces to the left or the right, straighten, turn his head to one side, pause again, move his head to the other side, pause for a shorter, or a longer, time, crouch, move a few paces forward, and so on.

They took a while to get there but were less than thirty paces away before she began to show any detectable signs of nervousness. At the moment she did, they both rushed forward as one, right arms raised high, each man with three fingers and a thumb gripping the knobbed end of his woomera, each with his index finger holding the shaft of the spear in its launching pad.

Their feet pounded across the side of the hill like a rapid thumping of padded clubs against a hollow log. A flock of bright green budgerigars exploded from an expanse of tussocky grass to one side of them. Then, as if controlled by a single external force, each man broke his headlong dash to skip once, twice, thrice, prop on his left foot and hurl his spear.

The shafts sang as they quivered through the

morning air. Three heartbeats later, a double thump and then the crash of a heavy body striking the ground was accompanied by a tumbling, kicking flurry of ungainly legs amidst a ballooning cloud of leaf and grass debris and a shower of flying stones and clods of earth. A few seconds later only a cloud of lighter debris was still moving.

Gunroi stood over the still-twitching body of the animal and pressing the end of his woomera against the soft fur, examined the two wounds. Good. Both spears were embedded high in the side of her chest. Her stomach and intestines were untouched. They would remain intact and shrink into a tight ball sealing their contents away from the flesh when they put her in the coals of a fire. There would be no need to waste time gutting and cleaning her. Nunderri's aim was improving.

Gunroi turned and gave his brother an approving nod. The younger man's face immediately broke into a beaming smile that flashed brilliant-white in a blast of light that speared at them from between thick bunches of leaves in the trees on the opposite side of the gully.

As they made their way back along the bank of the stream towards their camp, turning occasionally and shielding their eyes from the glare of the rising sun, an incident occurred that would trigger a succession of events that would ultimately link their lives with that of a white woman, who at that very moment was standing on the deck of the *Weymouth Bay*, shielding her eyes from the glare of the setting sun as it sank into the smooth copper sheen of the Atlantic Ocean.

Nunderri was walking ahead of Gunroi whose turn it was to carry the wallaroo. The younger man was carrying all four spears and the two woomeras. Because he was leading the way his eyes were continually sweeping from the path ahead to the stream. He scanned the path warily, always on the lookout for the deadly brown snakes that lived in this area, and he eyed the stream inquiringly for any sign of fish in the shallows—dim, barely discernible undulating shadows among the similar but at times out-of-phase undulations of the ribbons of grey-green weed.

At a place when a bend in the stream placed the sun above the opposite bank, a movement directly below the sun caught the attention of both men. They froze in mid-stride and stood watching the spot. Nunderri was the first to move but only to raise one of the woomeras and hold it horizontally above his eyes to shield his gaze from the glare.

The stream was not cleanly separated from the opposite bank at this point. The bank itself was low and waterlogged as a result of a small creek joining the main stream here in a series of reed-choked marshes that extended for about half a mile back to where the creek emerged from the mouth of a narrow gorge and spread out to spill down a broad natural stairway of moss-covered rocks. The sun at this angle had converted these marshes into an eye-smarting expanse of fierce light.

As the two men stood stock-still watching through the fine quivering lines that now separated the lids of their eyes, with all their senses focused on the centre of this conflagration, the rumbling gurgle of the stream was gradually consumed by a strengthening roar. And although both of them knew that this was merely the sound of the rising wind trapped in the forest that climbed away into the hills flanking the river, Nunderri began to tremble, and strands of hair on the back of Gunroi's neck lifted slowly away from his flesh.

It was unlikely when they were younger and were sitting listening to the tales of the story-tellers that behind their wide eyes their individual imaginations would have crafted and refined exactly the same image of a yoowii. But it was likely that both would have expected the creature to have some kind of human form and be dark and covered in lank wet hair, with eyes like glowing coals, slavering jaws and sharpened fang-like teeth.

As youngsters huddled around a winter campfire, their eyes reflecting its flickering light, they had no difficulty in imagining the creature was lurking out there somewhere; perhaps in the cold grey expanses of the night-time plain, or perhaps within the thick black shades of the forest. With the ebb and flow of the shadows of both plain and forest barely held at bay by the uneven beat of the flames, not only was it easy for the youngsters to imagine that an evil creature of indefinite size and configuration was out there, it seemed also probable that he could rush forward at any time of his choosing to seize one of them and drag him away.

For Nunderri, a yoowii would definitely be the black spirit of death, part-man part-devil; the same creature who carried off the first man on earth to die, the man the clan called Jerrabi, because his real name was forbidden to be mentioned by anyone but a select group of the elders, and then only during the most sacred of bora ceremonies.

For Gunroi, a yoowii was possibly also part-man part-devil, but as he grew older a yoowii was also a doubt. And a doubt was a worry, here on the edge of the plains, where the winters were cold, the summers fiery and the rainfall uncertain. Old Gaidimi had warned him that one doubter was enough for the Great Spirit Biamie to turn his back on the entire clan.

So obviously a doubt could be more of a danger than a part-man part-devil, Gunroi told himself—unconvincingly—as he stood on the bank of the stream looking towards the sun for he knew not what, with the small hairs on the back of his neck standing away from his flesh. If old Gaidimi is right about doubt, of course. And would doubting that he was right compound the danger? It hasn't rained since before the new moon before the new moon. And the budgerigars are a worry, so far from the truly dry country. He contemplated these matters for a moment and decided that doubt was a troubling confusion with no start and no end. A huge spiky tangle of roly-poly weed.

At this stage neither man was certain that he had noticed anything that did not have a rational explanation. The movement that caught the corner of their vision had caused concern, but exactly why, neither of them could determine. And there had been no repeat. Perhaps what they had seen was something quite normal, distorted by reflection from the water, or obscured by the glare. A flock of ducks landing perhaps. Or a cormorant diving. Perhaps even a dingo leaping from the water to hide in a clump of reeds on the muddy bank.

Gunroi was still contemplating these and other rational explanations when he was suddenly left in no doubt that whatever it was he was now observing it was certainly no ordinary creature or circumstance.

About three hundred paces directly ahead of them the marsh suddenly erupted in a gyrating shower of mud and water in an untidy column that seemed to stand twice the height of a man. The eruption continued unabated, with the glare and reflection turning it and the surrounding clouds of spray into a sparkling conflagration.

Despite the roar of the wind in the surrounding

forest seeming to choose that moment to press down on them with extra force, the men could clearly hear the furious slap-splash of disintegrating columns of mud and water tumbling away from the centre of the maelstrom and crashing back upon the surrounding surface of the marsh.

They were so startled and so preoccupied by the totality of the disturbance they did not immediately notice the creature within its midst. When they did they both staggered as if they had been slapped, and stood staring with their mouths agape.

It was tall and dark and was leaping and twirling so that it appeared to be perhaps fashioned from the flying mud and spray within which it was moving. Both men began to edge backwards away from the bank of the stream.

'I think it's seen us.' Nunderri whispered. 'It's coming closer.' As if on cue the creature suddenly raced towards them.

Nunderri cried out in alarm, dropped his weapons, spun on his heel and dashed across the riverbank towards the forest. The arched back of a large driftwood log momentarily blocked his path but he leapt high above it, clearing it easily without breaking his stride.

Gunroi dropped the wallaroo. But whereas his brother's fear gave wings to his feet, his own fear charged him with a tenacious resolve to avoid at all costs being dragged down from behind like the victim of a dingo pack. So with his heart pounding he dashed across the bank and scooped up one of the discarded spears, and in a continuation of the same movement swung around to face the creature.

His breath expelled in a rush of relief when he saw that it had turned back and was still about two hundred paces away, and now seemingly leaping about at the one spot. Gunroi turned away and was about to race after Nunderri, who was beckoning him from behind a large boulder, when something he had seen in the creature's movements caused him to pause and then turn back and shade his eyes in an attempt to see it more clearly. It was still thrashing about, but in an area that was less muddy.

Taking his eyes off it only momentarily, he squatted down and quickly picked up his woomera and another spear. He then straightened and fitted the butt of one of the spears against the spike of the woomera.

'No,' Nunderri called out from behind him when he saw his brother's intent. 'No. No.'

But Gunroi was already moving towards the stream. He waded across carefully, keeping his eyes on a clump of reeds through which he could still see the creature. He moved carefully, feeling with his feet to avoid putting his full weight on to a sharp stone or on to any of the large smooth boulders that were covered in slippery weed. When he reached the other side he moved towards the creature in a circulatory route, stooping and keeping himself partly concealed behind low mounds of turf and bunches of tussocky marsh grasses.

Whatever it was, it was still thrashing about, but less violently, and although he caught glimpses of it only occasionally it now seemed to spend more time rolling among the reeds than leaping into the air. As he came closer he could hear it grunting and gasping and releasing harsh coughing sounds like the exertions of a gusty wind poking away at a burning stack of hollow logs.

At the point where he was about to climb on to the last low bank that separated them, and from where he would be fully exposed, he glanced back and saw that Nunderri was now standing in the open, his arms akimbo, his stance projecting utter bewilderment and hopelessness.

Gunroi checked that the butt of his spear was securely fastened to his woomera, took a deep breath, and stepped on to the bank. The creature saw him and stood erect, black mud and water sliding jerkily down its thick, dark fur. Gunroi raised his spear high and ran forward, his toes gouging divots in the surface of the soft grass-encrusted mud that coated the bank. He skipped once, twice, thrice, propped and hurled his spear with all of his strength. For the second time that day the air vibrated in harmony with the song of a quivering shaft.

Thump! The blade buried deep in the creature's chest. It staggered from the blow but did not immediately fall. It clawed violently at the shaft for a moment, before pitching forward into the water. The water then erupted as they had first seen it, as the creature hurled itself upright and leapt high into the air with the now broken shaft of the spear protruding from its chest. Gunroi was so surprised by what seemed to be its resurrection that his hands trembled as he fitted the second spear into his woomera.

Again he leapt forward with his arm raised high and hurled the second spear. It struck inches from where the blade of the first was embedded. Again the creature clawed at the shaft and again it pitched forward into the marsh. But this time, although it did repeatedly attempt to rise, there were no further explosions of mud and water.

In its death throes it continued to kick fitfully for a while and a number of times it managed to lift its nose above the surface of the water. But it died eventually, and the surface of the marsh gradually settled to lap gently against those parts of it that protruded from the surface: the expanse of its broad back and the powerful thigh muscle of one of its legs.

Gunroi sank down on his haunches and squatted for a while on the bank, watching it. Finally he straightened and beckoned Nunderri to join him. His brother approached warily.

'Is it dead?' the young man asked when he finally drew near.

'Yes.'

Nunderri crept forward, his feet feeling for the earth as Gunroi's had earlier felt for the bed of the stream. When he reached his brother he stood staring at the two dark mounds of fur that protruded above the surface of the water as if they were perhaps beasts of prey lying in wait for him to move closer. His legs were trembling.

'You killed the spirit of death?' His voice was a hoarse whisper, crammed with a mix of fear and admiration.

'No,' Gunroi replied.

'No?'

'I killed a black wallaroo. A big one. And that's all I killed.'

'A black wallaroo! A black wallaroo?' Part of Nunderri's consciousness was obviously having difficulty accepting that what he was looking at was not his fearful devil-creature. 'A black wallaroo?'

'A big one. Bigger than any I've seen. Big as a grandfather grey kangaroo.' Gunroi held a hand head-high.

'But what ... what was he doing?'

'He was trying to escape from the bull ants that were attacking him.' So saying, Gunroi picked up a clod of earth and threw it at the larger of the exposed mounds of fur. Where the clod struck and disintegrated, big red ants emerged from the fur and raced across to examine the point of impact. Some of them reared back raising their front legs and nippers belligerently to challenge the broken clumps of mud that were sliding towards the water.

'Bull ants!' Nunderri was swept by a jolting shudder.

'Big and angry.' Gunroi pointed with his woomera. 'See the surface of the water. Among the broken reeds. The ones he managed to dislodge are everywhere. Like the stars in the sky. More than I've ever seen. He must have fallen asleep beside a big camp of them. And when they started to bite he jumped into the marsh to escape them. But there were too many. All through his fur. Biting, biting, biting, biting. Each bite a burning coal. A wasp inside his ear. So many bites would have driven him crazy. Would have killed him if I hadn't killed him.'

Nunderri stepped back quickly from the edge of the stream, his eyes darting backwards and forwards into the grass near his feet.

Gunroi stood looking at the body of the animal, perhaps contemplating whether or not to try to retrieve the spears that were hidden somewhere beneath the surface of the water.

Then a shudder similar to the one that had assailed his brother rippled across his own shoulders, and apparently thinking better of it, he turned away.

'A black wallaroo?' said Gaidimi.

'Yes, Grandfather.'

'You could tell? Before you crossed the stream?'

'Yes.'

'But Nunderri couldn't tell.' The old man glanced across to where Nunderri was sitting in the shade of a clump of saplings some distance away. 'Or so he says.' Nunderri was surrounded by an expanding group of young men, some of whom had drifted in through the afternoon haze in ones and twos from the plain, wading across what might have been a shimmering lake, their bodies for a time liquid, and their limbs dismembered.

Gunroi shook his head. Nunderri had told the tale of the morning's adventures so many times, undoubtedly with extra refinement at each telling. His voice would soon be as harsh as the yoowii's.

Peals of laughter broke out from Nunderri's audience when he described how he crossed the river at Gunroi's behest to view the yoowii. The young man had a natural propensity for comedy, particularly when spurred on by others, and in the manner of the more gifted story-tellers of the clan he was a brilliant mimic and an apt exponent of sign and body language. He was now using all these resources to give greater dramatic and comic weight to particular words and phrases.

What elicited the mirth of his companions was when he said, in effect, 'If you'd been there you would have seen how reluctant I was to cross that river.'

These were not his actual words, of course, nor

are they a direct translation; but they do convey his meaning more succinctly than quoting him verbatim.

In the language and style of speech of his clan, what he actually said with words and signs was more along the lines of, 'You see me at that river. I step into the river. I step out of the river. I step into the river. I jump out quick. I look along the bank this way. I look along the bank that way. I look up at the sky. Birds flying this way, flying that way. I look at Gunroi. He say, "Come quick, what are you doing?" I look up at the sky. I scratch my bum, I step back in the river. I jump back on the bank.' And so on.

Gaidimi turned back from watching him. 'Nunderri says that when it first showed itself it was impossible to tell what it was.'

'I was closer than he was.' He felt and sounded uncomfortable. And his gaze dodged past Gaidimi's face when the old man turned back.

'Was it your eyes that told you it was an ordinary animal? Or was it your stomach?' Had Gaidimi lived on that side of the earth that was now swathed in the shades of night, he may have said 'heart'.

'I'm not sure.'

'Think carefully before you answer. Were you more sure it was an ordinary animal, or more sure it was not a yoowii?'

'I think I was more sure it was not a yoowii.'

'Why?'

'Yoowiis are more scarce than ordinary animals.'

'More scarce?' The old man watched him carefully. And for the first time in a while Gunroi met his gaze.

'I've never seen one.'

A fire momentarily flickered in Gaidimi's eyes and Gunroi immediately regretted his remark.

'And who are you that the Great Spirit Biamie would choose to have you see one of his forbidden creatures? You, who have been to—how many?—only three, perhaps four bora ceremonies in your entire life. Why would Biamie waste his time? Men twice, three times your age have not been so honoured.'

'I'm sorry, Grandfather.'

'And so you should be. I don't know why I waste my time on you.'

'I'm sorry, Grandfather.'

'If I was your true grandfather I would have kept a closer eye on you when you were younger. I would never have let these dangerous notions enter your head. At the first sign I would have beaten them out of you. You know what I'm talking about, don't you?' Although his anger and frustration seethed about him like an invisible aura the old man did not raise his voice or change his tone.

'I'm not sure, Grandfather.'

'You're not sure, but you have a good idea, don't you? Like the day you took the others to see the howling of the dead in the gorge of the dead.'

'But that was not forbidden, Grandfather. If it was forbidden I would not have gone.'

'You were a boy. How old? Twelve summers? The howling of the dead should have terrified you. It's terrified many people older than you. And I'm not sure that if it was forbidden that you would not have gone.'

'No, Grandfather. Never. I would never defy the law.'

Gaidimi leant forward and peered into his eyes as if he could determine the accuracy of this assertion.

'It was only the wind, Grandfather. And the echo of the wind.'

'I know that, boy. But who told you?'

'I think I guessed.'

The old man threw up his hands in exasperation. 'That's what I mean. You guessed. You guessed. Well, you shouldn't have guessed. You shouldn't have guessed it was the wind, as you shouldn't have guessed the croak of the giant frog at the end of the gorge was a loose boulder rubbing against another whenever the stream was rising.'

'But that wasn't forbidden either, Grandfather. If it was, I would not have taken the others there either.'

'Wouldn't you? I sometimes wonder.'

'No, Grandfather. I would never do that.'

'How did you know about the boulders? Who told you, or was that also a guess?'

'I noticed the noise was there only when the stream was running faster than normal.'

The old man's shoulders slumped and his body seemed to assume a more relaxed attitude, as if some of the tension had been eased from the fibres that held it together. He stretched out both legs and leaned back, supporting himself on his elbows. 'I would feel more comfortable if you guessed less about some of these matters and believed more.'

His gaze turned to Nunderri and the group surrounding him. 'I would then feel more confident that you would never one day challenge any matter that was truly forbidden. You know that no other young man in the clan is held in the esteem that you are. No other. What worries me is that with the younger ones I'm not sure how much of the respect they have for you is because you challenge the conventions of the clan. And if you were ever to challenge the law rather than the conventions they might be tempted to challenge the law as well. The consequences for the land could be disastrous.'

'I would never challenge the law. Never.'

Gaidimi turned and looked deep into his face for an age. Finally he said, 'You must always remember that your soul is as fragile as a small bird that you have been entrusted to protect from dangerous creatures who wish to eat it.'

He held out one hand, palm-uppermost, and cupped it as if perhaps nursing that bird within it. 'To protect it you must hold it gently but firmly. If you squeeze too tightly you will kill it yourself. If you hold it too loosely it will fly away and be devoured. But protection is not enough, it will still die if you do not nourish it yourself. Every day you must feed it and keep it warm.'

Gunroi wished that he could find appropriate words to reply. He could feel Gaidimi's gaze probing him, seeking a response. But he could think of nothing that would not probably increase the old man's concern, so he remained silent and turned away, feigning interest in Nunderri and his audience.

'You must never lose your spiritual sight, my son,' said the old man quietly. 'Do you know what I mean by your spiritual sight?'

'You mean my faith, Grandfather.'

'Yes, your faith. Faith in the existence of the Great Spirit. Faith in the law. Faith in the teachings of your elders. It is faith that makes us stand apart from the animals.'

He was silent for a while. And then he said quietly, 'With spiritual sight one day you may be able to see as far as the end of the earth. And to see as far as the end of the earth will be to understand all there is to understand.'

Gunroi glanced back and saw that Gaidimi had his eyes closed. The old man's chest rose and fell heavily before he continued.

'Think for a moment how difficult it would be to understand what was happening about you if you had knowledge only of those things that were within the reach of the length of your arm. Now consider how much better it would be to have knowledge of those things about you that extended as far as you could throw a spear. Contemplate for a moment how much better would be your chances of survival in the second instance compared to the first. Do you understand what I'm telling you?'

'Yes, Grandfather.'

'Now try to imagine what would be the breadth and the depth and the extent of your understanding if you had knowledge of all of those things that extended as far as the end of the earth. Imagine then what would be your chances of survival. Perhaps with that level of understanding you could survive forever.'

When Gaidimi fell silent, Gunroi again could find no appropriate response and remained silent himself, inwardly cursing an ignorance that he now felt certain was a symptom of his lack of spiritual completeness.

The two men were sheltering in the shadow of a big river gum that robbed the nearby soil of much of its moisture, so that when Gaidimi dropped his gaze to his feet he allowed it to rest for a while on where his toes were partly immersed in a fine carpet of dust. 'The land needs rain,' he said absently and appeared to contemplate this for a long time before sinking lower to the ground and closing his eyes.

A comforting aroma of burning eucalyptus drifted in from the cooking fires near the stream. Gunroi glanced across at them in time to see a young woman with a deft backhand sweep of her wrist flick a twisted piece of wood at an over-inquisitive dingo pup, causing it to yelp in alarm and leap for safety away from the smouldering food.

Gunroi smiled. If that pup has any sense at all it should heed her warning well, he mused. The woman was his wife, Coranga.

He turned back and sat watching the closed shades of Gaidimi's eyelids, and the ache that had materialised in the pit of his stomach while the old man had been talking began to affirm its presence with increased intensity. The old man was right to be troubled. For Gunroi, the yoowii was like a final confirmation of the legitimacy of his strengthening distrust of most of the claimed mysteries of his world—and dare he even think it—his distrust of the related teachings of the clan elders, including old Gaidimi himself.

No wonder I am so ignorant, he lamented in a moment of contrition. I am obviously completely bereft of spiritual wisdom. I'm amazed that Gaidimi pays me any attention at all. I am utterly undeserving.

As he sat watching Gaidimi's relaxed counte-nance his own jaw stiffened and his shoulders suddenly quivered in the grip of a deep-seated shudder that rippled through his torso like a personal earthquake. Forgive me, Biamie, but I can't help myself.

That night he dreamt of the eagle.

He was sitting by the stream at the edge of the camp, but although the location was familiar, with the water tumbling over the ledge of rock that partly dammed the entire flow at this point, the form of the stream and the land on either side was softer, more rounded, than he knew it to be in reality. The rocks were less jagged, the contours of the ridges less severe, the hills less steep, the grasses softer, and the earth itself more gentle and less threatening.

The eagle was white. Or at least mainly white, with darker shoulders. And it could speak. Speak! With the voice of a man. It sat a short distance from him on the same arched log that Nunderri had jumped over earlier that day. How the log was now at the campsite was a mystery of sorts but not one that he allowed himself to dwell upon. What he was now experiencing was a tangle of circumstances and mysteries of much greater interest than displaced logs.

For instance, he found himself more surprised that there was such a thing as a white eagle than the fact that it could speak. In the curious logic that dreamers will bring to bear on such matters, he found himself rationalising that it could speak only because this was a dream, and in a dream all things were possible, but he was unable to apply the same rationalisation to the matter of its colour. It was white! White! He found this so distracting it was some time before he realised that it was talking to him about his spiritual vision.

'What? What?' he stammered when he finally realised that he was being addressed. He tried to divide his attention between listening to what the eagle was saying and trying to recall what it had already said.

'You're too close to the ground,' said the eagle. 'Your sight is impaired. You can't possibly have the vision and thereby the wisdom that I have. I can see so much more than you. Down here there are too many obstructions. Trees, rocks, hills, smoke, women.' It bobbed its head towards the plain. 'Dust and haze. To see into the distance you need to be higher. You need to be above the ground. High above the ground. High, high above the ground.'

The eagle had a habit of regularly repeating whole groups of words, Gunroi noted, not just single words which of course was necessary to explain large amounts. But he was uncertain how he was aware that the bird regularly repeated itself, being able to recall it doing it only once.

'But I've been high up in the hills where I could see a long, long way,' he replied. 'Right out on to the plain.' This was the first time he addressed the eagle, and he was suddenly embarrassed by what the others might think if they saw him talking to a bird. He glanced about quickly and reassured himself that no one was close enough to notice.

Nunderri was still holding council with the young men some distance away. Coranga was the closest of the women, tending to the fires on the bank of the river, and only occasionally did she glance in his direction.

Other than the eagle the only creature that seemed to be taking any real notice of him was the dingo pup that had been trotting around behind his wife. It seemed to be looking directly at him with an expression that suggested it knew exactly what was going on. He tried to recall if it was a female and found himself wondering if it, too, could speak. He concluded that it probably could. Under the curious circumstances that prevailed, it would probably be more surprising if it couldn't.

'What could you see from the mountains?' scoffed the eagle. 'The trees on either side of you. And a glimpse of the plain between those trees. What I'm talking about is high above the ground. High up above the mountains. Haven't you ever looked up and watched us circling in the sky?'

'I've never seen a white eagle before.'

'Any eagle. Haven't you ever watched and wondered how far we could see?'

'No.' A lie. And from the bird's expression he could tell it knew.

'I can take you up there and show you. Would you like that?'

'How could you? You're not big enough to lift me.' But even as he was saying this he could see that the eagle was indeed big enough. It was huge, with claws that easily encircled Nunderri's log, and although its wings were furled, he estimated that when they were stretched out they would easily span the river.

He found it strange, but not troubling, that he had not noticed its size when it first spoke to him. Then he had looked upon it as a big eagle, but not an overly large creature. Big enough to lift a bandicoot or a small possum perhaps. But certainly not big enough to lift a man.

But now? If it wanted to, I'm sure it could lift me in one claw and Nunderri's log in the other. Which solves the mystery of how the log arrived, he suddenly realised. The eagle had obviously brought its own perch with it.

At this point in his dream Gunroi found himself in idle contemplation of a matter that had preoccupied him many times: the incredible neatness of dreams. How dreams neatly solved the most complex mysteries, and how they neatly drew together all the loose ends of the most diverse and tangled stories.

Gunroi found himself being lifted by the eagle high above the camp while he was still contemplating the infallibility of dreams, so he assumed he had

214

agreed to the flight even though at that moment he had neither a memory of doing so, nor a chance to reconsider.

'Now you can see the difference,' said the eagle. 'From down there your whole world is a part of your camp, nothing more; a few cooking fires, a little bit of the stream, and a few men and women who are not hidden by the trees and the rocks and the slope of the ground. But up where we are now—even from this low height—your world becomes the whole camp, three, four bends of the river, and the trail of where the stream used to run and only visits when it floods.

From up here you can see that the river is deep on the outside of the bends and shallow on the inside. And you can see from where it used to run that it digs deeper into the earth every year and is moving away from the rocky ground into the softer muddy ground. You can see all these things from up here.'

'I can see those things from down there.'

'Not at the one moment. Not with the one glance. But I'll tell you something you can't see, even from up here. You can't see one ghost, one yoowii, one bunyip, or any other mysterious object that can't easily be explained.'

'I can see you. How can I easily explain you?'

'You know I'm a dream. I exist only inside your mind, just as all those other mysterious creatures exist only inside your mind.' With this the eagle chuckled. 'Now I'll show you what you can't see from anywhere but up here.'

He then beat his wings furiously, and the streams and hills below them began to grow smaller and smaller. 'There, now what do you see?' he called out above the roar of the wind as he gradually slowed his ascent, and arching his wings held them motionless so that he and his passenger soared in a great circle high above the land.

'I see how the Rainbow Serpent's long body shaped the mountains as it moved across the earth,' said Gunroi. 'And over there at the gorge of the dead I see how the land was split in two when the Serpent swiped its tail in anger because of the foolishness of the Madirigee people.'

The eagle laughed. 'You don't really believe that nonsense. And you don't fool me for a moment. What you really see is how the rivers have shaped the mountains. And how the earth has slipped along the length of the gorge of the dead in exactly the same way you have seen the outside bank of a bend in the river split and fall away when the stream has cut into it during a flood and caused it to grow too steep.'

'I know what I see.'

'I know what you see, too. And I know you can't see all of this from the earth.'

'I've seen parts of it from the mountains. I've heard stories of what I haven't seen.'

'Then have you seen this?' Again the eagle flapped its wings and they soared higher into the sky. Soon the earth was the colour of distant hills and the streams became like the fine meandering tracks of insects on the trunk of a blue-grey gum tree.

'You've come too far,' said Gunroi. 'I can no longer see the land I am familiar with.'

'But what you can see makes sense, doesn't it? The curves and contours of the earth from here are as explainable as the shape of a sandbank that has been exposed by a flood and then worn down by the rain and the wind. There is nothing mysterious in the curl of the mountains. There is no magic in the course of the rivers.'

'The land is no less wondrous from up here than it is from down there,' said Gunroi. 'I see the hand of the Great Spirit Biamie everywhere, and the influence of the Rainbow Serpent on Biamie's creation.'

'You're either blind or you're a liar,' snapped the eagle.

It was at this point in his dream that Gunroi began to wonder whether it was wise to argue with a creature that was carrying him high above the earth. He did not have to wonder long.

'It doesn't matter much to me whether you're one or the other: blind or a liar. But if you're blind, you won't need your eyes. So I'll remove them and keep them to remind me of your stupidity.' With this he held Gunroi out in front of him with one claw, and neatly plucked out his eyes with the talons of the other.

And as his sight vanished, Gunroi was swept

with a crushing sense of dread. His buffer that this was a dream was snatched out of his reach. He struggled to retrieve it—in vain—all his attempts simply reinforcing the prospect that indeed this was not a dream, but was real. And he was blind. Great Biamie, why have you deserted me?

'And if you're a liar,' continued the eagle, 'I'm not interested in wasting any more of my time.' And with this he opened the claw that was clasped around Gunroi's waist and allowed him to fall. Down, down, down, down he plunged, with the air rushing past him in a deafening roar.

And then suddenly he was sitting bolt upright, gasping for breath with his heart pounding.

'What is it?' Coranga was awake beside him. He turned and saw the moonlight caught in her wide eyes.

'I can see,' he whispered. The relief that swept through him was tempered by his vivid recall of the horror that had gripped him only moments before. Vestiges of his fear still clung to him like the strands of an invisible spider-web.

'The eagle said these things?' Gaidimi asked. 'Said that there was no mystery in the land?'

Although Gunroi kept his own gaze on the distant hillside, he could feel the old man's gaze probing deep into his flesh.

'Yes, Grandfather.'

'And you argued with him? Reminded him how these things were created?'

'Yes.'

'A white eagle?'

'White as the sacred white clay from the Goonoo Goonoo marsh.'

Gaidimi kept his gaze locked on the younger man for a while longer, and when he finally turned away it was to lower himself from the elbow on which he had been propping himself, stretch out on his back, and close his eyes. Gunroi stretched out beside him and waited. Thin veils of smoke drifted past. Eucalyptus. Comforting. He could sense the gentle rumbling of the stream in the soft earth beneath his back.

'You must find the white eagle and retrieve your sight.' Gaidimi's words jolted Gunroi, and he realised that he had been dozing.

'What?' He glanced across at Gaidimi and saw that the old man was still lying flat on his back with his eyes closed.

'The words he used to argue with you were your own thoughts. The words you used to defend the law were not what you truly believe.'

Gunroi did not speak for some time. When he did it was to ask, 'Why do you think the eagle was white, Grandfather?'

'White eagles live beside the great water that lies to the east. The message is clear. Biamie requires that you undertake a long journey.'

Gunroi lay without breathing for some time before his chest finally rose and fell heavily. 'You have been there? You have seen them?'

'No. But you are not the first person to take a journey in search of your soul. Over the years I have seen many travellers on similar quests. Some of them stayed with us for a time. Those who chose to tell of their travels spoke of many strange creatures they had encountered, including white eagles.'

'Far to the east?'

'Yes. But you must travel to the north first. The Djungatee have a feud with the Kamilaroi and will not permit anyone from the west to pass through their lands.'

'When will I go?'

'When it is warmer. It would not be wise to cross the mountains while the nights are cold. You are young, and young people are not strong in matters of the cold.'

Gunroi smothered a smile. Later he asked, 'Should I travel alone?'

'No. Alone would be dangerous. You might get lost.'

'I would never get lost.'

'There are many ways a young man can get lost when travelling alone. You must take a companion. Someone to watch your back whenever you need to bend down to drink in an unfriendly place.'

'I'll take Nunderri.'

'Nunderri. He's so young.'

'Not so young, Grandfather. Only two summers younger than me.'

Gaidimi glanced at him. 'Exactly. An older man would be more sensible.'

'I would feel better with Nunderri there.'

'The decision must be yours.'

'And Coranga. Should I take Coranga?'

'Would she go with you? Would she leave her friends?'

'She would be very angry if I refused to take her. She would demand to go.'

'Demand?' Gaidimi sought the younger man's gaze.

'Coranga, Grandfather!'

The intonation was enough. Gaidimi shook his head. 'If you take Coranga then Nunderri should take Mori.'

'Would her father agree? She is truly young. A child.'

The old man smiled to himself. 'Only a child,' he repeated quietly, also to himself. He studied the young man for a time before shaking his head and adding. 'I will talk to him.'

'What will happen to me if I don't find the eagle?'

'Sometimes the purpose of a journey is the journey itself.'

'Do you think it will be dangerous?'

'Perhaps. White is a sacred colour. But it is also the colour of death.'

Will Noling stood on the quarterdeck of the *Victory* watching tiny white specks on the horizon that showed where eight French ships of the line were emerging from Toulon to protect two frigates that were being harried by a small section of the British Fleet.

'Come on, La Touche-Tréville, come on,' Nelson encouraged the French Admiral as the British ships turned and moved away in apparent retreat. 'Come on. Bring out the rest. Keep coming.'

But, to his consternation, as soon as their frigates were covered, the French turned back and sought again the sanctuary of the harbour.

Will was left with mixed feelings. The tingling combination of fear and excitement that had coursed through him when the battle appeared imminent was certainly real relief from the mind-numbing boredom of the blockade. But as he swung into his hammock that evening, the relief that he did not have to face death and was still alive and uninjured was equally real.

EIGHT

Four degrees below the equator and about 80 miles off the eastern tip of Brazil, three ships were becalmed on a motionless sea and locked on the still pools of their midday shadows. Under the blast of the tropical sun the ocean had taken on a smooth, oily appearance, as if a transparent membrane had been stretched across it to stifle any potential disturbances from above or below.

The chaotic nature of the forces that brought them here placed two of the ships within less than 400 yards of each other, and the third more than four miles away. On the ship that stood off from the others, two women, each carrying two leather buckets, paused briefly as they met each other on the after companionway leading to the cabins. Elizabeth Crowling was the woman descending the steps. Her buckets were full, her shoulders drawn down by the weight. The tendons above her wrists were as taut as the ship's rigging, and her face, arms and legs were glistening with a sheen of perspiration.

Jessica Glider was the woman ascending the steps. Her buckets were empty, and the tendons of her forearms for the moment were relaxed. But, as with her companion, all of her that was visible shone as if draped in a film of light.

'This be warm work, lass,' said Elizabeth.

'Aye,' agreed Jessica. 'I hope he appreciates it.'

'If he don't, I'll clout 'im with one of these buckets.'

It took some time to fill Angus Donwald's bath and as they made their many journeys to and from his cabin, their activities attracted the attention of a good number of observers, including about an equal proportion of fellow convicts, marines and ship's crew.

Although the bath-filling episode itself was of interest, the activity mainly served to remind the observers of the circumstance where the first officer of one of His Majesty's convict transports was sharing his cabin with two comely convict wenches, almost certainly in contravention of the Royal Navy's, or whoever's, Standing Orders, or Codes of Discipline, or whatever regulations pertained, to the—presumed—advantage of all three players.

Not that the breach of regulations was of prime interest to any of the observing parties; most of the men and a good proportion of the women had been involved in illicit liaisons of one kind or another since sailing from Portsmouth, although not many of these involved the same apparent degree of permanence or comfort as enjoyed by the first officer and his women. What was of interest was that two female convicts were apparently receiving preferential treatment in exchange for their favours, and living in a style denied most of those on board.

Curiously, the observers of all ages were about evenly divided between those who viewed this situation in a disagreeable and negative way, and those who were sympathetic and positive in their attitude.

None of these observers—female, male, opposed or supportive—was aware of the real state of play in the first officer's cabin, and most of them were wrong in their assumptions in this regard. Fanciful images that any form of a lustful *ménage à trois* existed were misplaced. The relationship that had developed between Donwald and Elizabeth had been strictly monogamous. While the couple spent their evenings on a broad palliasse mounted on a combined bunk-stand and foot-locker recessed into the bay-window-like extensions of the cabin that projected about three feet beyond the ship's side, Jessica spent her evenings in the alcove behind the chart table on the opposite side of the cabin.

This area, which was barely big enough to accommodate her bedding, had originally been part of a passageway that provided access to three smaller adjoining cabins that had since been converted into the surgeon's quarters. While the alcove had no door and was not completely isolated from Donwald's cabin, at night it did provide him and Elizabeth with a level of visual, and partial audible, privacy, and Jessica with a snug and much appreciated sense of security.

Donwald's bath was a high-backed metal tub. Earlier in the day he had a trio of broad-backed seamen haul it up from a store in the orlop and place it in the centre of his cabin. The women had filled it with seawater to about a handspan below the rim.

As a consequence of the uneven depth and diverse quality of the glass in the window panes mounted in the bulkhead screens along the port side and after end of the cabin, the interior was interlaced with slivers of light of various hues. Pale pink and yellowish patches were framed in equally pale and distorted spectrums. Some of these fell on the trembling surface of the water in the bath and rebounded to paint ghost-like clouds across the sweep of the deckhead.

'I think we've overfilled it,' said Jessica after emptying her last bucket. 'When he steps into this it will overflow for sure.' Above her, exploding showers of fragmented light and shade were now coursing backwards and forwards across the panels of the deckhead.

'I'll tell you what, m'darlin',' said Elizabeth

spreading her arms and looking down at her perspiration soaked frock, 'I've a good mind to leap into it right now, rather than wait for 'is nibs to take 'is turn. I'm soaked right through.'

'Don't you dare, though,' said Jessica, spreading her own arms and looking down at herself. 'If you upset him I mightn't get my turn. Look at me. I think I'm wetter than you. How can anybody survive in this kind of heat?'

'They take regular cool baths is how,' replied Elizabeth. 'And stand naked under waterfalls out in the jungle. Here, how does this feel?' With this she reached down and smacked the surface of the water with a scooped hand, splashing her companion with a generous burst of cool water that struck her squarely in the chest.

'Liz, you cow!' Jessica stood frozen in shock for a moment with her arms spread wide, looking down at the front of her dress. 'Look at me! Look at what you've done!'

What Elizabeth had done was to render the garment useless with regard to any concerns of modesty Jessica may have harboured. Her breasts were as exposed as if they were draped in a transparent film; her nipples threatened to breach the confines of the fabric.

'Look at me!' she repeated, turning her gaze on the other woman and then staring at her intently with her mouth locked open wide.

'I am lookin' at you, m'darlin'. And you're a wonderful sight, I must admit.'

'I'm naked.'

'Noooo ye're not.' With this Elizabeth suddenly splashed her again.

Jessica squealed as the water struck her, this time in the midriff. She responded immediately, leaping forward and smacking the surface herself to unleash her own watery missile. Elizabeth squealed and twisted away, receiving only a glancing blow on her hip. But she, too, retaliated immediately, slapping the water with extra vigour to fire off a third round. This one struck Jessica squarely in the crotch.

Both women froze. They stood staring at each other as if transfixed, their limbs motionless, their eyes wide, their mouths agape. Several seconds passed. Finally Jessica lowered her gaze and observed the damage.

Elizabeth giggled abruptly. 'I'll tell y'someat, lass, y'mightn't have been naked before, but ye be God's truth naked now.'

With this, both women burst into shrieks of laughter.

'What in God's name is goin' on here?'

Their heads swung around as one. Angus Donwald stood in the cabin doorway. He strode across to them and stood glaring at them with his hands on his hips. 'Well?' He waited, his eyes moving from one to the other. 'Now you've filled m'bath you plannin' t'empty it before I can use it? Is that it? And at the same time tryin' your best t'turn m'cabin into one of the seven bleedin' seas. Is that what you're aimin' t'do?'

Elizabeth was turned partly side-on to him with her head and shoulders drawn back, and a spread hand raised in front of her chest somewhat defensively. Jessica was facing him squarely with one hand flattened in front of her crotch and the other attempting to shield her breasts.

Both women stared at him silently. But then a clipped bubble of mirth broke from between Elizabeth's tightly clamped lips. And then another. She recovered for a moment, but the second one had triggered a tremble in Jessica's cheeks. Both managed to control themselves for a lingering moment. But then as if a floodgate had been breached, they suddenly and simultaneously unleashed an explosion of unrestrained laughter, and writhed from the pain of it.

Jessica's hands immediately flew to clamp over her mouth as if she feared her cheeks would split. This action exposed those parts of her she had been protecting, causing Elizabeth to shriek with extra gusto. Realising what had happened, and continuing to be racked by uncontrollable rib-bruising shrieks, Jessica was then caught in a flurry of indecision, switching her hands backwards and forwards from her body to her mouth as she was assailed by alternating and conflicting concerns for which part of her, in the interests of propriety, most required concealment at any one moment.

For a while Donwald looked as if he might be

on the verge of slapping some sense into them, but then shook his head resignedly.

When the clamour finally abated and fragmented to irregular spates of giggling, he said, 'So what's your excuse? The deal as I understood it was that I would bathe first.'

'We 'aven't yet bathed, m'petal,' replied Elizabeth. 'All we've done is cooled off a bit. It were warm work fillin' this 'ere tub.'

'Seems it were wet work an' all.' He turned his attention to Jessica. By this time she had given up trying to shield herself, but under his steady gaze one of her hands did drift from where it had rested below her hip to hover over a more central location of her anatomy.

'That were my fault,' said Elizabeth. 'She seemed to be sufferin' worse'n me from the heat. She'd come over as pink as a scalded lobster.'

'She's still a bit pink in places.'

For a while no one spoke or moved. And although it may have been that up until then they had not noticed whether or not they could hear any external noises, the entire ship seemed to grow suddenly quiet.

Donwald was the first to break the silence. 'Did you cut your hair again, Jessie? It seems to be shorter than Liz's.'

'No.' Jessica ran the tips of her fingers through the hair on her crown and glanced at Elizabeth. 'I think it's about the same as yours, isn't it?'

'Aye,' Elizabeth replied, glancing from one to the other, and touching her own hair. 'Much the same, I expect.' She measured the length of a few strands against one of her fingers and then examined that finger. 'It takes a while t'grow, even in this weather.'

'Mine's wetter than Liz's,' said Jessica. 'I expect that's all.'

'Looks shorter,' Donwald persisted. 'Turn around.'

She turned. 'Looks shorter at the back as well.'

'How do our bums compare?' Elizabeth asked.

Donwald turned and matched her gaze. 'I believe your eyes have turned a shade greener today, Liz. Or is it the light in here?'

'I expects it's the heat. The tropical heat does funny things t'some people.'

'Is that right?'

'So I've been told.'

He looked down at the bath. 'I have to check the forward meat store this afternoon. They tell me some of the salted horse has gone off. If it has, I'll have to make sure the lads get rid of it, rather than try somethin' shifty like tradin' it f'favours with your good lady friends. Now, climbin' around down there and throwin' stacks of beef about won't be somethin' I'll be doin' after I've had a bath. So I'll have the bath when I'm finished.'

'How long will you be?' Elizabeth asked.

'Maybe the rest of the day.'

'Do we really have to wait until then before we can have ours?'

He looked from one to the other.

'You know we've been washin' regular,' she added hopefully.

He shook his head. 'I suppose not, seein' you're half bathed already. But only on the condition you replace any water y'spill. And if you do get it dirty I'll have you refill it completely. Agreed?'

She smiled. 'You're a pushover, Angus Donwald. For all your talk and y'struttin' about like a Scotch lord.'

'Scots laird,' Donwald snarled, 'you ignorant Sassenach.' He strode from the room.

'That's a turn-up,' said Jessica. 'I didn't think he'd agree.'

Elizabeth stood watching the door. 'What?'

'I didn't think he'd agree so easily. But I wish you wouldn't tease him. I'm never sure that he won't fly off the handle.'

Elizabeth turned back. 'Sorry. What were ye sayin'?'

'Never mind. Do you want to go first?'

'No.' Obviously still distracted, she made a conscious effort to concentrate. 'No. No. Like 'e said, ye're half bathed already.' She stood motionless with her gaze locked on her companion.

'What is it?'

'No wonder he was so taken by you, lass. In that wet frock ye're a sight that would take anybody's breath away.'

'Shush!' Jessica responded, ducking beneath the remark. 'He wasn't taken by me. That's silly talk. He was just surprised to find us both in the state we were.'

Suddenly Elizabeth stepped towards her and, leaning forward, kissed her gently on the lips.

Jessica did not move, and when Elizabeth drew back, their gazes remained locked. 'Why did you do that?' Jessica said quietly.

Elizabeth shook her head. 'I ... I don't know.' And then lifting a trembling hand to her face she suddenly burst into tears.

Jessica moved close and held her. Elizabeth's sobbing gradually subsided. For an age they stayed where they had come together in the centre of the cabin, with their arms locked around each other, their heads lowered, and each with one damp left cheek resting against another.

When they did finally part, Elizabeth stood for a time with her gaze averted and then with an apparent conscious effort to restore her equilibrium, she turned her gaze on the bath for a moment and then turned to Jessica.

'You go first, Jess. Ye really are half bathed. Ye might catch cold standin' here in the draught.'

'You've got to be jokin'! Draught! There hasn't been the hide nor hair of a draught around here strong enough to bend the flame of a candle in five days.'

'If we're goin' to stand around arguin' about it, you'll still be sittin' there when 'is nibs gets back.'

She held out a hand. 'Give me your wet frock and I'll get you a dry one for when you get out.'

Jessica glanced back at the door.

'What's the matter?' Elizabeth asked.

'I don't feel quite right about this, Liz, gettin' stripped naked in the middle of the day. What if someone comes?'

''Is nibs'll be the only one likely t'come, and not for a while. And even if he did, he's not goin' t'see much more of you than he's seen already today.' She bobbed her head at her companion. 'Ye've dried off a bit, but I can still see most o'you that ye're feelin' worried about. Come on, give me your frock.'

Jessica did not move for a moment, and then with a grimace of resignation and with some difficulty, she pulled the dress over her head.

Elizabeth's gaze rested on the other woman's breasts as they rose and fell with the motion. She then took the dress from her and held out her free hand. 'Here, take m'hand while you step in.'

Jessica complied, and suddenly feeling very vulnerable, released her companion's hand and quickly began to lower herself into the water. But the moment her buttocks dipped below the surface, the water rose to the rim of the tub and a wave sloshed on to the deck.

'Yoiks!' she exclaimed and immediately stood up. 'It's way too full. I can't sit down.' She made moves as if to step back out.

'No, stay there, the deck's wet enough already,'

said Elizabeth, and reached for one of the buckets. 'And ye'd be lucky if you didn't break ye neck an' all. I'll get rid of some.' She dipped the bucket into the water and partly filled it. 'Now don't move, and don't try to step out,' she cautioned. 'Ye'll go arse up like a turtle on its back f'sure. This'll only take a couple o'trips.'

So saying, she walked across to the after end of the cabin where she stooped over and carefully poured the contents of the bucket into the flared mouth of a scupper that was mounted flush with the deck. The normal function of this and other scuppers evenly spaced around the cabin was to drain any water that might enter during rough weather, or when the deck was washed down after it was holystoned.

'Or maybe three trips on account of your bum bein' a bit bigger than we'd allowed for during the fillin' of the tub,' she added as she straightened.

'There's nothin' wrong with the size of m' bum,' Jessica retorted, running a hand absently over one damp cheek of the object in question and raising her jaw defensively as the other women turned back to face her.

'Nothing indeed,' a voice behind her concurred.

As if all her actions were controlled by the release of a clockwork spring, her head swung around, her left hand clamped over her crotch and her right forearm crushed back against her breasts.

'Don't be alarmed, Jessie, 'tis only me from over the sea said Barnacle Angus Donwald.' He strode

235

jauntily across to the port side, hardly casting so much as a courteous glance in her direction as he moved past her. 'The antics of you two caught me off guard last time and I completely forgot why I had come back here.'

He moved to the footlocker beneath his bunk and kneeling down opened it and extracted a rumpled flannel shirt. When he stood up, he stripped off the shirt he was wearing and dropped it on to the bunk. He then walked back towards the others as he examined the garment he had retrieved from his locker. 'I wasn't about to be wearin' my one decent shirt while I was scramblin' around that filthy meat store. This one has seen better days, so it won't matter so much if I get it covered in dust and grease.'

He stood in front of Jessica and matched her gaze, with a smile tugging away at the corners of his mouth.

'There's no need to be so shy, lass. It's not like you're hidin' from me any bits and pieces of you I haven't had a wee glimpse of before. But only a wee glimpse, mind you.' He raised the shirt he held bunched in front of him with both hands, and patted it against his neck to absorb thin rivulets of sweat that were tracking away from the soft line of his beard.

Amidst an overwhelming sense of light-headedness she found herself trying to recall if she had ever seen the beard develop much past a light fleecing of downy whiskers that followed only the line of his jaw, or whether she had noticed before how ruggedly handsome he was.

She was suddenly aware of a curious stirring deep within her, an itch whose location she could not determine; a conflicting mix of comfort and frustration. She blamed the heat that pressed in on her for the sense of intoxication. And the nakedness: her complete example and his partial. Her head was swimming. This was a dream.

'The heat's gettin' to you, Angus,' said Elizabeth. 'You're talkin' like a child tha's tryin' to make a point but who ain't too sure what point he's tryin' to make. And put your shirt on, or I'll think ye're tryin' to show off your hairy chest.'

''Tain't so hairy,' said he, with most of his attention still on Jessica. 'Just enough so to lessen the risk of bein' mistaken for one of you two.'

'You cheeky bugger,' Elizabeth growled with her eyes narrowed.

He shook open the shirt and pulled it over his head. As he tucked it into the waist of his trousers he said, 'I've got to go now and clamber around in the meat locker. I wouldn't be surprised if the heat kills me. Or at least drives me mad. If not the heat, then the dust or the grease. One or t'other's likely to put me over the edge.' He stood looking directly at Jessica for a moment before adding, 'I reckon if you were to take your hands away for a moment, Jessie, m' gel, and give me more than just a glimpse of those bits of you that you're hidin', it might help me to make it through this terrible day I'm facin'. Take my mind off it, if you know what I mean.'

'Angus Donwald!' Elizabeth protested. 'You low bilge rat! You be on your way sharpish, or I'll box yer Scotch ears.' She stood with her hands on her hips glowering at him, daring him to turn and face her.

But his gaze remained on Jessica. 'Scot's ears, yer Sassenach bint. And why would you? What have I done wrong?'

'Actin' like a sly dog, that be what. A weasel. Look at you, gawkin' at the poor girl. Lowerin' yourself to the likes of them scum out there. What ye're doin' be unfair. You know the lass be beholden t'ye for givin' her safe refuge. Ye know the last thing she'd be doin' on normal road would be showin' herself t'you. Ye know she'd never do nothin' like that unless you forced her. Used your position. Harassed her like a good-for-nothin' bully boy.'

'Is that right, lass? Is that what you think?' His gaze did not move from Jessica's face. Nor did he show any sign of damage from the onslaught. He seemed to be perfectly relaxed.

'Tha's what I think.'

'Well, I'll tell you somethin', m'love. I think you're wrong. From what I've seen in m'travels, whenever more than one woman is beholden to a man such as m'self—a good-hearted man who protects'm well, doesn't demand too much in return, doesn't knock'm around—if he's a fair man, a straight man, and ain't too damagin' to the eyes when the light's on him right, it's been my observation that when there's a few women, say four or three, or maybe even two young ones such as yourselves that are indebted to him, that every one of them will seek his attention whenever they have the chance.

'And not only the game ones. What I say goes for the quiet ones as well. What I've noticed is that even the prim, proper and shy ones will rarely pass up a chance to try and gain an extra bit of attention if they can. Catch their protector's eye. Gain his favour. His good graces.

'I've been told it comes from way back when we lived in tribes like the poor black people in Africa. It's a breedin' urge they can't help. And the someone who told me ought to know, havin' been a slaver most of his seagoin' days. And havin' done a fair bit of breedin' when he was ashore.'

'Breedin' urge!' scoffed Elizabeth. 'Breedin' urge! And lived in tribes? When did we ever live in tribes? I've never heard such stuff 'n' nonsense!'

'I've heard it's true. Way back.'

'You've studied this, 'ave you?'

'No, but I've observed it. Among many other things I've observed over the years, bein' the observant type that I am.'

'Well if that be the way it works between men and women, then it shouldn't be the way it works. And if it be that way, then it be that way because of men. And men should be damned ashamed of

239

'mselves for forcin' women to act that way. Not that I'm sayin' they do. The women that is.'

'It's not all men's doin'. And some men such as m'self are so appreciative that this is indeed the way of the world that we make sure we don't offend any of those women. With men such as m'self—if I can—I see to it that each one of them benefits.'

'You're an arrogant bastard, Angus Donwald. Are you sayin' that not only would I vie for your good graces—whatever they might be—but Jessie here would do the same? Just so you wouldn't kick her out, or treat her bad? Be that what ye're sayin'?'

'No. And I'm not necessarily talkin' about this Jessie in particular. I'm talkin' about all Jessies in general. And I'm sayin' they'd do it for more than just to stop someone like me from kickin' them out. Although reducin' the prospect of bein' kicked out would be part of it.'

'What would the rest of it be?'

'They'd be vyin' for my attention because it would pleasure them to attract it.'

Elizabeth's mouth fell open. 'Pleasure them?' She looked at Jessica. 'Can you believe this man's conceit, Jess? Are you bein' pleasured by this attention he's giving you?'

'I'm bein' uncomfortabled by it. I'll fall over if I have to stand like this much longer. Hurry up and empty some more water so I can sit down. Or at least put a cloth over that spill on the deck so

I can step out and get away from here.'

Elizabeth seized Donwald with her gaze. 'You really believe she be enjoyin' this?'

'I said I'm not talkin' about this Jessie. I'm talkin' about all Jessies.'

'She be one of them Jessies, for Jesus Christ's sake. And you can't tell me she brought on herself this attention she be gettin' now. Or that she be enjoyin' it.'

'She's probably not enjoyin' all this talk. For a start it's delayed her bein' able to show me those parts of her that I would like to see to help get me through the rest of the day.'

'She won't be showin' you anythin'. Not unless you force her.'

'Well, I won't force her, because that's not the way of me, as you well know. But what I will do is this.' He stepped towards Jessica, and raising his hand to touch her lightly beneath the chin, he lowered his head and kissed her on the lips.

As he drew back, Elizabeth said quietly, 'You think that proves somethin', Angus Donwald? Kissin' a woman who can't move for fear of either offendin' her modesty or slippin' and breakin' her neck, or more likely both. You think that proves somethin'?'

He turned as if to leave and then hesitated and turned his gaze back on Jessica. 'It's terrible hot where I'm goin', lass. Are you goin' to grant my request? It's only a request, mind you. It's not a demand.'

Her head was still swimming. She felt as if she was draped, from her crown to where the water encircled her knees, in a warm syrupy blanket. She glanced across at Elizabeth and gave her a look that was charged with a mix of anguish and apology, for she knew what was going to happen, and she felt there was nothing whatsoever that she, or Elizabeth, or anyone else on earth could do to stop it. She turned back and, locking her gaze on Donwald's, lowered the arm she had clamped across her breasts and moved both hands to rest at her sides.

Donwald stood looking at her without moving for a length of time that none of them could later estimate with any certainty. No one spoke. And the light that spilled through the screened bulkheads seemed to take on a different hue, a softer, rosier colour that filled the entire cabin with a glow they could almost touch.

They became aware of a distant musical accompaniment that had sounded a number of times before, deep within the ship's core, but up until now they had not noticed. The cause was a succession of mild, resonant vibrations passing slowly through the central beams of the keel from bow to stern that released a chorus of low notes that could have been the murmur of the wind caught within the bigger pipes of a cathedral's organ.

At last he said, 'In keepin' with what I was sayin', Jessie, trust me and stay absolutely still.' With this he stepped close to the bath and, raising his hand, ran the tips of his fingers slowly from just above the damp tangled triangle of her pubic bush to just below the swell of her breasts. He then stepped back and placed his fingers to his lips. 'Just as I thought,' he said softly.

'Just as you thought what?' Elizabeth demanded. And although her voice was also soft, there was still fire in her eyes.

But his gaze was on Jessica as he backed towards the door. 'My heart-felt thanks, Jessie. I doubt I'll now have any trouble with the rest of m' day, leastways with the heat, the dust or the grease.'

'Just as you thought what?' Elizabeth repeated, and although she did not raise her voice, the level of her agitation was obviously on the rise.

He turned away and walked to the door where he paused and looked back at her.

'Just as you thought what?' she persisted. 'What did you mean?'

'You know what I meant. She tastes as sweet as you, m'lovely.'

'You bastard, Angus Donwald. You and your stupid talk. You don't know nothin' about women. Nothin' at all.'

'When I leave, ask Jessie if she would have preferred that I had not kissed or touched her. Or would she have perhaps preferred that I had kissed her again. Or, heaven forbid, touched her more intimately. And if you're game, ask yourself the same questions.'

He raised his hand in a salute. 'Best wishes until I see you later, my little lovelies. And feel free to talk about me when I'm gone.'

He turned and left the cabin.

After he closed the door behind him, both women stood watching it. Elizabeth eventually shook her head and, picking up one of the buckets, bent down and dipped it into the bath. 'Damn men!' she muttered, perhaps to herself. When she straightened she kept her gaze averted from Jessica. 'One day it will be different, lass. God willin'.' She turned and stood for a moment looking back at the door. 'He deserves to be flogged for forcing 'imself on you like that. Intimidatin' you. Using his position. The rat!'

Jessica said nothing, and as Elizabeth emptied enough water so that the younger woman could sit down, Elizabeth either did not notice or chose to ignore that her companion was trembling. Neither of them spoke while Elizabeth busied herself mopping the deck with a large cloth.

They both remained silent for some time. Finally, Elizabeth said, 'I don't believe I've ever met one of them who was more conceited than this one. Anywhere. Have you?'

'No,' Jessica replied quietly. She cleared her throat. 'Although I knew one who had more reason to be as conceited, but wasn't.'

Elizabeth glanced at her and their gazes touched for the first time since Donwald had departed. But only for a moment. 'Your man? The one who was pressed?'

'Aye.'

'Then he was a rarer bird even than this one. This one be rare enough. But yours be rarer still. Rare enough, I'd wager, t'come lookin' f'you.'

'I pray that he doesn't.'

'Why on earth not, lass?'

'There'd be no point, would there? Even if he were to come lookin', who he'd find would no longer be me. I haven't been me for a long time now. And I don't believe I will ever be me again.'

Elizabeth was lost for a moment as she pondered over Jessica's words. 'You know someat, Jess,' she offered at last, 'I don't think I've ever been me. Not for one moment.' She then tried to busy herself wiping the deck again, but her face suddenly crumpled and she looked despairingly back at her companion.

'Oh, Jessie!' she exclaimed softly, and then rose and moved quickly across to the bath where she sat down on the deck beside it. 'He means to swive you, and I think you means to let him.'

Jessica reached out and they clasped hands over the edge of the bath. 'I don't know what's happenin', Liz. My life's been so turned upside-down this last year I'm not even sure if all this is real or a dream. And this heat doesn't help. I'm so light-headed I don't think I can tell any longer what's right or what's wrong, or what's true or what's false.'

'I can tell you somethin' that be true, lass,' Elizabeth replied. 'He means to have you. As you means to have him.' She bit her lip. 'And for the love of me, I know I'm goin' to be torn apart by the good I feel about that, and the bad I feel about it.'

She was right on both counts. When Donwald returned and took his bath he did have Jessica, and she did have him. On the port side bunk, bathed in the rays of the setting sun that flooded into the cabin through the after windows along with a spread of softer light that bounced from the golden expanse of water that stretched away to the horizon. And while this was going on Elizabeth for the most part was curled in Jessica's sleeping compartment on the opposite side of the cabin, with her head lowered, her arms locked around her knees, and her mind in the turmoil she had predicted.

After Donwald had bathed and they had all eaten supper and had drunk a healthy draught of brandy, Elizabeth had bowed to the inevitable by feigning an attack of dizziness and retiring to Jessica's compartment to sleep.

But she knew she could not have slept, even if she had tried. Nor could she shut herself off from the events that were unfolding in the cabin, although this had been her intention when she had departed. But the moment she was alone she immediately positioned the bedding so that she could place her head close to the hatchway. Then with her heart pounding and her hands trembling, she tried to catch every muffled word.

So intense were her emotions that in the image that was projected on to the retina of her mind's eye, she—rather than Jessica—could have been the one who was presently being kissed, first on the lips and then on the throat in a practised piece of choreography she remembered well.

And as she closed her eyes and leaned towards the hatchway, turning her head to one side so that her left ear became the leading edge of her body, it could have been her arms she was watching in her mind's eye that were lifting high above her head to remove her frock. And it could have been her bare breasts that rose and fell back as the frock caught for a moment on her head before slipping clear of her shortly cropped scarlet crown.

She sank lower into Jessica's bedding, spreading her legs slightly to make herself more comfortable.

He's not rushing, she decided. But then he wouldn't. He'd be very mindful of her last experience with matters of this kind. He'll take his time. After all, he has all the time in the world. The bastard! He'll let her feel her way. Encourage her. Arouse her to her very limits while holding himself back. Induce her to take the lead. The rat!

Suddenly she held her breath and leant closer to the hatchway. They're chatting! Like lovers at a bleedin' picnic! She cringed as she was stabbed by the first truly painful barb of jealousy. And then found herself reflecting on this, and decided she was a strange creature indeed to be upset more by them idly exchanging conversation than by the sounds and hushed words that she earlier believed were the prelude to lustier pursuits.

It was at this point that she risked taking her first peep into the cabin. With her eyes turned sideways she carefully moved her face to the very edge of the hatchway. In a surge of fatalism, to sum up the required courage to risk releasing the final glide of her head that would expose her to anyone looking in her direction, she told herself that if they saw her she wouldn't care.

The couple were bathed in bright light pouring through the after screened bulkhead. Jessica was stretched out fully on her back beneath the port side windows with her head and shoulders hidden behind Donwald who was lying on his side and propped on one elbow facing her. Both were naked. Elizabeth's mouth suddenly became dry and she was immediately gripped by a surging flush as her eyes adjusted to the glare and she saw that Donwald's free hand lay across Jessica's belly with his fingers curled over her pubic mound, and their tips immersed in the folds of flesh beneath.

She drew back quickly and sank back down into the bedding, pulling the sheet over her head. She remained frozen in this position for an age. When she did finally lower the sheet it was to gulp in deep breaths of fresh air. She then made a vow that she would not look into the cabin again, and to this end she pressed one ear firmly against her mattress and jammed a pillow against the other.

Elizabeth could not recall exactly what it was that eventually drew her back, but some time later she found herself moving quickly away from the bedding and bringing her face again to the edge of the hatchway so that she could peer back into the room. The light had faded a little but the scene that confronted her burned itself into the deep recesses of her consciousness.

Donwald was lying on his back and Jessica was sitting astride him with her hands spread on his chest. His hands in turn were gripping her waist. Her head was lowered towards him as if in prayer and Elizabeth heard them exchange a few brief words. And then shortly after this Jessica began to rock slowly backwards and forwards.

Elizabeth's mouth opened and remained open as she continued to watch. By the time Jessica's breasts were rising and falling as if riding the waves of an incessant surf, and her breath was bursting from between her lips in short urgent gasps, Elizabeth had stopped breathing altogether. And when Donwald reached up suddenly with both hands and cupped those rolling breasts, Elizabeth, with her head swimming and her heart pounding, partly sank, partly fell back on to the bedding and curled into a foetal-like position where she remained for an age with her arms locked around her knees.

From that day until the ship reached Sydney some three months later, the fanciful images conjured up by the observers of the first officer and his women were not as far removed from reality as they had been previously. By the time they reached Sydney, miraculously, neither of the women was pregnant, although Elizabeth did have one or two scares and, equally miraculously, all three remained on reasonably friendly terms.

The *Weymouth Bay* ran into a succession of gales as she swept in a wide arc around the south-eastern tip of Van Diemen's Land and headed north, with the result that the first time those on board caught sight of the coast of New South Wales was when they were approaching Sydney heads. By then they were sailing alone, having lost sight of one of the supply ships a few weeks after leaving Rio de Janeiro, and the other in the Great Australian Bight.

It was a bright, cloudless day. The seas had abated and Jessica and Elizabeth stood side by side on the quarterdeck watching plumes of spray from the groundswell pawing at the foundations of the line of high cliffs that flanked the entrance of the harbour.

'Looks like a bloody prison an' all,' said Elizabeth.

'Looks warmer than the ones back home,' said Jessica. 'And cleaner.'

'What's the matter?' Elizabeth's gaze probed the

sea of faces watching them from outside one of the storehouses directly opposite the beach as they disembarked from the longboat on the western side of Sydney Cove. 'Did you see someone you know?'

Jessica was holding a hand to her forehead and was averting her face as they made their way towards a line of waiting wagons.

'The man in the broad-brimmed hat.'

'My God!' whispered Elizabeth. 'The tall one. Who is he? Old Nick hisself or 'is brother?'

'I don't remember his name.' She suddenly began to shake.

'Jessie, are you all right?'

'He's a friend of the man who had me gaoled. Lizzie, I'm frightened. I'm so frightened.'

The woman ahead of her turned around and looked her up and down. 'Did ye say you was frightened, my pet. No need to be frightened, my sweet. With them looks you'll be taken by a wealthy one f'sure and certain.'

'What are you talkin' about?' Elizabeth demanded.

'Your friend'll be assigned to one of them lot over there. Why d'ye think they've come? You too, with your looks, m'lovely. Senior officers and their cronies, an' thems with enough money to sweeten' the deal 'ave the pick of the crop. Tha's where you two'll end up. Livin' a life of leisure, if I be any judge. Spare a thought for a poor old scruffy mott like m' sel'. God knows where I'll end up. Breakin' my back for some ex-lag more'n be likely.'

'Are you saying' they have private prisons?'

'Prisons? I didn't say nothin' about no prisons, m'pet. I said you'll be assigned. Assigned to whoever makes first claim on you. You'll live with them until you be granted a ticket of leave, or until you finish y'sentence if'n you 'aven't been behavin' yourself and don't get your ticket first.'

'Do you mean we won't be locked up?' Jessica asked, continuing to tremble, and more certain now that she had real cause to be concerned.

'Why would you be locked up? There ain't nowheres to go, m'lovely. If you be unlucky they might lock you in at night. Or if you play up. But my guess be that if you two plays y'cards right you'll be free to go as you please durin' the day.' She suddenly released a low cackle. 'Providin' you don't give y'master no trouble whenever he crocks his finger in your direction come night-time.' Her face suddenly hardened.

'And providin' you don't get a bad one, o' course.' She glanced across at the group of bystanders. 'If you get on the wrong side of a bad one he could take it upon 'imself to make you pay extra dear.'

NINE

On a point of land a few miles west of Sydney Cove, and still within the flooded valley that was called Port Jackson, stood a large single-storeyed house. It was on the northern slope and just below the crest of a low ridge that ran generally east and west, terminating at its western extremity where it turned sharply towards the north and plunged vertically into the harbour. Below the house the land fell away gently to one of the harbour's many beaches, this one a scimitar of pale sand, broad enough to careen any ship afloat, and extending from the bluff that marked the western extremity of the ridge for a little over 300 yards to a series of broad but shallow natural stone steps that reached out into the water to form a hidden shoal.

The sun had risen less than half an hour earlier and as yet no craft disturbed this part of the harbour. Nor was there any wind, nor any clouds in the sky. Consequently the surface of the water was a motionless pale-blue sheet of glass that mirrored so perfectly the distant shore and a number of closer rocky outcrops, that if the reflected image had not been inverted, an observer would have had great difficulty in identifying which one of the twin images presented was real, and which was illusion.

A small herd of long-horned and gaily coloured dairy cattle was grazing on the pasture between the beach and the front lawn. The lawn, which was protected from the cattle by a long picket fence, was presently being trimmed by three sheep: leggy, spiral-horned animals which the new owner had extracted from a large flock of Spanish merinos which were en route to a friend's property a few miles further west.

The house was bordered by wide verandahs on all sides, and, as a legacy of the former owner's wife, with the exception of the one that faced the south, all were bedecked in a profusion of flowers and greenery. At the lower levels a family of large ceramic pots—some of which were mounted on squat pedestals—were spaced along the perimeter of each verandah, and from these pots ferns erupted, and broad-leafed plants, caught and held immobile by the still morning air in a frozen cascading moment; as were flowering creepers that spiralled down from baskets suspended beneath the eaves. A grapevine encrusted with freshly budding shoots was suspended along the eastern verandah. Behind and between the foliage were clusters of cane furniture which presumably could be transported to the lawns if the weather permitted.

The house was the former residence of a senior officer in the New South Wales Corps who, together with his wife, had recently departed to take up duties in the newly established settlement of Port Dalrymple in Van Diemen's Land.

The lawns were bordered by serpentine pathways, and gardens crammed with flowering ground creepers and low shrubs. Clumps of larger plants and delicate ornamental trees were spaced at appropriate vantage points about the grounds.

At the rear of the house were a number of outbuildings including stables, a dairy and a blacksmith's shop. Connected to the back verandah by covered walkways were the kitchen and servants' quarters. Behind the stables and partly surrounded by a large clump of bamboo that towered some sixty feet into the air was a low shed, fashioned from heavy slabs of timber.

Behind the outbuildings was the edge of the forest: a confusion of white-flowering native apple trees and eucalypts—red, grey and scribbly gums, and yellow-top ash—that crowned the ridge and all of the land on the northern slope except that which had been cleared for the house and the few acres of pasture that surrounded it. More eucalypts and a mix of banksias, bottlebrush and casuarinas were perched on the rocky outcrops in the harbour and on the opposite side of the water where they cloaked the undulating landform like a great patchwork blanket of olive greens and greys.

From before dawn the raucous laughter of kookaburras had been sounding from the forest. But now as their throaty wake-up calls were becoming less frequent, currawongs and their magpie cousins—the maestros of birdsong—were engaged in a musical competition that charged the morning air with a symphonic farrago: a mixture of clarion calls sounding out above a thrilling undercurrent of endless choral medleys and variations.

At the back of the blacksmith's shop a large rooster paused regularly as it picked away at interesting bits and pieces among the splintered red chips that surrounded a woodheap. And after appearing to listen for a while to the music from its distant relatives, it would lean forward, stretch its neck, spread its wings, and with flashing spectrums rippling through its quivering blue-green feathers, release a battery of cock-a-doodle-doos.

Its attention for a time was arrested by the undulating whine of a blowfly hovering over a slick dark red stain on the grass beneath an iron triangle that rose more than six feet above the turf beyond the woodheap.

When the rooster suddenly darted forward and tried to impale the fly, the fat insect swept into the air at a speed that belied its shape, and for a time spiralled fitfully just out of reach of its attacker before spearing out of sight towards the clump of bamboo.

Some time later the rooster spied it again—or perhaps a relative—this time outside the barred twin doors of the low shed behind the stables. As before, the insect was hovering over a dark red stain on the grass, this one much smaller than the first.

As the rooster approached, the fly sped off. The bird clucked a number of times as it examined the stain. Here, where the sun had not yet crept into the deeper shadows of the shed and the partly encircling clump of bamboo, the grass was interlaced with silvery crystals of frost.

Suddenly the rooster froze in mid-stride with one claw suspended above the ground, its beak open and its head held cocked on one side as if transfixed. From within the shed came a repeat of the sound that had caught the bird's attention: a low moan, as if a child, or a small creature, was in distress. After spending some time scouting the edge of the door, the rooster moved away.

Later that morning a thickset woman supporting a metal basin against one hip and carrying a ceramic jug walked from the back verandah of the house and moved towards the shed. When she reached her destination she placed the jug and the basin on the ground, unlocked a chain from the bolt of timber that secured the doors, pivoted the bolt clear of its U-shaped supports, and opened one of the doors. She picked up the basin and the jug and entered.

The woman moved across to where something or someone was curled in the far corner beneath a grey blanket. Placing down the items she was carrying, the woman reached out and began to pull the blanket away from whatever was underneath. The air was immediately charged with a ballooning cloud of swirling dust particles that sparkled like a swarm of tiny fireflies as they passed through the thin slats of sunlight that were projected from the closed door.

'Please,' a hoarse voice whispered above a clinking of metal on metal, as slim fingers curled over the edge of the blanket from beneath it and tried feebly to prevent it from being removed.

'Let go,' the woman said softly. 'It's only me what's 'ere. An' I ain't 'ere to do you no 'arm.'

The fingers disengaged, and the woman pulled the top portion of the blanket down to reveal Jessica Glider. Although, if anyone who knew her had been there, they would have been forgiven for not recognising her in her present state. Her hair was matted and plastered against her scalp, and the flesh around one of her eyes was so swollen it was difficult to judge if the eye was open.

She was naked and was shivering uncontrollably. And although the front of her body did not appear to be marked by physical injury, angry welts on her shoulders and thin strips of broken flesh at the edge of her rib cage suggested the same could not be said for her back.

Her first words confirmed this. 'Why did he flog me? I didn't do anythin'.'

'You don't 'ave t'do anythin' with this one, lass. He 'ad ye flogged 'cause that be in 'is nature. Turn around so I can see the damage.'

As she turned so the woman could see her back, Jessica raised her manacled wrists and pulled the blanket back against her chest. The movement caused her to wince and to tremble more violently for a moment. 'I didn't do anythin'. I didn't say anythin'.'

'Wouldn't 'ave made no difference if ye 'ad.' The woman pursed her lips as she examined where Jessica's back was laced with a hatchwork of blood-encrusted welts. 'Don't look so bad if ye look close. Ye was lucky he 'ad 'Enry Langsmith use a clean hemp cat on yer. Not one with birdshot spliced in't. Or one made from bull's 'ide. He could've cut ye in half with bull's 'ide. I seen 'im do it once to a Fenian. But he's probably got other plans for ye than cuttin' ye in half. Tha's f'sure 'n' certain.'

'He had no right to flog me for nothin'.'

He ain't got no right to flog ye a'tall, lass. No right to even own a flogger's triangle. Only a magistrate can 'ave ye flogged. And then 'tain't likely ye'll be flogged if ye're a woman. Not less'n ye've done someat really stupid. But not 'avin' the right don't stop this'n. This'n don't care about no rights. If this'n wants to flog ye, he'll flog ye, come hell or high water.' She turned, and picking up the jug lifted it towards the other woman. ''Ere, drink this.'

'What is it?'

'Fresh cow's milk. What's it look like?'

Jessica placed a trembling hand against the side of the jug and sipped tentatively.

'Go on, take a good swig. Ye don't know how long it'll 'ave t'last ye. An' when ye've finished I'll clean ye up a bit. Get some of the dirt off ye. I 'ave some nice warm water 'ere that might help stop ye shiverin'. I won't touch y'back though. Best t'let those cuts lie. Touchin'm might stir'm up. We don't want'm to go bad on ye.'

'Why?'

'Why what?'

'Why are you goin' to clean me up?'

'Ye can't go into the house like y'are, lass. If ye could see y'self ye'd know that.'

'Why am I goin' into the house?'

'He wants t'see ye, don't he? Wants to see if ye're broke yet.'

'Broke?'

''Tis what he does with most he brings 'ere. Leastwise, thems that he 'as special plans for.'

Jessica shuddered and pulled the blanket against herself more firmly. 'What do you mean, broke?'

'Broke, broke. It's why he 'ad ye flogged for starters. And he'll keep 'avin' ye flogged until he's satisfied that when he looks in yer eyes he sees that ye're broke. That ye're won't try nothin' stupid. Like tryin' t'bolt. Tryin' to bolt would be real stupid.'

'You can't mean he'll flog me again?' She shook her head. 'He couldn't do that. Not again. Not without reason?'

'He can, ye know. He can do anythin' he likes. An' the sooner ye accept that the easier ye life will be.'

Taking a folded cloth from her shoulder, the woman dipped it in the basin of water and wrang it out. She then proceeded to sponge the grime from Jessica, starting with her hair.

Jessica winced when the cloth touched a bruise. 'But you don't know he'll flog me again f'sure. He might decide I am broke. I'll tell 'im I'm broke.'

'Tellin' 'im won't do no good. He'll want to be sure 'imself. While he 'as you in irons, there's every chance he'll continue to 'ave ye flogged regular, and left locked up in 'ere nights. When he 'as the irons removed, that's when you'll know he's decided you're broke. An' probably not before.'

Later, the woman lifted back the lower portion of the blanket and began to sponge Jessica's legs, pausing from time to time to pick away with the tips of her fingers the more obstinate trails of dried blood that were entwined around her thighs. 'One thing ye musn't do. Ye musn't try and deceive 'im. He's part devil an' can pick it every time. An' he'll make you pay awful bad for tryin'. Awful bad.'

'How long have you been with him?'

'Five years.'

'What was your sentence?'

'Seven.'

'But we were told we'd have a ticket of leave well before five years was up.'

'He 'as ways with that one. Anyone who leaves 'ere at all can count 'im or 'erself lucky.'

Jessica could not find the courage to pursue that one. Instead she asked, 'Did he do this to you when you first came? Flog you until he decided you were broke?'

The woman looked into her eyes for a moment, then turned away slightly and pulled down the back of her collar revealing a twisted coil of scar tissue.

Jessica winced and remained silent for a while before asking, 'What's your name?'

'Molly. Molly Clinger. Yours?'

'Jessie. Jessica Glider.'

'Where you from, Jessie?'

'Hampshire. You?'

'Kent.'

Later Jessica asked, 'What will my duties be?'

'Duties?' Molly chuckled. 'That be an interestin' word for them. Ye name it. That's what they'll be. And some.'

'Will they include . . .' her voice died.

'Swivin' him? What do ye think, lass? Ye've seen 'im, for Jesus Christ's sake. Ye only 'ave t'look in his eyes. If swivin' were prize fightin', Garth Barlester would be champion of all England.'

'Why's she got that blanket on, Moll?' Garth Barlester asked, his voice a grating rasp.

'I thought that's what ye wanted, sir. To stop 'er from catchin' somethin'. She's been shiverin' off 'n' on awful bad.'

Barlester stood in the centre of his drawing room with his feet spread and his hands linked behind his back. He was leaning forward slightly so that, to the two women who stood a few feet away from him, he appeared to be towering above them.

'I don't give a damn, Moll. It's a filthy rag. What d'you mean by bringin' a filthy rag into my house?'

The entire left side of Molly's face began to quiver. 'I'm sorry, sir. I thought I was doin' right. She were shakin' fit to . . .'

'Shut up, woman!' Barlester snapped. 'I don't care if she were shakin' fit to have her teeth pop out.' He turned and looked across to where a solidly proportioned man was standing near the doorway. 'That'd save us some trouble, wouldn't it, Henry?'

The man showed his teeth, but did not reply. Barlester turned back.

'See to it later, Henry, that Molly here is

reminded that it was stupid to bring a filthy rag into the house.' He released one of his hands and pointed at Jessica. 'Get out of here, Molly, and take the rag with you.'

Molly stifled a whimper, and taking hold of the blanket that was draped around Jessica, pulled it away from her and with some difficulty detached it from her grasp. Her gaze then briefly touched Jessica's before she turned away and fled the room.

'She is shiverin', Henry. I wonder why. It's not cold in here. Do you think it's cold in here, lass?'

Jessica shook her head.

'Well, why are you shiverin'?'

'I don't know, sir.' The chain that linked her manacles was now jingling in sympathy with the tremble in her arms.

'She says she doesn't know, Henry.'

'Move over closer to the fire. Yes, the fire. That way. What, are you dense or somethin', woman? Have you never seen a fire? Move closer. That's better. Can you feel it?'

She nodded.

'Is it warm?'

She nodded again.

'Well, for God Almighty's sake, stop shiverin'.'

'I can't ... I can't help it, sir.'

'She says she can't help it, Henry.'

Jessica gripped the chain and managed to stop it from clinking.

'I have it on good authority that this one's a

biter, Henry. Does she look like a biter to you?'

'Not that I'd pick it, sir,' Henry Langsmith, Barlester's overseer, replied. 'But you can't always tell with the sneaky ones.'

'You mightn't be able to tell, Henry. But I can. Always.' Barlester's gaze did not move from Jessica. 'And this one's a twice biter. Once in England. And once on the voyage out. A bad biter too. Near killed a man on the ship. He may have even died since. So I'd say she's past curin' by normal means. What would you say?'

'I'd say that's right, sir. Not by normal means.'

'And we can't 'ave a biter runnin' loose around here, can we? Never know who might get injured.'

'That be right, sir. You'd never know.'

'So did you bring what I told you to bring?'

'Aye, sir. I did. I have it with me here.'

'Let me see.' Barlester held out his hand to one side, palm uppermost.

Langsmith walked across to him and placed in his hand what appeared to be a pair of blacksmith's pincers.

Barlester looked them over and then held them out in front of Jessica. 'Do you know what these are used for?'

'What ... What are you going to do?'

'Do you know what these are used for, woman? Answer me.'

She shook her head and whispered a plaintive, 'Please, don't.'

'They're used for pulling out horses' teeth.'

265

'No.' She shook her head. 'Please don't.'

'We can't have biters wanderin' around, can we? So do you know what I'm goin' to do?'

She continued to shake her head.

'I'm going to cure you. I'm going to pull all of your teeth.'

'No.' This is a nightmare. This can't be happening. 'Please. For God's sake. No.' She began to turn away.

Barlester nodded to Langsmith who immediately walked across the room, stepped behind her and, gripping her by the upper arms, turned her back to face him.

'No,' she shouted, and tried to twist out of his grip. But he held her firmly.

'What do they call you?' Barlester asked. 'Jessie, isn't it? Well, Jessie, open wide.' He reached up with one hand and gripped her lower jaw.

She wrenched her head away and managed to break his grip. Her upper body whipped back as if driven by the release of a spring. Her head thumped into Langsmith's face. He gasped and fell away from her, releasing his grip on her arms.

Barlester stepped forward and tried to restrain her with his free hand, but she ducked beneath it. She then turned and made to dash for the door but her sudden lunge was arrested by her fetters and she crashed to the floor.

'Seize her,' shouted Barlester.

As she rose to her knees Langsmith sprang forward and swept a curling arm around her neck from behind. He then locked his wrist with his other hand and leant back so that his forearm cut into her jaw. Her head was forced up and her gaze locked with Barlester's as he moved to stand over her.

'Now do as you're told,' he growled, reaching to steady her jaw again with his free hand. 'Open wide or you'll lose pieces of your lip.'

'No,' she managed to gasp. 'Please.' She closed her eyes and reached up blindly with her manacled hands trying to fend him off. But the chain that linked them had been caught in the crock of Langsmith's arm, and all she could manage was to grasp either side of one of Barlester's legs above the flare of his massive boot.

'Open wide, Jessie. You're a biter.'

'No,' she cried again, and tried in vain to push him away.

His hand closed around her chin. Her eyes snapped open and she watched him lower the open jaws of the pincers towards her.

Suddenly she released the grip on his leg and manoeuvring both wrists to gain the maximum slack in the chain, she slipped her right hand between his legs and pressed it against his crotch.

'I won't bite again,' she gasped, her gaze seeking his. 'I promise. Never again. Please don't.' Her fingers moved into the coarse cloth of his trousers, feeling for him, and then finally came to rest cupped firmly against him.

He stood there for some time looking down at

her with the pincers still poised close to her face.

'Never again?' he said at last.

'Never again.' She shook her head. 'Never.'

He stepped back. 'Let her go.'

Langsmith unlocked his arm and straightened.

Barlester turned to him. 'Go and get your face cleaned up, Henry. I don't want you messin' the carpet.'

Langsmith pressed his hand against his top lip and then examined the swirl of blood that had collected on his palm. He turned his gaze on Jessica and for a moment it appeared he might move to strike her.

'Go on, Henry, get out of here and close the door behind you. I'll ring for you when I want you.'

When Langsmith had gone she placed both hands in her lap and sank back on her haunches. Her head began to sink slowly forward.

'Hey!' Barlester snapped.

Her head straightened.

'What's the matter with you?'

'I don't feel well,' she replied softly.

'I warn you, woman, if you even think about playin' games with me, I'll have you flayed alive.'

She shook her head and tried to say, 'I won't play games' but it came out more like, 'I ww . . . ames.'

He reached down and gripping her jaw stared into her eyes as if he was peering into the back of her mind. He then released her and walked across to a tall wooden cupboard, opened it, extracted a bottle and a small glass, filled the glass and brought it back to her.

'Drink this.' He held it out. 'Straight down. One gulp.'

She took it and complied, and then gagged and fought for breath as the liquid scorched her throat.

He laughed and took the glass from her and placed it on the table. 'That was probably your first taste of the currency.'

He drew up a high-backed chair and sat down in front of her. Then, with his gaze on hers, stretched out first one leg and then the other on either side of her.

'If it turns out that you still are a biter, Jessie, I won't kill you. That I promise. So don't think that to bite would be to suicide. A quick end to y'sufferin'. To bite would simply be t'open the gates o'hell, lass. To bite would be the start of your real sufferin'. And that's the truth of it f'sure an' certain.' He reached out and wiped a smear of dust from one of her breasts with the tips of his fingers. And then, moving his hand idly to the nipple, squeezed it, causing her to flinch, more from the unexpectedness of the move than from pain. 'If you do choose t'bite, not only will I remove all your pretty teeth with those pincers over there, but I'll also use them to remove every part of you that I can grip with them. Do you understand what I'm saying?' He moved his hand to her other breast and repeated his action.

269

She shuddered. 'I won't bite again.'

He watched her for a while, and then leaning back reached below his waist, and with both hands began to unbutton the wide flap at the front of his trousers.

Later, he pulled on items of his clothing that he had discarded and rang for Langsmith. When the overseer arrived Jessica was still sitting slumped on the carpet.

Barlester glanced back at her from where he was standing at the door. 'Bring her over here.'

Langsmith moved across the room and hauled her to her feet. 'Will she be movin' into the house?'

Barlester's attention was elsewhere at that moment. 'What?'

Langsmith brought her across to the door. It appeared that if he had not been gripping her firmly by her upper arms she may have slipped back to the floor. 'Will I take the irons off her?'

Barlester reached out and, gripping her jaw, turned her face towards him. He stood looking at her for a moment and then released her and shook his head. 'No. She ain't broke by a long shot. Bring her out to the triangle and give her another dozen with the cat.'

'What?' Jessica raised her head and stared at him in disbelief.

He turned away and, walking from the room, moved towards the rear of the house. 'And then you can throw her back in the shed,' he called out.

'I'll have another look at her tomorrow. At present she's still far too uppity for her own good.'

'What?' Jessica repeated, more for herself than the others.

Langsmith pushed her to get her moving and then kept pushing her as he drove her ahead of him, following Barlester out on to the back verandah.

Other people were moving about in the distance. Some stopped what they were doing and looked across at them. Then, realising that it was Barlester and Langsmith that had emerged from the house, along with a naked woman, they quickly averted their gazes and went back to whatever was occupying them before.

'What about her teeth?' Langsmith asked as he directed her down a short flight of steps and along a stone pathway, still in his master's wake.

Without turning, Barlester replied, 'I'll keep my options open on the teeth. For the moment I'll let her keep 'm.'

A small flock of crimson rosellas shrieked as they speared past, with their red, blue and green plumage flashing in the sunlight.

'This is glorious weather we're havin', Henry,' said Barlester.

'Aye, sir. Glorious.'

As the first stroke from the nine-tailed cat cracked across her back, Jessica released a choking gasp. For a few seconds she stood with her outstretched arms and legs stiffened and trembling, then she fell forward in a dead faint. As her head dropped and her legs gave way, she hung from where her manacles were looped over the apex of the iron triangle that supported her weight.

Langsmith swung his arm back to deliver the second stroke.

'Hold fast!' Barlester called out. He walked over to the triangle and looked closely at Jessica's back. The first blow had cut open many of the wounds from the previous day and a maze of crimson rivulets were tracking towards her buttocks. 'That will do her. Put her in the shed and get Molly to put a blanket over her. When she wakes she'll think she's been given another dozen. Which will work as well as giving them to her. And this way doesn't over-bruise the goods.'

Some five hundred miles to the north, Gunroi stood watching the large bird skimming the tops of the waves.

'It is white,' Nunderri confirmed, 'but is it an eagle?'

Gunroi made no immediate response. The sun was low on the hills behind him and the bird was passing through the edge of the shadows that spread across the water from the base of the cliffs. 'I'm not sure,' he said at last. Although there was nothing against which he could use to gauge the size of the bird, he sensed that it was huge.

Coranga and Mori called out again for both

men to come back from the edge of the cliff. But they remained where they were until the water darkened and they finally lost sight of the bird as it was immersed in the strengthening shadows.

When they rejoined the women Coranga asked, 'Which way? Have you decided?'

Gunroi nodded to the south, the direction the bird had been heading.

'As if we needed to ask,' said Coranga aside to Mori, as they gathered up their small collection of possessions and moved after the men.

TEN

The name of the inn was The Spinning Top. And to prove it, someone had driven a stake vertically through a keg that had once contained two gallons of rum or brandy, or perhaps even molasses—the original markings having long been obliterated—and had painted it red and suspended the result by a chain from a horizontal cross-piece attached to a tall post outside the front door. So that now, whenever the device turned because of the breeze, or from having an energetic patron leap up and strike it, it did resemble a top of sorts.

The inn sat about midway between Sydney and Parramatta on the dusty road that linked the two settlements along the southern reaches of the harbour. It was a single-storey building constructed from slabs of timber, with the gaps between sealed with wattle and daub. As was generally the case with the building materials used in the settlement, the wattle component of the mix had been stripped from the many varieties of acacia bushes that at this time of the year filled the nearby forests with a vast golden understorey.

The yard behind the inn was flanked by low scrub country that extended into the marshy southern extremity of what was officially named Hen and Chicken Bay; but probably not on account of the publican's fowls. They usually stayed in the general vicinity of the inn and its outbuildings: a stable, a communal three-seater toilet, and a fowlhouse.

On any night of the week, some indication of what could be expected inside the building, in terms of both the number and type of clientele, could be obtained from outside the building. On this particular one, a string of saddled mounts were tied to the hitching rails along the front of the verandah, and to assorted trees and fence posts. Most of these animals were an odd mix of some sprightly, but more often aging, hacks and ill-shaped part-draught animals of various sizes and hues that had probably spent more of their domesticated life pulling ploughs and drays than transporting their thirsty masters in ones and sometimes twos to the local hostelry.

There were also a number of horses at the back of the building, many of them partly concealed by the overhanging limbs and buttressed trunk of a huge fig tree to which they were tethered. Most of these had shaggy coats and tangled manes, rendering them more untidy even than their cousins at the front. Only a discerning observer, and in better light, would perhaps notice that the remnants of their winter coats hid the true conformation of their frames and disguised the quality of their blood lines. Most of these animals were tethered by long reins and easy to release slip knots. And unlike those in the front, during the course of the evening they remained wide awake and fidgeting. Occasionally one or two would slash at a neighbour with bared incisors, and whenever the back door of the inn flew open to release a staggering occupant the more nervous would dance on the spot until whoever had emerged had moved on; or as was more often the case, had re-entered the building after vomiting or urinating into the shadows.

Amidst the undulating clamour inside the main room of the building about thirty patrons were present. Some were seated at tables, others were breasting the bar and a few were propped against the broad columns of brickwork that flanked the open fireplace at one end of the room. Most were men, but at any one time about six women were also present, scattered evenly about the room.

Occasionally one of these women would rise and, accompanied by a man, would make her way between the tables and depart the room via an open doorway beside the bar. Usually after about five or ten minutes both would re-emerge and resume whatever it was that was occupying them previously. For the man this usually consisted of quaffing drinks and exchanging noisy banter with his companions; for the woman it often as not involved spending some time with the man's companions—perhaps as an act of courtesy expected during such tribal rites—and then either repeating her disappearing-and-reappearing act accompanied by one of the others, or moving on to a neighbouring group.

This was not an activity shared by all the women. Some of them never left the room—other than unaccompanied, and then almost certainly in response to a call of nature—and of these, some remained with the one group or with the same companion during the entire evening.

One woman who up until now had not left the room with any of the men during the course of the evening, but did move from one group to another a number of times, was an attractive redhead who had arrived by herself on foot shortly before sundown from the direction of Sydney.

If there was anyone present who had come to the colony some eight weeks before on the convict transport *Weymouth Bay*, they may have recognised her as one of the two women who shared the first officer's cabin during most of the voyage.

But it would be unlikely that they ever knew her name was Elizabeth Crowling. So it would be equally unlikely that they would have challenged that she was now calling herself Liz Arlington. But it was doubtful that anyone who knew her was present. She could not see anyone she recognised, and from her latest vantage point close to the front door it was possible to see most areas of the room. Although not always at any given moment.

Thick clouds of blue smoke would hide sections of the room from time to time, usually when groups of men chose to expel the contents of their lungs at about the same time. Most of the men in the room were smoking, with their pipes ranging from stylishly crafted clay varieties with thin curved stems, to those that had been fashioned from one of the local eucalypts. Of these, some had been crudely made, consisting of little more than a solid upright cylinder into which a heavy wooden tube had been inserted. But others had been painstakingly styled, and had gently rounded and polished contours that accentuated the grain of the timber.

As well as being armed with pipes, most of the men were wearing hats. Elizabeth had recently come to realise that these provided a reasonably accurate gauge of how long their owners had been in the colony. For instance, if the subject had been raised she would suggest that the darker variety of cloth caps and all varieties of tall narrow-brimmed hats usually topped the heads of the more recent comers, likely as not from the latest fleet.

Those who had been living in the colony for some time usually wore a straw hat or one plaited from one or other of the local plants, often as not the cabbage-tree palm, with the shape and styling of these hats depicting a chronological order. Those that resembled Spanish sombreros, with wide brims and tall tapering crowns, seemed to be favoured by the longer-term inhabitants, possibly first-fleeters. From then on, both brims and crowns seemed to have diminished in incremental steps, possibly aligned to the arrival of each subsequent fleet, down to the point where the more recent comers, when they got around to discarding their original headgear, would be likely to replace it with jaunty, low-crowned, flat-topped, medium-brimmed articles that usually sported coloured bands with twin ribbons trailing over one side.

'They're a wayward lookin' lot,' she remarked to her latest drinking companion shortly after she had moved to his table. 'Most of them be regulars, I s'pose?'

'They be regular enough,' the man replied, with more of his attention on her than on those she was referring to. She was certainly a handsome woman, he conceded, handsomer than most of the table-jumpers who worked the room; on this night or any other.

'Then you be a regular y'self?'

'Aye,' he conceded, searching her face for a sign of why someone with her attributes had chosen her profession. 'Regular enough.'

'Hey, Henry,' a woman called out from across the room. 'Stop wastin' ye time on that one. She be too expensive for a tight-arse like y'self.'

He showed the speaker his teeth, and she in turn stood up and, much to the amusement of those at her table, hauled down the front of her bodice and exposed her bare breasts. 'Why don't you come for a walk with me. My price be far more reasonable.' She shook her breasts and they bounced as if filled with springs. One of the men reached up and tried to fondle her. She squealed and slapped his hand away. She then pulled her bodice back up to her shoulders, sat down again, and berated the man enthusiastically.

Elizabeth watched her for a moment before returning her attention to the man beside her. 'I seem to have upset a friend of yours.'

'I don't have no friends.'

'None?' She watched him closely.

'None I'd want to have in this godforsaken shithole of a country.'

'Well, even if she weren't ye friend, she still be jealous o'me sittin' here talkin' t'you.'

'Why is that?'

'Why is what?'

'Why are you sittin' here talkin' t'me?'

'Do you want me to leave?'

'What'd she mean, ye're too expensive? How expensive are you?'

'Maybe I'm not f'sale. Maybe tha's what she meant.'

'Then if ye're not f'sale, what are you doin' here?'

'I'm lookin' for work. Someone over there said you're a man that hires and fires. Maybe you'll hire me.'

'Why would I hire you?'

'I'm a good house worker.'

'What kind of housework?'

'Any kind.'

'Like what?'

'Like kitchens.'

'How about bedrooms?'

'Like bedrooms. I'm extra good with bedrooms.' She allowed her eyelids to droop. 'So I've been told.'

He sat watching her intently for a moment and then crocked a finger at her. 'Lean closer.'

When she did, he inverted the finger, hooked it into the top of her bodice and, pulling it away from her chest, dropped his head towards her and peered inside. 'Who told you I was hirin'?'

'Nobody said you were. They just said you did.'

With his gaze locked on hers, he slipped his entire hand inside the bodice and began to massage her. She allowed him some leeway for a while, but when his fingers suddenly dug into her flesh she winced and extracted the hand.

'You be a bit game.' She sank back out of easy reach. 'They didn't say nothin' about that.'

'Where do you think you're goin?' Garth Barlester demanded, swinging the head of the tall black gelding around. 'And what the hell have you been doin' in there?'

He switched the gelding sharply beneath the withers with his riding crop. The animal skipped and threw its head in the air before moving off the pathway and heading back towards the woman who had just emerged from the servants' quarters.

As she turned to face the horse and rider, Henry Langsmith stepped from the building behind her. 'It's all right, sir. She's with me. She be lookin' for a job.'

Barlester reined his mount to a halt in front of them. 'What?' For a moment he seemed flustered. 'A job? What job? Who said we were looking for anyone?'

'She thought we were, sir. I've told her we weren't.'

'She stay here last night?'

'Aye, sir. I . . .' Langsmith rubbed a hand across his jaw. 'I thought it might have been dangerous her goin' back to town in the dark.'

'Horseshit, Henry. All you thought was that I'd be gone by now.' He propped the fist in which he held his riding crop on his hip.

For a moment Langsmith appeared as if he might protest his innocence. But under Barlester's glare he swallowed any words that had threatened to emerge and lowered his gaze. It flittered about for a while before settling on a location somewhere on the crest of the heavily wooded ridge that he could see through the crock of his master's arm.

'What are you going to do now, Henry? Feed her as well? We don't give free board and lodging at my place. You know that.'

The gelding chose that moment to throw its

head in the air and begin to turn away. Barlester wheeled it around in the opposite direction in the process of regaining charge of it. 'See to it she works off the price of staying overnight,' he snapped. 'She can help Molly in the kitchen. And I want her out of here by tonight.'

'Aye, sir.'

The gelding continued to dance nervously 'Tonight. Do you hear me?' With this, he cut the animal across the flank with his crop and, swinging its head back towards the rear of the outbuildings, moved off at a solid trot.

'My!' Elizabeth exclaimed impressively. 'That be one angry man. What's the matter with him? Surely you've had someone stay overnight before?'

'Plenty of times. And he knows it. He were just tryin' to cover up how stupid he felt for mistakin' you for someone else, tha's all. That and showin' you how tough he is. He likes to do that.'

'Who?'

'What do you mean, who?'

'Who did he mistake me for?'

'Never mind. Come on, I'll show you the kitchen.'

'There are no jobs, are there? You lied to me.'

'I didn't lie to you. There could be a job. I'll talk to him about it when he's in a better mood.'

'Where's he gone?'

'To Sydney.'

'Does he go often?'

'Every weekend. Most, anyways.'

'He was right then, wasn't he? You'd thought he'd be gone already.'

'I'll tell you someat,' he said ushering her towards the back of the house, 'ye've got a job today. He'll be checkin' on that when he gets back. And no matter what he says, there could be somethin' permanent here for you if you play your cards right. But there as sure as hell ain't a job for anyone who doesn't know when to hold her tongue. And when not to argue. That be God's truth certain.'

'I thought you said the house looked over the harbour.'

'It does. Out the front.'

'Show me.'

'Jesus, ye're a flamin' nuisance.' He directed her to the eastern side of the house and they both stood for a while observing the scene below them.

A cutter with its sails ballooning was making its way upstream powered by a steady north-easter. The fine twin lines of its bow wave were streaming out on either side and ruffling the shoreline a good quarter mile behind.

'Is that a beach down there?'

'A beach? Aye.'

'Why don't you have a jetty?'

'Don't need no jetty. Anyone droppin' stores can run a decent sized boat right up on the beach.'

'Don't you have a boat yourselves?'

'What would we want with a boat?'

'It'd be quicker to go to town by boat than by horse.'

'That'd be assumin' you wanted to go.'

'Your master goes every weekend, you said. Wouldn't it be quicker and easier for him to go by boat?'

'Maybe. If he was in a hurry. And didn't need a horse when he got there.'

'Where does he go?'

'He goes to see his cronies. Ones he was in the corps with.'

'He was in the Rum Corps?'

'How the fuck do you think he got a place like this elsewise? Come on, I ain't got all day t' stand around here. I'll show you where you can eat and where ye'll be workin'.'

'Y'ain't serious? About the workin', I mean. Not about the eatin'. I'm not interested in any work I don't get paid for.'

'Don't mess me about, girl. I'm not in the business of wastin' m'breath. And I'm not in the business of crossin' Garth fucking Barlester over someone such as y'self. Whether ye want to or not, you're goin' to do the best part of a day's work in the kitchen.'

'Am I just?'

'Aye, you am just.'

'I could refuse.'

'That'd be a bad mistake. Bad. And it would kill any chance you had of scorin' a cushy job out here.'

'There don't seem no chance of that happenin' anyways. Not accordin' to ye're high 'n' mighty master.'

'He's been known to change his mind. But not with some mott who's ever crossed him. When he said you're to help out in the kitchen, he weren't whistlin' no tune. He meant it.'

'There be smoke over there on the other side of the water. Where'd that be comin' from?'

He turned and looked. 'Blacks.'

'Blacks.' She mouthed the word and stood watching the spot for a time before suddenly shuddering and turning away. 'Ye're a long way from town out here. Do they ever come over?'

'Not often. Not thems that know what's good for'm.' He chuckled. 'And never closer than musket range. Not around this house. That's f' sure 'n' certain.'

Jessica was sitting at the kitchen table when they entered.

'Hullo,' said Elizabeth. 'I'm Liz Arlington. Are you Molly?'

'No she ain't,' snapped Langsmith. 'But she's the person who can show you where you can ladle yourself a bowl of that gruel.'

He picked up a plate from a sideboard and handed it to her. Then, returning his attention to Jessica, he snapped, 'Come on, woman, she ain't got all day. Where is Molly?'

Jessica stood up and walked across to the end

of the room where a long stove occupied most of the area beneath the broad sweep of a blackened brickwork arch.

Elizabeth immediately moved to join her. Jessica lifted a ladle from a hook above the stove, and from a large blackened pot served her an ample helping of a grey mixture that some would call porridge.

As she did, Elizabeth placed a hand over hers to steady it.

Langsmith remained at the doorway. 'I said, where's Molly, yer cloth-eared mott. Have you gone deaf or somethin'?'

'I think . . . I think she's gettin' the milk,' Jessica replied distractedly. 'She'll be back soon.'

'Tell her that as soon as ye've both finished y'breakfast t' put Liz here on helpin' you scrub the pots. All of them. And after that you both can do the floor. It's gettin' t' look like the deck of a whaler.'

He waited until they returned to the table and sat down. 'And tell her I'll be back to check from time t'time, and if I catch any of you slackin' I'll take it out on her.' With this he turned and left.

Only then did the women turn their eyes on each other.

One week and about two hours later in the day, Garth Barlester was again riding towards Sydney Town when an incident occurred that was to trouble him for some time. He had just crossed

Johnston's Creek about three miles short of his destination when a rider passed him heading in the opposite direction. Thin sheets of drizzling rain were sweeping in from the south and, like himself, the rider was wearing a hooded cape.

Had Barlester not at that moment been distracted by his customary enraged appraisal of the 300 acre grant that his former colleague, Major George Johnston, had inveigled the Crown to grant him on the north side of the road, adding to the 100 acres he already owned on the south side, he may have done something about it at the time.

As it was, he was so furiously engaged in his usual teeth-grinding lamentations at having missed out on the latest prize himself—a sweep of prime real estate that stretched to the southern end of Rozelle Bay—that by the time he realised the rider was a woman, and that the woman was Langsmith's redhead from the previous weekend, she was a good two hundred yards away—possibly three—and moving at a fairly steady gait up the long slope behind him towards the line of young Norfolk Island pines on the crest of the ridge.

He had only glimpsed a flash of an almost hidden profile, and what must have been a few strands of her hair. But it was enough. Although not enough to prompt an immediate response. Her complete image emerged from where his subconscious self had assembled it in the recesses of his mind while his conscious self was still engrossed in envious condemnation of Johnston's windfall.

I'll kill that Langsmith, he promised himself in consolation when he finally reined his mount to a halt and twisted in the saddle to look back at her. He thinks he can play me for a fool.

What he should have done there and then—he flayed himself repeatedly with this thought during the following months—was chased her. Ridden her down if he had to. Accosted her and demanded to know her business. Grabbed her by the throat if he had to. The bitch! That would have nipped it in the bud. Or so, with the advantage of hindsight, he had no trouble in convincing himself.

But it wasn't until later that evening that his moment of inaction began to really trouble him. Shortly after Wally Suttling approached him with a mud-skipper in tow.

'Garthie, old son!' Wally was a buffoon of the first order. But having to put up with buffoons was the price of staying in close touch with the corps. And staying in close touch was about the most financially astute activity that someone in his position could undertake in the colony these days. Particularly as they were in charge of the table where the highest stakes were being wagered; a table where all players lucky enough to be invited won. And where the winnings were paid in acres. Or concessions. Sometimes both. And where opportunities regularly existed to play the likes of Lieutenant Colonel William Paterson and Captain John Macarthur against each other, even at the risk of Macarthur putting a ball into Paterson's shoulder. But now that you've managed to buy yourself out of that one, Jackie, as soon as you return you could do us all a favour and put one in Suttling here. A bit higher up though. Betwixt the eyes would be appreciated most handsome.

'Ianie Chesterfield, meet Garthie Barlester. Ianie's been telling me a tale of his adventures on the high seas that I think you'd be very interested in, Garthie.'

Barlester there and then decided he couldn't wait for John Macarthur's return from England and made a silent vow that as soon as he had the opportunity to do so without too many witnesses present, he would garrotte Wally Suttling for all of his accumulated and boorish arse-aching misdemeanours, but for none with greater relish than the silly little man's persistence in calling him Garthie. Garrotte him, and stamp him into the earth.

Barlester swallowed a belch and, turning to the table, picked up a partly filled bottle of brandy. God save me from the military. How could I have put up with these supercilious morons for so long. Perhaps if he ignored these two they would go away.

'Ianie was in charge of marines on the transport that shipped your little redhead to Sydney.'

'Jessica Glider,' said Chesterfield.

'You remember her name?' Despite himself, Barlester failed to disguise a mild surprise.

'Oh, I remember her name all right.' Chesterfield pulled up a chair, sat down and leaned forward while Suttling braced himself against the back of the seat.

My God they've come to stay. Barlester poured himself a healthy portion from the bottle.

'Did you know she bit the nose off a man who tried to get friendly with her uninvited?' Chesterfield lowered his voice conspiratorially. 'Clean off.' He then leant back, raised his eyebrows, dropped his jaw into a reasonably good imitation of a smiling theatrical mask, and nodded enthusiastically. A trickle of spittle ran from the gaping hole in the centre of the mask.

Give me strength. 'Is that right? How come she didn't hang?'

'She didn't hang because I wasn't the first to get there after she did it, is why. Fast. Her feet wouldn't have touched the ground.'

'That's the best way to do it. Feet off the ground.'

'What?'

'So what saved her?'

'The Scotch bastard who was the ship's first officer is what saved her.' He closed a fist and bent his elbow. 'He took her under his wing, didn't he. Right into his cabin. And fucked her all the way from Rio de Janeirie to Sydney Cove. Her and the other redhead.'

Barlester raised one heavy eyelid with what seemed to be some difficulty against the hairy weight of the overhanging brow above it. 'What other redhead?'

'Elizabeth Crowling were her name. I remember that one as well. Two peas in a pod they were. And forever lookin' after each other's interests. It'd have taken a game jack-me-hearty to come on strong with either one without keepin' a wary weather eye out for t'other. Comely as any two wenches you'd see together in y' lifetime. And that prick fish-head had them both. God rot him, but he was a lucky bastard.'

'Where is she now?'

'Who?'

'The other redhead, for God's sake!'

'Crowling? If she's still in the colony she's workin' for Simeon Lord. Down at that hostel where he and those other thievin' ex-felons, Kable and Underwood, put up the crews of their sealers and whalers.'

'What d'you mean, if she's still in the colony?' Barlester's glass of brandy had almost turned over between his fingers. If he had not emptied it moments before, more liquid would have spilt into his lap than the thin trickle that was staining his breeches.

'Lord lets any of the foreign crews that he does business with bed down there. And I've heard he only keeps Crowling on a loose rein. Has done since she was assigned to him. If she hasn't already wangled herself a berth on one of those Yankee vessels that are always comin' and goin' I'll wager it won't be long before she does. Hey, steady on, old chap!'

Barlester had lurched to his feet, colliding with Chesterfield's legs and dislodging Suttling's grip on the back of the chair so that he fell forward and knocked his companion's chin on to his chest.

They were in the upstairs parlour of one of a number of the more comfortable hostelries above Sydney Cove where Barlester stayed on his regular visits to town.

By the time he reached the courtyard he realised that he was in poor shape to travel anywhere that evening. But this did not stop him from seriously contemplating choking the landlord for daring to caution him on the folly of setting out for home at that hour in such weather.

'It be as black as the inside of the belly of the Lincolnshire Ox out there, y'lordship. Blacker even. Ye'd be lucky to reach the toll-bar at Ultimo without breakin' y'neck. You wouldn't get a hundred paces past it without someone to light the way. And who could do that on a night like this?'

A flash of lightning above the rooftops behind the man's head gave credence to his assertion. And possibly saved his life.

When the landlord saw in his guest's face the turmoil that was besieging him, his jaw dropped and he quickly stepped out of range. 'But of course I'll get your horse now if that be your decision.'

'Wake me an hour before sunrise,' Barlester thundered. 'Not a moment later.' He turned on his heel and staggered towards the rear stairs. 'And have the horse saddled and ready to go.'

Only Barlester's hangover saved his horse. Several times the big man had to interrupt his headlong dash for home, and then dismount and stagger, with the horse in tow, to where he could support himself against a tree or a fence post, where he would vomit with such roaring fervour that anyone within hearing would believe that he was surely being torn apart by wild animals.

He need not have put himself through such torment. Jessica was long gone by that time. She had in fact been closer to him before he departed the inn.

Early in the evening she and Elizabeth had been assisted up a rope ladder slung over the side of a big three-masted schooner that was anchored in Neutral Bay on the north side of the harbour. At about the time Barlester reached Johnston's Creek the next morning, the schooner had hauled in anchor and was heading down harbour against a steady south-easter. She was the *Cobscook Bay* out of Portland, Maine, now en route to Calcutta via Batavia with a crew of fifteen, two female guests, and her holds crammed with sealskins.

When Barlester finally arrived home, Molly Clinger, blubbering and quaking behind raised forearms and spread fingers as she cowered beneath him in a corner of the kitchen, gave him the news he feared would greet him.

She told him how the woman from the previous weekend had arrived the morning before and had then spent most of the day in Henry Langsmith's quarters. And how shortly before nightfall she saw both of them walking in the gardens, and later near the dairy, so she assumed he was showing her around the grounds.

'They been drinkin', sir. Somethin' awful. 'Enry was still carryin' a bottle. Wicked t'see, it were. Shameless. They was clingin' t'each other like they had to just to stay on their feet. God help me, I said to meself then, that I wished you was 'ere to put a stop to it.'

She told him how not long after this she was surprised to see the woman and Jessica hurrying down the slope in front of the house towards the beach.

'I immediately went lookin' for 'Enry, sir. Honest I did. But I couldn't find him nowheres. By the time I got back to see what they was doin', they was on the beach an' gettin' into this boat with two men that I seen fishin' off the point most of the afternoon.'

She told him of finally locating Langsmith sleeping in the shed where Jessica had been placed when she first arrived.

'I had to get Albie to break the lock with a crowbar. Took him some time as well. We couldn't wake 'Enry at first. When we did he was like a madman. I never seen him worse. He knocked Albie down, an' this is what he done t'me. I can't see outta the eye at all. God help me. Albie saddled the bay mare for 'im and he rode off just on dusk. We thought he went to get you, but I s'pect he got lost in the dark. God knows where he be now. God knows where any of them be now.'

'There's been movement in Toulon,' Will Noling announced when he took his place at the mess-deck table on the lower gun deck of the *Victory*.

'Don't tell me they're comin' out at last?' someone muttered.

'They'll never come out,' someone else responded. 'We'll grow old and die before we see them sail.'

'Well, someone grew old and died before he saw them sail,' said Will.

'Who? Who died?'

'Admiral La Touche-Tréville. He's been replaced by Admiral Pierre Villeneuve.'

'Villeneuve? Never heard of him,' said Moth, the sailor whose 'Betty' would have been forgiven by many at the table for being glad he was at sea.

'Why would you have heard of him, Moth? He probably never called in on the Duck's Bum when you was a regular.'

'The expectation is that he'll break out as soon as the weather gives him the right cover,' said Will.

'Let's drink to that,' said Alley Gable, and raised his cup.

ELEVEN

Two shipwrecks—separated geographically by about two hundred miles, and chronologically by about two years—had a profound effect on the lives of Jessica Glider and Will Noling. Both wrecks were of a similar nature: collisions with hidden shoals that tore the ships to pieces in the dead of night. And with both, the first that most of those on board the vessels knew of their predicament was when they found themselves fighting for their lives in mountainous seas.

From the moment the weather-deck cabin of the *Cobscook Bay* disintegrated around Jessica and she found herself floundering in the ocean amidst shattered wreckage, until well into her fight for survival, she could not accurately determine which of her experiences were real and which were figments of her imagination.

During the voyage to Australia Angus Donwald had often helped pass the time by entertaining his women with tales of the sea. And although he added the customary fanciful embellishments that sailors' tales usually attract, his audience deduced that even the more unlikely were entwined with at least threads of the truth.

A number of times he told of shipwrecks and of the peculiar experiences of castaways, particularly those who had spent long periods in the sea. So Jessica knew something of the mind-jinking and hallucinatory effects of prolonged immersion. But as with nightmares, the knowledge that they exist provides little comfort when a demon has you by the throat.

Moments after the collision Jessica found herself in suffocating darkness. She clawed free and fought for breath, gagging and spluttering on the jagged knife-edges of salt water that were scouring her throat and grinding into the back-alleys of her nose. My God, I'm drowning!

An age later she managed to gulp in some air. But in the next instant her breath was choked off by a blast of mind-crushing terror.

She could sense them, see them clearly in her mind's eye, feel them brush past her bare legs: sharks the shape and size of overturned boats converging on her out of the inky gloom, huge cruising submarine jaws crammed with rows of razor teeth.

If she could have screamed she would have. But the intensity of her fear was as effective as a gag.

She was a steeplejack the moment after stepping into space; the moment of trying to turn back; the moment of embracing an empty bundle of air. She was a chimney-sweep with eyes, ears, nose and throat clogged with acrid soot, the moment after tripping and executing a tumbling head-first dive into the top of a smokestack. She was lost. Lost!

And then a cry found her, the sound of a frightened child. 'Is anyone there?'

Thank God! Her chest rose and fell.

'Yes,' she called out. 'I'm here. I'm here.' Again the sound of a frightened child. In that instant she realised the cry had been her own. She recoiled as if she had been slapped in the face. And a moment later she burst out crying.

'I'm sorry. Sorry,' she found herself saying, God knows why. And then screamed, 'Liz! Liz! Where are you? Liz! Liz! Anybody! Can you hear me?'

My God! My God! Nothing! Don't let her be dead. Please! Don't let her be dead. 'Liz! Liz!'

She clutched desperately around her trying to take hold of pieces of debris she recalled swirling about her earlier. But her hands and arms smacked against empty water.

She burst out crying again, and perhaps would have continued to cry had she not been distracted by the ribbons of bright blue–green phosphorescence trailing from the tips of her fingers and from her toes.

What is this? What are these fires that flare

as I move? Am I dead? An instant later they disappeared.

She fought desperately to clear her mind. Am I hurt? Injured? She did not think so, but was not certain, being unable for more than a fleeting moment either to keep her head out of the water or to use her hands to examine herself for pain.

This is ridiculous, she suddenly decided. So what if I'm injured? So what if I drown? To drown would be to end it. Peacefully. Angus said so. The best way to die. That's why sailors never learn to swim.

'Can you swim?' Liz had asked him.

'Yes,' he'd replied. 'My bad luck!'

My bad luck too, Jessie told herself as she felt herself riding up the leading edge of a huge wave. Up, up, up. She held her breath. Will and I and most of the Lowfoley brats could all swim like fish, having Pike's Hole so close to the village. Up, up, up.

She crested the wave and released her breath as she sensed it rolling on past her with a minimum of broken wash; the ridge of a fluid hill. And then she felt herself beginning to slide down its trailing edge. Down, down, down.

It was the local custom for kids, swimming in Pike's Hole. Down, down, down. Despite the threats of the adults. A custom's a custom. Like the threats. Half meant. Half believed. Down, down, down.

She felt herself reach the trough and after what

seemed an age begin to rise again. Up, up, up. She again held her breath. My God! She began to contemplate the sheer enormity of the forces that held her in their grip. How far was the ocean floor beneath her? One hundred yards? Two? A mile? Two miles? My God!

From the moment she found herself in the water she had been trying desperately to keep her head above it. When she had thrashed about trying to grab hold of something—anything—it was in response to Angus's advice that if ever they found themselves in that situation to find something to cling to. 'Anything that floats will help keep your head above water.'

'You can trap air in your clothes when they're wet,' he had also told them. 'A shirt makes a good float.'

And he was right. All she was wearing was a man's cotton shirt she had been given as a night-dress, and with a minimum of effort she found she could trap air within the arms and body of the garment as it ballooned about her.

What direction am I being driven, she wondered again. She forced herself to recall details from when she and Elizabeth were on the upper deck earlier in the evening. The moon had been in the east, she decided. Due east. It was low on the horizon off the starboard beam. And the sea? Which way was the sea running? From behind. From the south. She remembered her exhilaration when the schooner's stern had been lifted high a number of times so that it rode the huge waves like a surfing dolphin. Then I'm being driven north, she decided. I'll have to make my way across the waves to the west. She began to pull at the water with a flattened hand and a curved left arm.

By trial and error she found that she could make the least tiring progress by floating on her back and propelling herself along with rhythmic, frog-like kicks beneath the surface.

Perhaps the sea wasn't coming from dead astern, she mused at one point, trying to remember the exact direction. I seem to recall it coming more from the starboard quarter. In that case I could be heading towards the land anyway.

At some stage after she had begun to make an effort to influence the direction she was heading, the moon suddenly appeared high in the sky. If her directions were correct, it was still to the east of her. It soon disappeared again, but a glow remained to track its course behind thin cloud cover. She was relieved to note that over a period it appeared to be continuing its ascent, confirming her reckoning on direction. At the same time it was disconcerting to note that the sea was becoming increasingly choppy and that to the east regular bursts of lightning revealed the presence of great bundles of clouds.

A short time later the glow from the moon began to rapidly diminish and finally it disappeared altogether and she was forced to rely entirely on what she believed was the direction of the sea to determine her course. Despite her small misgivings on whether survival was worth the effort, and a fatalistic buffer that she did not really care much one way or the other, she found herself trying to suppress a rising anxiety about the approaching storm. If it arrived amidst a strengthening wind, the waves could come from any direction, she decided. She could be turned around and expend her energies heading up or down the coast. Or even out to sea!

As the storm drew closer, it was heralded by almost continuous flashes of lightning and by swirling changes of wind direction. In the bursts of flaring light she saw that flecks of foam were peeling off the crests of the waves and spearing like illuminated arrowheads across the surface of the water.

Within fifteen minutes rain began to fall and the crests of the waves themselves were detaching and slapping her in the face. Fifteen minutes later the mix of foam, seawater and rain was so dense, and the wave troughs so steep, she doubted she could survive another fifteen.

The sleeves and body of her shirt were still ballooning about her in the water and, unaided, were trapping good pockets of air. With all of her resources directed at keeping her head above water, she would have had no chance of keeping air in the shirt had this not been the case.

Earlier, perhaps to conserve energy, she had spoken aloud only on occasions. Now she found herself shouting. And although to shout was to swallow water, and on occasions to cough and choke and expend a wealth of energy, she continued to shout. Perhaps to test if she were still alive.

She shouted at the rain and she shouted at the sea. At times she cried out to Elizabeth, asking if she were safe; and at times she called out to Will, asking him the same. And at other times she cried out for one, or the other, or both, to help her. Finally she simply screamed into the teeth of the gale and cursed her misfortune, and cursed Rory Fitzparsons and Garth Barlester.

Barlester in particular she cursed with such a shaking vehemence that had anyone been in a position to hear her, they would surely have been concerned for the condition of her heart, and her larynx.

Finally her shouting subsided and for a long time she remained silent. And then she suddenly cried out, 'My legs, Liz. I'm too tired. I can't keep going.'

And Liz replied close to her ear, 'Keep your back to the wind.'

'What?'

'Keep your back to the wind.'

'I can't kick any more.'

'Don't kick.'

'I can't breathe.'

'Don't breathe.'

And then later, when the sea had the anger of wild surf she cried, 'We're drowning, Liz.'

'No we're not. We won't drown. We be survivors, you an' me.'

Her response was lost as the ferocity of the rain suddenly increased with the roar of a giant waterfall. Huge bullets of water pelted into the ocean with a force that exploded fragments of liquid shrapnel back into the air above the collision points. The surface immediately responded as if it had been draped in a chainmail blanket. Within seconds the spray and froth were gone, and within minutes the waves had subsided to a gentle undulation.

She was uncertain how long the rain lasted—she thought perhaps for more than half an hour—and for half of that time it was a deluge: the incessant roar that beat into submission all opposition from wind and wave.

She looked for Elizabeth but she was nowhere to be seen. She was too exhausted to call out. All she could manage was to press her head back into the water and drift with her nose and mouth gulping air that was now charged with pellets of fresh water but was free of the buckets of brine that had assailed her earlier.

When the rain stopped she managed to refill her shirt with air. The glow of the moon had returned. And what little sea was running appeared to be still moving towards the north-west. She wondered how far away the coast lay, behind that eerie opaque gloom. Had she lost or gained distance? Had she expended too much energy? Her limbs were leaden. Liz's would be the same. She looked for her again. 'Where are you, Liz?' she called out, and immediately was engulfed by uncertainty. 'Liz?' she queried, as if testing the sound of the word.

'Liz!' she called out again. 'Liz!'

During the hours that followed she caught herself drifting in and out of a dreamlike state and her efforts to keep a clear head were in vain.

Throughout that night and long into the following day she was often unable to determine what was real and what was not. But she was sure about one event: the incident that almost killed her was the incident that almost certainly saved her life.

It happened not long after the rain stopped. She was drifting, too tired to propel herself, too tired to risk any movement that could cause her to fight again to keep her face above the surface.

Something brushed her arm. Instinctively she pulled away, but in that instant realised that it was not a curious shark or other threat from the deep, but only a piece of wood. She reached out and grasped a small branch. There were leaves still attached, heavy with water. She broke one and put it to her nose. Nothing. Not a hint of a smell. Long dead foliage. She brushed past another branch, and another, and then a cluster of reeds.

'What's happening?' she cried out, a touch of panic in her voice.

'Floating debris,' Liz replied, close by. 'Probably from a river.'

The water was now thick with foliage: bushes, vines, leaves and grass.

'I don't like it,' she said. 'I don't like the feel of it.'

Liz replied that she did not like the feel of it either. But if there were large enough branches, perhaps even logs . . .

Whatever it was, it brushed past her ribs and caught in her shirt. And in catching the shirt, trapped her in a tightening vice. And it happened so slowly and with such gentle force she was unaware of the danger until it had her tightly in its grasp. It rolled slightly in the swell and she felt its weight. What's happening! She sensed huge invisible arms probing the darkness around her.

And then it bore down on her, slowly, inexorably driving her head beneath the surface. My God!

She kicked out. Her shin cracked against something solid. Timber. A tree, stripped of bark and foliage. 'Liz! Help me. Help me!'

'Get out of the shirt!' demanded a powerful male voice. 'Quick. Slip it over your head.'

Will! She could feel his strong hands helping as she fought to extract herself. She managed to drag the garment over her head and free of her shoulders but a tangle of material still trapped her arms. She then wrenched one wrist free and tore the shirt away completely, stripping it from where it was entangled with both of her arms.

Her head broke the surface. 'Are you all right?' he cried out.

'Yes.' She coughed to clear her throat and searched for his face in the gloom. 'Yes, I think so.' She couldn't quite make him out, but he was close. She could feel his hands under her forearms, lifting her towards the shadow towering above her. 'Is it a log?'

'Climb on to it. Quickly.'

Jessica was not so certain. 'It might catch me again.'

Dawn brought with it a grey day, a warm damp day devoid of colour. A heavy fog had descended during the night and now bathed the sea and its vegetable flotsam and animal jetsam in a murky diffused light.

She woke with a start and found herself alone and firmly entwined in a web of dread.

'Will!' she cried out. 'Will!'

She looked about her fearfully, trying to probe holes in the veils of mist that surrounded her.

'Will! Where are you? I forgot to tell you about Liz. Where are you?'

The sun was completely hidden and her range of view was so restricted and the swell so slight, she could no longer determine the direction of the sea. She was lost. And weary. Her arms, her legs, her eyelids could have been crafted from lead.

She next awoke with the roar of surf in her ears. The log heeled. She turned and grasped a limb for support. An instant later the log was lifted high on a breaking wave and began to slide down into the trough. As it gathered momentum she clung on for dear life. Moments later it burst clear of the shrouds of mist and charged towards a rocky shoreline less than three hundred yards away.

Huge boulders towered on both sides of her and rose like haystacks from the watery field ahead. With the crash of a lightning bolt the leading branches suddenly struck bottom. Timber snapped and splintered. The log stood on end and pitched forward. Jessica screamed and was speared across the water as if hurled from a catapult.

She plunged safely into waist-deep water. But the moment she came to her feet she was knocked over by the churning wash of the breaking wave. And for an age she tumbled along the stony bottom with her arms and legs flailing above and around her in the grip of a seething cauldron.

As soon as she was able to fight her way back on to her feet she was immediately knocked over again by a following wave and subjected to the same treatment. Three more times she was forced to endure this punishment before she finally staggered, bruised and bleeding, from the surf and collapsed exhausted on a sandy beach.

She lay hugging the fine dry sand for nearly an hour before she could gather enough strength to rise. When she did she rigorously scanned the waterline to the north and south, and then stared out to sea past the tumbling breakers and the endlessly dissolving spectrums of spray.

'Liz,' she mouthed a number of times, and perhaps 'Will.' But her words were softly uttered, if at all, and lost beneath the rumble of the surf.

Fresh water was her most pressing need. This reality was pressed home rudely when she tried to run her tongue over her lips. Her mouth could have been crammed with cotton waste.

Behind the blanket of low scrub that flanked the beach there appeared to be higher country to the north than she could see to the south. At a point she estimated was no more than five or six miles away, a low ridge swept down to the coast terminating in a high bluff that fell away steeply to the sea in stepped shelves of rock.

On the assumption that the lumpier the topography, the better were her chances of finding a stream, she set off in that direction, trusting she would not have to negotiate the ridge before she had quenched her thirst. She hoped she would reach there before nightfall and guessed she had less than three hours.

As she set off she admitted to herself that even if she had seen higher country to the south, she would probably have still headed north. It was unlikely that any of the dangers she might encounter ahead of her would rival the ones she had left behind. Or so she hoped.

Luckily, she found fresh water well before the ridge. When less than halfway to her destination she encountered a shallow stream crossing the beach amidst a scattering of low boulders.

Only when she stumbled forward on unsteady limbs, sank to her knees and spread herself flat on the sand so that she could place her lips directly into the water, did she realise the depth of her fatigue and how unlikely had been her chances of reaching the ridge before nightfall, if at all. Even as she was drinking she had to fight to prevent herself from fainting and perhaps drowning in the few inches of water beneath her face. An observer standing over her would have seen shallow vibrations passing through her body. From where they seemed to originate in the water that rippled across her fingertips the tremors passed up through her braced arms, across her shoulders and down her back. From the twin dimples riding below her waistline they rose over the curve of her buttocks and quivered down the long spread of her legs into the smooth arches of her feet, and finally out to the very tips of her toes.

They did not cease the entire time she was drinking. Only after she finally pushed herself clear of the stream and rolled over squarely on to her back, and lay there for an age gasping for breath, did they gradually diminish and finally disappear.

She spent the night huddled between the boulders and partly covered by a pile of sand. She was cold and hungry; but she was so exhausted that, from time to time, she did sleep soundly.

She awoke as the sun was climbing out of the ocean. Although her limbs were riddled with localised aches and pains that had her wincing, and on occasions crying out aloud whenever she overtaxed one of them, she did feel refreshed.

The sunlight, as weak as it was, provided such wonderful relief to her frozen extremities that her eyes immediately swam with tears of gratitude as she gave thanks to a god she no longer believed in.

Food had now become her most pressing need, and the shelves of rock beneath the bluff up ahead seemed to be a likely refuge for shellfish and crabs. Seaweed, even, she told herself as she set off. I'll eat seaweed if that's all there is.

She made her way determinedly along the compacted sand at the water's edge as the sun continued to climb away from the ocean. Shallow waves only inches high swept the way in front of her and occasionally bathed her feet and ankles in a cool frothy wash. A low mist, glowing fluorescent-white in the early morning light, extended along the entire length of the beach ahead of her. A number of times she turned and looked out to sea but she could keep her gaze on the broken water of the surf for only brief intervals, so intense was the rippling glare; patches of the surface sparkled as if strewn with tiny magnesium flares.

If she had noticed the puffs of pale smoke on the skyline past the bluff, she chose to ignore them, along with the pleasant aroma of burning eucalyptus that occasionally drifted over her.

TWELVE

When she saw them coming, Jessica was in the open, halfway down the slope of a high dune that flanked the beach. There was nowhere she could hide. She knew that to try and escape back up the steep slope with her feet ploughing knee-deep furrows in the unstable sand would be to risk living the nightmare of her legs having suddenly turned to lead.

Having recently had her fill of terrors—both real and imaginary—she stayed and watched, slumping in an outward reflection of the depth of her resignation; her breath expelled in a rush, her shoulders dropped and one leg bent forward as her weight settled back on the other.

From her elevated vantage point she missed nothing. When she first saw them they were still far enough away for her to perhaps believe that a strange pale animal was being pursued along the beach towards her by a group of darker animals; a herbivore perhaps, that having been cut from the herd by a pack of carnivores was now at the point of being run down by them.

At a greater distance she may have believed she was watching a deer being pursued by wolves; or a gazelle by lions; or even a kangaroo by the local variety of wolves or jackals whose mournful howls she had heard in Sydney. When she had been curled up at night in Barlester's house nursing injuries, both physical and mental, their melancholy cries had lifted the fine hairs on the back of her neck and provided a fitting accompaniment to her state of mind.

But the creatures she was now observing were soon close enough for her to recognise that although the hunted and the hunters were of different colouring, they were of the same species, and moved in a way that in her experience was unique among all of the creatures of the earth. For they were loping along on two legs, not four, and although she was aware that a kangaroo travelled on its hind legs, none of these creatures was hopping along like some giant frog, as she erroneously imagined a kangaroo would do.

These creatures were definitely men. All of them. Of course she had assumed as much from the moment she first noticed them. She would have preferred they had been anything but. So, as they drew closer, she had willed in vain that they prove to be something different. Even wolves. For there was something decidedly more sinister in the sight of a pack of men pursuing one of their own number than in any equivalent she could imagine in the animal kingdom.

They caught up with their quarry at a place where a number of shallow tidal streams crossed the beach close to the base of the dune on which she was standing.

By then she could see they were naked. All of them. Including the white man, who for some reason seemed in comparison to his pursuers to be more disadvantaged by this. Certainly more vulnerable. As if he was not vulnerable enough, she mused, his being outnumbered six—no seven, eight—to one.

One of them had run past him and was mocking his stumbling gait. It was their skin-colour, she decided, perhaps by way of distraction. Another had slowed temporarily to snatch up a club-like length of driftwood from the high-tide line. Naked blacks have a more natural appearance in the open. Naked whites are obviously abroad in alien territory. Unnatural. Definitely vulnerable. Like naked birds.

Her gaze for a moment dropped to her own nakedness. These breasts are hardly white, she noted sardonically, despite the crippling dread spreading within her. Beneath a thin film of perspiration and a scattering of more lumpy beads of moisture, her skin was a blotchy pink. Burnt tissue she could no longer sense; the former tingling discomfort was now at a level well below the threshold where her physical sensors were being activated.

When she raised her gaze she saw that another of the man's pursuers had picked up a piece of driftwood. All of them were now either running alongside him or had moved on ahead.

He stumbled and nearly fell as he entered one of the streams that crossed the beach, and then slowed abruptly. Two of the leaders immediately circled back around him.

As he stepped out of the stream he picked up his pace for a few strides but soon slowed again to little more than a stumbling trot. Either he no longer had the strength to continue his flight, she decided, or the futility of what he was doing had finally sunk home.

More of them began to circle him. Most were now armed with driftwood clubs. She could hear them laughing and calling out to each other. At the edge of the next stream he stopped moving altogether and stood with his head thrown back looking up at the sky.

As far as she could tell, none of them had seen her. She momentarily glanced back towards the crest of the dune and regretted not making an attempt to retrace her steps earlier. Whether or not they would have noticed her before was uncertain. But she had no doubts that any movement now would attract their attention.

Only when they began to kill him did they seem fearful of him. The tall man who had been the first to pick up the driftwood delivered the first blow. Raising the club over his shoulder, he danced in behind the man and struck him on the back of the head with such force that the makeshift weapon snapped in two.

Jessica's jaw dropped open. A moment after the man pitched forward the sound of the blow reached her and she was swept with such a cold wave of shock she would have been excused for assuming that the fine film of perspiration that cloaked her had suddenly turned to ice.

All the pursuers, including the man who delivered the blow, leapt backwards a few strides, as if they feared their victim would in some miraculous way turn on them and exact revenge. This was hardly likely, for he was sprawled face-down and motionless, with his head and shoulders immersed in the shallow stream.

Even so, when his attacker next approached him brandishing a new club he had snatched from one of the others, he did so warily. With his neck craned as if to give him a clearer view of his target, and moving in what might have been a parody of a ground bird, he crept towards his victim for a few strides before suddenly dashing forward and landing another blow across the back of his head. Almost in the same instant he leapt back out of range again—but of what, was a mystery.

Others then followed the attacker's lead and

danced in to land blows on the victim's body before scurrying away. Only after they had engaged in this activity for some minutes did they appear to relax and approach his inert form without any sign of fear. Probably because he would no longer resemble anything that had ever been capable of retaliation, she decided. Now he was simply a pale lump lying on a pale beach. A mound of clay. A piece of driftwood. Perhaps part of a stranded sea creature. Long dead and harmless.

Curiously, when she realised that one of the men had turned away from the body and was looking directly at her, she felt no alarm. For this action seemed simply the continuation of the macabre play she was watching. The opening scene of the next act. An inevitability.

Nor, for some reason, was she surprised that this man made no immediate attempt to alert his companions. It seemed appropriate that he simply stand there and stare at her, and that she in turn remain unmoving and stare back, as if both he and she—two players waiting in the wings—should for a moment remain immobile, while those out on stage moved as the sea behind them, and the birds above them continued to move in time with the progress of the tragedy. For the importance of the role of the players in the wings was surely worthy of a few moments' grace.

It was only after the man finally directed his companions' attention to her that she realised she was no longer standing on the slope of the dune but lying back against it, and probably had been for some time.

She pressed herself back into the sand as they made their way warily up the slope towards her.

A detached calm had descended on her. And she found herself wondering, abstractedly, that if she had a pistol, what would she now do with it? Would she use it to try and defend herself? Perhaps scare them off by shooting one of them? Or would she turn it on herself?

A knife even? Would she wave it at them? Entertain them for a few moments before they rushed at her en masse? Or would she plunge it into her own chest? Save herself from whatever terrors they had in store for her before they despatched her as they had despatched that poor wretch down below.

As the events unfolded, at times she was swept with a curious impression that she was observing what was happening from a short distance away. From behind her left shoulder perhaps.

As they drew closer and were able to see her more clearly, they grew bolder. By the time they reached her they were moving quickly, almost running, with the dry sand squeaking in protest around each deep thrust of their feet. She braced herself as they stopped a few paces short of her and jostled each other for the best vantage.

They watched her in silence for a time moving

their heads slowly from side to side, with the soft tissue around their eyes crinkling from the squinting intensity of their observation and accentuating the broad flare of their nostrils.

They were younger than she had been expecting. Only two or three of them—including the tall man who struck the first blow on the beach—sported fully grown beards, along with a light crop of body hair on their chests, arms and legs. And, except that some of them were wearing narrow belts of a coarse fibrous material from which hung assorted loops of twine and small netting bags, they were all completely naked. Their genitals hung like dried plums beneath the tight tangle of their pubic hair.

The first to move closer was the tall man. Jessica's sense of detachment disintegrated the moment he reached out a hand towards her face, and she began to tremble. As he took a strand of her hair between his fingers and tugged on it she sucked in her breath through clenched teeth.

His action seemed to be a signal for them all to move in. Hands reached out and touched her. Lightly, mainly, but at times inquisitively, probing and squeezing. And as they observed the colour of her hair and eyes, the texture of her skin, the conformation of her shoulders and breasts, they began to chatter among themselves. Passing comment? Criticising?

Once or twice she felt certain she was being asked a question. She was tempted to speak but was afraid her voice would open a breach that would render her defenceless. Until now, she had not been harmed. To speak would be to change what she had been doing, and perhaps change what they were doing. To speak could be to solicit harm. To do anything could be to do a last thing.

They spent a considerable time examining the newly healed scars on her shoulders and back, pressing her forward away from the sand so they could trace the extent of the damage. She sensed from their murmurs that they were impressed.

Occasionally one or other of her examiners would release a short, clipped chuckle, or an obvious exclamation. At one point her concern escalated when their attention was drawn to her pubic area. As they gently but firmly forced her legs apart and leant forward to examine her closely, her gaze made a swift circuit of the nearest dried plums. But her examiners' interests seemed more academic than lascivious and appeared to be centred more on the colouring and texture of her hair than on the genitals themselves. When a hand reached over her mound and she quickly intercepted it before a greater level of intimacy was established, her action was met by startled laughter rather than by complaint or anger from either the perpetrator or the witnesses.

By the time their attention moved on to her legs and feet, and finally back to her face, her level of preparedness had slipped a notch and assumed an archer's détente; she remained on guard, but allowed some of the tension to ease from the previously singing fibres stretching through the core of her body. However, despite the apparent lack of aggression in these men, she was well aware that she was firmly in their charge and that they were the same people who only a short time before had bludgeoned someone to death for no discernible reason other than perhaps because he was white. So she did not relax entirely during these events but simply allowed her body for the moment to breathe more freely, and her consciousness to settle back from remaining at full alert and suffering the consequences of its draining effect.

But any respite she did experience was short lived. When her attention was elsewhere, the tall man suddenly lifted one of her hands and slipped a noose of thick twine over her wrist. He then barked a command at the others and they reached down and pulled her to her feet. A few moments later she was being led down the slope like an animal on a leash.

They took her across the beach to where the shallow wash made for easier travel, skirting well clear of the motionless form of the dead man. She noticed that all of them except her captor kept their eyes away from the body, or cast only furtive glances in its direction when they passed by at the closest point, as if they were perhaps ashamed of what they had done. She, too, only looked across at the body for a moment in an attempt to see if she recognised the man. But his face was turned from her and fully immersed in the stream.

While she had been adrift in the ocean she had made estimates of how far the schooner had travelled. They had been sailing for almost four days pushed along by a steady south-easter. On the assumption they were making between five and ten knots, she calculated she would now be anywhere between five hundred and one thousand miles north of Sydney.

From what she had heard there should be no whites that far north, so she assumed the dead man had come from the schooner. And if she and one other person had made it safely ashore, there was every chance that more had survived.

As they moved along the beach, her eyes continually swept the rocky shallows and regularly skipped out past the crash of the breakers to probe the broad blue band beneath the horizon.

They had not gone far when they were joined by a number of boys carrying spears that they handed to the men. The boys then trailed along behind, exchanging excited bursts of conversation with some of those around her. Shortly afterwards, up ahead she noticed wispy columns of pale smoke snaking into the sky from within the blanket of green–grey scrub behind the beach.

Shading her eyes against the smoky red glare of the setting sun, Jessica estimated that their camp extended along the bank of the narrow stream for over three hundred yards. The dwellings consisted mainly of simple brush and bark lean-tos, either independently supported on a flimsy framework of crossed saplings, or propped against the trunks of trees and against boulders that had fallen from the rocky shelf that marked the border between the grass-covered bank and the low wooded ridge that climbed away darkly to the south-west of the dunes.

As she had been expecting, what appeared to be the entire population of the camp gathered to observe her, abandoning whatever was previously occupying them. Cooking mainly, she decided; enticing aromas drifted out from fires where the charred carcasses of small mammals or birds and the detached limbs of larger animals were roasting in the coals.

Her stomach growled and she was swept with hunger pangs that caused her head to swim suddenly and her knees almost to buckle. She recovered quickly. But only an extreme effort in deference to propriety prevented her from giving life to a sudden fantasy of breaking free, snatching a hunk of flesh from the coals and devouring as much as she could before she was apprehended.

Her stomach protested noisily at her inaction and she was momentarily shamed by the realisation that when confronting a host of dangers including some she dared not even think about, her only physical reaction to her circumstance was her maintenance of proper behaviour.

Children showed the most interest in her, laughing shrilly and jostling each other for the best position to see her as they ran beside the men. Of the older people of both sexes, only the women seemed to view her with signs of hostility, their expressions ranging from sullen curiosity to obvious belligerence. Some of them met her gaze momentarily and showed her their teeth. Others called out to her and to the men and waved their hands at her in gestures that obviously signalled for her to begone, or for the men to hunt her away. Perhaps worse.

Her hunger pangs were suddenly displaced by a deeper, more far-reaching discomfort, as if an invisible knife had entered her abdomen. I don't want them to kill me, she decided. I want to live.

And immediately she was besieged by conflicting emotions. Why should she want to survive? The utter hopelessness and wretchedness of her recent experiences, and the likelihood of a continuation of similar or worse treatment at the hands of these people should be more than enough reason to welcome an end to her suffering. To die would be to escape.

Liz may have been right. We could be survivors. And surviving could be a curse!

Thoughts of Elizabeth immersed her in guilt. How could she have completely forgotten about her companion's plight? Even for a moment! Where was she? Was she drowned? Did she reach shore only to be killed by these people? Liz! Liz! Where are you? Are you safe? I need you now. Are you here somewhere? Her gaze swept the mass of dark faces that pressed in on her.

All the people seemed to be naked except that some wore narrow belts made from the same material she had seen before. She had been told that the natives sometimes wore capes of animal skins to protect themselves from the cold, but none was evident here. Perhaps these people didn't feel the cold.

Not that this is what I would call cold, she observed defiantly, prompted by memories of colder times. And instantly she felt a prickle of goose bumps that gave lie to her bravado. She then shook for a time in the grip of a long, trembling shudder.

She noticed that although there were distinct physical similarities with most of the natives, there were differences. Broad noses were common but were not exclusive; some of the people had noses as narrow as her own. And whereas most were slimly built with long legs and short torsos, some were thickset with longer torsos and shorter legs. The older men also sported a variety of body hair from thick pelts to fine bristles. Some were bald.

A similar mix of shapes and sizes would be evident on any night at the Sir Francis Drake in Lowfoley, she concluded, her gaze passing over the well-rounded paunches on a number of the older men. Body shapes. Perhaps even personalities. She could see familiar stances and expressions. Definite counterparts to people whose ways she was familiar with. Gaunty Farlie and his cronies, for instance. Slouching, and observing her through half-closed eyes. Swearing. Sniggering. Taunting her with lurid suggestions. She shuddered.

And they aren't black. Least not all of them. Not black black. But some of them couldn't be much blacker, she conceded, as her eyes momentarily settled on the slim back of the man who was leading her. He was coated by a fine film of perspiration, and the sheen on a wet lump of coal immediately sprang to her mind.

But some had skin that was definitely of a lighter shade. And one pretty girl whom she estimated to be about thirteen, and whose face and brilliant smile she had noticed peeking at her through the press of bodies, was the colour of deeply polished mahogany. She could see her again now, moving with her, still smiling. So she smiled back, amazing herself that she was able to even sense, let alone transmit, a sign of anything but utter despair.

As she returned her attention to her captor she found herself in idle contemplation of what the girl's prospects would be if their roles were reversed, and she, the youngster, was being paraded naked past the locals at the Drake. Before she had hardly begun to create the image in her mind's eye she was again gripped by a rippling shudder. God save us all!

She was finally brought to a halt before a small group of older people seated outside a more substantial lean-to than any she had noticed elsewhere. The group consisted of elderly men of whom the oldest and most wizened—a thin, bald man she estimated could be in his seventies or eighties—appeared from the way the others treated him to be their leader.

The moment they arrived, her captor pulled her forward roughly with the cord attached to her wrist, and placing a hand on the top of her head, forced her to sit directly in front of the old man.

His name was Mungilong, considered by most of his clan to be their wisest elder. For a time he spoke only with those who had brought her and seemed to pay her no attention at all. The sun was directly in her eyes and her head had begun to ache. She did not wish to risk closing her eyes so she lowered her gaze to where her dusty toes were partly buried in the soil between the spread of her knees Other than to wave away an occasional fly from her face she remained without moving, with only part of her attention directed at the speakers, whose conversation seemed to be riding the rise and fall of a drumming sensation that she recognised as the relentless song of cicadas. The undulation was perfectly attuned to the intensity of the ache in the centre of her forehead.

When she began to believe that she may not have even been the subject of their conversation, the old man finally turned and spoke directly to her.

She raised her head and watched him closely. When he stopped speaking and was apparently waiting for a reply, she offered, 'I don't know what you're sayin'.'

He looked at her blankly for a few moments and then spoke again.

'I'm sorry, but I don't know what you want.'

The man who had placed the twine on her wrist turned around and without any warning struck her full in the face with a sweep of his open hand. The force of the blow knocked her on to her back and scattered those sitting immediately behind her.

Despite the unexpectedness of the assault, she instinctively sat up again so that she could better protect herself. But her assailant had already turned away and was speaking again with the old man.

Still fearful of being subjected to a repeat performance, she slipped the loop of twine from her wrist and moved in behind some of the others. At least now she was out of his reach. She knew he could attack her again, of course, but at least not without warning. Cold comfort, she mused, but for how long now has it been any different?

With her face smarting and her head ringing from the blow, she placed the flat of a trembling hand against her lip and examined the smear of

330

blood that came away on her fingers.

She became aware of a low murmur rippling through the onlookers. Most of those who had been sitting beside and behind her had stood up. And as a result she found herself surrounded by a forest of legs that allowed children, who until then had been held back by the press of bodies, to stalk closer to her. Some of them reached out and began to pull her hair.

But she made no attempt to fend off the outstretched hands. For the bulk of her attention was still directed at examining the abrasions in and around her mouth. The sharp tugs to her scalp simply served to fan a smouldering sense of outrage that was now being stoked by escalating discomfort.

The human cavern in which she was entombed had begun to stifle her. The odour of sweat, rancid grease and rotting fish, that up until now she had successfully managed to disregard—mainly because she was uncertain of her own contribution to the mix—pressed in on her in a concentration that threatened to choke her. Rivulets of sweat began to gather at the dusty base of her throat and snake down on to her breasts. Her headache was now a glowing poker that had worked its way in behind one of her eyes.

But as her breath became laboured and her head began to spin, it was the flickering sunlight that speared at her through the press of bodies that troubled her the most. Memories of intense, thinly sliced pain passing between the vertical planks of a slab shed.

Why did he flog me? I didn't do anythin'.

You don't 'ave t'do anythin' with this one, lass. Molly reminded her from somewhere back behind her. Back down the beach. Behind the waves. *He 'ad ye flogged, 'cos that be in 'is nature ... 'Cos that be in 'is nature ... In 'is nature.*

It would have been difficult to determine which of her torments was the trigger. Perhaps it was the teeth-jarring screams of the children who had managed somehow to place their open mouths against the very centre of her brain; or perhaps it was the simultaneous jolt her head received from each accompanying tug to her scalp.

A woman gave the alarm, screaming out a shrill warning. The group standing adjacent to Jessica were so surprised by this outburst—the sudden release of an almighty squawk that Jessica would later, in recall, associate with the teeth-jarring cry of a white cockatoo—that they leapt and stumbled aside to reveal that the strange white woman had risen to her feet. And as if perhaps seeking to play a more active role in the proceedings, she was advancing on the man who had struck her.

They stood and watched as if transfixed, perhaps more from shock at her audacity than from fear of her. But whether or not she intended to exact retribution on her attacker was never determined. Or for that matter, whether her fierce determination was more globally oriented:

whether it suggested she intended to try and simply walk away—regardless of the consequences—out of their lives forever, and away from anyone who might harm her.

She had advanced no more than two or three paces before her knees slowly buckled and she sank to the ground. After a few moments, during which she seemed to contemplate a spot somewhere above the heads of Mungilong and the elders, her eyes rolled back and she fell sideways in a dead faint.

Jessica sensed the blow coming before it landed. She threw herself to one side and the shaft of the digging stick caught her on the shoulder rather than squarely on the top of the head. She rolled and came to her feet with her own digging stick clenched firmly in both hands, held as she had often held a similar length of wood when playing stick-ball as a child in Lowfoley.

'What were you tryin' to do?' she shouted at her assailant. 'Kill me? Were you tryin' to kill me?'

As she had guessed at the instant she realised her danger, her attacker was Nandiwa, wife of the man who had brought her to the camp. The young black woman, having failed to land the blow where she had intended, was now facing Jessica in a crouch that mirrored her opponent's stance.

'Well I don't care! Do you hear me, you black bitch? I don't care!'

The two women circled each other bent at the waist and waving their sticks backwards and forwards in front of them like a pair of amazons performing some pre-battle ritual.

'But I'll promise you somethin', I'll make you work for it. Do you hear me? I'll make you work for it!'

Nandiwa's intention of disposing of Jessica with one blow had been thwarted. So, with her confidence waning, she would have preferred to detach as quickly as possible from this confrontation and bide her time waiting for a better opportunity. But she could not simply turn and walk away without risking serious injury to herself—as others had discovered when they made the mistake of treating this newcomer as a normal captive woman.

Nandiwa clenched her teeth. They'd had slaves before to carry firewood and bark. And to dig for yams and gather shellfish and beach-worms. Captive women or outcasts from other tribes. Women who were too old or too ugly to be taken up as wives by the men. Not that any of them were as ugly as this one, with her funny colouring and blotchy skin and her strange smell. Or as useless. She could never even gather enough food to feed herself.

Although Jessica's gaze was at that moment primarily directed at Nandiwa, she kept a loose surveillance on the other women. A group of about five of the younger ones were standing watching the combatants from the edge of the beach. But perhaps as a consequence of previous skirmishes, none of them seemed anxious to join their companion.

During those previous engagements Jessica had clearly demonstrated a particular abhorrence of being set upon by more than one. Whenever a second or third person lined up against her, her fury seemed to escalate proportionally. She would then hurtle herself at her assailants with such boundless determination, screaming and shouting and slashing at them with whatever weapons she could lay her hands on—sticks and stones and utensils crafted from both—that not only would she usually drive off her attackers, but also a good proportion of the spectators that had gathered to watch.

Nandiwa was obviously the leader of the younger women, but why she should have set herself up as her main antagonist, Jessica found bewildering.

Several times she had made what she believed were friendly overtures to the woman, only to be met by furious gestures of resentment and belligerence.

What was particularly worrying for her as they circled each other now, was that she knew that her own defences were weakening. With each new day her strength was diminishing. The diet of the few shellfish she had been managing to collect from the more easily accessible division of sea and land was inadequate, particularly during the last few days when a heavy swell had been running. And other than a few fatty morsels of possum or kangaroo flesh—or more often the grease from one or the other soaked in a wad of paperbark—that the children would sometimes bring to her bower of plaited casuarina branches on the fringe of the camp, she was receiving no worthwhile nourishment.

Try as she might to take on her proper share of food-gathering, she was almost completely unsuccessful. The black women collected far more shellfish; and they had an uncanny knack of locating yams deep in the soil and of discovering the hiding places of small furry animals in burrows and logs and in nests of matted grass.

Her enthusiasm for delving into some of these places received an untimely but cautionary setback when one day she withdrew a large brown snake from a hollow log. Luckily the snake was as shocked as she was and beat a hasty looping exit in one direction as she made a similar scrambling retreat on a combination of her hands, buttocks and feet in the other, much to the amusement of all who witnessed the performance.

She was now in her third week with the natives and she was beginning to doubt that she would last another three. So as these and other thoughts spiralled somewhere behind her eyes as she confronted Nandiwa, her immediate resolve to survive at all costs began to wane.

Had it not been for an excited shout from one

of the women standing in the background, she was at the point of straightening and turning away from her opponent and offering her an unprotected back as she walked away in disgust and resignation.

For Nandiwa the shout was the excuse she had been looking for to end the confrontation. Casting a quick glance behind her, she backed away a few strides from Jessica, before swinging around and walking across to the others. They were standing looking along the beach and shading their eyes against the mid-afternoon glare. Someone was coming. Strangers.

Other women began to hurry back in ones and twos from where they had been foraging along the rear of the beach. Then suddenly all of those who had gathered to watch turned away and began to run back towards the camp, a scuttling flock of women and children weaving through the shallow dunes in headlong retreat. And as they ran they began to wail. Jessica ran with them, and as the mewing cries of fear rose around her she found herself whimpering in sympathy.

By the time they reached the camp the men were moving out, bristling with spears, to form a cordon behind them.

There was no need for this level of concern, for there were only four strangers, two men and two women; tall thin people with the mark of long travel about them. And they had come in peace.

While their two women sat huddled together on the outskirts of the camp under the distrustful gaze of the women of the clan, the men held council with Mungilong and the elders.

As Mungilong examined the markings on Gunroi's message stick, Gunroi wondered if he could read anything at all in the whirls and shapes that old Gaidimi had placed there to help them obtain free passage through foreign lands. Or, as he had speculated on several occasions since setting out on his quest, would not any markings have sufficed? Not that it really mattered, he conceded, when Mungilong reverently handed him back the message stick and invited him to share the evening meal. If the function of the stick was simply to reveal peaceful intent and promote formal intercourse with the inhabitants of the regions through which they travelled, then the actual meaning of the markings—if they ever had any meaning other than in Gaidimi's eyes—was of minor importance.

What did assume a great importance on this particular occasion was the event that occurred while they were waiting for the meal to be prepared. For it was then that Mungilong, with other elders in tow, took his guests to the outskirts of the camp and showed them the strange white woman.

Jessica was sitting cross-legged in front of her shelter when the men approached. She held up a hand to shield her eyes against the setting sun as they stood and looked down at her. Her first reaction was one of surprise. When she had seen the newcomers from a distance as they entered the camp she had noticed that their leader was taller by far than any of the men in the clan, and he had walked with a bearing that suggested he had been much older than the man who now stood before her. His face was only lightly fleeced and she estimated that he was probably close to her own age. And his companion was younger still.

'Can she speak?' Gunroi asked.

Mungilong was not familiar with the stranger's language and, turning to face him, signalled a query with his curled fingers.

Gunroi repeated the question slowly and touched his tongue.

'No, she can only chatter like a magpie.'

'What is it that she has rubbed in her hair?' He touched his own.

'Nothing. That is its true colour.'

At this point Jessica stood up and the men stepped back so that they could see more of her.

'She's been nothing but trouble since she came,' said Mungilong. 'Trouble,' he repeated with his hand. He then chuckled. 'She has a temper. The women are afraid of her. Afraid of her temper. Afraid she will steal their husbands.' He again chuckled. 'They need not worry. Soon she will die. She does not know how to gather food.'

'Where is she from?'

'From across the water.' He swept his hand towards the ocean. 'Others were swept ashore with her. Men. They were lazy and tried to run away rather than work for their food, so the young men killed them.'

He stepped closer to Jessica and reached for her shoulder. For a moment it appeared she would duck away from it, but then chose to let it settle. He turned her around and showed the strangers her back. 'It was well that they died. They are cruel men on the other side of the water. Look how they treat their women.' He ran his fingers over her scars. She flinched when he touched the welt that Nandiwa had inflicted, and pulling herself free of his grip turned to face him.

'I'd appreciate your keepin' your hands to y'self.' She raised her jaw and locked her gaze with his for a moment before turning and looking closely at Gunroi.

'I think she does speak,' said Gunroi, touching his tongue again. 'Tell me,' he asked, leaning forward and looking down at her, 'are there white eagles in your land across the water? Large white eagles?'

'I don't know what you're sayin',' she replied, matching his gaze. 'But I can tell you somethin'. You have more of a way about you than anyone I've seen around here.'

That night the strangers camped about a mile along the beach and shortly after daybreak they continued their journey south. About that same time children in the camp reported that the strange white woman had disappeared.

THIRTEEN

When they first noticed that Jessica was following them they tried to hunt her away. Coranga in particular went to considerable lengths, assailing her with abuse and throwing sticks and stones at her. Curiously, it was Coranga's aggression that accelerated their acceptance of the strange woman.

Late on the second day that she was following them, one of Coranga's stones caught her a glancing blow on the rib-cage. For a time she was winded. But when she could respond, she screamed, snatched up a length of wood and raced at her assailant, brandishing the weapon and shouting her indignation.

Coranga was so startled by this turn of events she spun on her heel, dashed the hundred paces or so back to where the others were watching and ducked behind Gunroi.

'Go away,' he demanded, and waved the flat of a spear at her.

Jessica stood her ground and shouted her grievance, pointing first to where Coranga was crouching behind him and then to where a trickle of blood had gathered in a jagged cut below her left breast.

By rights he should slap her for her impertinence, he mused. But I doubt she knows any better. For a few seconds he was distracted by the contrasting colour of the blood and the paleness of her skin. The cut and the surrounding welt were the same colour as her lips. The same colour as her nipples. Her breasts were plump, he noted as she drew herself to her full height and continued to berate Coranga. He glanced across at his brother who flashed a smile at him. Standing beside him Mori had a hand clamped tightly over her mouth.

Suddenly the woman reached down and picked up a stone. He snapped a warning at her as she straightened and stepped away from him. Then she did something that none of them were expecting and was the subject of much discussion at the campfire that evening.

She turned and pointed at the pale trunk of a tall gum tree that stood more than twenty paces away. She raised her arm high behind her shoulder, danced forward two strides and hurled the stone at the tree. It struck squarely in the centre of the trunk at a point about head-high from the ground and gouged out a deep bite of soft bark. The woman then pointed at other stones lying at their feet, stabbed a finger back at Coranga, and after matching Gunroi's gaze for a moment turned and strode back the way she had come.

At first they thought she had departed, but afterwards they saw her again moving through the brush in their wake. She had apparently only gone back to retrieve her digging stick and a twine bag in which she probably had some yams or fruit. Perhaps even shellfish. Mori saw her chasing crabs earlier in the day before they moved away from the beach to skirt the last headland.

That evening when they sat beside their fire she sat at the edge of the clearing some thirty paces away. When it grew dark they sometimes caught sight of her pale form in the flare of a flame.

The next morning Jessica woke to find Coranga squatting beside her. The black woman spoke quietly to her while unwrapping a small parcel of bark no bigger than the palm of her hand. From inside, she extracted a creamy dark mixture which she gently smeared on the angry cut below Jessica's breast. When Jessica examined the substance more closely later, it appeared to be mainly a mixture of crushed charcoal and a eucalyptus-scented oily substance.

By the next evening she was travelling with them, and in the days that followed she shared their food. Soon, with gradually increasing ability, she was helping the women to forage. For a time Coranga remained somewhat reserved in her dealings with this newcomer, but Mori took an immediate and seemingly unreserved liking to her, continually seeking out her company and patiently guiding her in all unfamiliar activities.

One evening, after Jessica had been travelling with them for about three weeks, Nunderri returned to the camp with a collection of small birds he had snared. As Jessica was to discover, the snaring of birds was one of his specialities. The normal procedure when he returned with his catch—which he kept trussed up alive so they would not spoil— was for the women to kill them and place them directly in the coals. By the time the feathers had burnt away the flesh was crisp and tasty.

On this occasion Mori became particularly excited by the appearance of one of the birds, most of which were varieties of honeyeaters, Nunderri having set his snares in a clump of flowering melaleucas. The one that caught her interest was capped by crimson feathers. She held it gently in one hand and rubbed the fingers of her free hand across its head. She then reached out and stroked Jessica's crown in a similar manner.

Her message was obvious: Jessica and the bird shared the same gold–red colouring. But none of the others seemed to be as impressed by this as Mori herself. She continued to chatter away enthusiastically until Coranga brought the subject to a sudden end by lifting the bird from her grasp, snapping its neck with a quick flick of the wrist and placing it in the coals.

This event would not have been particularly noteworthy if it had not been followed several days later by a curious sequel.

Nunderri had again returned with a collection of birds just before evening, and while the women were preparing them Mori again discovered that one was of the crimson-headed variety. But this time, before Coranga had time to deal with it as she had done before, Gunroi suddenly stepped forward and took it from her. He then carefully unbound the snare from its feet and the binding from its wings. While the others watched with their mouths agape, he lifted the bird above his head, opened his hand and allowed it to fly away.

He offered no explanation for his action and after the initial shock of what they had witnessed had subsided and they began to speak again, none of the others seemed inclined to seek one. From then on, whenever Nunderri returned with a collection of snared birds, there was never a crimson-crested honeyeater among them.

Gunroi never did tell them of the dream he had the evening after the first incident. The dream where he fought frantically to ward off the great white eagle and prevent it from seizing the tiny red-crested bird he had been charged to protect. He awoke in a sweat, quivering with waves of fear and frustration coursing through him, not knowing whether or not he had been successful.

From the side it was a chain of slim ghosts weaving through the shadows of the light scrub that lined the outer border of the riverbank. From within that chain it was a single dim form moving through the gloom ahead, the soft pad of bare feet and irregular scrape of loose stones below, and an occasional rustle of leaves brushing against an arm or a shoulder at the side. Nunderri was leading the way and had chosen a route that avoided the adjacent riverbank.

The flatland was blanketed by a gurgling maze of tidal channels and sunken mud pans crammed with mangroves and entanglements of driftwood; another nocturnal maze of natural man-traps that Nunderri with the best night eyes of any of them was sensibly avoiding.

By dawn the mangrove thickets had begun to fragment into isolated strips that clung to the edges of the deeper tidal channels. Finally the mangroves disappeared completely to be replaced by broad sweeps of sand interspersed with islands of grass. Up ahead flocks of birds rose into the air as they approached, and Gunroi was reminded of the source of unease he had experienced before they saw the Djungatee warriors, the unease that prompted their night-time flight.

During the previous week the scarcity of animals and the timidity they displayed—an occasional blur in the distance or an invisible rustle of retreat through the undergrowth—gave clear indication of the regular presence of hunters. There were no pelicans here nonchalantly preening themselves in the shallows.

This was not unusual in itself, Gunroi pondered. But no one had approached them to demand their intentions. And this was of real concern. To be denied the chance to present Gaidimi's message stick would be to risk being speared from ambush. Why was no one fishing in the lagoons? Hunting in the forest? Digging for yams? The only explanation he could offer the others was that either the Djungatee were at war with a neighbour, or that two of their clans were fighting.

In either case he decided it would be prudent to pass through this area as fast as possible. What stopped them was the river that lay behind the low headland they reached late on the day they first became concerned. It was far too wide for them to cross at that point. So they decided to camp for the night and head upstream the following morning.

But when from the headland they spotted in the distance a number of heavily armed warriors approaching, Gunroi decided that it would not be sensible to wait and see if the newcomers were a belated welcoming committee. Instead he decided to break camp immediately, hoping that by morning they might be at an appropriate place to cross the river, and that by some time later that day they would be well clear of the area.

Shortly after the sun rose, Gunroi moved alongside his brother. 'We should try and cross soon.'

Nunderri shook his head. 'It's still too deep.'

Gunroi sensed his concern. The rivers they had encountered since reaching the coast were much larger than any they were familiar with and had a different appearance and feel about them. There would be no canoe made available to them by friendly locals on this occasion, and because Nunderri was the weaker swimmer of the two, and the women might need to be assisted by both of them, he decided to leave him with the decision of when to cross.

Also, he had only scant knowledge of Jessica's ability in water. He had watched her splashing about in the surf with the others, and she obviously could swim, but he was uncertain how she would cope with a swift running stream.

His gaze swept the surface of the river. His brother was probably right in being cautious. Where the water was not a tumbling torrent it was a murky green colour, too clouded to reveal more than a few feet of its secrets. And it was impossible to tell if sudden swirling ripples on the surface of the calmer areas were caused by eddies of wind from above, or by something of more ominous nature moving below.

But still it would not be wise to remain on this side too long. He turned and looked back the way they had come. Nunderri sensed his unease and glanced to where serpentine swirls of sand were now beginning to show above the shimmering expanse of water. 'Two walks,' he offered. 'Maybe less.'

Shortly afterwards Gunroi moved past the others and took the lead. He kept them moving at a quicker pace, allowing them to pause and catch their breath only infrequently, usually when he was forced to gather his bearings and choose one path upstream from two or more offered, the way ahead being blocked by a higher than normal sand knoll, or by a tangle of driftwood of hillside dimensions. Occasionally they had to skirt a lagoon, and at one point the spread fingers of a shallow intersecting stream.

Since leaving the camp the others had exchanged words and hand signals with Jessica only infrequently. An observer would have been excused for believing that they blamed her in some way for the need to take such precautions with the Djungatee. Perhaps one or other of them did blame her. This was the first time they had encountered problems with the people whose land they were passing through. And one of the few differences in the circumstances that prevailed was that she had joined them, and was obviously an alien creature.

They finally crossed the river where the sand bars almost bridged the water and left such shallow channels that wading from one narrow island to the next was a simple exercise. Only the last channel caused problems. It was about thirty yards wide and for a quarter of that distance the water was deeper than head-height and flowing quickly.

They threw their weapons and the women's digging sticks and dish-like coolamons across on to the stony beach on the other side. Gunroi hung back and directed proceedings.

With Gunroi watching them closely, first Nunderri and Jessica crossed the deeper flow. Both were swept about twenty yards downstream where they scrambled out into the shallows and stood waiting to assist the others.

Coranga then directed a hesitant Mori ahead of her with Gunroi following closely behind. One moment all appeared to be well, the next Mori for some reason tried to turn back. She collided with Coranga and an instant later both girls disappeared beneath the surface in a tangle of flailing arms.

Gunroi and Jessica immediately plunged in to assist, while Nunderri snatched up a spear and ran alongside them in the shallow water. Gunroi managed to get hold of Mori and drag her towards the bank. But Jessica took longer to locate Coranga who was being tumbled along the riverbed weighed down by the force of churning water. It took Jessica several attempts to wrap her arms around the other woman, her back and shoulders brushing against rocks as she tried to kick clear of the bottom. Weeds or something of similar texture grabbed at her legs. Her mind was assailed with images of giant eels converging on her with jaws agape.

The moment her head broke the surface a great tentacle suddenly wrapped around her throat. She dragged air into her lungs and released a mighty scream, a cry of fear and anger she prayed would frighten the monster off. Almost in that same instant she realised that it was Gunroi's arm. He muttered soothingly in her ear.

Coranga was unconscious. Together they dragged her into the shallows. Nunderri extended the shaft of his spear towards them and helped haul her on to the bank. They then placed her beside Mori who was hugging her knees and sobbing pitifully.

Jessica immediately checked Coranga's throat was clear of any obstructions, and lying her on her face thumped her solidly with clasped hands three times in quick succession in the middle of her back. She then lent forward to check if she was breathing. Finding no indication that she was, she repeated the process.

She had never done this before, but whenever one of the Lowfoley kids was dragged unconscious from Pike's Hole, this was the treatment she had witnessed. It usually worked.

After the fourth battering, Coranga suddenly began to cough. Shortly afterwards she was breathing evenly.

She retched for a while, and cried a little, but recovered quickly. Mori, on the other hand, took longer to regain her composure. Nunderri moved to sit beside her and, wrapping his arms around her, murmured soothingly close to her ear. Gradually she stopped trembling and after a while began to whisper replies to his questions.

At one stage while this was happening Jessica turned and saw that Gunroi was watching her. She matched his gaze for a few moments before turning her attention back to the others.

'Is she a god?' he wondered.

After checking that both Coranga and Mori could walk they prepared to leave, and collected their possessions.

To get a better view of the terrain to the south, Gunroi stepped on to the grey trunk of the carcass of a tree that was partly buried in the sand. Beyond the bank of the river a plain extended to low hills on the south-western horizon. The forest of trees that had once blanketed the plain was a gaunt blackened graveyard of smouldering stumps.

They trudged through a carpet of ash. Jessica, who knew about standards of distance and time, tried to gauge and stack mile upon completed mile, hour upon completed hour; Gunroi, on the other hand, glanced occasionally at the sun and at the strengthening definition of trees and rocky outcrops on the distant hills.

Silent explosions of powder rose about their ankles and encased their legs in fragmented grey stockings. On either side, the black remnants of the forest stood silent watch, a broken backdrop robbed of even the whisper of leaves or the lament of a bird. Besides the regular thump of the travellers' feet, the only sound that disturbed the stillness was the occasional spit and crackle of escaping gas from a smouldering log.

During one period Gunroi's gaze remained on Jessica as she moved ahead of him. Just below her waistline two slight indentations, not quite dimples, sat on either side of her backbone. He watched those not quite dimples riding smoothly above the rhythmic rise and fall of the swell of her buttocks, and he marvelled again at the symmetry of her form and at how wonderfully she moved. Similar in many ways to Coranga, but with more balance, more self-assuredness.

He masked a smile. Who would have believed he would encounter another woman with more confidence than Coranga?

The morning sun bathed Jessica as she topped a slight incline. Her down trapped the light and encased her form in a silvery outline. Her flesh glowed.

His gaze moved from her shoulders to her thighs, touching the fine scratches and bruises she had collected during the past few days. The smudges of soot and dust on the ball and heel of each foot. The streaks of soot on her calves. Where did she come from that this land marks her so easily, he wondered. Paints her in so many colours? She *is* a god, he decided. Some kind of god.

He felt a sudden catch in his throat and resisted

the urge to move forward and touch her. When they crossed a dry gully they took the opportunity to rest on low boulders that were strewn along the far bank. Gunroi brushed away a film of ash from the surface of the boulder beside his leg and then deliberately smeared it with perspiration from his forearm. Deep red, shot with ribbons of quartz. I know you, rock, he mused, I've seen you before. He stepped on to the boulder and looked back at the hills that rose above the plain to the west.

Although we've been gone seven months, we've travelled only about one and a half months north, he calculated—gauging distance rather than days—one month east and now one month south. Our homeland is there behind the mountains. Less than two months away.

Nunderri approached him as he turned and looked back to the south, and perhaps guessed what was on his mind. The younger man pointed to the west where the closest of the ridges extended out on to the plain. 'We could reach the foothills over there before dark. But if we continue travelling south we'll have to spend the night on the plain, without cover and probably without food.'

Gunroi looked back to the west, and for some time his gaze rested on two eagles circling high above the closest ridge. 'But it's to the south they said we would find the nesting places of the white eagle,' he said finally.

'Do you think they really knew?'

'Why would they lie?'

'They could see we were heading south. Maybe they just wanted us to keep moving. Wanted to be rid of us.' Nunderri looked back to the west. 'Our home is beyond those mountains.'

'Yes,' said Gunroi softly. 'But it's too soon to go home.'

Both then turned and watched Jessica as she stepped on to a boulder and stood looking towards the west. Her attention may have been attracted by the changing play of light on the mountains. A shifting bank of clouds moved across the horizon to reveal deep valleys flanked by an undulating weave of rolling hills that were here and there topped by massive spires of rock. The entire area was gradually being flooded with an eerie mauve light that clung to ribbons of mist that swathed the spires and streamed from the crests of the ridges.

The two men continued to watch her as she stayed unmoving for an age, framed by the back-drop of the mountains and waves of changing light. When she finally stepped down Gunroi glanced back to the south for a moment and then returned his gaze to where she had rejoined the others. All three were bending forward and kneading their calf muscles. 'You're right,' he said. 'The women need to rest. And it wouldn't be wise to spend the night on the plain.'

Nunderri watched him closely as he added, 'And

perhaps we should spend some time having a closer look at those mountains. We can head back to the sea when it suits us.'

They turned back to the women.

'Coranga and Mori seem to have recovered from their fright,' said Nunderri.

Gunroi nodded. But their eyes were not on either of them. Both were watching Jessica as she leaned over and carefully extracted ashes and leaf debris from the curl of her toes. One breast was pressed against her thigh.

Nunderri moved closer to his brother and caught his eye.

'What?' said Gunroi.

Nunderri placed spread fingers on either side of his mouth to check the spread of his cheeks.

'What?' Gunroi repeated, a touch of irritation now riding the edge of the query.

'I'd like to lie with her,' he said softly.

Gunroi's head snapped around so that he faced the other man squarely.

Nunderri's eyes sprang wide in alarm. 'What?' He lent closer to his brother and whispered, 'Unless you were planning to yourself. Tonight, I mean?'

'Tonight! No.' Gunroi looked across at the hills. 'Of course not.'

'Then what's wrong?'

'Nothing's wrong.'

'There is, I can tell.'

Gunroi returned his attention to Jessica. 'I'm not

sure she would want you to, that's all. Whenever we do it with the others she hides.'

Nunderri flashed a smile. 'Not want to? Why would she not want to?' He looked back at her. 'She isn't a child. It must be many years since she was initiated. Her wounds will have long healed.'

Their eyes remained on her as she attended to the other foot.

They emerged from the fire-scarred plain about an hour before sunset and made camp beside a small stream tumbling from a ridge that blocked out the northern sky. They dined on a small wallaby the women had caught at the fringe of the plain. Its legs had been injured in the fire and it was unable to escape from their combined scurrying pursuit.

Not long after the meal Jessica suddenly grew weary and moved away from the others so that she could stretch out on one of the broad ledges of rock that flanked the fire. Leaning back on her elbows she turned her gaze to where the sun had not long disappeared. Her eyelids drooped.

From a fiery hub on the horizon broad shafts of crimson light radiated across the darkening sky like the spokes of a giant chariot. She closed her eyes. The breeze from the stream drifted over her, and her nose was touched by a hint of eucalyptus on the edge of the smoke.

She carefully lowered herself squarely on to her back and stretched out her legs, spreading her knees slightly and pressing her flesh down to make maximum contact with the surface of the cool rock. The breeze whispered across her body and between her thighs. Suddenly aware of the extent of her nakedness and the vulnerability of her posture, she opened her eyes and saw that Gunroi and Nunderri had moved closer together and were watching her.

Behind them, Coranga and Mori were talking quietly to each other. The faces of all four were framed by the shallow undulations of her slightly splayed twin insteps and the gentle curl of her toes. As she watched, Coranga and Mori also turned to look at her. Time stood still. The artists who painted the grand pictures she saw at Duckwick Hall would have caught them thus, she mused; no breath escaped them.

When she did finally move it was not to roll on to her side as she may have expected herself to do, or even to raise a protective knee; instead she uncurled and stretched her toes, languidly, sleepily, a simple seeking of relief from the faint discomfort she noticed there, the legacy of the miles they had travelled. Then she closed her eyes and settled even closer to the rock, turning her hands palms-up and spreading her fingers. And she made no move whatsoever to assume a less exposed or more defensive attitude.

As she began to breathe evenly again she sensed that so did they, and that their eyes remained on her. Close at hand the air carried the song of a cricket and in the distance she heard the faint cry of a night-bird. She felt a curious sense of euphoria. Of being light and unencumbered, free of the burdens and worries of that other world. Her body could almost have been an extension of the smooth, cool rock itself, and of the land that surrounded it. And she knew she was being consumed by a growing acceptance of her circumstance. Knew that she could do as little to change the air that she breathed as to escape the events that unfolded around her. She cared not whether they chose to travel east, west, north, or even south. Her chest and shoulders suddenly rose and fell with a heavy spontaneous sigh of contentment.

She must have dozed off, she deduced later. For she next recalled that someone was sitting close beside her. Was leaning over her. Her eyelids fluttered. Nunderri? She then realised his hand was cupped between the spread of her thighs, his fingers invading her.

The next morning as they prepared to break camp she could not recall how she had managed to grab hold of the piece of wood. So she surmised that it must have been lying close by. The sequence of events as she remembered them shed no light whatsoever on where it had come from.

One moment she had almost certainly been dozing. The next she was waking and was aware of Nunderri's disturbing presence. And of course the very next she was swiping him on the side of the head with the lump of wood that had miraculously materialised in her hand.

Even the events that followed were something of a blur. Nunderri's startled cry of pain. The women's shriek of laughter. Gunroi's cautionary murmur when for a few moments it appeared his brother might seek some form of retribution. Her own apologies and moves of reconciliation by helping Mori salve the wound with Coranga's ointment. The young man's heart-wrenching embarrassment.

Even now he was suffering. And the others were not giving him any peace. The women continually breaking into sudden bursts of giggling. And Gunroi failing to hide the beams of amusement that were triggered by their outbursts.

Nunderri led them up the slope of the nearest ridge, undoubtedly grateful to be back at the head of the column and not having to look any of them in the eye. The three women followed him in single file with Jessica trailing the others. Gunroi as usual brought up the rear.

From time to time Gunroi's gaze again rested on the indentations riding smoothly above the rhythmic rise and fall of the swell of her buttocks.

He felt somewhat confused, unsure why it was that he was more pleased than disappointed by Jessica's rejection of his brother. If Nunderri had succeeded in his intentions, the way would have been open for him, too, to lie with her. And that was certainly a prospect he had been contemplating seriously for some time now. Only the mystery of her had stayed his hand, caused him to be uncertain.

Nunderri surprised him when he declared his intentions. Perhaps he does not see the mystery. Surprised him, and troubled him.

Why troubled? Why would I be troubled by his wanting to lie with her? He lies with Coranga from time to time, as I lie with Mori. This is the way it should be with brothers. Brothers and good friends. Nunderri is both. So why am I troubled? Why am I pleased she refused him? Despite himself, he suddenly smiled as he recalled her reaction.

He watched her as she negotiated a fallen log, stepping on to it first and—as Mori had taught her—checking the ground on the other side before stepping down. The log was high, and as she stepped up and then down he twice caught a brief glimpse of the morning sun flaring in the tight gold–red foliage between the wide stretch of her thighs. As on the previous day he felt a sudden catch in his throat and again resisted the urge to move forward and touch her.

As he stepped on to the log himself he turned and stood for a time looking back the way they had come. When he turned again he saw that she had stopped and was looking at him, perhaps waiting to see if he had noticed any danger behind them. They watched each other.

Finally she swung away and moved quickly after

the others. He allowed his gaze to stay with her for a time before he turned his attention to the high ridges that surrounded them.

These are mysterious hills, he decided. I might not find the eagle there, but I believe I will find something. His gaze returned to Jessica's retreating back.

Coranga was the worst offender, Gunroi fumed. Giggling and nudging the others whenever he had to fall behind or leave the fire and pretend to be busy with some activity where he could better conceal the state he was in. Nunderri was no help either, smiling and craning his neck whenever he looked across at him. If he had been back with the clan he would have let their childish behaviour pass by him. But he wasn't back with the clan, and Jessica was obviously embarrassed.

Coranga was certainly the one who brought the entire episode to a head, he often conceded later, usually with a begrudging sense of gratitude.

They were camped beneath the skyline of a fire-scarred ridge. Rain had fallen earlier and clouds of mist drifted in occasionally from the east bathing the clearing in a smoke-like haze that was tinged with a red glow from the setting sun.

Several times on the climb out of the valley he had been forced to drop well behind the others. And again when they settled down around the fire, he repeatedly had to leave hurriedly.

On the last time he returned, Coranga and Mori, whether spontaneously or by some prearranged agreement, kept their eyes away from him and sat with straight backs murmuring politely to each about how—because of the prolonged journey—various parts of their bodies were being subjected to aches, pains, twinges and, of course, uncomfortable swellings.

Jessica, on the other hand, had a distracted air about her and seemed to be either ignoring the other two, or was completely oblivious of them. She was sitting quite still with her legs folded and her hands on her spread knees. Her gaze seemed to be resting on Gunroi's feet, or more accurately on where his long toes were curled into the thin layer of dust and soot that carpeted the clearing.

Perhaps Coranga and Mori would have been able to carry off their tongue-in-cheek charade had not Gunroi turned to Nunderri and blamed his hasty departures on the figs he had eaten that morning. This was too much for Coranga. Although she managed to pinch her lips together and contain her mirth for a few seconds, when it did break free it exploded from her lips in a great expanding bubble. She fell forward on to her knees shrieking with laughter and for a time rolled around hugging her sides.

When she finally recovered she rocked back against the other women in mock exhaustion. They tried to push her off, and when she resisted all three were soon jostling and wrestling and releasing shrill squeals whenever the clutching fingers of one dug into the rib-cage of another.

But when Coranga in her excitement began to modify her version of fairly conventional catch-as-catch-can technique, by groping obscenely for whichever of her opponents' more sensitive parts came within easy reach, Mori squealed and quickly wriggled away from her clutches. Jessica, on the other hand, was not fast enough to avoid a hand being cupped firmly between her thighs.

'No!' she cried, wrenching herself free. She lurched to her feet and backed away from the other woman, shielding her crotch defensively behind clenched hands.

Coranga sat looking down at the palm of her own offending hand.

A sudden silence descended on the scene.

Jessica stood looking down at Coranga for a moment and then spun around and hurried from the clearing, passing through a swirl of red-tinged mist as she disappeared into the forest.

They sat there in silence for a while and then Gunroi stood up and strode off after her. As he reached the edge of the clearing Nunderri picked up their spears and followed him. The women exchanged glances before scrambling to their feet, grabbing up their possessions and hurrying after them.

Gunroi caught glimpses of Jessica from time to time as she strode purposefully up the steep slope ahead of him. On either side of the narrow animal-track they were following, the forest understorey was wrapped in bundles of the red-tinged mist, blocking out all but a few feet of the dense foliage. Leaves that brushed against them as they passed were slick with moisture. Within the mist huge columns of shadow towered away from them and were consumed by the haze. Perhaps these were the edge of rocky outcrops, or even a forest of giant trees. There was a sense within all who climbed through the mist that day that they were passing through massive portals that loomed just out of sight on either side of them.

The top of the ridge had been razed some months before by fire. The blackened trunks and limbs of the trees and bushes beside the track were festooned in bundles of fresh green leaves. A thick coating of ash lay on the ground.

When Gunroi reached the crest, he saw Jessica ahead of him in a large clearing, sitting on the ground amidst ash and leaf debris. He moved across and sat down beside her. Her hand was clamped beneath her breasts, her chest was heaving, her body was bathed in a sheen of perspiration and swathed in ribbons of soot. Rivulets of moisture gathered beneath her throat and tracked down her chest. She kept her eyes away from him.

He reached out and gently plucked a small dead leaf from where it clung to one of her breasts, and then with the back of his fingers he brushed away a smear of dust close to her nipple. 'No,' she whispered, turning towards him. 'I can't.'

But she was exhausted from the climb and did not have the strength to prevent him from pressing her back on to the ground. The mist must have been lifting, for when he loomed over her, his hair was ringed in a fiery halo from the setting sun. Beyond his silhouette she could see wisps of gold lace in the sky. She felt the flat of his hand press against her belly.

'No!' she protested again, and twisted away from him on to her stomach.

But he stopped her before she could rise to her knees and held her, murmuring to her softly until her moment of panic had passed. Then he rolled her on to her back once more and, still murmuring quietly, painstakingly began to remove all of the debris that clung to her damp skin.

She watched him in silence as he alternately employed first the tips of his fingers to lift off each piece of foreign matter, and then the sides to brush away the underlying smear of soot or dust. She made no protest when he spent some time picking out and brushing away a collection of leaves and ash that was entwined within the tight curls of her pubic bush. And when his hand moved on, and his fingers became employed in activities that were not exclusively involved with removing dust and debris, she spread her thighs a little to accommodate them. Shortly afterwards she reached up and placed her own fingers on his lightly fleeced chest, and ran them slowly down over the hard horizontal ridges of the initiation scars that marked him in two even strips from his pectoral muscles to his waist.

But as Gunroi spread her legs even further and lowered himself between them, cutting out all light in the sky behind him, she was suddenly engulfed by a wave of revulsion. Reacting impulsively to the induced weight of aeons of prejudice, superstition and fear, she pushed back on his chest with all the strength she could muster and, struggling from beneath him, lurched to her feet.

As he rose and stood beside her, his eyes seeking hers, she hesitated, uncertain and confused. Suddenly ashamed of her action, she looked up at him, her face a mask of anguish and apology.

A noise at the edge of the clearing sent her gaze darting to where the other three were standing watching them.

She quickly turned away from them and her breasts brushed against him. 'Tell them to go away,' she whispered.

He looked at her enquiringly.

'Tell them to go away,' she repeated. Her legs began to tremble and she placed her forearm on his chest and moved against him, partly to steady herself, partly to conceal his erection. It pressed into her stomach, a salient reminder of their carnality, of the reality of what was happening here. He murmured close to her ear, and then called out to the others.

She then sensed them moving away. But she caught something in the low murmur of their voices that told her they were not leaving completely. When she looked again she saw that they were further away and did not appear to be taking any interest. They were sitting partly concealed by a clump of bracken. Motionless. An extension of the deepening shadows of the surrounding forest, the hills, the rocks.

She continued to tremble and press herself against him. And then she was uncertain if it was he who lowered her to the ground, or she who drew him down on top of her. But she was aware that it was her hand that was encircling that salient reminder of their carnality, urgently, wantonly. And it was she who was guiding it into her.

He paused to brush a fall of hair from her eyes, and then began to ride her, steadily at first and then with increasing vigour. She arched her back and wrapped her legs around his.

In the shadows, the other three stood up so they could see what was happening. After a few moments Mori raised her chin, and pursing her lips began to utter a soft undulating trill. Following her lead, Coranga soon joined her in a rippling duet. Nunderri rubbed the back of a hand across his mouth and, although his attention primarily was centred on the lustful activities that were under way in the clearing, from time to time he self-consciously glanced away, feigning interest in the surrounding bush.

They're watching, some part of Jessica's consciousness told her. But why should that trouble me, defended still another part; they're simply players in this dream. This terrible, glorious dream that I've been caught up in.

He was a giant towering over her. She could no longer see his face. His head was a moving silhouette against the darkening gold lace in the sky behind him. She turned to where the sun had set behind a high domed rock on a neighbouring ridge. He could be hewn from one of these great rocks that protrude from this land, this giant towering above her. His beat was relentless.

Of course that was only the beginning. Twice more during the evening the two of them reached for each other. And during the months that followed they continually employed the flimsiest of excuses to duck off by themselves, coming together with such seemingly monotonous regularity in the eyes of the others that they frivolously speculated on whether or not an oft-mentioned part of Gunroi's anatomy would one day snap off.

The events of that first evening had perhaps a much greater impact on Gunroi than they did on Jessica. Mainly on account of what was revealed when the mist drifted completely away and the sun rose the following morning.

The revelations that confronted him were so astounding that it took him some time to come to terms with them.

The two trees first caught his attention when he happened to glance towards the rising sun and saw that it was framed between their massive trunks. Never before had he seen their like. He was so captivated by their size that it was some time before their significance became apparent.

They stood just below the crest of the ridge on either side of the track along which Jessica had led them on to the ridge the previous evening. Then they had been hidden by the mist. Now they could be observed in all their glory. One of them was a blackbutt and the other a flooded gum: eucalypts that were not normally forest giants of this dimension. But as a consequence of their roots breaking into a deep store of super-rich nutriments, and their foliage having to fight for sunlight during their early development, both now towered more than three hundred feet above the forest floor.

A hint of their significance dawned on Gunroi as he absently observed the width of their massive trunks, one charcoal-black, the other a gleaming white. His gaze suddenly shifted to the sun as it climbed between them, and then he spun around and looked back to the west, past where Coranga and Mori had joined Jessica, and all three women were sitting engrossed in quiet conversation.

They looked up as he strode towards them. Nunderri moved away from the edge of the clearing and called out a query as his brother moved on past the women and stood looking at the huge dome-shaped rock on the adjacent ridge that had caught Jessica's attention the previous evening.

All eyes were now turned towards him as Nunderri moved to his side and asked, 'What's wrong? What can you see?'

Gunroi glanced back for a moment at the two trees behind him, and then returned his gaze to the huge rock. 'Namulami, the birth stone. The navel.'

'Namulami!' Nunderri whispered, his eyes on the rock. 'Are you sure?'

Gunroi turned and nodded to the trees. 'Gaidimi described it as it is. The black and white spirits escorting the rising sun.' His eyes suddenly grew wide.

'What?' said Nunderri.

'The bora ground. It must be here.' He strode back towards the women, his eyes traversing the ground. They stood up as he approached.

'Here, where?' Nunderri asked.

'Here, where we are. Right here. The most sacred bora ground of all.' He looked back at the trees. 'How far is it between those trees?'

'A good spear-throw. Why?'

'Gaidimi said that Biamie placed the black and white spirits three strides apart, and then stepped out four strides from each to mark where the ancient ones should place the centre of their bora ground.' Glancing up at the trees and then back to the clearing a number of times, he began to walk slowly towards the women.

They both saw the outline at the same moment.

'What are you looking at?' Coranga asked.

He raised his hands. 'Get back out of the clearing. Quickly.'

'Why?'

'This is the Namulami bora ground.' He ushered them ahead of him.

'Sacred,' said Coranga in response to Jessica's query as the three of them sat where Gunroi had directed, at the edge of the ridge facing back into the forest. 'Forbidden.'

Jessica looked up as a small leaf spiralled down towards her from the upper reaches of the flooded gum. As it came within reach she snatched it out of the air and, holding the stem between her thumb and forefinger, twirled it and watched it flash as it caught the light.

Behind them Gunroi and Nunderri traced out the low circular bank that marked the perimeter of the bora ground.

Nunderri picked up a burnt branch and threw it towards the edge of the clearing. 'Why is it so overgrown? Why hasn't someone been maintaining the bank? It's almost worn away.'

'It's only used for the most sacred ceremonies,' said Gunroi. 'Many years might pass without it being used. And perhaps those who were last charged with its care have died.' He looked back towards the women.

Nunderri moved to his side. 'Do you think Biamie will punish you?' he whispered. 'You lay with her here. All night.' He glanced furtively to where the forest climbed away darkly along the ridge. 'Do you think I'll be punished? I lay with both Mori and Coranga on the sacred path.'

Gunroi turned and looked at him for a moment and then glanced back at the centre of the clearing. 'Perhaps it was Biamie's doing that she led us to this place.' He raised his eyes to the ridge opposite. 'Brought us to the birthplace of all peoples.'

'But she's a woman.'

'She led us along the sacred path. Between the spirits of life and death. Perhaps she is no ordinary woman. Perhaps she's a god. Perhaps it was Biamie's doing that she and I . . .'

Nunderri looked at him closely. 'But you're not even sure you believe in gods.'

Gunroi returned his attention to the women. 'If gods don't exist, then it doesn't matter, does it? Whether or not she's a woman. Whether or not I lay with her here.' He turned back and gripped his brother with his gaze. 'Or whether or not you were greedy and lay with both Coranga and Mori on the one night, and without my permission.'

A sudden breeze roared momentarily in the upper reaches of the two forest giants and a huge flurry of small leaves exploded into the air. Far below, five faces looked up to observe, perhaps in wonder, the myriad tiny flashes of light that were descending on them out of the sky.

Jessica, not Gunroi, was the last to turn away from the grandeur of the massive cylindrical columns—one black, one white—that towered above them.

That evening Gunroi painted vertical black stripes down Jessica's left cheek and left breast, and similar white stripes down her right cheek and breast. Then, disappointed with the smudged appearance of the black stripes, and the lack of contrast against her skin of the white stripes, he replaced them with stripes of red and yellow ochre.

The five of them wandered through those hills and sheltered in the valleys for over a year before they finally made their way back to the coast.

He sensed something was wrong as he and Nunderri neared the place where the women had prepared the camp. There was a stillness in the air. The cry of the birds was sporadic. Hesitant. Querying. The cicadas were silent. So were the crickets. Only the breeze was continuous, whispering moanfully through the tops of the tallest trees.

As one, and without exchanging any verbal communication, both he and his brother knelt and carefully unloaded the game they had killed: Nunderri the two brush turkeys, and he the small brush-tailed rock wallaby. Again as one they fitted spears into their woomeras, raised the weapons above their shoulders and crept towards the clearing.

Mori lay where she had fallen, the grass beneath her head coated with a slick crimson stain that was alive with the whine of blowflies. A similar sound emerged from the back of Nunderri's throat as he knelt over her and brushed her eyelashes with his trembling fingertips, desperately willing those staring eyes to blink back at him.

Gunroi moved on past the body and knelt to examine the crumpled turf. A low wail from the brush ahead brought both of them to their feet, their spears raised high.

Coranga stumbled into the clearing and ran towards them, falling to her knees as she reached them and renting the air with her cries of distress. Gunroi immediately ran past her to protect her from pursuers. When he satisfied himself that there were none, he returned to where she was crouched beside Mori, wailing pitifully and tearing at the flesh of her own arms with raking fingernails.

When she was able, she told them how they were set upon by a large group of white men garbed in blood-coloured skins. She described how Jessica ran into the bush and how they chased after her and dragged her back. And how they examined the marks on her ankles before binding her wrists with thick twine.

She told them how Mori had tried to stop them from taking her away, how she wrapped her arms around Jessica and refused to let her go. And how finally one of them struck her with his fist and knocked her to the ground. And how when she tried to rise, another had stood over her and driven the butt of his club on to the back of her head.

At this point Nunderri rose to his feet, threw back his head and unleashed a wild cry of despair and anger that rang through the surrounding brush and rebounded off the nearby rocks. Birds within earshot suddenly found themselves launched into flight. Small creatures in the undergrowth ducked their heads and remained locked frozen in mid-stride until well after the last ringing echoes of the fearful sound had died away.

The great canoe lay in the mouth of the river. Was this his eagle, Gunroi wondered as the three of them crouched in the undergrowth and observed it with alternating waves of awe, fear and anger coursing through them.

It has some of the appearance of a bird, he decided, great many-layered wings furled one above the other. But it has none of the movements of a bird. It does not soar, it wallows. It sits heavily on the surface of the water with waves lapping at its sides as if it was attached to the earth somewhere beneath those waves.

'Can you see her?' Nunderri asked.

'No.'

'There are many white ones,' said Nunderri. 'Too many to fight.'

'Yes,' Gunroi conceded.

'Then what do you intend to do?'

Gunroi did not reply immediately. After a time he released a heavy sigh and stood up. 'I will go there and tell them she is mine. I will ask them to return her to me. I don't know what else I can do.'

'But they'll kill you as they killed Mori,' Coranga whispered shrilly.

'I won't go so close that they can reach me with their clubs.'

'But they won't return her to you,' she responded. 'She's one of their people. They'll say you have no right.'

He remained silent for a time. 'I'll explain that she is no longer one of their people,' he said at last. 'She is now one of us. I'll tell them of the bora ground. I'll tell them that the Great God Biamie has sanctioned that she become one of us.'

'Perhaps they don't know of Biamie,' said Coranga. 'Perhaps they are a godless people.'

'Then I'll tell them of Biamie.'

Coranga scoffed. 'Why will they believe you? You don't even know if you believe yourself.'

He turned on her and for a moment it appeared as if he might strike her. She stayed her ground and matched his gaze.

'How will you go out there?' Nunderri asked, to relieve the moment.

'I'll take one of the Djungatees' canoes.'

'The one we saw was damaged.'

'There'll be others.'

They brought her on deck and the captain of marines took a firm hold of the coarse shirt of the sailor's garb in which they had dressed her, and led her to the ship's side. When her eyes had adjusted to the light she saw that the crew were preparing to sail and had already hauled in the anchor.

'Do you know that man?' he asked, directing her attention to a solitary figure sitting in a bark canoe some fifty feet off the port quarter.

'Oh no,' she breathed when she saw who it was. 'Please don't hurt him.'

'Yon nigger's a special friend, is he?'

Gunroi saw her at that moment and called out to her.

'Tell him that the death of the woman was an accident,' said the captain of marines as Gunroi began to call out his request. 'Tell him we want no trouble from the tribes of this area. Tell him that when we return we will pay compensation for her death. Do you hear what I'm saying?'

'When you return?' she said distractedly, most of her attention being taken up with Gunroi's words.

'One day we will be returning with surveyors to inspect all of these larger rivers.' He turned his attention back to Gunroi. 'What's that black savage rambling about?'

'He's asking you—politely—to release me.' She turned to him. 'Please do as he says. Please don't take me back to Sydney.'

'Don't be ridiculous, woman. You're an escaped felon.'

'You don't know that. You don't know that I haven't served my time.'

379

'As soon as we return and I find out who you are I'll know.'

'But you don't understand. I can't go back.'

The ship suddenly heeled as the loosened top-sails filled with air. The man holding her was momentarily knocked off balance. Before he could recover, Jessica thrust her shoulder into him and, wrenching herself free of his grasp, threw herself at the guardrail. Two other marines immediately sprang to apprehend her, one of them managing to grasp hold of her baggy duck trousers.

She kicked out frantically and the trousers slipped below her buttocks. The man clutching them fell back heavily on to the deck.

Gunroi in the meantime had sprung to his feet and had notched a spear into his woomera. The canoe trembled precariously beneath his feet. Jessica, now trouserless, grabbed hold of the main's rigging and hauled herself on to the guard-rail. At the moment it appeared she would jump, the other marine grabbed her by an ankle. The captain of marines had by now recovered and leapt forward to assist.

Gunroi bounced his spear up and down above his shoulder in exasperation at being unable to release it for fear of hitting Jessica. Finally he hurled it into the midst of a group of redcoats who were running to assist the others.

A cry of pain rang out as the spear struck one man a glancing blow on the chest and remained embedded in the folds of his jacket.

'No!' Jessica screamed as she was hauled back on to the deck and several marines pushed past her to level their muskets on Gunroi.

The ship had now picked up speed and was turning towards the river's mouth. In a few moments his canoe would have slipped behind the stern. He had already snatched up another spear and was straightening to full height when a volley of musket fire boomed out across the water. Jessica screamed in anguish as his hair suddenly flew upright and he pitched backwards into the water.

The image that remained with her as they dragged her below decks was of the upturned canoe bobbing in the swell.

FOURTEEN

The first time Amanda Dalrymple saw Will Noling was on the Atlantic Ocean off the coast of Brazil, just out of sight of the Fernando de Noronha Islands and not far from where the *Weymouth Bay* had been becalmed two years before, almost to the day.

But on this day there was a breeze, and something of a swell, although the combination of both failed to tear the crumpled dark blue blanket that stretched to the horizon and there was no sign anywhere of its white underside.

Amanda and her uncle Sir Peter Dalrymple were en route to New South Wales as paying passengers on the convict transport *Tynemouth*. Will Noling was not one of the paying passengers.

Amanda's attention was drawn to him by the amazement of one of the ship's officers, Lieutenant Cotter, when he spotted Will among the convicts who were exercising in the waist of the ship.

Witnessing Cotter's astonished reaction, Amanda

and her uncle immediately moved closer to the break to get a clearer view over the heavy iron and oak barricade that had been placed between the waist and quarterdeck.

The primary purpose of this structure was to provide the marines with a defensive wall should they ever need to quell a riot or an attempted mass escape. But it also served to give some privacy to the paying passengers whenever they were on the upper deck, and at least a measure of visual protection from the daily spectacle of gaunt and dishevelled men, some with weeping sores on their ankles and wrists, exercising their cramped bodies on the deck below.

Not that all the passengers sought this protection. Depending on the weather and the direction of the prevailing wind, some of them treated the spectacle as a form of entertainment. They looked upon the shuffling serpentine dance of these wretched creatures as they were brought into the fresh air in rotation—sealed compartment by sealed compartment, deck by deck—as one of the few amusing distractions available on the voyage, a diversion to while away the hours. These same passengers also found it entertaining when one or more of the convicts—or sometimes even a member of the crew or a marine—was flogged until his flesh hung in strips from his back and the deck beneath him was awash with his blood.

This particular brand of entertainment, however, was not regularly available, nor would it be on this voyage, so it could not be relied upon to ease the tedium very often. All because the captain was a backsliding reformist, a weak-kneed old woman who by now would have had his throat cut while he slept, if it had not been for Lieutenant Gordon, the Captain of Marines, being made of sterner stuff. Or so that very same Lieutenant Gordon told Amanda and Sir Peter Dalrymple one night after dinner, and—on his part—a copious consumption of brandy.

Amanda and Sir Peter had decided shortly after leaving Portsmouth that the misfortune of the convicts was not a circumstance that either of them found entertaining, so whenever they were on the upper deck at the same time as their less fortunate fellow travellers, they made a point of directing their attention elsewhere.

Naturally they dealt with the Captain of Marines in a like manner, and during the remainder of the voyage both of them managed to exchange no more than one or two words with him. Assisting them in this regard was Lieutenant Wallis Cotter, formerly of HMS *Victory* and now temporarily seconded to the *Tynemouth* while in transit to New South Wales to take up a posting on the staff of the new Governor, Captain William Bligh, formally of HMS *Bounty*.

Cotter and Gordon had taken an almost instant dislike to each other and the Dalrymples exploited this by seeking out the naval lieutenant's company whenever they could, thereby improving their chances of holding his marine counterpart at bay.

It had been many weeks since either Amanda or her uncle had so much as glimpsed the scene in the waist. So it was, as they stood at Cotter's shoulder and looked down at the wretched creatures that made up the bulk of the slowly rotating human cyclone below them, that they both fell silent and remained that way for some time.

Sir Peter was the first to speak. 'You say he was on the *Victory* with you?'

For Amanda, who was completely immersed in images of the misery that was etched into the faces of the men below, her uncle's words initially had no meaning; they served simply to gently bring her back from whatever layer of the underworld she had been visiting.

'Yes.' Cotter's voice was brittle.

The *Victory*! Amanda craned her neck as she recalled the question and realised its significance. She found herself leaning to one side attempting to gain a clearer view past the shoulder of one of the number of marines who were deployed along the top side of the break with their muskets at the order. 'The tall man with the red hair?'

'Yes.'

'He obviously hasn't been a prisoner as long as most of the others,' said Sir Peter. 'Was he at Trafalgar?'

'Yes. He was with Lord Nelson when he was shot. I believe Noling was wounded at about the same time.'

'Noling?' Amanda still could not see him clearly. She moved on to her toes and craned her neck.

'William Noling. He was on Nelson's staff.'

'So he was an officer?'

This was more a statement than a question, but Cotter replied with a distracted, 'What?' Then, with part of his attention still obviously else-where, 'Sorry. No, he was ... I'm not sure what he was. An able seaman probably. He was the Admiral's scribe.'

'His scribe?'

'Mostly, I believe. He worked with the two Scotts, Nelson's secretaries. The Admiral's good eye was failing. By the time we got back from chasing the French fleet to the Caribbean, he was almost totally blind in some light.' He looked about him and held up one hand. 'Please don't ever repeat that.'

'I believe it was known,' said Sir Peter, his gaze still on Will Noling.

'I'd still prefer that you did not repeat it.'

'Of course. Tell me, how is it that an able seaman can be an Admiral's scribe?'

'I have no idea. It was a mystery to many on board.'

'Perhaps he did something similar before he joined the navy?' Amanda offered.

'No. Apparently he was a farmer. And he didn't join. At least not voluntarily. He was pressed.'

The three of them remained silent until Amanda said, 'It seems as if he's been pressed again.'

'Yes,' Cotter agreed. 'I'll have a chat to the captain and see if I can look at the records and find out why.'

The captain's records did have the bare details of why Will Noling was being transported to New South Wales. But a letter amongst the mail on a ship that departed for Sydney some three months before the *Tynemouth* gave a more detailed— albeit distorted—account of the sequence of events that placed him on board. It was sent by Sir Rory Fitzparsons to his cousin Garth Barlester.

Again deciphering the spelling and making allowance for the terrible punctuation, the letter read, in part:

Be warned, Garth, the redheaded rooster will soon be on his way to New South Wales. I am talking about Will Noling, the friend of your little robin red breast. He tried to kill me, and should have hung, and would have hung for sure and certain if the damned navy had kept its nose where it should have been kept rather than sticking it into the business of honest men. They sent a stuffed shirt chaplain called Scott and a letter from that upstart Hardy, who thinks he is on his way to the House of Lords because of being with Nelson during that battle off Cadiz you have probably heard about by now. The letter saved the scoundrel's neck, but it could not save him from being found guilty of trying to kill me with my own pistol like the low cur he is, even though he had the gall to claim it was the other way about and that I shot myself in the leg when we were fighting for the pistol. As if I could not easily have held him with one hand and slapped him senseless with the pistol any time I wanted, if he had not caught me by surprise. His council was no match for the Crown. When he tried to discredit me, the rogue revealed that he obviously thought he had cause to do what he did, and was guilty by his own omission by claiming I had something to do with having him pressed and that I had lied at the trial of the robin, causing her to be transported. The Crown tore that last one apart, revealing I was the one who petitioned the court to have her sent to New South Wales rather than be hanged like she deserved. I still have the scars. The bitch! The Crown also had some Portsmouth locals testify he had assaulted them and accused them of taking money from my man Mactaggart to hand him over to the press, which was utter rot of course. As if I would go to so much trouble with the low upstart. But it was enough to convince the jury he meant to do me harm when he stormed into my house and attacked me, whether they believed that what he said about me was true or not. I had been warned and had a pistol ready but the scoundrel used a ruse to distract me and grabbed it from me. He would have killed me if I had not knocked it aside. The ball broke my leg which I now have to drag around. If I could get my hands on the cur I would flay him alive for what he has done to me. It is an outrage he did not hang, coming into my house like a corsair and doing what he did. His council told the jury that he could have killed me then if that had been his intent, but I convinced them that the loss of blood caused me to faint and that the scoundrel thought I was dead, which saved my life. For your information only, before I did faint he vowed to find his little robin red breast if it took him the rest of his life. Because the stupid judges were swayed by the navy he will soon be on his way to Botany Bay rather than hanging in chains across the harbour at Fort Blockhouse where he should be, with the gulls feeding on him. He might well get the chance to meet up with her unless you take steps to stop that happening.

'Did you know him?' Sir Peter Dalrymple asked Wallis Cotter the next time Cotter joined him and his niece when they were observing Will Noling exercising in the waist. Several days had passed since Cotter had brought Will to their attention, and this was the first opportunity they had to discuss him again since Cotter had given them the brief details of Will's incarceration.

What Cotter had learnt from the sparse records that were carried on board—apparently for security purposes more detailed records were both held and shipped separately—was that Noling had been convicted of the attempted murder of a local dignitary and had been sentenced 'to be transported beyond the seas for and during the term of seven years'.

As Cotter pointed out, this was highly unusual for such a serious offence. Mindful of the upheaval in France, the death penalty was practically a mandatory sentence in British courts for any form of attack on people of prominence, including for far less serious transgressions than attempted murder.

As he explained to the others over supper the evening he brought them his findings, 'I can only assume that the judges thought there were extraordinary mitigating circumstances, or that they were petitioned by some persuasive authority, perhaps the navy.'

From that day on, the Dalrymples had looked for Will whenever the convicts were exercising. With more contribution from Amanda than her uncle, they had even passed some time by conjuring up possible scenarios that might have explained how he came to be on Lord Nelson's staff, and afterwards be convicted of attempted murder and receive a sentence of a mere seven years.

One of Amanda's bolder suggestions, certainly in the opinion of her uncle, was that Will was the brother of Nelson's mistress, Lady Hamilton. As soon as she had offered this explanation Sir Peter had interrupted her immediately, stating that as far as he was concerned, refined young ladies should not even have been aware of Emma Hamilton's existence, let alone be prepared to discuss her openly.

But Amanda pooh-poohed his concern and——

although she knew it was not the case—treated his call for decorum as a joke in keeping with her tongue-in-cheek suggestion. She pressed on to argue that her solution had real merit. She explained that if she were correct it would then be reasonable to suppose that when Nelson found out that his almost brother-in-law had been pressed into the navy, rather than further antagonise his own enemies in England by seeing to it that the young man be put safely ashore, he elected instead to have him placed in the *Victory* where he could at least ensure he would not fall foul of any home-grown harm.

With regard to his sentence, she suggested that the man Will had attacked could have been one of those in high places who was making life difficult for Lady Hamilton now that Nelson could no longer protect her; hence his light sentence from a sympathetic court.

'You're far too knowledgeable for your own good,' Sir Peter had admonished with not more than a twinkle of humour in his countenance. 'I don't believe that even Sydney Town is ready for such modern and outrageous self-assuredness from a lady of such tender years.'

'Splosh!' countered his niece.

'Splosh?'

'I don't know what the fuddy-duddy matrons of New South Wales would consider proper, but what nonsense it is that someone with intelligence should pretend to be ignorant of matters that have been one of the prime topics of conversation in the drawing rooms of the country for years, simply because she's a woman.'

'Fuddy-duddy!' Sir Peter released a hearty laugh. 'Fuddy-duddy! Splosh!' He then released an infectious burst of mirth that had Amanda fighting to restrict the extent of her resulting beams of enjoyment. 'And I thought that the currency lasses of New South Wales were at the forefront of this new female assertiveness that threatens to shake the world to its very foundations.'

'Currency lasses?'

'Those that were born there. Although it's a bit of a misnomer at the moment. For the present currency is rum, and the sprightly lads and lasses of the colony are certainly not the product of rum. Which brings me to my theory on yonder young man with the ruddy thatch.'

He had then gone on to construct one of his more interesting alternative scenarios. He proposed that Will was a spy for the navy and that his sentence was an elaborate charade to place him in New South Wales in a position where he could gather sufficient damning information on the corrupt elements within the Rum Corps to spike their guns once and for all. The navy could then ship the ringleaders back to England in chains.

'Rum Corps?' Amanda queried.

'Hasn't your Granville told you that's what they call his corps?'

'No. Why do they call it that?'

He looked at her for a moment and then turned away. 'It's not important.'

'Tell me. I'll find out when we get there. Uncle Peter, please.'

He turned back and looked at her again, without speaking, for a time before saying, 'I'm afraid, my girl, that notwithstanding that you plan to marry one of them, they have within their midst as corrupt a clique of greedy opportunists as ever donned the King's uniform. They control most of the distribution of goods and services in the colony, including the allocation of convict labour, which they predominantly assign to their own cronies. They already own or control most of the land, and they own about sixty percent of all the livestock. And now that rum is the currency, they control the distribution of that as well, and have set up their own illicit still.'

She looked back into the waist, 'Then if our friend is to be the spy that will bring the corrupt clique undone, that will be for the good. I would not want Granville associating with anyone who was less than honest.'

'I'd like to think that someone was planning to bring them down. But I suspect it will take more than a fresh-faced youngster with a thatch of red hair.'

These flights of conjecture for a while provided some diversion from the monotony of the voyage. But for Amanda the result was that she regularly found herself being preoccupied with highly fanciful speculation not only on Will's former and present circumstances, but also on what might be in store for him in the future.

Sir Peter had told her of how a number of talented former convicts had taken advantage of the lawful opportunities available to them in the colony and had become prosperous members of the community.

'And respected?' she had asked at the time.

His reply had been along the lines of, 'At this point let's be content with prosperous. But in a few years, who knows?'

Amanda decided that to a degree she enjoyed Lieutenant Cotter's company. However, she did find some of his ways annoying, particularly a habit that whenever he found himself in familiar territory, or was relating an obviously well-practised anecdote, he would affect a pompous air and a theatrical flourish in his delivery, that brought him to the very edge of being a crushing bore.

She forgave him for this as well as she was able, excusing the quirk as the unavoidable consequence of the military's obsession with theatrics.

She and her uncle learned that he was the youngest of three sons of a modestly landed family from Somerset. From as early as he could remember his brothers and other members of the family would equip him with uniforms and toy weapons. And if it had not been apparent then what was expected of him, when he found himself at sea as a midshipman at the age of thirteen, he began to realise that the course of his life had been fairly securely set in place.

The posting to the *Victory* had been to his benefit, and with the problems with Bonaparte likely to continue for some time, his prospects for promotion had at least seemed sound. However, his financial situation was by no means secure. The young woman of means that his family had hoped would become his partner had become engaged to another while he was away with Nelson.

So, although he and his family had misgivings, when the opportunity arose to join Bligh in New South Wales, he decided he had better prospects of improving his finances in the colony than in England. From all accounts the prospects for military personnel being able to improve their financial lot were propitious, to say the least.

His plans for his future may well have been refined to include Amanda Dalrymple had she not been accompanying her uncle to New South Wales to join her fiancé, an officer in the New South Wales Corps, with a view to marrying him as soon as was practicable.

Amanda and her fiancé's families had been neighbours in Sussex and she had known him since she was a child. They had become engaged when he had returned home on leave. Originally they were to marry when he returned to England at the end of his posting. But, confronted with the combination of the unexpected death of her widowed father, and the equally unexpected acquisition by her fiancé of a prime piece of real estate in the colony, she accepted his invitation to join him in New South Wales and be married there.

The invitation was delivered by her uncle. Sir Peter had been living in New South Wales for more than eight years and had amassed a considerable fortune as a wholesale merchant. Whenever he returned to England he stayed with his brother, Amanda's father, and during these visits a warm relationship had developed between himself and Amanda.

When he learned that his brother was gravely ill he had returned to England but had arrived too late to see him before he died. He was, however, just in time to assume the role of Amanda's surrogate father. This immediately loaded him with conflicting responsibilities.

As the messenger of her fiancé he felt obliged to deliver the young man's proposal and present the argument of why she should accompany him back to New South Wales, if not entirely enthusiastically, at least impartially. He also accepted that the death of his brother reinforced her fiancé's argument.

But as her surrogate father he found himself tempted to reveal that he believed her fiancé to be a shallow young toady upon whom it would be unlikely that she could ever rely should she be confronted by real crisis. Also, it would not surprise him if the young man was involved with the corrupt clique that ran the corps.

However, since he also believed that it would not be wise for her to remain in England alone, he hoped that before she was married to her fiancé some circumstance might occur that would delay the event, perhaps indefinitely.'

These and other sentiments were bouncing around in the far reaches of his consciousness as he now turned from Cotter and looked down on young Will Noling.

'I did not know him very well,' Cotter replied. 'It was not usual for us to have dealings with any of the men, other than those we came in contact with in the course of our duties.'

'But you remembered his name as soon as you saw him,' said Amanda.

'He was on Nelson's staff.' As it did not seem as if he was going to amplify this remark they assumed he believed it was sufficient.

'Perhaps you could talk to him,' said Amanda. 'Find out what happened.'

'I'd rather not. He may not remember me.' And then a little later, 'I'm not too good at that sort of thing. And he might try and take advantage of it in some way.'

She gave him a searching look. 'I can't see it would do any harm just to ask.'

He kept his gaze away from her and shook his head. 'No, I wouldn't risk it. You never know with these people.'

'These people! You said he fought beside Nelson. He was wounded. He's not these people, he's your people.'

He turned then and met her gaze steadily. 'I'm sorry, Amanda, but I'm not going to approach him. I would feel awkward in doing so, and possibly he would feel awkward as well.' He waved a hand at the barricade. 'Divisions of that kind are there for a dual purpose. They protect us from them and they protect them from us.'

'Wallis!' Amanda exclaimed with a smile that Sir Peter immediately recognised, and steeled himself to intervene if it was necessary 'I do believe you've just ventured into political territory. Are we talking literally now, or ideologically? Are we talking about this barrier that stands between us and the convicts down below, or are we talking about barriers that stand between us and all people who are less fortunate than ourselves?'

'I suppose we could be talking about either.'

'And you agree they should exist?'

'They serve a purpose.'

She met his gaze for a moment and then turned away momentarily to catch her uncle's eye. 'Uncle Peter says that the barriers are coming down in New South Wales.'

'I doubt that is a good thing. Look at France. And I doubt it will last. In New South Wales or France.'

She turned her gaze back to the tall young man

with the unruly shock of bright red hair. 'So you won't speak to him?'

'No.'

'I'd like to speak to him.'

'Well, that will be impossible, for the captain would never allow it.'

He was probably right. As progressive as Captain Mortimer Percy Stevens was in refusing to keep the convicts in chains, in ensuring that every one of them spent as much time as possible on the upper deck during daylight hours, and in insisting that the decks below were aired regularly, it was unlikely he would agree for any of the male, let alone female, passengers to converse with any of them.

For a start it would be highly unlikely that a convict would have anything of interest to impart, other than to offer an offensive suggestion perhaps. And for this reason, if for no other, it would be sensible to protect the sensibilities of the more genteel people in his charge.

But he had in mind a plan that would by default result in a number of the convicts, including the young man in question, addressing the entire company of passengers.

And so it was that a few days after leaving Rio de Janeiro he set his plan into action with the words 'Mr Cotter, I require your assistance.'

A few days afterwards, late in the afternoon, half the convicts on board were crammed into the waist of the ship. As directed by the marines, most of them were squatting on the deck facing aft. But as there was not enough room to accommodate them all in this manner, some of them were occupying slightly higher positions including between the set lines on the main mast's rail, the combing beside the companionway and the edge of the skid beams that held the boats.

The marines were obviously agitated by this disruption to their normal routine and were in a surly mood, lashing out with truncheons at anyone who was slow to obey an order or move out of the way as they occasionally waded through the wash of bodies.

At the head of the short flight of steps that led up to the quarterdeck, the gate in the heavy barrier that divided the two decks was propped ajar against the guardrail. The Captain and Lieutenant Cotter were standing with their backs to the gate, talking. From that position they could be seen from both the waist and the quarterdeck.

On the quarterdeck, still shielded from sight from those in the waist by the barrier, the entire contingent of paying passengers, with the exception of the only two children on board and their nanny, were sitting on two rows of seats facing the gate.

The absent children were the twin daughters of Janette Randall who was travelling to Australia to join her husband, a member of Governor Bligh's staff, who had recently accompanied Bligh to the colony. Besides Amanda, Janette and her daughters' nanny were the only women on board.

'Are they all here, Mr Gordon?' the captain finally called out into the waist.

'Yes, sir,' replied Lieutenant Gordon, who was standing at the rear of the assembled convicts, before he turned away to glower at the marine standing closest to him and mutter a profanity beneath his breath.

'Well, then,' said the captain in a voice directed across both decks, 'you will be wonderin' why I've assembled you here. It is hoped that this'll be the first of a number of such events during the remainder of the voyage. Tomorrow it will be the turn of your friends down below that we couldn't accommodate on the upper deck today.

'You may not know it, but our own Mr Wallis Cotter was in the *Victory* at the battle of Trafalgar. Why we are all assembled here is so that Mr Cotter can tell us about the greatest naval battle ever fought and about the death of one of the greatest men ever to die in defence of his country, Horatio Lord Nelson. I'll now hand you over to Lieutenant Cotter, Royal Navy.'

A low, assenting murmur immediately spread through the assembled convicts as the captain moved away and Cotter took his place.

Glancing first back at the group assembled on the quarterdeck and then into the waist, Cotter cleared his throat and started his story with the words, 'For two long and wearying years the Mediterranean fleet under Lord Nelson cruised off

401

the French port of Toulon hoping to engage the French in a decisive battle that would once and for all put paid to Bonaparte's plans to invade England. Fruitlessly.'

'Fruitlessly,' someone echoed from the waist. And then with a chuckle, 'Yer didn't have no fruit?'

'Silence!' roared Lieutenant Gordon from the rear as a ripple of laughter drifted around the bedraggled assembly.

Captain Stevens stepped back closer to Lieutenant Cotter and looking down at the sea of faces that were turned towards him held a finger to his lips. The laughter died, but many smiles remained. Stevens smiled back, as if acknowledging that this uncommon creasing of their faces was a sign to him of their appreciation, which in most cases it probably was.

Cotter cleared his throat again and continued, 'But the French fleet refused all Lord Nelson's enticements to come out and fight.'

'Come out and fight, you French bastards,' someone called out. The resulting laughter died quickly as Lieutenant Gordon waded into the group and prodded the speaker with the end of a heavy leather-encased truncheon.

Captain Stevens again stepped forward and, still smiling, held up his hand and said, 'We have ladies present, lads. Keep the language down and let Mr Cotter tell you his story without interruption. You can ask him questions when he's finished.'

This was met with a brief surge of muttering, perhaps from those who had been unaware that there were women on board. But by the time Cotter began to speak again most of the noise had subsided.

He first told of the French fleet's escape from Toulon and how Nelson chased Admiral Villeneuve to the West Indies and back.

By the time he reached the eve of the battle of Trafalgar, the assembled throng were hanging on his every word. And at appropriate moments, despite Gordon's warnings, the more adventurous continued to release noisy cries of support. When this happened Captain Stevens would step back beside Cotter and pat him enthusiastically on the shoulder, and both men would then stand beaming down at the excited throng waiting for the noise to abate. Occasionally they would glance back at the group of smiling passengers seated on the quarterdeck.

Amanda Dalrymple's gaze was locked on Cotter and when he cast a quick and somewhat embarrassed glance in her direction she decided that there was much more to him than she had at first realised. For a start he was more attractive than she could recall. Perhaps it was being able to see him so clearly in the afternoon light and watch his every move and expression without interruption and without appearing forward.

'Silence!' thundered Gordon, when intermittent bursts of cheering and shouting broke out as

Cotter began to describe the activities preceding the battle.

As the noise died Cotter cleared his throat and continued.

'After a hurried three-week refit in Portsmouth, the *Victory* was armed with one hundred and two guns total, including two bastard 68-pounder carronades on the fo'c'sle.' He cast a sudden and sheepish smile at the passengers beside him. 'Sorry. I mean unauthorised 68-pounder carronades.'

'What's a carronade?' someone called out from below.

'It's called a "smasher",' another voice responded. 'And it fires a great big ugly cannon ball about this size. And if you want, a keg of musket balls as well.'

Cotter peered down at a squat brawny man who was scooping his arms above a head that was so completely devoid of hair it could have been carved from a block of beech and then sanded and polished smooth.

'Able Seaman Barkman?'

'Aye. One and the same, sir.' The speaker rose into a part crouch and gave Cotter what was probably a gap-tooth smile of greeting, but what would have appeared to most creatures on the planet as a threatening snarl.

Captain Stevens moved to Cotter's side. 'Was this man in the *Victory*?'

'Aye, sir.' Cotter shook his head. 'I had no idea he was on board.'

'Were you at Trafalgar?' Stevens called out to the man.

'Aye, sir. I were there with bells on.'

'But did you have your balls on after the battle?' came a less than generous query from the back of the group.

'What were you?' Stevens asked above the rattle of laughter.

'I be captain of a 24-pounder on the larboard side of the middle gun deck, sir. That be what I be then. But that ain't what I be now. Now I be a traveller to Botany Bay, sir.'

'Why?'

'I thought I might like to see what t'other side of the world looked like, sir.'

This was met with some derisive laughter and calls for him to sit down.

'Are there any others on board who were there?'

The man turned around, still at a half crouch, like a wrestler, with his arms now scooped in front of him as if he was perhaps still indicating the size of the carronade's ball. 'Jamie Turnberry over there, he were a gunner in the *Neptune*. Will Noling's down below. He were with me in the *Victory*. In fact he were with Nelson on the quarterdeck at Trafalgar.' A hand went up in the middle of the press of bodies. 'What's yer name again? Wilters. Wilters over there. He were in the *Belleisle*.' He looked about. 'Don't think there were any others.'

'Who did you say was with Nelson?'

'Will Noling, Cap'n. He be with them still down below.'

'What do you mean he was with Nelson?'

'He were with him when he were hit, Cap'n. And he were in the cockpit when he died.'

Stevens turned to Cotter and asked quietly, 'Noling? Wasn't he the man you were checking on?'

'Aye. That was Noling. I thought I mentioned he was on Nelson's staff.'

'The significance didn't hit me.' He turned back to face the man in the waist. 'One day soon we might have this Mr Noling tell us of his experiences.'

'Get him now,' someone called out, and others endorsed the demand.

Stevens held up his hand. 'Quiet, lads. We have a long trip ahead of us. Mr Cotter will now tell you of the battle.' He looked back at the man standing below him. 'Thank you, Mr Barkman. We may have to get you up here one day as well.' He stepped back and with a warm sense of well-being turned his attention for a moment to the passengers seated behind the barricade. This was going much better than he had hoped. Everyone seemed to be caught up in the spirit of the occasion. Young Miss Dalrymple was obviously enjoying herself. Her face was flushed and she had a firm grip on her uncle's arm.

As Barkman manoeuvred his broad stern with some difficulty back on to the deck he was accompanied by a chorus of encouraging shouts and bursts of merriment. By this time Lieutenant Gordon had given up trying to stop all but the more boisterous behaviour and stood scowling at the back of the group and occasionally muttering to himself.

When the noise had died to an occasional oath or a stifled chortle, Cotter stepped back to the edge of the break. He paused again and for a time appeared to be gathering his thoughts.

'Come on, tell us about the battle,' someone prompted impatiently.

'For three weeks we waited for the combined French and Spanish fleet to emerge from Cadiz. We knew she would, because she was clearly seen preparing for battle. And then on the morning of the nineteenth of October we received the word back from our frigates: the enemy were loosing their topsails and preparing for sea. I can tell you all that when we received that message the hair on the back of my neck fair prickled most peculiar.'

'And the hair on mine, an' all,' the former Able Seaman Barkman called out from below. 'Not that I have much on the back of me neck. But I have plenty on the back of me back.'

Cotter waited until the brief spate of sporadic and seemingly nervous laughter that followed this had died down. 'We kept them under close watch throughout the day and night of the twentieth, and into the dark hours of the morning of the twenty-first. They were lit up like the Thames Embankment during the night, while we were blackened, and stalked them like a pack o' wolves ready to pounce as soon as it was light.

'And when the sun came up and we could see'm stretched right across the eastern horizon, the order swept across the fleet: "Prepare for battle".'

A hoarse cheer erupted from the waist.

'By the time I arrived at my station on the lower gun deck, my gun captains had their crews clearing away the guns and running them out loaded with double shot. Centre guns treble shot. From that moment on all I saw . . .'

His voice died suddenly and he lifted a hand to the side of his head. 'All I saw of the battle were my guns' crews firing, loading, and firing again.' As he began to speak again he dropped his hand and his voice soon returned to normal. 'Men were cut in half by balls that breached the gun ports. Others were blinded or near skinned alive by splinters. The decks were awash with so much blood the shavings were swept away. We lost too many men and had to send for more.

'Marines finally arrived from the upper deck and stripped off their jackets to help make up the numbers. Within minutes they were joining in with the wild yelling of the tars with each loading and firing. Savage, crazy cries that got louder the deafer they became. Later, when the need for the marines was greater elsewhere, it took much coaxing to get them to stop and rejoin their parties.'

'Hurrah for the marines!' someone called out

from the port side behind the gathering. Lieutenant Gordon's head snapped around.

'Sponge and load,' came a hoarse cry from the centre of the group, arresting Gordon's attention and probably saving the hide of his errant subordinate.

The brawny Able Seaman Barkman was back on his feet and bent as before in a crouch, but this time with one hand curled in front of his waist and the other curled beside it as if gripping the shaft of an invisible pole.

'In goes the mop. Wet and sloppy.' He thrust out his hands. 'Slosh, slosh, slosh. All embers out. Back comes the mop.' Back came his hands. 'In goes the charge.' Forward went his hands. 'You know what a charge be, Billy? A silken bag of coarse black powder, that be what a charge be, Billy, he says. Smooth as your mother's left cheek, he says. In goes the wad. In goes the ball.'

He twisted his body so that his hands were positioned over a new location and twisted a clenched hand against an open palm. 'Into the vent goes the worm. Twist, twist, twist. Out comes the worm. In goes the goose. You know what the goose be, Billy? A quill crammed with fine black powder, he says. Stand back!' He straightened and held his left hand straight out from his shoulder, and his right arm crocked below it. He bobbed his head to the left. 'This hand be the aimer.' And to the right. 'This one be the lanyard.'

He began to raise, lower and tilt his left hand.

'Come left. Come left. Come up. Come up. Fire!' He pulled back his right hand and then clamped both hands over his ears. 'Whoompaaah!' He then threw both hands up in the air and kept them there for a time, frozen in that position. Finally he smiled and looked about him sheepishly, and then manoeuvred back down to the deck amidst a mixed ripple of mirth and derision from those around him.

The captain was back at Cotter's shoulder. Smiling broadly he clapped his hands together a few times and nodded in Barkman's direction.

Cotter, too, nodded, but his smile was tighter, and when he raised his gaze and began to speak again his voice had changed, as if his throat had become constricted. 'Soon after we engaged the enemy our rigging became entangled with the rigging of the French ship *Redoubtable*, and for most of our battle we were locked against her, hull to hull.

'But that didn't stop them or us from firing broadside after broadside into the other. Afterwards, those of us that weren't deaf were half deaf, and all of us were stupid from the shock of the explosions.' He cupped his hands over his ears and stood stock still for a time before he lowered them. They waited for him to continue.

'Tell us about Nelson,' someone called out, perhaps to aid him.

Amanda found herself almost aching from the effort of willing him to start speaking again.

'I'm ... I'm sorry,' he managed to stammer finally. 'I did not recover my hearing for many weeks. Nor my full senses. My battleground was the lower gun deck. I knew little at the time of what happened elsewhere. I have not felt inclined to seek for the detail since.'

'He thinks the lower gun deck were a nightmare,' Able Seaman Barkman called out, rising again into his familiar crouch. 'It were a nightmare of a kind, I'll wager. But the mother and father of a nightmare were on that middle gun deck where I were. It were a thunderin' hell. The blastin' were so bad it were like bein' hit with an iron bar square twixt the eyes. You could taste the pain of it like sippin' bitter wormwood.

'The blasts came at you like a blacksmith's hammer. From below. From behind. From above. From ahead. On that deck your head was bruised from skin to core.'

'Sit down, Barkie,' someone called out.

'Tell us about Nelson,' another called out to where Captain Stevens was again talking to Cotter.

The mood had changed. There was no more laughter. No one was smiling.

'Yeah, we want to hear about Nelson.'

Cotter moved away from the break and Stevens turned and held up his hands for silence.

'Mr Cotter is not feeling well so I'm afraid that concludes his address. We will do something similar to this in the near future, providing all of you behave yourselves as you return to your quarters.'

'We want to hear about Nelson,' someone persisted, and this cry was taken up by others.

'At another time,' said Stevens. 'Now quieten down and return to your quarters.'

'Why don't you get Will Noling up here,' called out Able Seaman Barkman who was back on his feet. 'He can tell us about Nelson.'

'Aye, get Noling,' someone seconded.

'We want Noling.' The chant was taken up by a good proportion of the group and persisted for some time, despite Lieutenant Gordon and a number of marines moving into the fringe and shouting for silence as they prodded away at a number of men with their heavy truncheons.

'All right, all right,' Captain Stevens called out finally, fanning the palms of both hands at them in a downward motion. When they eventually quietened he said, 'If you all settle down I'll have someone fetch him. But I warn you if there's any repeat of the clamour I just heard, I'll end the proceedings immediately.'

He looked across their heads. 'Mr Gordon, would you fetch Mr Noling please.'

Will came into the light blinking like a miner coming off the midnight shift. He was not surprised by the size of the group squatting in the waist. He and the others who were still below had been promised they would be assembled the following day to hear an address, presumably from the captain, so he had been expecting to see such a sight.

What he had not been expecting was to be led to the front of the group and up the short flight of steps to the quarterdeck where the captain seemed to be waiting for him. Nor had he been expecting a smattering of cheers from the assembly, and to be assailed by a barrage of demands of 'Tell us about Nelson', and similar cries.

'What were his last words?' someone called out.

'Kiss me, Hardy,' another replied.

'Kiss me, Hardy, kiss me arse!' a more derisive voice repeated with a chortle. 'What were he, a Nancy boy or someat?'

Behind them Lieutenant Gordon was on the verge of wading into the crowd and collaring the offender but checked himself. Instead he turned a belligerent gaze on the captain and declared silently, let it be on your stupid head, you old fool.

'Mr Noling, Mr Cotter over there has been telling us about the events leading up to the battle of Trafalgar. We have been told that you were on the quarterdeck with Lord Nelson. We would all appreciate it very much if you would describe the battle as you saw it. And perhaps you could also tell us about Lord Nelson's last moments.'

'Were he really a Nancy boy, f'r instance?' the familiar and persistent voice demanded from the group below.

Will looked down and stared coldly at the

leering face of a thin man whose top lip was curled back in a smiling leer as he stared back unflinchingly at him.

Did he say Cotter? Will turned back to the quarterdeck and looked across to where Cotter was pulling up a chair beside a group of well-dressed people including one, two women. Two women! Where in the bright blue blazes did they come from?

His gaze then locked on Cotter and the two men watched each other for a moment.

'Come on, Noling, tell us about Nelson,' cried the undernourished haranguer in the waist.

Stevens stepped to the edge of the break. 'Keep quiet, that man, or I'll have you in irons.' He then turned to Will. 'Would you describe the battle for us, Mr Noling? We would appreciate it.'

'Aye, I'll tell you of the battle,' Will replied in a steady voice that acquaintances would have recognised was loaded with double, perhaps treble shot.

He turned away for a moment and, gathering his thoughts, looked about him, allowing his gaze to sweep the faces of the people on the quarterdeck beside him. The young woman at the end looks like she's been crying. Why would that be? If that's her husband's arm she's clinging to so tightly, he's a lucky man indeed. She's lovely and he must be twice her age.

He glanced across at the captain. 'Where do you want me to start?'

'Mr Cotter took us up to the moment the enemy

was sighted on the morning of the twenty-first. But that's the last he saw of them. He was able to give us a sobering description of the scene on the lower gun deck, which we very much appreciated. But what we'd like to hear now is a description of some of the major events of the battle as seen from the quarterdeck. Can you do that for us?'

Will's gaze for a moment touched the still snarling face of the man he had observed before. And then in a voice that carried easily to all of those who were assembled he said, 'First, I'll tell you something about Lord Nelson.

'When we arrived back at Portsmouth after two years of battling black storms in the Mediterranean, and after chasing the French to the West Indies and back, every one of our ships was afloat and riding high. And every man jack of us was in finer fettle than when we'd left England. That was Nelson's doing. And no other man could have done it.

'When he went ashore in Portsmouth with the *Victory*'s salute booming across the harbour it was a miserable day. Cold and wet. But a whole host of people came running from every direction to watch him disembark. And they stood in the rain and cheered themselves hoarse. It was as if he had already saved them from Bonaparte's invasion.

'On the morning before he rejoined the *Victory* he had breakfast at the George Hotel. When the people of Portsmouth learned he was there, so many of them flocked to see him the streets of the port were jammed tight. He would have had little hope of walking to the dock, so he arranged to be picked up near Portsea beach. And then he departed the hotel by a back door.

'Many of those who couldn't get near the dockside had gathered at the beach hoping to see his boat leave in the distance. When these people suddenly realised that he was among them, many of them were so overcome they were unable to speak let alone cheer. They just stood there and stared. Others began to cry openly. Some sank to their knees in prayer.

'And then as his boat pulled away, and those at the dockside realised what was happening, they rushed down to the beach to see him. Some of them ran straight into the water up to their waists.

'Then they began to cheer. And the roar swept across the harbour to Gosport like a roll of thunder. And they didn't stop cheering until he was out of sight.'

Will stood stock still for a moment looking past them. Then he ran his gaze first over those below him and then over those beside him. There was not a sound from any of them.

'Now I'll tell you about the battle.'

And so, after gathering his thoughts, he told them of the battle. Occasionally those who sat and listened called out a question. Or when it was appropriate they loosed a resounding cheer, or a cry of approval or dismay. But most of the time in the waist and on the quarterdeck they sat quite still and leant forward with their breath regularly held in check so that they would miss nothing. Some of them cried from time to time. Others trembled uncontrollably from when he started to speak until long after he finished.

He told them of seeing the topgallants of the enemy ships on the horizon: 'The sun was on them before it was anywhere else. They could have been a row of signal flares mounted on top of a long grey wall. Nelson told his signals Lieutenant, Mr Pascoe, to run up the order "Prepare for Battle".

'The men had been held in check for two and a half years for this day. They hit the decks at a full gallop. The pipers and drummers played "Heart of Oak".

'Most of the gunners were stripped to the waist and had bandannas tied around their ears. Marines sharpened their blades. Boys distributed fire buckets. Others spread sawdust and wood shavings on the decks and checked that the hammocks stowed in the nets along both sides of the upper deck were secured tight enough to stop a musket ball. Powder monkeys dampened down the fire curtains in the magazines and ran out the first cartridges to the guns. The guns' crews loaded their guns. The gun captains checked that all the shot garlands around the hatchways were restocked with cannon balls. The surgeons prepared the cockpit for amputations.'

He told them of Nelson's special signal to the

men: 'When we were still a mile or so off, Nelson told Mr Pascoe to run up the message "England confides that every man will do his duty. And be quick about it," he says, "for I have another of importance concerning the battle."

'Pascoe near came down with apoplexy over the "confides". He would have had to spell it out letter by letter. By the time he'd raised it we'd have been ducking cannon balls. So with Nelson's permission for the change, he ran up instead, "England expects that every man will do his duty".'

'I don't think any of us thought much of it until it was up there. But as it caught the breeze and stood out, a roar went up from the crew of the *Temeraire* on our larboard quarter, and then another from the *Neptune* on our starboard. And as it was relayed back down the line the muffled roars of approval came back to us on the breeze. By then our own crew had their fists in the air and were shouting themselves hoarse.'

He shook his head. 'And although my fine hairs were standing rigid, for the life of me when I think back on it, I don't know why. I suspect we were all more caught up with the shouting than the message. For none of us needed to be reminded of our duty.'

'It weren't the message, Will'm,' Able Seaman Barkman called out, running a hand over his smoothly sanded pate. 'It were the moment. And like the Bard said about Agincourt, it were a moment that them Englishmen who weren't there to share it will curse forever whatever it was that kept them away.'

Will told them of the *Victory* coming under fire:

'The *Bucentaure* began to fire ranging shots at us as we came within range. The first two fell short. But the next tore straight through the main's topgallant. A moment later about eight of them opened up with full broadsides. A wave of cannon balls crashed into us. Within seconds the top of the mizzen and all of the studded sails and booms had been blown away. We also lost sails, yards, booms and rigging from the foremast and main. And half the wheel was shot to pieces.

'Before we reached their line we'd lost about sixty men on the upper deck alone. About a dozen marines were cut down on the poop by a single double-headed shot that went through them like a scythe.

'The moment we crossed their line we swung around the *Bucentaure*'s stern and opened fire. First up Billy Willmet, the bos'n, fired the smasher on the larboard side of the fo'c'sle straight through their cabin windows. He had it loaded with one 68-pound ball and a keg filled with about five hundred musket balls. A few moments later we raked her with a treble-shotted broadside that brought down all three of her masts. A huge cloud of hot black smoke came back at us like it had been belched from the gates of hell. Which was fitting. Those opening shots killed upwards of four hundred of her crew and blew twenty guns off their mounts. Between the rolling thunder of the guns we could hear the screams of those that weren't killed outright.' He held up a hand and opened and closed it. 'The air was chock full of burning debris and scorched flesh. You could feel it. Taste it.

'The black smoke was then blasted away by billowing blue and white smoke. Flaring crimson. Laced with trails of flying lumps of metal and shattered pieces of timber. One cannon ball fired at point blank range from the *Redoubtable* sliced through the hammocks in the waist, knocked the end off the launch, shattered the timbers at the break, and knocked a buckle from Captain Hardy's shoe.

'Nelson told him, "This work is too warm to last long, my friend."

'But it lasted long enough. When Mr Scott, his secretary, moved to talk to him, a cannon ball whistled between Nelson and Hardy and almost tore the poor man in half. Those parts of him that weren't blown to kingdom-come hit the deck with such force you'd have sworn they'd been fired into it from the mouth of the cannon itself.'

He paused and looked somewhere past them all. 'He was a good man, Mr Scott.' And his voice faltered as he added, 'A friend. Before what remained of him was scooped up and thrown over the side, his blood painted a broad crimson stain on the deck a few yards aft of the quarterdeck hatchway.

'Then Lord Nelson himself was hit. Shot by a sniper perched in the *Redoubtable*'s rigging. The ball struck him near his shoulder and lodged against his backbone. He went down as if his legs had been blown from beneath him.' His voice faltered. 'He ... he lay where Mr Scott had fallen and his jacket was stained with his secretary's blood. He was conscious, and from the way he fell he was certain his backbone had been shot through. He told Hardy this. I didn't see him fall. I didn't hear what he said. I was told this later.'

'What were you doing?' someone called out.

Will was momentarily distracted. 'What?'

'What were you doing? Where were you?'

'I was lying on the deck a few feet away with a sore head and a broken shoulder.'

They all watched him in silence waiting for him to continue.

He turned and ran his gaze over the people assembled on the quarterdeck, allowing it to rest on the young woman he had noticed earlier. Her cheeks shone as if she had recently rubbed tears from them. Perhaps not, he conceded; perhaps it was simply the play of light on her face. He glanced at the end of the row of seats and saw that Lieutenant Cotter had both hands clamped together tightly on his lap and appeared to be trembling.

'Did they take you to the cockpit?' someone prompted from the waist.

'What?' He looked back.

'Were you anywhere near Nelson when he died?'

'Yes.'

'What were his last words?'

He shook his head. 'The cockpit was a red nightmare. Dancing shadows. Lanthorns sweeping backwards and forwards. Rasping bone saws. Men screaming and groaning. We were still locked against the *Redoubtable*, and at times you couldn't tell what were screams and what was the screeching of our splintered timbers.'

'Did he say, "Kiss me, Hardy"?' someone called out, but not the man Will had earlier admonished with his stare.

Will did not reply immediately, and when he did it was to shake his head and say, 'He took a while to die and was in great pain towards the end. He spent most of the time talking quietly to Chaplain Scott and Dr Beattie. From time to time Captain Hardy came down to report on the battle.'

'Did he say, "Kiss me, Hardy"?'

He sighed and said quietly. 'I doubt it. He sometimes used the word *kismet*. I think the skipper misheard him.'

'Tell them what happened at Gibraltar,' Able Seaman Barkman called out. 'Tell them what happened when they tried to send him home in a frigate.'

So Will told them of the final act. 'When Lord Nelson died his body was placed in a cask of brandy. When we arrived in Gibraltar, Surgeon

Beattie drew off the brandy and replaced it with stronger spirit to preserve the body for the journey back to England.

'Admiral Collingwood sent a message across to *Victory* to transfer the body to the frigate *Euryalus* so that it could be returned to England immediately. When Hardy told the crew of the Admiral's order, they gathered on the upper deck and Billy Willmet said something along the lines of, "We lived with His Lordship for two and a half years. He fought and died alongside us. We'll take him home. No others have the right. And we'll take him home in his ship. This ship. HMS *Victory*. That way we'll make sure he gets there safely. The frigate might be taken by the French. How could we live with ourselves if that happened? But there's no way on God's earth they'll ever take the *Victory*. Not with us here and him still on board."'

In the waist Barkman came to his feet. '"No fuckin' way are you goin' to take him from us", is what he also said. "And if you try it'll be over my dead body, and a good number of those that comes for him." They backed down, didn't they? And I don't blame 'em. Who'd have wanted to look down the wrong end of a smasher with old Billy Willmet at the other end of it after what he'd done to the *Bucentaure* and after he wiped out the entire boardin' party trying to climb over from the *Redoubtable*. Later they hushed up what happened, didn't they. Mutinies are no good for anyone's career.'

'There was no mutiny,' said Will quietly. 'Strong words don't make a mutiny. Not unless someone objects to them enough to try and do something about it.'

'Is it true that some of the men toasted his memory with the brandy that was drawn off when the *Victory* returned to Gibraltar?' The questioner was Sir Peter Dalrymple.

Will looked the man squarely in the eye for a lingering moment. Finally deciding that there was no malice in the question, and that it was a reasonable one, he shook his head. 'Who knows what sailors will do who've lived through such a battle, and wish to pay their respects to such a man?'

He then turned his gaze to the young woman. Her eyes stayed on his for a moment. But then she lowered them and turned away. The shine on her cheeks is definitely from tears, he concluded. I wonder who she is.

FIFTEEN

As the *Tynemouth* was manoeuvring to enter the harbour at Cape Town she passed close by the American brig *Pemaquid Point* heading out of port en route to Boston. Although both vessels were being buffeted by a solid westerly and their upper decks were being scoured by fine sheets of drizzling rain, a number of civilians were visible on the upper deck of both vessels.

On the *Tynemouth* two of those civilians were Amanda and Sir Peter Dalrymple, who together with a handful of the more intrepid paying passengers were braving the elements in the hope of catching sight of Table Mountain.

On the *Pemaquid Point* the sightseers were looking the other way. For they were hoping to catch a glimpse of some of the unfortunate felons who were being transported to New South Wales on the *Tynemouth*.

All were to be disappointed, for the convicts on the *Tynemouth* were locked below decks and would remain there until well after she anchored; and Table Mountain was locked beneath a damp shroud that would remain in place during the transport's entire stay in port.

One passenger on the American brig who was paying particular interest to the *Tynemouth* was a young woman who was wrapped against the weather in a sailor's anorak. The very sight of the transport, and intimate knowledge of the likely conditions that were being endured by those on board, filled her with a curious mix of trepidation and longing.

As the ships passed each other, a gust of wind pulled back the oversized hood of the anorak exposing her head and shoulders. An obliging tar had earlier wrapped the garment around her when, having heard that the transport was approaching, she had rushed on deck ill-clad for the conditions. With her attention completely taken up by the other vessel, she had mouthed a *thank you* to the gallant seafarer and simply hugged the coat against her body with her folded arms to prevent it from being blown open.

Amanda Dalrymple happened to look across at this woman as she was struggling to pull the hood back around her ears and secure the leather tie-cord beneath her chin.

Other than to note that she was young and that her hair was long, Amanda did not dwell on the incident. Actually, she did spend a few seconds in whimsical contemplation of the validity of the notion that the lives of people on ships that pass in the night—or in this case *near* night—can sometimes be mysteriously linked.

Had Will Noling been on deck and seen the woman, and had the bleak weather not robbed the day of its colour, it is likely the incident would have had a much greater impact on him than on Amanda. Because he would have seen that not only was the woman's hair the colour of Jessica's, but that she had a remarkable resemblance to Jessica, and at that distance it would have been difficult for him to determine whether or not it was really her. Certainly the sight of her would have caused him great anxiety. But of course Will was not on deck, there was no colour in the day, and the woman was not Jessica.

She was Elizabeth Crowling. And if the full implications and significance of that had been known by Will and others it would have caused a few tingles to run up and down their spines.

The American brig had picked up Elizabeth and three other survivors from the *Cobscook Bay* in Batavia.

When the schooner had struck the submerged shoal on the northern coast of New South Wales, Elizabeth and those who were with her had been caught up in the wreckage of the hull. Unlike Jessica, who had been hurled well clear of the main structure of the vessel along with the shattered remains of the weatherdeck cabin.

While Jessica was being swept away in the wash of the breakers that were crashing over the shoal, Elizabeth and six members of the crew managed to launch and scramble into the pinnace before what remained of the hull was torn completely apart.

During the night they hauled in two more survivors. The next morning they were able to rig a makeshift sail that allowed them to run before the wind, but they had not salvaged enough rigging to allow them to turn around and beat back into it so that they could search for others.

When they reached the mainland two days later and some one hundred miles further north, they had loose intentions of either waiting for the wind to change so that they could try to sail back to Sydney, or perhaps attempt the journey on foot. An attack by natives put paid to both of those options.

Two of the men were speared and the survivors barely managed to launch the boat and escape. They then reluctantly continued their journey north, Elizabeth more than any of the others suffering as a result of this decision. The greater risk of her being recaptured—had they been able to make their way south—was of no consequence to her when measured against the knowledge that they were now abandoning any chance of finding her companion. *She's alive, I tell you. Alive!*

By the time they reached the town of Kupang on the south-west corner of Timor there were only five of them left. And incredibly, shortly afterwards they lost another man while crossing to Batavia in a native prau. He was a straw-haired former wheelwright from Nantucket, and no older than Elizabeth. Having survived all the terrors they had faced up until then without seeming to suffer any more than the others, he chose to throw himself into the smooth waters of the Java Sea.

The hidden shoal that destroyed the *Tynemouth* was about two hundred miles to the south of where the *Cobscook Bay* had foundered two years before. Both mishaps were similar in many ways, but there were some notable differences: whereas the *Cobscook Bay* went down some ten miles from shore, the *Tynemouth* foundered off the point of a small rocky island slightly less than two miles from land; and whereas all that remained of the *Cobscook Bay* was splintered wreckage scattered on the ocean, great lumps of the after end of the *Tynemouth* were cast upon the aforementioned island. Along with some of the crew and most of the paying passengers.

The majority of the convicts and crew and a small number of passengers did not fare so well. Mainly as a consequence of where they were located on the vessel at the time of the collision, they were cast into the wild torrent that separated the rocky outcrop from the mainland. The crew members who found themselves in this situation had either been on the upper deck or were bedded down in the fo'c'sle; the few passengers who found themselves similarly disadvantaged had also been on the upper deck; and the convicts, of course, had all been secured below decks.

The ship struck with such force that it tore right across the broad surface of the shoal, screaming as if in agony as the aging timbers of its keel were torn apart. It finally came to a shuddering halt with its forepeak suspended above a churning tumult of wind, wave and spray beyond the rocks.

The sliding mountain of water that the ship had been riding effortlessly lifted the stern and swung the entire vessel around abeam of the sea. Like a great dying seabird, the old ship trembled for a moment in the wash of the monster that had brought it there, and then it fell slowly on its side and broke in two.

Almost in the same motion, and accompanied by a continuation of the teeth-jarring battery of exploding timbers, a following wave then picked up the forward section and hurled it over the shoal into the chasm beyond. Moments later the trailing edge of the wave lifted the after section, held it for a moment, and then slammed it down again on to the one visible section of the shoal.

The gale from the south that had converged on the ship outside of Sydney some four days before, and which had prompted Captain Stevens to turn away from the high rocky headlands of the harbour and run before the wind, continued relentlessly to batter what remained of the vessel.

Beyond the shoal, water swept into the forward section through the break in the hull and through a jagged wound of shattered and missing timbers that extended along the entire length of what remained of the keel. Within minutes it had begun its death dive, sliding beneath the surface and leaving, billowing in its wake, a fat black geyser of air and debris and a small collection of human refuse.

It then spiralled slowly down through one hundred and fifty fathoms of jet black water, trailing a snaking comet-tail of expanding black bubbles. Inside, the convicts howled and screamed silently into the face of the tumbling darkness that crushed in on them with relentless, merciless and ever-increasing pressure.

Just before the remains of the vessel struck the bottom, it levelled out and ploughed upright along the seabed, forcing a bow wave of sand to run before it and to rise high about either side of the keel. Finally it came to a stop and lay there, creaking and heaving from the exertion of its death-throes.

When it gasped its final defiant breath, great cumulus clouds of sand and debris, charged with a myriad shattered bubbles, remained swirling fitfully in the water around it.

Of the collection of human flotsam that remained high above on the surface, some were dead, some were dying, and some were clinging to whatever buoyant debris they could grab hold of.

They included a small collection of crew and passengers who had been on the upper deck at the time of the collision, and a larger assortment of convicts who had been secured close to where the timbers of the hull had parted when the ship had snapped in two.

Very few made it safely ashore. Most were drowned in the first few minutes. Some were assisted in this regard—intentionally and accidentally—by others clinging to them, and at times even trying to climb on top of them in the desperation of their struggles to survive.

Two people who did reach shore, after spending that night and most of the following day clinging to a shattered spar, were Amanda Dalrymple and Lieutenant Wallis Cotter. At the time of the collision they had been sheltering in the lee of the mizzen-mast. What was almost certainly a contributing factor in their being hurled into the ocean together, and then managing to hang on to each other, was that at the moment of impact Cotter had just locked Amanda in a crushing embrace and was kissing her. Although later, in reflection, Amanda was uncertain if she had not been the more active participant in the event, or at least had not initiated it.

She recalled that one moment she had been clinging to Cotter's arm for support, with a mixture of fear and exhilaration coursing through her each time the stern of the vessel rose and snaked backwards and forwards on the crest of the wave it was riding, and the next moment both her arms were around his neck and she was kissing him and being kissed in return. But the exact sequence of events was as unclear in recall as it had been at the time. Particularly when within moments of embracing—or so it certainly seemed—they found themselves fighting for their lives in the ocean.

Her first attempted recollection of her role in the matter was prompted by Cotter's insistence, while they were struggling to keep their heads above water, that she shed her heavy woollen gown, before—as he claimed—the damned thing pulled them both under. His tone and manner seemed to presume that they now shared a level of familiarity that suggested she might have been more than a passive participant in the preceding events.

Despite their predicament she was momentarily concerned that false impressions may have been given. But she complied anyway, not so much because their survival may have depended on it, but because she knew that in this stifling darkness there was no way he could see through what she imagined would be her now transparent camisole and petticoat; and being swept along and battered by mounting turbulence, she was reasonably confident that by morning either she or he, or both, would be drowned; in which case her nakedness would be of minor consequence.

Shortly after she abandoned her dress they were swept against the broken spar and managed to secure themselves in the tangled remains of that part of the rigging that was attached to it.

So with enhanced prospects of surviving the night—but at the cost of being exposed to his gaze come dawn—for a short time she did find herself revisiting the matter of the kiss and its implications.

However, by dawn all such concerns of propriety and modesty had been long forgotten. Both of them were so weary that almost their entire attention was taken up in trying to keep their faces out of the water. Neither of them could muster enough energy to glance more than occasionally at the other. Even then it would have been unlikely that Cotter would have caught sight of more than the back of Amanda's head, or possibly part of her face with broad strands of her hair plastered against it. The occasions on which any other part of her anatomy did broach the surface were rare, and then those parts were usually swathed in ballooning fabric.

Throughout the day they were caught in surging rip tides, and were swept backwards and forwards adjacent to the breaking waves that swept curving arms towards the shore. Eventually they drifted into the outer fringe of the surf where almost immediately they found themselves being lifted high on a rising wave. They were still halfway up the leading edge when the crest suddenly began to peel away and curl over them. The next moment a cliff-face formed beneath them and they were pushed over and into the sliding chasm beyond.

They were then propelled through acres of seething white water with their former life-saving spar leaping and bucking about them and threatening at any moment to either impale them or batter them to death. When the wave finally passed over them, for a few moments they remained bobbing and gasping in its wake. But any sense of relief at having somehow survived was cut short when they were picked up by a following wave and subjected to a repeat performance of the nightmare ride.

Twice more they were picked up and buffeted before they managed to stagger out on to a broad strip of sand where they collapsed and lay gasping for breath like stranded sea creatures.

Only when they recovered sufficiently to sit up did Amanda's concern for her state of undress return. And with a vengeance that took her breath. Not because of Cotter. But because of the prospective attention of the four ragged figures that were making their way along the beach towards them. So she tried in vain to close her torn camisole and detach the drenched material from where it was plastered against her torso and rendering the fabric almost transparent.

'Wallis!' she whispered, glancing across at him to make sure he was aware of them.

'I see them,' he confirmed.

Fighting the twinges of pain in her aching joints, she stood up and was momentarily surprised that

Cotter did not also come to his feet. She then saw his injured leg and for one brief instant her vision swam.

'My God!' she whispered, recovering, and quickly bent to assist him as he struggled to rise.

He managed to stand by placing his weight on his good leg and steadying himself against her.

With one eye on the approaching men, she dearly wished she had the strength to tell him to sit down again. But, 'How?' was all she could manage.

'One of the fittings on the spar.'

The men were now less than two hundred yards away. One of them was carrying what appeared to be a stout pole.

Her eyes darted to the rear of the beach. Beyond a light fringe of grass and bushes, a ridge laced with sharp rocky outcrops climbed away too steeply to provide an avenue of retreat. Her eyes then swept the ribbon of weed and debris along the high-tide line a few paces to one side of her.

'Can you stand without me for a moment?'

She sensed his nod, and left him for a moment to scoop up a stout length of driftwood.

'Leave me,' he whispered as she pressed back against him and took his arm. 'Run away. Quickly.' She could feel his weight suddenly beginning to settle on her, and realised he was probably fainting.

'No, don't,' she pleaded. 'Stand straight. Don't fall. I can't hold you. Oh God!'

But he fell anyway, almost dragging her down with him, and lay sprawled at her feet. Oh God! God! She tried unsuccessfully to avert her eyes from the long torn strip of flesh below his knee with what might have been a bone visible within the wound.

The men were about fifty yards away and were approaching so quickly one of them had broken into a trot to keep up with his companions.

As the first one reached her, she was engulfed by an impression she was being set upon by some strange species of wild creature that was not quite human, not quite animal—a shambling primate with sunken eyes and cheeks, and skin like creased sailcloth.

'Stay away!' she cried, brandishing the driftwood. She may have tried to swing it at him but the effect of any contact was lost as he collided with her and drove her to the ground.

'Let me go!' she screamed as he pinned her beneath him.

'Let her go!' Cotter shouted in endorsement, and tried to rise.

But the man carrying the pole, a solid length of driftwood, stepped in close and swiped him across the side of his head with it and then pinned him to the ground by jamming the heavier end against his chest.

'Steady, matey, steady. Or I'll brain you where you lie.' He chuckled. 'Might do it anyway. After we've swived your little lady.'

One of the others moved in and kicked Cotter in the ribs. 'Might swive you as well if it takes our fancy t'do so, eh lads? Before we brain you, that is.'

It was doubtful that Cotter heard any of this. His eyes were still open but his lids were flickering like the wings of a moth.

The kicker then turned his attention to where his companion was still struggling to subdue Amanda. 'Come on, Spider. If ye ain't man enough to swive her without 'elp, get outta the way and make room for someone who is.'

'Who's this?'

The query from the fourth member of the group caught the attention of the others as effectively as a shout.

A figure had appeared on top of a low shelf of rock that crossed the beach about two hundred yards away, chopping off all visibility to the north.

'He's got to be one of us.'

'I think it's Noling.'

'Jesus, one of ya,' snapped the man on the ground, 'will ya grab hold of her legs or somethin'.'

'Aye, Noling.'

'What's he want?'

The three who were still on their feet stood and watched the newcomer approach.

'Somebody grab her bleedin' legs, for Christ Almighty's sake.'

'He be a right funny prick, Noling. I don't trust the bastard.'

438

'He can't do us no harm. And he's one of us, ain't he? For all his stuck-up ways.'

'Yeah, but he were in the navy, weren't he? With this'n.'

'Aye, the navy.'

'There's four of us, for Christ's sake. So what can he do?'

'Nothin'. An' he'd be stupid to try.'

'Aye, stupid.'

'Jesus!' gasped the man wrestling with Amanda as she managed to butt him squarely on one ear, breaking the skin. 'Will someone give me a hand with this bitch?' The blow was probably accidental as she had both eyes clamped tightly shut. He tried to hit her but she had a double-handed grip of one of his wrists and his other arm was trapped beneath him. Somehow she had managed to wriggle around from under him so that they were now both lying on their sides.

He was known on board as 'Spider' for no known reason other than that was what he called himself. He was a pickpocket from London, and despite his undersized and undernourished frame, there was a time he would have been more than a match for the woman. But years of malnutrition had robbed him of much of his strength and during the last few days when the ship had been riding out the storm, he and the other convicts had received even fewer rations than normal.

'Hullo, Noling,' one of them offered as Will walked up to them. 'The weather's on the up.'

'Aye,' Will replied, with his gaze briefly touching Amanda and Spider and sweeping on past Cotter's prostrate form before finally resting on the curtain of fine mist beyond the breakers. 'How many others have you come across?'

'There be about four or six or seven or so live ones gone lookin' for water back there. An' about the same number who've had their fill of the briny blue variety an' won't ever be needin' any again. Not by the way they be rollin' around in the shallows.'

The speaker was a broad-jawed man whose flesh hung in folds on his lean frame, suggesting that a fair proportion of his former self was no longer present. Also absent were most of the teeth from one side of his mouth, so that when he spoke he sprayed fine jets of saliva at his listeners. Hence he was known among his fellow travellers simply as 'the spitter'.

'Aye, and a couple of His Majesty's finest who won't ever be needin' no water neither.' This was the man who had the pole pressed against Cotter's chest. His flesh had a taut pinched appearance that suggested it had always been stretched over a lean frame. As did the twist of his nose and the curl of his top lip suggest his face had always been distorted by a long-frozen sneer. He chuckled as Will turned back and gave those on the ground a more thorough appraisal. 'But they did need some convincin' of that.'

'Shut it, Farrad,' spat the spitter, watching Will carefully.

Will turned to the fourth member of the group. 'Is that you, Barky?'

'Aye, Will. 'Tis indeed. Hale and hearty, as always,' replied Able Seaman Barkman, one time captain of a 24-pounder cannon on the middle gun deck of HMS *Victory*, as he ran a hand over his shining bald pate. He looked anything but hale and hearty and was obviously the oldest member of the group, or at least the one on whom life's misfortunes had left the heaviest imprint, although all four had the stamp of prolonged incarceration on them: the stoop, the pallor, the sunken eyes, the stench of decay; and like herbivores at a water-hole, the regular flick of the head to the left, right and behind.

'Didn't expect to see you this side of those big green thumpers out there,' said Will. 'You must be a better swimmer than I'd have picked.'

Barkman chuckled, 'Didn't have to swim, Will'm. Not after the years I done floatin' French goods into Poole Harbour.' He pinched the pale wrinkled flesh of one hand with the other. 'After a while this turns into cork. You couldn't push me under water if y'tried.'

Will nodded to where Cotter was struggling to open his eyes. 'That's something else I wouldn't have picked. I wouldn't have picked that such a gentle soul as yourself would be joining up with these bold lads.'

Barkman's smile froze a little and he cast a nervous glance at the spitter. 'You never know who you might need to team up with to survive in these distant parts, Will'm.'

'That's true. That's true.' Will stepped closer to Cotter and looked down at him. 'How are you feeling, Mr Cotter? You look a little peaky.'

Cotter tried to find him but was obviously having trouble focusing. 'Noling, is that you?'

'Aye.'

'Where?'

'Here.'

Cotter's gaze finally steadied on him. 'Ah, there you are. Would you tell Dr Beattie I'm feeling much better today, thank you.'

'Dr Beattie?'

'He's been a bit concerned.'

'Well I suppose he has good reason.'

Cotter closed his eyes again. 'I'll just rest a little longer.'

'Aye,' Will replied, returning his gaze to Farrad. 'Did one of you bold lads do that to his leg?'

'His leg?' Farrad's query was genuine. Up until then he had not noticed the wound. 'I didn't touch his stuffin' leg. Anyone say I did's a liar.'

The spitter shook his head. 'Shut up, Farrad.'

His name wasn't really Farrad. Nor was it so much a nickname as a misunderstanding. The only name he knew himself by was 'Ferret', the legacy of his unfortunate expression. 'Farrad' was a result of others on board misinterpreting his mumble.

'Looks like it might be broken,' said Will.

'Couldn't care less if it fell off,' replied the spitter.

In the meantime Amanda and her opponent —amidst gasps from her and grunts and profanities from him—were still locked in an almost immobile embrace. Her opponent seemed to be even further from his initial objective; she was now almost behind him. And to ensure that she remained there she had locked his upper thigh in a crushing scissors grip with her legs.

Will studied them intently as if noticing them for the first time. 'What's going on here?' he asked. 'A Devonshire wrestlin' match?'

Barkman chuckled. 'That ain't Devonshire style, Will'm. That be Cornish style. Pit rules. 'Ceptin' this one ain't never been down no pit. Not with skin like that. Ain't been nowhere rough with skin like that.'

Amanda's camisole, now torn to her waist, and one bare breast were crushed against the side of her opponent's shoulder.

'Jesus!' gasped Spider. 'Will you lot stop squawkin' like you was at a flippin' picnic and give me a bleedin' hand.'

'I'm a bit surprised one of you wasn't helpin' him,' said Will. 'Seein' he looks like he could do with some help.'

The spitter flared. 'One of us would've been helpin' him, wouldn't we, if you hadn't stuck yer bleedin' nose in?'

'Why are you worried about me? What do you reckon I'll do?'

'That's what we don't know, do we? We don't know what you might flippin' do.'

'Give me a for-instance.'

'I wouldn't trust you not to try and help your navy mate here.'

'I never noticed he was much of a mate.'

'The mott, then. You might try and play the hero or somethin' stupid.'

'Not that it would worry us much,' Farrad offered. 'There bein' four of us to one of you.'

'Run the bastard off,' Spider called out. 'Then give me a bleedin' hand, for gawd almighty's sake.'

'I don't know where you get four of you. Your friend on the ground would hardly count, would he? If I were to try and play the hero or somethin' stupid, that is.'

'We wouldn't need fuckin' four,' Farrad snapped. 'Three would be plenty to see the likes of you off. Two to hold and one to kick the livin' sheart out of ya.'

Will glanced across at Barkman. 'I don't think old Barky over here would be too keen on bein' one of those three. What do you reckon, Barky? Would you be keen to be one of the holders, or maybe even the kicker? I can't imagine you takin' on one of those tasks with a lot of enthusiasm. What do you reckon?'

Something of a smile brushed over Barkman's

wizened countenance. 'I reckon I'll keep my options open.'

'So that leaves two of you. One to hold and one to kick. Which means I wouldn't have to play as big a hero, would I? Up against only two of you. What would you be, Farrad, the holder or the kicker?'

'Maybe I'd be the hitter. With this.' He raised the pole momentarily from Cotter's chest.

'That's a big pole. Once you got it swinging you could easily swipe the wrong person. Your mate here, maybe. That would make the odds a lot more interestin'. Up against only one of you.'

'What are you ravin' about, Noling?' the spitter demanded. 'Are you sayin' that you are goin' to try and play the hero?'

Will smiled. 'I must admit I'm tossin' it over in my mind.'

'What for, for Christ's sake? You don't owe this lot anythin'. If you had any sense you'd be gettin' in line to fuck her yourself.'

'I don't think anyone's goin' to fuck her. Not now you've wasted all of this time.'

'What are you talkin' about?'

Will turned away slightly and cast a glance back the way he had come. 'There's a party of blacks makin' their way along the beach back there. I don't think they spotted me. But by the time they reach that rock shelf they're going to get a pretty good look at anyone still hanging around here-abouts.'

445

They stood staring at him for a few seconds before the spitter blurted, 'Horseshit, Noling! You're just tryin' to scare us off.'

'Feel free to go back and have a look. That should waste another few minutes of good gettin' the hell out of here time.'

'If what you say be true, you wouldn't still be hangin' aroun'. You'd be gettin' the blazes out of here yourself.'

'I intend to do that. But for old time's sake I think I'd better take Mr Cotter and his friend with me. Now that I've had time to think about it. I wouldn't feel right leavin' them behind.'

'You're lyin', Noling,' the spitter snarled. 'There ain't no blacks.'

Farrad began to walk backwards away from Cotter, dragging the pole with him. 'I don't think he be lyin'.'

'He is. I know he is.'

'They could be cannibals. Oh Jesus!'

'Did you really see blacks, Will'm?' Barkman asked.

'I did, old son. Unless my brain got waterlogged and I was seein' things. Big bastards, they looked. Carryin' long spears.'

'Jesus, let me up,' Spider cried out.

'He's lyin',' the spitter insisted, his voice an octave higher than before, his eyes less steady.

Farrad threw the pole to one side. 'I don't give a sheart if he be lyin' or not. I'm gettin' outta here.'

He turned and began to run back along the beach the way they had come.

Barkman stood matching Will's gaze for a moment. 'I'm half inclined to stay with you, Will'm. For old times' sake as well. His nibs here bein' an old shipmate an' all. Usin' the term very fuckin' loosely, mind you. But there's more of these bad bastards than there is of you lot. So I think it's in my best interests to stay with them. Least in the short run. So I'll wish you all the best and get the hell outta here, smartish. Stay healthy!' With this he turned away abruptly and trotted after the other man.

'God rot you if you be lyin', Noling,' growled the spitter, before swinging away and also striding after the others.

'What about your mate here?' Will called after him.

'Fuck him!' the spitter called back over his shoulder as he broke into a shambling run.

'That's not very charitable,' said Will as he reached down and grabbed hold of the collar of Spider's coat and the waistband of his trousers. After a number of attempts he managed to detach him from Amanda and pull him to his feet. He immediately had to push him out of the way as Amanda also lurched to her feet and rushed at them with her claws extended.

'Steady! Steady!' Will cried out as she slashed at his face. He grabbed hold of her wrists and pinned her arms to her side.

'Stop it!' he yelled as she tried to bite him. 'You're safe. Safe. Do you hear me? They've gone. Gone!'

They had indeed gone. All of them. Beyond her shoulder he could see that Farrad, Barkman and the spitter were already a couple of hundred yards away and that Spider was in stumbling pursuit.

He stared into her wild eyes. 'I'm going to let go your arms. But you must stay calm, do you understand? Don't try and hit me. I'm a friend. Do you understand?'

He let her go. She immediately attacked him again, this time connecting with one claw and raking him across the cheek before he again managed to restrain her.

'Jesus!' He shook his head to try and dislodge the pain. She tried to bite him for the second time. Her eyes were like the eyes on the statue of a raring horse: wild and frightened, and blind! He released one arm for a moment and slapped her across the face. Her mouth fell open and only then did her gaze falter and reveal a flicker of awareness. A moment later she burst into tears.

The release drained her of her remaining strength and, as her knees sagged, she fell against him.

'Is that you, Will Noling?'

Will turned his attention to the man on the ground.

'Aye, 'tis indeed.'

'There are blacks comin', Mister. See to it quick

that Miss Dalrymple is put safely back in the jolly boat.'

'There are no blacks comin'. And as sure as sunrise, there's no jolly boat.'

'Don't be absurd, Noling, I brought her ashore in it. And I saw the blacks myself. Makin' their way along the beach. You saw them too. I heard you mention it.'

Will lowered his head closer to Amanda. 'Your friend's had a nasty blow to the head. I want you to help me get him off the beach and under cover. Do you understand what I'm sayin'?'

She nodded

'If I let you go, do you think you can stand?'

Again she nodded.

She was wrong.

'Jesus!'

SIXTEEN

With difficulty, Will managed to assist Amanda and Cotter across the sand to take shelter among a cluster of boulders that were exposed in a dry wash at the rear of the beach.

There they discovered that Cotter's leg was not broken and some time after Amanda bandaged it with strips of cloth torn from the hem of her petticoat he had recovered sufficiently to hobble about with the assistance of two makeshift walking sticks.

'We should rest tonight and set off at first light,' he declared confidently.

He was probably concussed. Even so, it would be difficult for him to ignore the implications of having such a large chunk of flesh gouged from his calf. So it was likely that the unspoken question that helped glaze the expressions of the other two was aligned to one flickering somewhere behind his own eyes: how long would he be able to hobble about?

'You must stay with us, Noling, and help me protect Miss Dalrymple.' His voice was pitched higher than normal in keeping with the elevated level of what had to be forced enthusiasm. 'If you remain with us it will stand you in good stead with the Crown once we reach Sydney. Give me your word you'll stay.'

All Will gave him was a glance that said 'settle down', before he stood up and strode across the beach to the water's edge.

'Rum chap, that Noling,' said Cotter, as he and Amanda sat watching his retreating back. 'Glad he's come on board.'

Now it was Amanda's turn to touch him briefly with a similar glance to Will's, but hers combined anxious appraisal with the transmitted caution.

For a time Will scouted the shoreline gathering small crabs from shallow scars and craters in a string of sea-battered shelves of rock scattered along the beach.

When he returned he and Cotter tried unsuccessfully to light a fire using a magnifying lens they salvaged from a small rattling pie-shaped object that had once served as Cotter's pocket-watch. But the spot of brightness they took turns in aiming into crunched-up piles of dead leaves and grass was too diffused in the failing sunlight and failed to generate sufficient heat. So the three of them ate the crabs uncooked, using lumps of rock to break them open, and thin slivers of wood to remove the flesh from the tighter

451

crannies of their shattered armour-plating.

Having to dine on cold unaccustomed flesh did not seem to impede the appetites of any of them, though Amanda did take some time to pick cautiously through her share. When they had finished, nothing remained but pieces of splintered shell.

After the meal Will tracked along the high-tide line and returned shortly afterwards with two narrow poles. While the others watched he placed the end of one of these between the V-shaped divide of a split boulder and, taking some care to ensure the timber began to part to his liking by prising the fibres apart with the edge of a large shell, he carefully snapped the pole in two. He then held up to the fading light the silhouette of a lance that was tipped with what might have been the threatening blade of an otter baiter's steel pike.

'Good man, Noling,' said Cotter. 'That's a fine weapon you've crafted.' He lifted the heavier of his two walking sticks. 'You with your pike and me with my mace, we could hold an entire army of filthy transportees at bay.'

In the deep shadow beside him, Amanda cringed.

Will walked across to her and handed her the pole.

'This one is for the lady.'

'You're not serious, man,' Cotter responded. 'You don't expect Miss Dalrymple to have to defend herself.'

'Miss Dalrymple can do as she pleases.' Will

walked back to the rock and repeated the blade-shaping exercise with the remaining pole. 'But who knows when you or I might be otherwise occupied.'

A sea breeze sprang up shortly afterwards and they moved further into the dry wash where they received some protection within a dense copse of melaleucas. The pleasant eucalyptus-like aroma that wafted from Amanda's hands after she absently crushed a leaf touched within her what might have been a memory. Of more significance to their comfort, they tracked down and located a shallow gurgle of fresh water where what remained of the stream that had formed the wash was showing itself briefly beneath an undercurve of one of the boulders.

During the night each of them took turns to keep watch while the others tried to catch up on some sleep. With varying degrees of success. All three managed somehow to filter out the crash and rumble of the surf and the creak, snap, murmur of the bush. But each time they began to drift off they were usually assailed by a jumbled confusion of distorted images from the preceding days that shook them awake and left them gasping from the assault.

As is often the way, sleep came easiest shortly before dawn. And just on sunrise, when Will alerted the others to a solitary figure approaching from the south, he had to wake them both from their first moments of deep slumber.

When he saw that the newcomer was Barkman, he handed his lance to Cotter and moved out on to the beach to meet him. 'Where are your friends, Barky?'

'They ain't no friends of mine, Will'm. You know that. An' you know there was no blacks nowheres yest'y.' He squinted up at the other man. 'Was there?'

'There was some smoke. I expect they weren't far away.'

Barkman turned and pointed up the slope. 'Some of them lookin' for water said they could see near to the horizon to the north, an' di'n't see hide nor hair of no one.'

'Where are they now, your friends?'

'Don't call'm that. Jesus! Friends! They're back there a'ways.'

'Why have you come?'

'Me and some of us others are headin' for China. We want you to join up with us, Will'm. Truth is some of us want you to lead us. You've had more book learnin' than all of us put together. You can show us the way.'

'China?'

'Hoopie Watson says he heard it ain't far.'

'Hoopie Watson?'

'Will you come?'

'China's not near here, Barky. China's halfway back to England, for Lord Jesus' sake.'

'Sheart, Will, don't say that. It can't be that far.'

'I wouldn't lie to you.'

'You lied to me yest'y.'

'That wasn't for you, Barky. That was for your mates.'

'Mates! Jesus, Will!' He spat on the sand. 'Halfway back to England.'

Will moved closer to him and lowered his voice. 'I can't join up with you, Barky. I have to get to Sydney. And for the moment I'd best stay with these two.'

'Which way is China?'

'I don't know where we are exactly.' Will pointed to the north-west. 'Even so, I reckon it would have to be somewhere in that direction. Across a lot of land and a lot of water.'

'Water?'

'Aye, water.'

'If China's too far, where else should we be headin'?'

'There's nowhere civilised anywhere hereabouts. Not that I've heard of. You might be able to live off the land. I don't know. There's nowhere close. Maybe your best move would be to head for Sydney yourselves and turn yourselves over to the Crown. As long as you don't commit any more crimes I've heard life can be reasonable.'

'Turn ourselves over! You've gone soft in the head, Will'm. Jesus! I can't tell'm that. They'd skin me alive.'

'That's all I can suggest.'

'And you won't come?'

Will shook his head.

Barkman began to turn away and then looked back and said quietly, 'I'm not sure it's real wise stayin' with these two, Will'm. You know what some of them bad lads are like. Like as not they'll come a'huntin' for the little lady again. They're talkin' wild and crazy at the moment. Comes from suddenly findin' 'mselves free, I reckon. Say they're goin' to be pirates. Goin' to fuck and plunder their way from here to China. And from China back to England. The spitter an' his crew mainly. I reckon' they would, too. Worse'n pirates they'd be. Given the chance.'

Will raised his chin and stepped closer to the other man. 'Worse than pirates! You think that worries me? You think that worries Cotter over there? Lieutenant Cotter, Royal Navy. Jesus, Barky! When was the Royal Navy ever frightened of pirates, for Christ's sake? We eat pirates. You know that. Who chopped up Ned Teach? We did. Cut his head off and stuck it on a pike. Who captured Kidd? We did. You were with us when we ran down those Barbaries in the Med. That was just to relieve the boredom from the blockade. Hung them high and handsome, those we didn't put to the sword. That didn't even rate an accurate description in the log of what really happened. The Royal Navy hardens its blades on pirate's blood. Pirates are fair game, Barky. You know that. Always were. Tell your friends to pay us a visit any time they want a lesson on how the Royal Navy deals with pirates.'

'Jesus, Will, there's only two of you.'

'Two would be enough.'

'You've got a pistol, 'aven't you?' Barkman glanced across at the other two. 'Got it off a drown'ded flatfoot. A cutlass as well, maybe?'

'Is that what they sent you to find out, Barky?'

'God's strength, Will. What do you think I am? I told you straight why I come. Me and some of them less excitable lads back there want you to come with us.'

Amanda moved closer to Cotter. 'What do you think he wants?'

'More than likely he's trying to talk Noling into joining them. Or perhaps even bargaining for him to hand you ... to hand us over.'

'But he wouldn't, would he?'

'I don't believe so. Not Noling. But we musn't drop our guard. If there's one thing I know about these people ... ' he gasped as he moved his leg into a more comfortable position, eliciting a concerned glance from Amanda, '... through no fault of their own, mind you, but simply because they lack the appropriate cultural heritage and social upbringing ... ' Another gasp and another concerned response, '... it's that if they ever think they have the upper hand, you can never completely trust them. Never.'

'What?' Amanda struggled to deal with conflicting concerns.

'That's why we must ensure he always knows who's in charge.'

'That's unfair, Wallis. I'm not sure what exactly happened yesterday, but I believe we owe our well-being to him.' She shuddered. 'And I feel sure he's still putting himself at risk for our sakes.'

'It's my experience that ambitious people from the lower orders always have a selfish reason for what they do. Always.'

'Lower orders! My God, Wallis!' She swung away for a moment and then returned her gaze to the two men standing on the beach before continuing. 'I know there are people from all social classes who are intrinsically good. And often act for no other reason than to do what they believe is right. I know that.'

'Noling's hardly the religious type.'

'I'm not talking about religion. I'm not talking about people doing what they're told to do. Or taught to do.' She placed the flat of her hand between her breasts. 'I'm talking about doing what they themselves know is right.'

'You're too generous, lass. I'll wager that everything Noling's done to date as far as we're concerned, he's weighed up as being to his own advantage.'

The spark that he had ignited within her flared. 'If you think that, why don't you simply tell him to go his own way?'

'We can use him is why. Look at him now. Culturally speaking, he's a natural linguist. He speaks all languages. Theirs, ours. Whatever is required of the moment. People of all walks readily accept him as one of their own. That's his strength. I'm beginning to understand how he managed to attract Lord Nelson's approval. He's such a natural schemer he would probably not even be aware that he is one.'

'I don't believe you.'

'That's because you're young.'

This had her wondering again about Cotter's age. And then the state of his leg. Shadows of despair began to converge on her once more and eventually pushed aside her anger.

'Where are they at the moment, the others?' Will asked. 'The more excitable ones?'

'They're all together. They found a fresh water-hole behind them sandhills. They reckon they could see a river to the north. When I get back and tell thems that might be interested you won't be joinin' us, that's where I reckon most of 'm'll be headin'.'

'How many of them are there, all up?'

'About a dozen.'

'And how many of them might we need to worry about?'

'Probably half.'

'Well, tell them what I said. Tell them that if any of them comes within grabbin' distance of us we'll do worse to them than any eye-gougin' gut-slicin' pirate they've ever heard of. Worse than

Teach. Worse than Gow. Worse than a boatload of Barbaries. Tell them we'll kill every man jack of them without a prayer. Without giving them one chance to back down. See that lance that Cotter's holdin'? Tell the spitter and his mates we'll feed them on to lances like that one and leave them to roast in the sun like pigs on a spit.'

Barkman stared at him open-mouthed. Then dipped his head towards the others. 'Yer mate don't look too sprightly. Can't see 'im doin' too much damage no matter how he's armed.'

'Don't be fooled, Barky. His lot always look like that. Even when they're as fit as fiddles. They practise lookin' pained. It's in their breedin'. He'll be there if needed, make no mistake.

'But I'm the main one your friends should worry about. If they get my dander up I'll give them pirates in spades. They'll think they've run into mad Frank Lolonois himself. They'd rather be in a pit with three black bears. Tell 'm that.'

Barkman opened his broken mouth and released a hearty guffaw.

'Tell 'm what I said, Barky. Tell them they've got enough worries. Tryin' to find China, for one. Tryin' to stay out of some cannibal's cooking pot, for two. Tell them to steer well clear of us. They can do without our brand of trouble.'

'They mightn't take too kindly to me tellin' them anythin'. That's what I'm thinkin'. They might take it into their heads I'm dancin' to your tune.'

'Explain what you're sayin' is for their own

good. They'll listen if they've got any sense.'

Barkman turned and looked back the way he had come. 'I don't know so much. Wouldn't trust 'm an inch.' He turned back and looked long and hard at the other man. 'Why are you doin' this, Will?'

'Maybe I'm stupid.'

'Maybe you're somethin'.' He began to turn away again. Then suddenly he propped, turned back and pointed to seaward. 'Them that spotted the river say what's left of the ship is stuck on a reef out there. Out past them curlers. You might see it from that hill a'hind ye. They say it's worth a look. Worth seein' where the scum from the arse end have been washed up. They say they're on a bitty sandbar off the end of the reef. And if they can't scrounge any food from the wreck, all they'll have to eat when they gets real hungry in a couple o' days' time will be each other. And not much else.' He chuckled coldly. 'The lads say their biggest problem will be findin' some straws so they can draw lots on who'll be first.'

He stood looking at Will for a moment and then he laughed abruptly and shook his head. 'Frank Lolonois! Jesus, Will!' He lowered his voice and bobbed his head at the others. 'That old Frenchie would have fucked and eaten both them two by now. You're no Frank Lolonois. But you're game. I'll give you that.' With that he left.

Cotter insisted that they help him see the wreck and the survivors for himself. But the ground was far too loose for him to struggle up the slope unaided, even with his sticks, so the other two had to practically carry him.

'Noling, I need your word that you'll stay with us.' There was more of an order than a request in Cotter's tone. His mood was now one of acute agitation. His forehead was spattered with beads of sweat and his eyes were threatening to pop from his head. A mini-cyclone of small black flies that he could not wave aside while gripping his walking sticks were swirling around him and alighting on his face in relays to drink his sweat. 'We must get help as quickly as possible for those poor wretches out there. We must immediately head for Sydney.' A bunch of the insects clung to his upper lip like a small moustache.

Will stood looking at the island. It seemed to be less than a few hundred yards across and little more than a detached and slightly higher elevated extension of the shoal itself. Possibly at high tide it would also be submerged. Jesus Christ!

'Which way is Sydney?' he asked.

Cotter settled back against the slope so that he could free his hands and swipe at his tormentors.

'Which way do you think it is, for God's sake, man? To the south, of course.'

'Why "of course"?'

'Because we were off Sydney when the storm hit us and drove us north, weren't we? Where'd you think we were, for pity's sake, man? You were there, weren't you?'

Will turned and looked down at him. 'Aye, I was there. But I wasn't paradin' around on the upper deck admirin' the view and sniffing the wind.' He raised his head and exchanged a glance with Amanda before turning back and scanning the broad strip of sand at the base of the slope.

'If you're heading south, the easiest road would be the beach,' he said at last. With this he started back down the slope.

'What do you mean, "if *you're* heading south"? You're coming with us, aren't you?' Cotter called after him. 'By God, man, you had better.'

Amanda watched him go. And then turned and helped Cotter struggle back to his feet.

Will gave her his shirt and averted his gaze as she put it on. Only when she had concealed her breasts and her upper torso as well as she was able did she somewhat guiltily point out that he now had insufficient protection against the weather himself, should it slide. But she made no move to give the garment back. Having already lost most of her underclothing in dressing Cotter's wound, shivers of vulnerability were at this moment her more dominant prompt. And, of course, Will still had his trousers, or what remained of them, and even if they protected him only to the waist, he was a man. So what if his chest was now completely bare?

Bare and well-formed, she could not help but notice, despite her efforts at directing and keeping her gaze elsewhere. Nor could she ignore his smell. Fresh. Salty. The smell of the sea at high tide. Obviously he had spent about the same time in the water as she and Cotter. But Will's was an aroma that was wafting on a warmer carrier than she had noticed on either herself or Cotter. A hint of more freshly bathed and still wet flesh, perhaps.

So she chanced a glance and saw that the flesh of his upper arms and at the base of his throat was gleaming beneath a fine film of perspiration. She also saw that his chest was coated in a light fleecing of burnished curls. Her fiancé's chest was as hairless as her own. Or so was her recollection from the one fleeting, fumbling and ultimately unsettling occasion during which she had been in a position to compare them both. Hers with his.

She was suddenly troubled. Her gaze leapt back to the island as waves of guilt surged across the pool of dread that had been lapping blackly against the underside of her consciousness. How could she dare toy with such frivolous distractions when her dear uncle could at this very moment be lying at the bottom of the ocean, or floating dead or dying out there beyond the surf?

They were resting in the shade of serrated-leaved bushes in the saddle of a ridge that climbed away to low rolling hills along the western horizon. The pommel of the saddle was a sharply domed headland that had abruptly blocked their path about five miles from where they had set out.

From their elevated vantage point they could

once more see what remained of the after end of the *Tynemouth* straddling the shoal that had harpooned her. They again caught glimpses of some of the survivors from the after end of the vessel, though from this distance the only signs of life were an occasional flash of white cloth against the ribbons of black rock that protruded through the sand on the low island adjacent to the wreck, and some ant-like movement along the perimeter of the sand.

She glanced at Will and saw that he was looking back the way they had come. A knife of fear entered the pit of her stomach. 'They're not coming, are they?'

He shook his head but made no other move.

Thank God! She turned and looked at Cotter's sleeping form. He must rest. And then less benevolently, otherwise we may have to carry him. Her gaze touched his wound. But it was other wounds that sprang into her mind's eye as the blade of the knife within her slowly began to rotate.

A head sitting on the hot sand. A crimson skull. Empty eye sockets. Gaping mouth. Anchored there by the body buried beneath it. Screeching gulls. Snarling dogs. Will running and swiping with his lance. Get away! Get away! The gulls lifting into the wind and shrieking in protest. The tawny-yellow dogs slinking away reluctantly. Will kneeling. All three of them, for a time staggering away and retching, gasping for breath. The dogs watching from a distance, their jaws open and grinning at the spectacle. Dingoes, Uncle Peter had said they were called.

Thank God the man was dead, she had breathed when this was, with some difficulty, confirmed by the men. Thank God!

Beneath Barkman's wounds, inflicted by the beaks and teeth of his winged and four-footed tormentors, Cotter briefly examined the earlier handiwork of less innocent creatures. The missing eyelids and ears. Neatly severed. The not so neatly severed tongue. 'Who did this?' he demanded. 'Who in God's name did this?'

Will lurching to his feet with tears of anger and frustration spilling down his cheeks, and bellowing, 'I did!'

Cotter demanding, 'What do you mean: you did?'

Will firing back, 'I gave him the message they didn't want to hear. I treated him as a friend. I deserted them.' His waving a hand in frustrated dismissal before striding across to the ocean's edge and standing there for an age as if he were another wind and wave–swept rock protruding from the sand.

Her aching with the need to go to him. To soothe his hurt. Her hatred of her own inaction and of Cotter's glance in her direction. The upward roll of his eyes that assumed her endorsement of God knows what: some condemnation or other of his behaviour.

And later, Will piling rock upon rock over and around the head, burying it under a squat cairn. His ignoring of their every offer to assist. His eyes fierce. Ordering them to stand clear.

'Do you think they will come?' she asked, with her gaze on what had become rivulets of sweat tracking down his back as he stood scanning the way they had come.

'No, they've gone.'

She was tempted to ask how he knew. She suspected that the answer lay in the manner of the killing of the man on the beach. A parting declaration of defiance or retribution, perhaps. Not wishing to revisit that particular nightmare, she asked instead, 'Where do you think they've gone?'

He was about to reply, 'To Hell,' but instead shook his head and said softly, 'To China.'

Cotter was able to walk after he had rested. But with some difficulty, and in obvious pain.

At the southern side of the ridge they were met by a panorama that under other circumstances might have delighted them with its majesty. Immediately ahead the terrain fell away in a succession of gentle slopes to a heavily wooded plain, a latticework of greens—from dark rhubarb to pale lettuce—bounded on the east by another long ocean beach and on the west by a succession of interlocking waves of high mountain ridges. The beach was flanked by a tangle of grassy dunes and narrow snaking waterways. It stretched away to disappear into a mist of spray and summer heat that clung to another low headland on the horizon. There was no smoke to be seen nor any other sign of human presence.

'Again, the beach seems to be the best road,' said Will.

Despite Cotter's protestations they assisted him down the slope. After a short rest, and with unspoken misgivings that it was the route that would more readily expose their presence to distant observers, they made their way along the very edge of the water where the travelling was easiest.

They were able to quench their thirst a number of times from shallow streams that cut the beach, and they rested often in the shade of the dense brush that flanked the sand. But by the time they reached the next headland Cotter was almost fainting from pain and exhaustion.

His wound had begun to bleed again. Despite his protestations Amanda insisted on replacing the bandage. While the injured man lay back in the sand beside a shallow tidal stream Will helped Amanda to remove the soiled bandage and bathe and clean the wound as best they could.

'If it gets so bad I can't walk, you two will have to go on alone,' said Cotter as they carefully removed scraps of dark material that could have been either dried blood or dead flesh, the state of the gaping hole making it impossible to tell.

'Don't talk nonsense, Wallis,' Amanda snapped,

trying in vain to keep her gaze away from the angry red streaks that ran up his thigh, and to ignore the ripe smell emanating from the blue–black flesh that surrounded the wound.

They somehow were able to get him over the headland and down to the beach behind it. But that was as far as they could manage. By then they were carrying him. When he was not unconscious he was delirious, one moment swamping them in tearful appreciation of their assistance, the next assailing them in spiting vehemence for their stupidity.

With the sun still high in the sky Will was able to start a fire easily with the watch lens. He collected some oysters and other likely edible shellfish from the ledges of rock that formed a ruffled skirt around the base of the headland. While he placed these items in the coals and shifted them about with a green twig Amanda joined him to hold important council.

'He's sleeping now,' she said softly, 'but he's becoming weaker by the minute.'

'That's because the wound is gangrenous and is rapidly poisoning the rest of his body.'

'What can we do?'

'Nothing.'

'But if we do nothing, he'll die.' She waited for him to respond. When he remained silent she declared, 'We must do something.'

'If the wound was smaller we could have tried to cauterise it, but it's far too big.'

'Cauterise?'

He prodded the coals. 'Sear it with fire to burn away the dead flesh and seal it.'

She shuddered. 'But we can't just let him die. Can we try?' Tentative. Fearful of the reply whatever it would be.

He shook his head. 'All we'd do is kill him quicker.'

Their eyes met for a moment and then they both turned away and stared out at the pounding surf. Gulls were making their way along the shoreline from the south, gliding on the sea breeze, with one or more dipping a wing occasionally to dive and skim inches above where the bubbling froth of a broken wave expired on the beach.

It took Cotter two more days to die. And he died badly. Shrieking in agony at times and extolling the others to kill him. Neither of them wanted to talk nor even think about his last few hours as they moved trance-like along the beach the following morning. Ahead of them the sand extended like a taut line hooked on the blurred arc of spray and mist that was the southern horizon.

Later that day they had their first encounter with the local inhabitants.

Shortly after midday, as they moved away from the beach to traverse a series of sandy mangrove-bordered lagoons in water shallow enough to wade through, Amanda suddenly realised they were not alone.

She made to reach out and touch Will's shoulder, arresting the movement a moment before her hand would have contacted his bare flesh.

'Mr Noling,' she whispered urgently, 'someone's following us.'

'Aye,' Will responded, 'I know.' He glanced back to where three or four liquid shapes were pulsing in the heat and spearing fitful reflections towards them across the mirror-sheen of what appeared to be pools of water spread throughout the dunes.

'You know? Why didn't you warn me?'

'I was worried enough for both of us.'

'How dare you keep me in the dark,' she flared. 'If you think we are in danger I demand that you tell me immediately. This is my predicament as well as yours. You have no right to patronise me.'

Their eyes met. 'All right,' he conceded. 'I'm sorry.'

'My God!' she breathed. Her gaze had locked on a point past his shoulder.

He turned and saw that there was a large group of natives—upwards of fifty—clustered in and around where the mouth of the lagoon they were crossing emptied into the ocean about three hundred yards away.

'Keep moving,' he said quietly. 'Don't slow down or stop. Even if they call out. Let them see that we're bent on passing through. That we pose no threat.'

The men in the group were either standing or

471

swimming in the surf and seemed to be drawing in a large net around a boil of fish. Women and children were gathered on the beach opposite the bight of the net, obviously preparing to help land the catch. Flashes of silver lightning swept backwards and forwards across the churning surface of the water. A whirlwind of gulls spiralled and dipped overhead.

All the natives were so engrossed in their task that either they had not noticed the strange couple wading through the shallows of the lagoon, or they were choosing to ignore them. Any shouts of excitement that managed to pierce the continual crash-thump of the surf seemed to be entirely associated with the landing of the fish.

The travellers moved out of the lagoon and made their way through a band of light brush that bordered another series of dunes extending to the south. They quickened their pace. The figures that had been trailing them were now no longer visible. Perhaps they had joined the others. Perhaps they had not realised that those they were following were aliens in this land. Perhaps here there *were* no certainties.

As Will and Amanda emerged from the brush a spear thudded into the sand ahead of them. Four natives, armed with an assortment of spears and clubs, were standing watching them from a rise of land fifty yards away. One of them had a spear raised above his shoulder, holding it in what was apparently some kind of launching device.

'What should we do?' Amanda whispered.

'Nothing too sudden,' Will replied. 'Just follow me closely.'

He pointed at the man who was threatening them and addressed the largest of the natives, the one who appeared to be in charge. 'Tell that man to lower his weapon,' he said evenly, and demonstrated with his lance, lifting it above his shoulder momentarily, taking care not to point it at the natives, and then lowering it to his side. He then began to walk slowly towards them, repeating both his command and his action. Amanda remained a step behind.

The natives made no move until they were about ten paces clear of them. Then suddenly the largest man shouted what might have been either a demand that they stop, or a command to the others.

They stopped anyway. For at the man's shout all four of the natives assumed an attacking stance with spears raised threateningly above their shoulders.

Again the man shouted, and shook his own spear as if he were at the point of releasing it.

'Don't get excited,' said Will calmly. 'We mean you no harm. We're simply passing through.' He slowly moved the point of his spear around, keeping it horizontal to the ground, and pointed it to the south. 'We're going that way. We'll keep going. We won't stop. We mean you no harm.'

Again the man shouted, and again he shook his

spear. This time one of the others seemed to echo his words and shook his own spear with even more vigour.

'This doesn't seem to be working too well,' said Will softly. 'If they attack, follow my lead and rush them. They won't expect that. And use your lance as a pike. Thrust with it. Don't try to throw it. And try to knock their spears aside with it. Don't release it, whatever you do.'

'Couldn't we offer them something?' she replied. 'Give them something to show we come in peace?'

'What have we got they'd want?'

'Cotter's sovereigns.'

'I doubt they'd be interested.'

'What have we got to lose?' She rested her lance against her shoulder and fumbled with a handkerchief she had knotted to a cord around her waist.

'Only remove one,' said Will. 'Don't let them see the others.'

The natives preened their necks and moved their heads from side to side attempting to get a better view of what Amanda was up to.

'Here.' She passed Will the coin.

The large native shouted again.

Will held up the coin between his thumb and index finger and turned it so that it caught the light. 'This is a token of our sincerity that we mean you no harm. It carries the likeness of our king. Here, I want you to have it.' He walked forward purposefully with his hand extended.

All but the man he was addressing fell back and

watched him warily. The large man stood his ground and locked his gaze with Will's for several seconds. Then he lowered his spear and, reaching out, accepted the coin.

Will pointed at the coin as the man turned it over in his hand. 'That's His Royal Highness George the Third.'

The man gave a sudden cry of amazement when he noticed the likeness of a man's head on the strange object that had been handed to him. He turned and holding it up said something to the man standing closest to him. The man lowered his spear and moved closer so that he could see more clearly what was being shown to him. This was apparently too much for the other two, and soon all four had their spears propped against their shoulders and were passing the coin from one to the other, peering at it closely and chatting among themselves.

'All we want to do is pass through your land,' said Will. He raised the end of his lance and once more indicated the route to the south.

The large man looked at him closely and then exchanged a few words with the others. Finally he turned back and held out the coin.

'No.' Will shook his head. 'You keep it. It's payment for crossing your land.'

The man snapped a response and thrust the coin forward.

'Yours,' said Will. He waved his hand in front of the coin.

The man suddenly reached out and grasping Will's hand placed the coin in his palm. He then stood back and pointed to the south.

'I think we've been given clearance to travel,' said Amanda.

'I think you're right,' Will replied. He stood to attention and nodded formally to the man before turning away and ushering Amanda to move ahead of him. They both then raised open hands in farewell to the natives and moved off at an even pace.

'Are they following?' Amanda asked when she noticed Will glance behind after they had travelled several hundred yards.

'No, they're still standing there.'

She released a heavy breath. 'Thank goodness for that. I don't think I could have remained braced for the impact of a spear for a moment longer.'

'Nor me,' said Will, releasing a similar exhalation. 'Nor me.'

Three more times during their travels south the ceremony with the coin was repeated in similar circumstance. In each instance the coin was returned.

The object itself and the markings on it were of small consequence; what was important was the ceremony: the act of formally presenting obvious credentials of peaceful intent.

SEVENTEEN

Will had seen few tall forests, so nothing prepared him for the size of the trees that now confronted him. Most were far broader than the broadest sweet chestnut he had ever seen in the New Forest on the far side of Southampton Water; and two, three times the height of the tallest oak.

Seeking a pool of fresh water deep enough for easy drinking on the day after they encountered the natives, he and Amanda had followed a trickle that crossed the beach in a thin film that afforded them only a gritty draught if they were prepared to press their lips directly against the sand. When the watercourse widened they found themselves at the edge of a forest that spilled down from the slopes of a low ridge in the lee of the rocky portals of a high-sided gorge.

The trees were so large that Will found he could not properly gauge the size of the closer ones, their buttressed bases extending out and beyond the periphery of his vision. The largest of these giants, which seemed to be crushing a host tree and some smaller neighbours within entwining cords as thick as full-grown elms, towered towards the forest canopy in a column broader than a two-laned high road.

Around its base were boulders the size of fishermen's cottages that it gripped in a vice-like tangle of massive roots. Dappled vines hung down from the overstorey, some straight to the forest floor, others coiling like great snakes around each other and around the trunks of the trees. The air was alive with the songs of birds and crickets.

The warbling murmur of water trickling over rocks and tumbling into a pool drew them to the base of a boulder. As they approached, a small animal, possibly a ground bird, scurried through the undergrowth on the opposite bank. They found the pool partly hidden beneath the boulder and surrounded by ferns. Will quickly scanned the perimeter for snakes, then dropped his lance beside him, leant forward, and bracing himself on his hands, drank deeply.

'Nectar,' he proclaimed when he finally drew back. He moved aside to allow Amanda to put down her lance and stretch forward to drink. He noticed that like his own limbs, beneath the remnants of her shredded clothing, her arms and legs were swathed in bruises and scratches, legacy of the dense brush they were forced to traverse shortly after their encounter with the natives.

When she had taken her fill and began to rise

he reached out to assist. But she suddenly snapped her arm away from him. The eyes that locked with his were momentarily filled with ire. And then seconds later with confusion. A sudden loud beating of wings overhead took their attention away from the moment. Above them large shadows skipped through the foliage and disappeared into the gloom. When the noise subsided they both separately busied themselves brushing away dust and dead leaves from their hands and knees.

When Will straightened he stood for a time looking at the forest around them.

'I don't like it here,' said Amanda.

Something scurried through the undergrowth again, perhaps the same animal as before. Will did not like it here either. Not in the least. Unknown dangers were a concern; unseen and unknown dangers were a compounded concern.

'We'd better get back to the beach,' said he.

They retraced their steps in silence. Before they had gone far, Will paused to break off a slim sapling and fashion himself a rod of about a three feet in length. So that we can light fires when it's cloudy, he mused. He immediately chided himself for what was probably an unrealistic expectation. Many times he and other Lowfoley children had tried to light a fire by twirling an arrow-like length of wood with a makeshift bow, which they had heard was an ancient method. But never with any success.

A little later, when he paused again, this time to test the strength of a thin piece of green bark he stripped from a ground creeper, he explained what he was doing.

Amanda made no reply, her attention being mainly taken up with concern over her behaviour when he had moved to assist her in the forest.

Why did I react that way, she agonised. What must he think of me?

Her prime worry was that she had hurt his feelings. He had gone out of his way to protect her. Risked injury. Perhaps even death. And she had reacted as if his very presence offended her. She groaned inwardly and her gaze played on the faint crisscross scarring on his back as he moved on ahead of her, and she rehearsed the words she might use to try and erase any misunderstanding.

How could she explain that her action had almost certainly been an unconscious attempt to stem the flow of events that seemed to be propelling them unswervingly towards each other? An instinctive reaction to avoid a collision or injury. Like a duck of the head, or a blink of the eye.

How could she explain that he had preoccupied her thoughts since she had first seen him in the waist of the ship. No other person had so dominated her idle moments. Not her fiancé *in absentia*, nor Wallis Cotter in ready attendance.

How could she explain that he had been the subject of numerous fanciful discussions with her uncle? And—with a blush triggered by the recall even now creeping up from her neck and stinging her cheeks—that he on many occasions had played a prime and exclusive role in more intimate fanciful scenarios that she conjured up to help ease the discomfort of sleepless tropical nights.

She cringed. And now he almost certainly believes I couldn't even stand to have him touch me. That he's too far beneath me. Culturally. Socially. That I, someone of position and privilege, perhaps resent having to depend for my well-being on him, a lowly transportee. She released a quiet groan and for a moment was fearful that he had heard her.

Perhaps he's right, she considered with her confidence plunging to an even lower plane. Perhaps I reacted as I did because I subconsciously believe our differences are irreconcilable.

Later that day they were forced to climb the steep side of a rocky knoll that blocked their way. Several times when Amanda had to negotiate a sharp rock, or a particularly steep or slippery part of the ascent, she expected that Will would turn and offer his assistance, or at least check to see that she could manage. But he did neither. He simply strode on purposefully up the steep slope ahead of her. He did not even give her the chance to wave him away, she noted ironically, with a sense of increasing anger and frustration swirling within her.

Since leaving the forest he had cut a pace that

she had difficulty matching. A number of times she was forced to break into a trot so that she would not fall too far behind.

When they reached the top, both of them stood for a time looking at the view. On the seaward side of them row upon row of gigantic parapets plunged away almost vertically to the pounding surf. The stone from which they were hewn was a deep blue crystalline sheen of solidified magma, shot with long narrow ribbons of white quartz. Boulders of the same material were strewn around the top of the knoll.

To the west and south a dark forest of dense brush extended from the coastline to low hills on the western horizon. To the south the country was swathed in various hues of foliage that bordered silvery swirls of lagoons and marshland. Closer to the coast, serpentine tidal creeks and dunes were flanked by low blankets of mangroves. Beyond them a large river lay across the coastal plain like a giant scimitar, gleaming where it caught the light.

Amanda stood staring at the view. Her hands were on her hips, her chest was heaving and her entire body was laced with rivulets of dusty perspiration. After a while she placed her hands on her knees and lowered her head.

Behind her, Will watched her for a time, and then placing his lance and fire-making materials on the ground, he climbed on to one of the boulders, where he stood for a time staring out to sea.

'What are you looking for?' she asked when she noticed him.

He shrugged and stepped down. 'Perhaps a ship.'

He picked up his lance and the other materials and headed for the southern slope. 'If we want to gather some seafood before dark we'd better not waste time.

'Damnation!' she whispered beneath her breath, surprising herself. She released a frustrated sigh and, picking up her lance, moved off after him.

As she crouched prising oysters from a rock-shelf she looked across at where Will was standing with his back to her. She saw within the shredded remains of his trousers that he was sunburnt on the buttocks and glanced at where her own were clearly visible through similar gaps in what remained of her petticoat. And, like his, her flesh was bright pink. She would be sore by nightfall. She stood up and looked along the sweep of beach to the south.

At that moment he turned towards her and, noticing that what he could see of her buttocks was sunburnt, checked his own. He would be sore by nightfall, he decided, and tapped the pink flesh lightly with his fingertips.

Amanda turned back in time to see him do this. She blushed deeply as she realised what had probably prompted his action and quickly crouched down to continue the hunt for oysters. She was now used to their near-nakedness; but the thought that her glowing backside had caught his attention caused an embarrassment she could have done without.

Will walked from the light brush adjacent to the beach and placed several coiled lengths of vine beside a small collection of driftwood, bark, stripped saplings and odd-shaped shells. Before he sat down he glanced to where Amanda was bathing in a rock-pool close to the shore. Behind them the sun was a red disk hovering close to the horizon.

He attached a strip of vine to both ends of a sapling, looped the vine around an arrow-like length of driftwood, trapped one end of this arrow in a hollow length of softer wood which he had crammed with pulverised bark, trapped the other end in an oyster shell cupped in the palm of one hand, and gripping the sapling with his free hand sawed it backwards and forwards, causing the arrow to spin.

This dexterous performance would have been much more impressive had it not begun some two hours before, and this was not his eighth attempt to get something to ignite—at this stage he did not mind what; the bark, the wood, the arrow or even the damned vine—before it broke again or his arm gave way from exhaustion.

With the water in her natural bath surging rhythmically around her waist, Amanda washed away the dust of the day and tenderly sponged her cuts and bruises with bunched leaves of soft seaweed. She gradually began to relax, but the shadows that had dogged her since Cotter's death were still hovering.

Her prime concern now was Will's attitude since the incident in the forest. Obviously she had offended him. And she was bereft of ideas on how she could make amends, other than perhaps to confront him and reveal that she had been suddenly frightened by the relentless march of events that was bringing them together.

She cringed at the thought of having to make such revelations. But there did not seem to be any alternative. They must still be many hundreds of miles from Sydney. She couldn't bear the thought of his continuing to act as he had acted since the incident. A wave of anger surged through her as she recalled that behaviour. How dare he be so intolerant! So assuming!

And then suddenly she saw how she could cushion her embarrassment. She would reveal why she had acted as she did, and then immediately assail him for his childishness. With a prickling discomfort still churning in the pit of her stomach, she rose and climbed from the pool.

Pausing for a moment to squeeze water from her clothing and close as many gaps in the sodden fabric as she was able, she took a deep breath and strode resolutely across the beach towards him with the sun in her face.

By the time she reached him her uncertainty had completely evaporated and her determination had blossomed into outright belligerence. So that when she finally stood in front of him, her stance was unabashed and open and her demeanour decidedly aggressive. Some part of her that hovered in the background as a neutral observer of her actions wondered why. Why was she suddenly displaying such uncharacteristic hostility? Why was she challenging him in this manner? Practically thrusting her nakedness at him? What was happening to her? She was angry. But never before had her anger caused her to abandon the tenets of normal civilised propriety expected of someone of her upbringing.

Will would certainly have been surprised had he looked up at that moment. But he was too engrossed in the thin wisp of smoke that had suddenly begun to spiral up the spinning arrow between his knees. His body glistened as if oiled as he laboured. His breath was pronounced but even. And his shoulders, glowing crimson in the failing light, rippled as he worked. She was reminded of a well-balanced machine. Her resolve to confront him rapidly began to wane.

'Quick, get the bark,' he said urgently.

'What?' She was caught off guard but welcomed the diversion.

He bobbed his head to one side. 'The bark. Over there. Quickly.'

She moved to comply. 'Where will I put it?'

'Crunch it up a little. Rub it between your palms. That's it. Put it beside the log. Now . . . keep your fingers crossed.' He lowered his head beside the spinning arrow and began to blow gently on the small hollow log. The spiral of smoke began to thicken. A few moments later he suddenly cast the bow and arrow aside and lowered his mouth to almost touch the log. Continuing to fan the seat of the spiral of smoke with his breath, he then picked up the bark and began to feed broken pieces into the hollow of the log. The smoke continued to thicken.

'I think I can see a glow.' Amanda knelt in front of him. 'I can.' There was excitement in her voice. 'There is a small flame. You've started it. Don't let it go out. Gracious heaven, don't let it go out!' Behind them the forest climbed away like a great black blanket.

'Quick, get some more bark.'

She leapt to her feet and quickly gathered a small armful of bark and twigs. By the time she knelt down again he had tiny flames licking at his fingertips. He immediately fed them with larger pieces of fuel he plucked from her cupped hands.

'We have a fire,' said he. And then with more enthusiasm. 'We definitely have a fire.'

'We do indeed,' she agreed. 'I'll get more wood.'

She returned a few minutes later with a bundle of twisted sticks, some quite large, and dropped them beside the small fire which was now eating hungrily at the tepee-shaped stack of bark and twigs that he had built over it.

'Now, if you would keep it going, I'm going to have a look at those shallow tidal pools. If any decent sized fish are ever going to move into them, it should be about now.'

As he moved away she sat back on the sand, watching him.

Will held his breath as the big cod nosed its way carefully through the narrow opening that led to a series of shallow rock-pools at the edge of the beach. With a wild cry he leapt into the water and smacked the surface with a heavy driftwood club.

Amanda stood up beside the fire as he continued to whoop and thrash the water. The fish darted from side to side. Gradually he managed to force it into the shallower pools. As it crossed through an ankle-deep wash, he suddenly leapt forward and brought the club down across its back. But the blow was deflected by a rock. The club shattered and the big cod bucked and writhed and kicked its way back into deeper water. With this he cast aside the remnants of the club and threw himself at the fish, groping for it with outstretched hands. He managed to hold it for only a moment before it began to slip from his grasp. He yelled loudly and tried to throw it into shallower water. As it hit the surface he leapt on to it again. And again he managed to grasp it and throw it closer to the shore. He then leapt on to it once more and, scooping it into his arms, threw it clear of the water and out on to the wet sand. And still it was able to flop back into the shallows. But he was not going to let it escape now.

With one final whoop he scooped it up and hurled it on to dry sand well clear of the water. He rushed after it, hauled it up by the gills and ran across the narrow beach to where Amanda waited beside the fire.

'What do you think of this little beauty?' he asked. He was flushed with the thrill of the hunt. His chest heaved. His face was alive with excitement. His jaw rode high like a Greek dancer's and his gestures were expansive. 'Tonight we'll dine like gods,' he promised with enthusiasm.

'Surely we shouldn't cook it without cleaning it first,' Amanda said as Will lay the fish in the coals and began spooning glowing embers over it with a flat piece of wood.

'Without a decent knife, it's safer to cook it whole. Its stomach will shrink into a tight ball and seal the contents clear of the flesh.'

Amanda pushed aside her uncertainty when the enticing aroma that was already emanating from the pile of coals began to trigger embarrassing growls of hunger in her stomach.

Will had built the fire beside a rocky stream that skirted the southern edge of the knoll. The water was ice cold and had a mild soda flavour.

After about twenty minutes of continually

rolling and reburying the fish in glowing coals, Will used a twig to break away a piece of flesh. Then bouncing it from one hand to the other a number of times he put it to his lips. Amanda leaned forward watching his reaction intently. He nibbled and paused, and nibbled again.

'What's it like?' she demanded impatiently.

In answer he broke in half what was left in his hand and offered it to her. 'Careful, it's hot,' he cautioned.

She took it from him, bounced it a couple of times as he had done and nibbled tentatively. His eyes were on her when she turned to him. 'It's delicious,' she said softly. 'Truly delicious.'

And so they attacked it in a manner fitting half-starved diners denied the luxury of eating utensils and the appointments such a feast deserved. They plucked and tore, tossed, juggled, sipped and bit, and they sucked and licked and swallowed. Their entire performance, from the first breaking of singed skin to the final discarding of the skeleton and bundle of innards, was accompanied by an undulating undertone of pleasurable murmuring interspersed occasionally with sudden painful intakes of breath.

'You were right,' Amanda said, after they had cleaned away in the stream all remnants of the meal from their flesh. 'We did dine like gods.'

When they sat down again at the fire Amanda turned to speak to Will and saw that his attention was elsewhere.

He was sitting stock-still with his head cocked on one side. When he finally turned towards her, stiff-necked, still listening, his eyes touched hers and his index finger went immediately to his lips. She could hear nothing save the gurgle of the stream and behind her the heavy pulse of the surf.

He came to his feet quickly, cat-like, and carefully picked up his lance.

'What is it?' she whispered. She was surprised how dark it had become. The low scrub bordering the beach was a black curtain beneath the gaily painted swirls of the sunset. Her heart was pounding.

Will pointed to where the stream broke from the foliage about ten yards away. She heard it now: a low rustle in the undergrowth, an occasional scrape of stone upon stone. Whether the animal was stalking them or had stumbled on to them by chance was uncertain. What was certain was the intensity of the collective shock experienced by all three participants in this drama when the beast suddenly rushed from the brush, apparently intending to seize the discarded remnants of the fish.

Amanda unleashed a blood-freezing scream. Will fell backwards on to the sand. The animal leapt high into the air, twisting so that as it landed it was well positioned for a hasty retreat. But it did not retreat. It remained staring at them with its feet spread and its shoulders hunched. Its head was low to the sand, its jaws were open wide and its fangs gleamed in the firelight.

Will struggled to his feet and lowered the tip of his lance at the creature. Amanda scurried to the opposite side of the fire.

'It's a dingo,' she hissed. 'Uncle Peter said they won't attack humans unless they're cornered.

The animal's eyes were locked on Will as it pulled back its jowls into an evil smile and released a low, grating growl.

'In that case,' said he, 'don't do anything that might cause it to think it's cornered.'

'What if I throw a burning brand at him,' said Amanda, reaching for the fire. Immediately the dingo swung its head to face her.

'No, don't move,' said Will. 'And it's not a he, it's a she. With a litter of pups to feed by the look of her teats.'

'Perhaps she doesn't know she's not supposed to attack humans.'

'Well, we can't stand here all night like this waiting to find out,' he replied, and tentatively poked the point of his lance at the animal. 'Go on. Get out of here, you ugly creature.'

The dingo responded by unleashing a ferocious snarl and lunging at him. He stepped back and almost collided with the fire. The dingo immediately swung away to the side, and in a blur of movement snatched up the remnants of the fish and then spun around and dashed back into the thicket beside the stream.

'It definitely didn't know it's not supposed to attack humans,' said Amanda when she had recovered from the shock.

'I think that was a feint,' said Will. 'It was after what was left of the fish. And it meant to have it at all costs.'

He sat down beside the fire and placed his lance close by his side. He then picked up a small log and threw it on to the flames. 'We had better make sure the fire stays burning brightly tonight.'

As on previous evenings, they both gathered for their bedding bunches of soft rubbery leaves from the bushes that grew along the fringe of the dunes. As usual they stacked the leaves into two thick mattresses that radiated from the fire with an angle of about ninety degrees between them. Rather than being in accordance with any prearranged agreement, this arrangement seemed to satisfy naturally their needs of maintaining contact for defensive purposes, but not such close contact as to impinge on their space and privacy requirements.

As they settled down for the evening, Amanda was aware that despite the distractions of the fish, the fire and the dingo, the tension that dominated the earlier part of the day was still with them. A number of times she resolved to broach the subject and try to clear the air.

Finally she tentatively offered, 'Mr Noling, I believe a misunderstanding may have risen between us. When I . . .'

'If you don't mind, Miss Dalrymple,' Will interrupted. 'I'd prefer we dropped the subject.'

'But I don't want to drop the subject. I'd like to explain . . .'

'There's nothing to explain. Truly. You have nothing to fear from me. I simply intend to accompany you to Sydney. My intentions as far as you are concerned are completely honourable.' With this he stepped around the fire and strode across the beach towards the water's edge, leaving her with an open hand raised towards his retreating back and her eyes clamped tightly shut in frustration.

'You have no idea what I wanted to say,' she finally declared evenly, angrily. But by then he was too far away to hear. 'Men!' she exclaimed, and flopped back on to her mattress of leaves. Tomorrow, she promised herself. Tomorrow he'll hear what I want to say if I have to sit on him. Which proved to be somewhat prophetic.

In the meantime Will had walked out on to the rock-shelf where he had earlier caught the fish and for a time stood looking out across the breaking surf. When he turned back he saw that Amanda was lying down. He moved to where she had earlier collected the oysters. It was now too dark for him to see clearly, so he groped around blindly in the shallow water until he found one that she had missed. The shell was only lightly closed and he was able to prise it open with his fingers. He put it to his lips and ate the contents. Not the best oyster I've ever tasted, he decided.

What he did not know was that Amanda had discarded that particular oyster because it was open when she found it stranded clear of the water.

During the previous evenings, after the sea breeze had died, the weather had been mild. So they were able to spend most of the night lying on top of their spongy mattresses. But usually, shortly before dawn, both of them would bury themselves beneath some of the layers.

When Amanda awoke the next morning she was somewhat surprised to find that Will was still buried deep in his mattress and still sleeping soundly. Usually he was up and about before her.

She walked to the water's edge and at a place where she was sheltered by high surrounding boulders, she bathed in a deep rock-pool. When she emerged she rubbed the excess water from her body and for several minutes stood with her arms akimbo facing the sun, watching it rise slowly out of the sea above the thunder of the breakers.

The tide was out and the surf was pounding through low clumps of exposed reef. The wash was slopping creamy-soft back over itself and coating the surface of the water below her in a soapy web. At another time, she knew, she would have enjoyed the beauty of this place; revelled in it even. There was much of the stuff of paradise here.

She occasionally glanced over her shoulder to where Will was still sleeping beneath his bundle of bushes near the remains of the fire. He should be awake, she decided with a return of some of her irritation. Their discussion the previous evening had done nothing to clear the air and she again resolved to have him hear her out. But later. When he was wide awake.

She looked along the beach to the south. At a point some four or five hundred yards away, gulls were swirling above a stretch of rocky shallows in a similar manner to those they had seen above the boil of fish the natives had been landing. She turned and walked back across the sand to where Will was sleeping.

'Mr Noling,' she said loudly, 'there's a large flock of gulls along the beach a'ways. I think a school of fish could be trapped in the shallows.' She immediately averted her gaze when she saw that beneath the thin cover of bushes he was naked. She then noticed that his wet trousers were draped over a boulder near the stream. Obviously he had washed them during the night.

'Mr Noling. Wake up. I believe we can catch some fish if we hurry.' She picked up her lance and began to move off. She glanced back at him as he mumbled something again and rolled away from her on to his side.

Please yourself, she responded silently, and was

suddenly attracted by the idea of presenting him with a healthy catch of fish by the time he got himself moving and caught up with her. So, without a backward glance, she strode off purposefully across the beach, heading for the wet sand.

She was unaware that Will had woken during the night in the grip of violent stomach cramps and had staggered into the bushes behind the beach where for over an hour he endured an almost crippling attack of diarrhoea and vomiting. Wave after wave of nauseous flushes left him drenched in sweat and shaking from head to toe. The pain in his abdomen for a time was so severe he truly felt that he could die. Eventually, believing that he was over the worst, he had cleaned himself and his trousers in the stream and crawled back under his covers. But he had then slipped into a coma, and when Amanda had tried to rouse him, he knew little of what was happening.

EIGHTEEN

Despite the shadows at the back of Amanda's consciousness, she felt a sense of exhilaration as she strode along the beach. She lifted her lance, jiggled it, and tossed it in the air a number of times. Smooth and clean. Each time she caught it, it whipped and bounced in a ringing oscillation. It was light. Naked and unencumbered. Like me. Like him. She groaned in recall of their last conversation.

When she reached the spot where the gulls were swirling she found that they were indeed attacking a boil of fish. But to her disappointment the fish were not trapped in shallows as had appeared from a distance; they were caught where a number of large boulders formed a deep hole between the pounding surf and the rock-shelf. The water was far too deep and surging too violently for her to even contemplate entering. So she decided to wait for Will. Perhaps he could use his lance to spear one or more. The water was so charged with hurtling black shapes and flashes of silver that she was tempted to try to do this herself but finally decided not to risk losing her weapon. Particularly now that when she looked back to see if Will was coming, she felt some unease at having put such a distance between them.

There was still no sign of him and the first hollow twinges of concern began to nudge her in the pit of her stomach. Where was he?

She moved away from the water's edge and crunched across a carpet of crushed shells through which a number of low boulders protruded. Choosing one of them for a seat she sat down to wait for him.

She ran back along the beach, her toes gouging small furrows in the wet sand beside the footprints that marked her progress in the opposite direction. At her side, the ends of her lance bounced up and down with each stride in perfect time with the undulating rise and fall of her breasts.

Something was amiss at the campsite. There could be no other explanation. Unless, of course, he had deserted her.

No, she could see movement. But the moment of relief was short-lived. For the movement looked wrong. Unnatural.

She was still too far away to see why, so she tried to pace herself. To stride easily, rhythmically. Not knowing what she might face, she did not wish to be suffering from complete exhaustion when she arrived. An image of the animal that had startled them the previous evening was firmly implanted in her mind's eye.

Something was moving among the darker shapes she knew were the remains of the fire and the piles of bushes they had used for beds. One of these was larger than the others. Will was still lying there. Still asleep! How could he still be asleep? She was now less than two hundred yards away.

'No!' she gasped aloud when she realised that what she had seen moving was indeed the dingo. She raised her lance and began to sprint across the sand. 'Stop!' she shouted. 'Stop! Stop!'

The animal snapped its head towards her and froze in mid-stride. But it did not back away, even when she rushed to within five yards of where it stood. So she slowed to a walk and lowering her lance held it out in front of her with both hands.

Out of the corner of her eye she confirmed that Will was still lying beneath his bundle of bushes. Surely he must have heard her shout. 'Wake up, Mr Noling,' she cried loudly. 'Wake up.' He did not move. My God! I'm too late! It's already killed him. 'Wake up!' she cried. 'Please wake up!'

With its eyes still on Amanda and its nose testing the air, the dingo began to edge towards him again. Amanda immediately stepped forward and lunged in its direction with the tip of her lance, more in threat than attack. It immediately propped and released its familiar snarl.

'Shoo,' she yelled. 'Get away, you ugly beast!' She jabbed out with her lance again, again in threat, well clear of the target.

The dingo crouched nearer the ground. Amanda stepped closer and shouted at it again. Suddenly it rushed towards Will. Perhaps it was seeking to escape, but Amanda's first thoughts were that it was meaning to seize some part of him. She screamed and hurled the lance with all her strength. The point hit the ground between its front legs and the shaft whipped forward and struck it on the side of the head. It gasped and leapt back towards the remains of the fire.

Amanda snatched up Will's lance from the ground and lunged at the animal again. It leapt to the side but tripped over as its legs became entangled in the stack of driftwood that lay beside the fire. Before it could regain its balance, Amanda swept Will's heavy lance like a club and caught the animal on the side of the head. It yelped and sprang away, tripping again as it landed on more loose logs.

Amanda lunged again, and missed. The dingo was now in full retreat. Without a backward glance it bounded across the sand and disappeared into the brush beside the creek.

Amanda's chest was heaving as she dropped to her knees beside Will and pulled the bushes from his upper body. He was alive. His mouth was partly open and flecked with pale dried stains, but he was breathing heavily. Thank God, her mind rejoiced. Thank God! Thank God!

Will was desperately trying to quench his thirst. But every normal water source he tried was either dry, or failed to satisfy him, regardless of how much he drank. He tried tanks and wells, streams and dams. He even tried to drink from the horse-trough outside the Francis Drake and from the puddle that was seldom dry beneath the gate to the bottom paddock. All to no avail. His throat and chest remained parched.

To add to his troubles, his head felt as if it had been caught in the jaws of a vice and he could not place his limbs anywhere to relieve the ache that seemed to twist into every muscle in his body. He became aware on at least one occasion that he was lying on a beach somewhere and admonished himself for being so stupid as to venture out of doors when he was so ill. He fantasised about being able to lift the top off his head and place a handful of frozen snow inside.

Eventually someone spoke to him and he momentarily forced open his eyes against the glare of the sun to see a figure approaching him.

'Do you have any water?' he asked, as a shadow fell across his closed lids. He felt a pressure against the back of his neck and something brushed his lips. And then water, cool and wonderfully refreshing, trickled into his mouth. He gulped and tried to devour more than was available. His teeth and tongue detected wood.

'I'll refill it,' his mother said, or was it Jessica?

He felt his head lying back again on the soft leaves of his bed and wondered if he could lick any moisture from them. Again he felt pressure at the back of his neck, and more delightfully cool water trickled down his throat.

'More,' he said without wishing to offend his mother, or Jessica, or whoever it was. It seemed rather pointless wasting words when he was probably dying.

Amanda had built a makeshift bower from branches to shield Will from direct sunlight. She found the best vessel for carrying water to him was a partly hollow piece of driftwood, blocked at one end with a crude wedge. It leaked but it worked. By dusk his colour had improved, his fever was down, and he breathed more easily. She also managed to resurrect the fire from its ashes. Now that light was fading she began to add more wood.

She sat watching him as he slept and remembered how she had held him earlier, his weight pressing heavily against her breasts. She remembered the fear when she thought he was dead; the elation when she knew he was not; the return of the fear when she thought he was dying.

She woke with a start. The fire had died to a pulsing glow. She came quickly to her feet with the lance already in her hands. Her eyes were on the low black curtain of foliage that bordered the beach.

But she could hear nothing save the burble of the stream, the whine of crickets, and the low groan and incessant thump of the surf. Will was stretched on his back and seemed to be breathing freely. She placed a hand on his forehead. No fever. She touched his lips with the back of her fingers. He needed more water.

She manoeuvred a log on to the fire and added a number of smaller pieces of wood to encourage a speedy increase in the level of light. She remained standing until the flames began to send beating waves of colour into the surrounding gloom. Then picking up the wooden bowl with one hand, and directing her lance generally at the spot where the dingo had earlier emerged, she moved to the stream and refilled the bowl with water.

Returning to the fire, she knelt beside Will and touched him on the shoulder. 'I have some water here. Can you sit up?'

'Yes,' he replied. There was more strength in his voice than earlier when he had bade her give him some privacy so that he could attend to calls of nature. She had soaked some of the rubbery leaves of the bedding in the stream and filled the drinking bowl so that he could sponge himself. She had then walked to the water's edge.

When she had returned he was back in his bedding and there was no sign of where he had been, or where he had disposed of anything. He had even apparently taken the trouble of sweeping the surface of the sand with a bush. But the effort had obviously weakened him. He was paler than before and was lying very still.

'Are you all right?' she had asked.

'I'll be all right soon. I'm a bit tired.' Shortly afterwards he was sound asleep.

Now as he sat up to drink, he was obviously still very weak but his colour was better. 'Thank you,' he said, and lay back. 'I didn't realise oysters were such dangerous animals.'

'Did you know that another dangerous animal came back to visit us?'

'The dingo?'

'I was able to hunt it away. But I wouldn't be surprised if it hasn't gone far. It doesn't frighten easily.'

'Because of her pups, I suppose.' He raised his head. 'Where's my lance?'

'I'm keeping it handy in case I need an extra one.'

He managed a weak smile. 'I'm sorry that I'm not much help at the moment. I should be all right by tomorrow.'

Amanda opened her eyes. The sky was grey. She lay without moving for several seconds and then as she raised her head and looked across at Will her breath caught in her throat. The dim figure of the dingo was crouching beside him and pressing its nose into the bushes that partly covered him.

She carefully reached out and curled her fingers around the shaft of her lance. Then she lurched to her feet and screamed, 'Get away! Get away!'

The dingo came at her across the sand as if fired from the mouth of a cannon. She swung the point of the lance to bear on it. Whether or not the animal was attacking her, or meaning to race on past to the safety of the brush, was uncertain. What was certain was that the point of the lance struck it squarely in the base of its throat.

The impact knocked her down and the lance was jolted from her grasp. The dingo gasped and hurtled into the pile of firewood where it immediately lost its footing and crashed heavily on to its side. She threshed out violently with her arms and legs, as much to ward off an attack as to bring herself into a sitting position.

As the animal fought to regain its feet amidst an eruption of sand and flying pieces of driftwood, she managed to retrieve her lance. She came to her feet as the dingo speared out of the woodpile and collided with Will's bedding. She screamed as the animal became entangled with Will for a time and seemed to savage him before leaping away.

She lowered the point of the lance as the dingo then raced back towards her. Her knuckles were white. The lance was trembling. As in the first instance the dingo may well have been attempting to escape. But she was taking no chances. This time she aimed at its head and thrust with all of her might. The tip passed between its gaping jaws and imbedded deep in its throat.

She was immediately knocked into a sitting position and driven backwards across the sand. But she bore down on the butt of the lance, and as it caught in the sand the dingo was brought to a shuddering stop. Blood gushed from its mouth. It stumbled and fell on to its side. The shaft of the lance bowed for a moment and then the end that was buried in the sand suddenly came free. It swung in an arc and cracked against the side of her head. She fell back, dazed.

As she came to her knees she saw that the dingo was standing watching her. Its head was lowered, its face a fright-mask of retracted jowls and gleaming teeth. A thin trickle of blood ran from its mouth and painted a black stain on the sand. The lance was lying between them.

She screamed loudly, as much to boost her own resolve as to distract the animal, and throwing herself forward snatched up the lance and fell back onto her haunches.

There was no doubt now of the dingo's intent. Had it wanted to escape it could have done so. But instead it rushed at her with its jaws agape.

She lunged and caught it flush in the chest with the point of the lance, and again managed to bury the butt in the sand. The shaft bowed and snapped in half. The dingo tumbled as it landed, catching her on the shoulder and knocking her off balance.

She grasped one piece of the broken shaft as the

animal scrambled back on to its feet and lunged at her face. She just managed to thrust the shaft sideways into its mouth. It was on her then, crushing her, gasping, spraying blood and saliva between incisors that whipped the air only inches in front of her face.

Gripping the shaft in both hands she forced it back against the bite of its jowls. Its back legs clawed at her shins in its efforts to reach her. To protect her legs she immediately wrapped them around its body and locked her ankles behind its back. She then squeezed her thighs as if she had some chance of crushing the life from its body. She had more chance than she knew. Within its bloodied chest the ends of broken ribs ground past each other and penetrated vital tissue. Within its throat, torn sinew opened and released vital blood. The animal died minutes before she realised it was dead.

After a time she rolled on to her side and released her legs. She then struggled from beneath its body.

As she came to her knees her gaze immediately leapt to Will. 'Mr Noling, are you all right?' She scrambled to her feet and rushed to his side.

He was trying to prop himself on his elbows. His throat and chest were covered in blood. She dropped to her knees beside him.

'Gracious heaven!' she whispered, placing trembling fingers against his throat.

'What? What's wrong?' He squinted into the

sun that was climbing out of the ocean behind her.

'You've been bitten.'

'Where?' He felt for himself, his thumb and forefinger pressing down on hers. 'My God. What's that?'

'That's me.' She withdrew her hand.

He released his breath in a rush. 'Thank goodness. I thought my throat was torn.'

'So did I.' She sank back, closed her eyes, and raising a clenched hand to her bottom lip, began to tremble. Tears spilled from her eyes and cascaded down her cheeks.

He reached out quickly, and gripping her forearm, squeezed it gently. Both of them remained like that for some time. Neither of them spoke.

Finally her shoulders rose and fell in a heavy sigh. She took a couple of deep breaths and opened her eyes. Her cheeks were damp. Avoiding his gaze she returned her attention to the swathes of blood gathered beneath his throat and matted in the hair of his chest.

'You are bleeding.' She ran the back of her index finger gently across the base of his throat. 'From scratches mainly. But I think most of this blood is the dingo's.'

He bobbed his head at her. 'And that is as well, I trust?'

She glanced down at her own body. Her camisole hung in shreds from her shoulders. She immediately made a half-hearted effort to close a few

509

of the larger gaps, but when they immediately fell open again she gave up.

Within the garment her breasts were spattered with tiny crimson spots and smeared with swirling streaks. Her stomach and thighs glistened with so much blood an observer could have believed she was surely haemorrhaging from a mortal wound.

'Most of this mess is the dingo's blood, thank God. I have a few scratches, that's all.'

'Where is the dingo now?'

'Over there.'

'You killed it?' He propped himself up further and looked across at the bloody carcass. 'You killed the dingo!'

She leant forward to peer closely at his shoulder. 'You have been bitten, you know.' She screwed up her face in sympathy with his discomfort as she realigned a piece of torn skin over the wound. 'It will have to be cleaned so that it won't fester.'

He looked down at the wound. 'It will have to be fired so it won't fester.' He winced in anticipation. When he noticed that Amanda's reaction was similar, he added, 'It won't be anything to worry about. A quick touch with a hot ember to seal the edges, that's all. I've seen it done many times at sea.'

'I'd better clean that blood off you so we can check for others.'

He began to rise. 'I can do it.' The bunches of leaves that covered his lower body slipped away revealing more scratches and swathes of blood clinging to his abdomen. He suddenly closed his eyes and sank back on to his elbows. 'In a moment I'll do it.'

'No you won't. You'll stay where you are. You're still not well. I'll bring some water.'

She rose, and gathering up the crude driftwood bowl she had used earlier, she filled it from the stream. As she returned she paused for a moment to look down at the body of the dingo.

'You're a brave lady, Miss Dalrymple,' Will said softly, watching her.

His words caught her by surprise. 'What?'

'I said, you're a brave lady. What I didn't say, but what I was thinking just now, is that you are also a beautiful lady.'

She was gripped for a moment in a surging flush and self-consciously lowered the bowl to shield her lower abdomen.

'Don't be silly, Mr Noling. You're still delirious.' Avoiding his eyes she moved quickly to his side and knelt down.

As she busied herself sponging him with a wet bunch of soft leaves she became acutely aware that she was basking in the grip of a tingling euphoria that caused her to be swept at irregular intervals with pleasurable waves that from time to time made her eyes sting, her chest swell and her breath catch in her throat, as if in spontaneous response to an unexpected ovation.

And these sensations continued uninterrupted,

as if they were separately controlled and located somewhere beneath the surface of the activities that now occupied her: sponging away the blood from his cuts and bruises, discarding and replacing the soiled bunches of leaves, refilling the bowl with fresh water, taking some of his weight each time she needed to move him, and covering his loins each time one of those movements exposed him. She sensed that some of these surface activities, like the regular release of a clock spring, gave impetus to the waves of euphoria.

Suddenly she was gripped by a need to gather her thoughts, and abruptly stood up and walked across to where a copse of melaleucas overhung the back of the beach. As she stood looking into the dense brush, forcing herself to breathe evenly, she absently grasped a handful of leaves and crushed them in the curl of her fingers. Immediately she was immersed in the pleasant eucalyptus-like aroma she had noticed on the first day. And as on that occasion it touched what might have been a memory.

'Uncle Peter,' she suddenly said aloud, and placed her open palm under her nose.

She stripped a number of small branches from the closest bush and carried them back to Will.

'What do you have there?' he asked as she knelt beside him.

'I think they call it tea-tree. My Uncle Peter claims the oil from the leaves will cure a wooden leg.'

'I don't understand.'

She crushed some leaves and held her hand close to his nose. 'The colonials use it to help heal cuts and sores. He had a small bottle. I remember the aroma.'

As he was speaking she began to crush a number of fine leaves between the tips of her fingers, and reaching out rubbed them against an angry band of scratches below his neck.

'There's no need for you to do this, Miss Dalrymple.' He struggled into a sitting position. 'I'm feeling much stronger. If you'll give me a few moments to myself I'll clean away the rest of this mess in the stream and pull my trousers on. And then I'll rub some of your miraculous oil into my wounds.'

'No you won't. I don't want you fainting where I won't be able to move you.'

'But I'm feeling very exposed at the moment.'

'How do you think I feel? And I have no trousers to pull on.'

She placed her hand on his shoulder. 'Lie down and I'll attend to these scratches you can't see around the base of your neck.'

'But what about you? You've been scratched as well.'

'Not deeply. Mainly on my legs. I'll see to them later.'

As she gently began to smear the sap from the leaves into the cuts and welts across the top of his chest, the pleasant tingling sensation that had earlier applauded her victory over the dingo began to reaffirm its presence.

'Hand me some of those leaves,' he said when she began to attend to wounds lower down his chest. 'I can help.' He began to lean forward.

She placed a hand firmly on his shoulder again and prevented him from rising. 'Tell me, Mr Noling, how is it that you were being transported to New South Wales?'

He lay back. 'I was convicted of attacking the man whose lies caused my fiancée to be transported.'

'You have a fiancée?'

'Yes.'

'And she's here?'

'Yes.'

They were silent for a while.

Then he asked, 'And what about you, Miss Dalrymple? Why were you travelling to New South Wales?'

'My fiancé is here as well. I was coming out to be married.'

They turned and watched each other in silence and remained unmoving for some time. And then, as if responding to a signal, or practising a move that had been choreographed, they leaned towards each other and kissed. When they drew back they watched each other again for some time before he reached out and ran the back of his fingers slowly down her cleavage. They kissed again, and as she came on to her knees both his hands moved to cup her breasts and release them from their inadequate covering. A short while later she rose higher and, stepping across him, sank back astride of him. Her sudden concern for what this activity might have on his state of health rapidly evaporated as she sensed his strength.

At one stage during the events that then took place, she lowered her head and watched with an expression of incredulity at the rhythmic collision of their bodies and each sympathetic jump of her stomach and bounce of her breasts. And within her the sensation that had gripped her since she killed the dingo became a deep-seated itch that was now being urgently worried. And with each exquisite stroke the core of her body vibrated with a rising intensity.

Later she sat on a small boulder beside the rock-pool. For a long time she wallowed in pleasurable recall of how the invisible fibres from which her itch was constructed had gradually stretched to their very limits and then had exploded one by one in long rolling oscillations.

But then she grew sad. And after a while she looked down at the dried blood congealed in her pubic hair and coating her stomach and thighs. The dingo's, she wondered, or mine? Or his? Perhaps all three.

When he came and sat beside her, her gaze was on the breaking surf. She kept it there, refusing to look at him. So he filled a soft piece of

seaweed with water and sponged away, and
scrubbed away, all the blood and grime and other
physical remnants of her morning's adventures.
And when she was clean again, he held her while
she cried.

NINETEEN

Gunroi's gaze probed the heavier darkness that climbed away to the north. Regularly, when he detected a change in the whisper of the forest or the murmur of the wetland, his head would suddenly cock to one side and he would swing his spear around to better ward off an attack from that direction. Often he would wince in recall and expectation of being struck by another lightning bolt. An exploding burst of pain in the centre of his head. A rolling clap of thunder in his ears.

A number of times, and lasting for several minutes, the background murmurs of the night rose in strength to fill his mind like a full chorus of cicadas while images of the red-coated white men and their huge canoe swirled around the periphery of his consciousness.

And deep within him there remained a continual ache, a hollow discomfort that gnawed at the very core of his body. An ache more deep-seated than the ache of the wound he tentatively touched.

Deeper than this raw crease of bruised and broken flesh that lay beneath the crusted mix of dried blood and matted hair on the crown of his head. So deep, he knew, that no amount of probing with his fingers could reach and worry it. Could scratch the itch and blunt the edge of the pain.

There was a remarkable similarity about all journeys at night, he decided. Whether through his own country, or this distant country, or any in-between country. There was a degree of sameness that at times had him struggling to dispel the notion that the time and the place and the circumstance were not in most ways identical. That the great spirit Biamie had not plucked him up and placed him back in the middle of a previous experience. Or a future experience. Or had in some mysterious way woven the time space and circumstance of all night-time journeys into a singular experience.

Several times his eyes probed deeply into the back of the dim figure moving ahead of him to confirm that he was indeed looking at Coranga, and not at the paler form of the strange white woman who had come into his life and had altered it irrevocably. And each time he did this the ache in the pit of his stomach intensified to a degree that almost caused him to groan aloud.

Not that the name of the white people's huge camp was of any significance to Gunroi, it was Newcastle, not Sydney, that he and his fellow-travellers encountered some six weeks later. The former Coal River penal settlement had recently been re-established at the mouth of what was now called the Hunter River.

As well as providing a place of punishment for secondary offenders, the community serviced the burgeoning coal-mining and timber industries of the district. Unofficially the local garrison also provided protection to serving and former members of the Rum Corps who had prematurely taken possession of prime land-holdings along the Hunter in anticipation of it being released for pastoral development.

What was of significance to Gunroi was that huge canoes, similar to the one that had carried Jessica away, were tied up in the river. And that among the people who inhabited the strange dwellings that were stacked in rows on the hillside opposite the canoes were many white men who wore the same blood-coloured skins as those who had stolen her from him.

Naturally, he and the others were wary of these savage people who killed and stole women, and who were powerful enough to build canoes as big as the rock that stood at the river's mouth, and knock people down—perhaps even kill them— with bolts of lightning. So they approached the huge camp with caution, skirting to the south and keeping to high county where they could move in through dense brush unobserved and look down on what was going on from positions of cover.

They were surprised to discover that small

groups of other black people had set up a number of camps around the perimeter of the settlement. They were even more surprised to see some of these people occasionally mingling with the whites.

They were not surprised to see how brutally the whites treated their slaves, mainly old men of an inferior race with stooped frames and shrunken bodies, and skin even whiter than their masters. The tasks these unfortunate people were forced to perform seemed to consist mainly of mindless activities such as hauling large logs and stones from one place to another, and digging a great hole in the side of one of the cliffs that overlooked the sea.

Even though most of these wretched creatures seemed to carry out these tasks to the best of their abilities—with their bodies often trembling and their eyes rolling back into their heads from their exertions—they were repeatedly set upon by those in charge and kicked and beaten until the blood ran freely over their pale white skin and they cried like injured children.

They came across the sick woman on the third day. They had encountered other blacks in the woods while they were carrying out their initial surveillance of the place, but usually only fleetingly. Little more than the sighting of a startled face before the owner disappeared amidst a rustle of bushes and the steady thump of retreating feet.

Similar in many ways to suddenly coming face to face with a kangaroo.

She was sitting with her back propped against the trunk of a tree and, unlike the other encounters with locals, as she watched them approach she gave no sign of surprise. To the contrary she smiled weakly as if perhaps she was expecting them.

She seemed to be in very poor condition, having perhaps wandered away from those who might have been able to assist her, and had been forced to fend for herself. Badly. Her hair was matted and caked with grime, her body was covered in weeping scratches and insect bites, and a great clump of hardened mucus was clustered beneath her nose. They deduced from her hand signs and mumbled replies to their questions that she probably belonged to one of the southern Kamilaroi clans, or perhaps was a Catarn. Coranga, whose mother was Kamilaroi, was able to get the most sense out of her. But as well as having no idea what was ailing her, the woman appeared to resent any suggestion that she was ill. She did indicate, however, that she came from a nearby camp where a small creek flowed into a tidal arm of the river.

Despite her protests, Gunroi and Nunderri lifted her to her feet. Then, partly carrying her and partly supporting her between them, they made their way through the brush to where they expected the camp would be sited. Coranga, carrying her own utensils and their weapons, brought up the rear, grumbling whenever she lost control of any of the items she was carrying or when one of the spears caught in the underbrush. With good reason. Twice she dropped the entire load, despite, on each occasion, performing a complicated dance that involved stepping rapidly from one foot to the other while simultaneously raising the opposite knee to steady the trembling odds and ends. She also managed to grab and dexterously juggle for some time those items that began to tumble away from the main cluster.

The camp was where they expected, but what they did not expect was its condition. From well before they reached it they began to encounter refuse lying in untidy piles on either side of the track, mainly rotting carcases of partly consumed animals. Why the inhabitants had not dumped them in the one place downwind was a mystery. Some of the waste had even been thrown in the shallow creek upstream from the camp.

Their noses also told them that the camp's inhabitants had been equally casual with their disposal of their own waste. And by the time they reached the camp proper they were taking extra care of where they placed their feet.

But even the state of the surrounds did not adequately prepare them for the condition of the camp itself. About half of the brush and bark lean-tos had collapsed and had not been properly raised again, even though they were still being used. The poles and saplings that had been used for their frames had been left lying where they had fallen. From all appearances those who were still using them had simply propped them up high enough for them to crawl under the sheets of bark and layers of foliage.

At some stage a shallow trench had been scraped in the sandy soil around the dwellings at the lower end of the camp, presumably to drain off rain water. But a small log had apparently fallen or been thrown into the drain, and a build-up of refuse and sand behind it now caused the entire lower end of the camp to be awash with green, foul-smelling water.

Gunroi silently promised himself as they approached that they would stay only as long as it took to unburden themselves of the woman. Obviously she was not the only person suffering from a sickness. The entire place smelt of decay.

A man approached them as they placed the woman on the ground. Although his demeanour did not appear to be overly belligerent and he carried his spear with its point lowered, both Gunroi and Nunderri turned away so as not to confront him head-on, and as casually as they could do so in the time it took him to reach them, they retrieved their weapons from Coranga. With the exception of the spare spears, she lowered the remainder of her burden to the ground.

The man stopped as he reached the woman and after lifting his jaw a little higher than Gunroi felt comfortable with as he appraised both him and his brother, he looked down at the woman and spoke to her harshly.

Gunroi, continuing to face slightly to one side of him to demonstrate his own neutrality, glanced across at Coranga. 'Tell him we found her lying in the brush. Tell him the sickness she's suffering from has made her very weak.'

Coranga spoke to the man, who replied with a laugh and waved a hand dismissively above the woman's head.

'Is he saying she's not sick?' Gunroi asked, picking up what he believed was the gist of the man's comments.

'He says she's . . .' She turned and asked the man a question. 'He says she's stupid from something the white men have given her to drink.' Again she sought clarification with the man. Turning back to Gunroi, she fluttered the fingers of one hand before her eyes. 'I think he means it's like she chewed too many leaves from the pijirri bush.'

The man walked to the side of the clearing and stooping close to the water's edge picked up one of a number of ceramic bottles that were scattered among the roots of some young mangroves. He returned and waved it at them causing it to flash as it caught the sunlight. They had never seen anything like it.

'Rum,' said the man, and inserting a finger in the neck tipped it up and then placed the finger in his mouth. He handed the bottle to Gunroi.

Gunroi leant his spear against his shoulder and ran his free hand over the smooth surface. 'Is it stone?' he asked, reversing his hand and tapping it with his finger nails.

Nunderri and Coranga moved closer and both reached out and felt it.

A small amount of liquid ran on to Gunroi's hand as he tipped it over. 'Ask him is it poison?' he said as he studied his damp flesh closely.

Coranga spoke to the man.

'Poison!' he retorted. 'Tell him we're not so stupid we'd drink poison. Tell him to taste it. It's good.' He leaned towards Gunroi. 'It's good, you fool. Good.'

Gunroi placed his hand to his lips.

'Let me try,' said Coranga, placing a finger in the neck of the bottle and rubbing the liquid on her own lips.

'It's sweet. Like honey.'

Gunroi spat on the ground. 'It burns the throat. Ask him if it's so good, why is the woman too sick to stand up?'

'Because she drank too much,' he replied when Coranga passed on the query.

With this he leant over the woman and shouted, 'Too much!' And then struck her on the top of the head with his closed fist. The blow seemed to hurt him more than it did her, for she made no sound at all, while he gasped in pain. Complaining and wringing his hand he walked across to the mangroves and picked up a heavy stick about the size of a woomera.

Gunroi noticed that he walked as if his legs were injured in some way, and that when he straightened, clutching the stick in one hand, he stumbled and had to use his spear for support to prevent himself from pitching forward into the mangroves.

When he returned he again bent over the woman and shouted, 'Too much!'

Her eyes rolled back as she tried to look up at him. He then lifted the stick high and brought it down solidly across her back. She gasped and he shouted at her before striking her again. She began to wail and tried feebly to fend off the blows as he struck her repeatedly, shouting at her all the while, with bursts of saliva flying from his mouth.

Gunroi threw the bottle away and glanced at Nunderri. And then turning to Coranga said, 'Ask him why he's beating her.'

When she spoke to him he stood back and looked at Gunroi with his chest heaving. 'She drank all of the rum the white men gave her.'

'Why did they give her rum?'

'So she would let them lie with her.'

The woman wailed something, and picking up a handful of dirt tried to throw it up at the man, but most of it spilled back on her face.

The man again lifted his stick but Gunroi quickly stepped in front of him.

'She's my wife,' the man retorted, raising his jaw and staring into Gunroi's face.

The woman interrupted her wailing to assail the

man with a long burst of apparent accusation.

'She says he gives her to the white men in return for rum, and keeps it for himself,' said Coranga.

Although he was a head shorter than Gunroi, he was much more solidly built. But his eyes were rheumy and flickering and his shoulders and arms were quivering. Whether his condition was on account of sickness or fear, Gunroi was not concerned. He was confident he could deal with him in any manner he pleased and was in no mood to truck any nonsense from him.

'Ask him why do they live in such squalor. Why don't they clean the place, unblock that drain and put those shelters back up?'

The man scoffed and waved a hand above his head.

'He says this is not their camp. It was like this when they arrived. If anyone should fix it, the people who built it should fix it. He says there's no reason why their women should waste their time on it. He also says it's none of your business, and you have no right to interfere between him and his wife.'

'Tell him he beats his wife because he's a coward, and it's safer to make war on women than on people who might fight back. And that if he doesn't leave us now and crawl into whichever one of those stinking rats' nests he crawled out of, I'll put this spear of mine straight through him.'

When Coranga relayed the message, the man leaned forward and hissed something at Gunroi who noticed that his breath gave off a strange heat, similar to the woman's.

'Tell him to get out of my sight,' said Gunroi. 'Now! I won't warn him again.'

The man tried to match Gunroi's gaze but soon began to tremble uncontrollably. Then suddenly, he spun on his heel and dashed back across the clearing, weaving from side to side as he ran.

Is it his sickness that prevents him from running in a straight line, Gunroi wondered. Or does he believe this is how he will best avoid having my spear thud into his back? The man finally dived into one of the shelters and scurried out of sight.

Their attention then turned to a young boy who staggered from behind another shelter and stumbled to the creek where he lay down on his side and began to vomit.

Gunroi watched him for a time before turning away and shaking his head. 'Come on,' he snapped angrily and began to move off along the path they had arrived by. 'I can't bear to look at this place a moment longer.'

Before Coranga gathered up her possessions, she moved to the side of the clearing and, picking up another bottle, poured out the remaining few drops of liquid it contained on to the palm of her hand. She then licked them off.

The big white man pressed his back against the tree and scratched himself by rocking his shoulders from side to side. And no wonder, Gunroi mused as he sat watching him from the opposite side of the fire. Although his strange wrapping was the colour of blood, it appeared to be made from the same stuff as Coranga's blanket. And despite her claims that it was the most wonderful thing that she had ever possessed—even now as she sat beside him she had it wrapped snugly around her shoulders—he found that it prickled his skin and he couldn't bear the feel of it brushing against him for more than a few moments.

For a time Gunroi had seriously considered whether or not he should kill the man. After all, he was from the same race of people who killed Mori and took Jessica away. And it would be a simple thing to do. The man was completely unprepared for trouble. His thunder club was propped out of reach against the tree along with the one that belonged to his companion, who was somewhere at the back of the camp with a woman belonging to Coolbee, the head of the camp.

A quick thrust of a spear. The thump of a club. His companion would be easier still. He was even more stupid from drinking rum than this one. And this one could fall over at any time. Even with his great legs spread wide and propped in front of him to help keep him upright.

What probably stayed his own hand, he decided, was that this man was also Coolbee's guest this evening. If he did choose to kill him, it would be better that he do it at some other time, and well away from the camp.

Coolbee had warned him, when he first heard of his grievance with the white men, that they were terrible in their anger if one of their own were killed. He told him that the camp where they left the sick woman had once been occupied by a Catarn clan, one of whom had speared a white man. And although the injured man did not die, a great number of the whites attacked the camp and killed everyone they could catch, including women and children.

The people who now occupied the camp, he told Gunroi, were mainly outcasts from a number of clans: men who had broken tribal law, women whose husbands had grown tired of them, and sick and crippled people. Curiously, this had some effect on raising Gunroi's spirits, which had plummeted to new depths after their visit to the sick woman's camp. At least there appeared to be some excuse for its condition and the lifestyle of its inhabitants.

Coolbee's camp was in much better condition and was sited beside a clean stream on the very edge of the settlement itself. As soon as he saw Gunroi and the others approaching he went out to meet them and invited them to join his group.

Although he did run an appreciative eye over Coranga, his prime motivation was profit. He recognised that both Gunroi and Nunderri were in better condition than any of those he had earlier recruited to help him retrieve escaped convicts in return for a steady supply of rum and flour from the garrison store.

He and his cohorts were also allowed to set up camp where their women were assured of a steady supply of red-jacketed visitors, an exchange of goods for services that compounded the benefits. Occasionally Coolbee was rewarded with a barrel of what the whites called 'salted horse', which was actually salted beef. Not that whether the whites rightly or wrongly named the tasty substance was of any great interest to Coolbee and the others. There were a few live examples of horses and cattle in and around the settlement, and both species looked equally appetising.

Coolbee's white guest was apparently an important person, signified by the three stripes on his jacket. Coolbee explained to Gunroi—assisted where necessary by Coranga—that because both he and the white man had good knowledge of each other's language, they were the most important link that existed between the white and the black communities in the district. Therefore it was in the interests of both communities that he and this man maintain a friendly relationship. Or to put it another way, Coolbee had explained, 'Don't, whatever you do, go belting him over the head with a club, or running a spear through him.'

After he finished scratching his back, the man drank deeply from a bottle of rum he kept close by his side. He then wiped the back of his hand across his mouth and began to speak to those around him, punctuating his words with expansive gestures and occasional bursts of laughter. The fact that only Coolbee understood what he was saying seemed to be of no consequence to him.

Coolbee translated some of his words, and Coranga in turn translated some of these for Gunroi and Nunderri.

Apparently he was telling them that they were not to trouble those white men who were venturing deep into the countryside to cut down trees and erect dwellings, no matter how far they moved away from the settlement. He also told them that they should not spear any of the white men's animals.

Gunroi decided he was an arrogant man not deserving of any respect, and his thoughts returned to whether or not he should kill him.

At one point Coolbee burst out laughing at something the man said. According to Coranga—who must have misunderstood Coolbee's explanation because her words made no sense whatsoever—the man said that there were two ways to prevent rum making you sick. One was not to drink it and the other was not to stop drinking it. He then leant forward and passed his bottle to Coranga. She smiled shyly and in response to his hand gestures to drink, she placed it to her lips and swallowed some of the contents.

Gunroi's expression did not change and he continued to stare without moving at a point in the brush somewhere behind the man's head. I will kill him, he decided. But not tonight. And how she can swallow without gagging is a mystery. Perhaps she's had more practice than she admits to. When I've been away looking for Jessica, and when Nunderri's been away with Coolbee. She also seems to be more interested in this man than he deserves. She's hardly shifted her eyes away from him since he arrived. And whenever he laughs, and the clumps of yellow hair on his cheeks bounce up and down, her eyes widen, her mouth springs open and her own cheeks bounce in sympathy. She even looks around at us as if to confirm or encourage our support for the fool.

He was momentarily distracted by the strange material that covered the man's lower torso and legs and grudgingly acknowledged that this was a garment that would have more uses than simply keeping out the winter's chill.

His anger began to escalate. She's been blinded by these strange wrappings he hides himself behind, he decided. His blood-red cloak. The shiny stones that hold it together. The strips of gleaming kangaroo hide, painted white and stretched across his chest, painted black and wrapped around his feet. Can't she see that beneath these fancy skins he's as soft and spongy as a baby? Most of him.

Suddenly Gunroi stood up, and without a backward glance at any of the others, strode out of the camp. If I'm to spare him tonight, he told himself as he headed for the river, I must get far enough away so that I can no longer see him, hear him, nor even think about him.

He stopped when he came across a large log partly buried in a sandbank and sat down. Lights from fires on the opposite bank wiggled snake-like across the water towards him. Could she be over there, he suddenly wondered, the night momentarily casting a fanciful cloak over his more rational judgement. Of course she's not over there. She's been taken somewhere else. Perhaps to this other place they speak of. Further south. But what if she isn't there? What if I go there and they say there's another place still further south? And what if she hasn't been taken south, but north; and each day I travel further away from her? What if she's been taken to the land across the sea where the white men came from?

He raised his head and turned to the north-west where great bundles of clouds were being embraced by spider webs of silent lightning. If she managed to escape would she look for me? And where would she look? Where would she go and wait? His gaze remained locked for a time on the bundles of cloud and he knew very well where she'd go.

He settled back against a broad limb that stood upright from the log and closed his eyes.

Gunroi's despondency increased over the following weeks to a point where he could no longer stand what was happening around him in the white men's camp. He decided it was time to return home and told Nunderri and Coranga to gather whatever they wanted to bring. But both of them seemed reluctant to leave.

At first he attempted to be persuasive. Taking a handful of twigs and breaking them into even sizes, he squatted before them. 'When we left home we travelled about two months to the north.' He placed two of the twigs in a straight line. 'We then travelled about one month east to the coast.' He placed another twig at right-angles to the top of the others. 'Allowing for the time we spent in the mountains, we then travelled for about three and a half months a little to the west of south to reach where we are now.' He angled three more twigs down from the right-hand side of the last. 'Which means we are only about one month from home if we travel to the west of north.' He placed down a final twig to complete a small enclosure.

'Only one month!' said Nunderri, bending forward as if observing the twigs at closer range might reveal the flaw in his brother's surprising revelation.

'Perhaps one and a half months,' Gunroi conceded. 'I think this river is the one travellers from the south-east of our land speak of. If we follow it back to the mountains I'm certain we'll find our homeland on the other side.'

'But you haven't found your eagle,' Coranga protested. 'You haven't found Jessica. You haven't found anything you've been looking for.'

Gunroi squatted before them and, dropping his gaze to the ground at his feet, remained unmoving for a time. 'What are you saying?' he asked finally, his voice brittle. 'You want to stay here?'

Coranga pulled her blanket around her shoulders. 'What's wrong with this place? We have all we want to eat.'

'You mean you have all you want to drink,' Gunroi flared.

'It's warmer here.'

'When? Whenever your fat sergeant lies on top of you and you have your arms wrapped around him?'

She squatted in front of him and pressed her face towards him with her jaw raised.

'Yes. Warmer than you are at night, lying by yourself and trying to wrap your arms around the ghost of Jessica.'

He struck her with an almost involuntary sweep of the back of his hand. She fell backwards, releasing her blanket, and then scrambled naked away from him as he stood up and advanced on her.

She cowered, whimpering beneath him as he stood over her. 'Gather your things. We're leaving now.'

'I'm not going,' she mumbled.

'What?'

'I'm not going with you. I'm not going back to be your slave and the slave of the old men. I'm warm here. I don't have to burn myself in the coals

of a fire to keep myself from freezing. I don't have
to break my hands digging for food. I don't have
to break my back hauling firewood.'

'But you have to lie with the white men.'

'Back home I have to lie with the old men.'

'That's not true.'

'It was true before I learned how to avoid them.'

'It's a lie since we were married.'

She met his gaze. 'Not always.'

He swung away and stared into the brush.

'And I'd rather lie with the white men.'

'Get up. You're coming with us.'

'I'm not. I'm staying.'

He turned back and raised his hand.

'What are you going to do, hit me again? You
never used to hit me.'

'You never disgusted me before.'

He swung away and strode past Nunderri.
'Come on, we're leaving.'

Nunderri looked back to where Coranga
remained squatting on the ground with her arms
wrapped around her shoulders. 'You're going to
leave her?'

'She can do as she pleases. She always does.'

TWENTY

Will and Amanda followed a stream away from the beach seeking a path around an abrupt headland that blocked their way. Will was concerned about dark clouds moving in from the east and suggested that if a squall did arrive they would have a better chance of finding shelter in the lee of the headland than if they tried to scale it.

He was still uncertain of the state of his health. So that he could start the evening's fire without having to use too much energy, he carried embers from their previous fire in a small hollow log balanced on his hip and supported by a strip of vine around his shoulder.

Amanda was very quiet, usually speaking only when he addressed her. Several times during the day he noticed that she was weeping quietly. Not knowing what he could say to comfort her, for a time he said nothing, and then tried to direct her attention to their surroundings.

The squall did arrive, just as they reached a place where the stream opened into a series of shallow marshes surrounded by dense forest. With raindrops the size of acorns assailing them, they scurried up a gentle slope to a rocky outcrop that flanked one side of the stream and scrambled beneath a long overhanging shelf.

Satisfying himself that it provided ideal shelter, Will dashed out and quickly gathered several bundles of dead branches and small logs and stacked them beneath one end of the overhang.

He soon had a fire going, positioning it so that the smoke drifted out of the shelter. The heavy rain abated not long after it started and as it eased to a light drizzle small flocks of waterfowl moved in and began to feed in the shallows of the nearest marsh.

Seizing the opportunity to test his trapping skills, Will fashioned a number of small snares from lengths of fibre he stripped from vines that grew along the edge of the cliff. He briefly left the shelter and set the snares among reeds where the birds had been the most active. Using a stick, he broke away sections of the soft earth in the bank of the marsh and stirred up the mud around the snares.

As soon as he returned to the shelter the birds swooped back to attack the insects and worms he had disturbed. Within minutes three birds were trapped and he dashed back down the slope to retrieve them.

The rain stopped completely about mid-afternoon and he and Amanda ventured out to stretch their legs and survey their surroundings. He reset his snares in the shallows and dug some earth from the surrounding bank to release more insects and worms. This realised a bonus meal when he disturbed four small freshwater crayfish.

After they had gathered a store of wood for the fire, Will suggested they explore the terrain immediately upstream from the shelter. Although he did not say so, he believed they would probably rest easier if they extended the perimeter of the zone that separated them from the unknown surrounds.

On the way they disturbed a small mob of wallaroos feeding on the lush grass that bordered the stream. The animals took fright the moment they were sighted and, dashing across the bank, pounded away up the hillside leaving behind an audible wake of tumbling stones.

To the west clouds had drifted away from the sun and the two of them stood for a time shielding their eyes from the glare that bounced off the water. Beyond a rocky bend the marshes seemed to extend back to be engulfed by a rainforest that swept down from higher ground, but the sun in their faces turned the afternoon shadows ahead of them into gloomy veils that cloaked the exact divisions of land and water. Spears of light that penetrated the higher branches of the trees on the skyline scattered small fires across the surface of the marshes near them. The observers were like players on a brightly lit stage seeking in vain to observe the far reaches of the stalls.

'We would never know if there's anyone or anything out there watching,' said Amanda, and shuddered.

'There was no sign of smoke earlier to suggest there was anyone,' Will replied. 'And with regard to dangerous anythings, my guess is your dingo was an exception. With a decent fire going I'm sure most animals will stay well away.'

As they were returning to their cave Will walked across to a copse of broad-trunked melaleucas and stripped off a thick wad of the spongy bark. Finding that it was dry, he suggested that they gather a bundle large enough for their bedding.

He passed it to Amanda. 'It's like layers of soft paper. I haven't seen any soft-leaved bushes like the ones we have been using. And they weren't anywhere near as soft as this stuff.'

Amanda agreed, so with some trial and error use of the flat of their hands they began to shear away wide blankets of bark from the nearest trees and place them in a pile on the ground.

At one point, as he moved to help her manage a large sheet that she was removing, he said, 'A few more and we'll have a bed over a foot thick.'

Despite what had happened between them, his use of the singular 'bed' caused her cheeks to sting. She turned quickly away from him and feigned interest in the forest.

After the pile had grown to about the level of

her knees, Will flicked off two cicada shells that were clinging to one sheet and said, 'I think this is about as much as we can carry.' He gathered up the top few sheets. 'Hold out your arms and I'll load you.'

The birds he had caught had webbed feet and although their bills were more pointed than flat, he was certain they were a variety of duck. After they had been roasted in the coals they certainly tasted like duck, with crisp golden skin that they eagerly stripped from the flesh, and sticky juices that clung to their lips and fingers as they devoured every morsel. They attacked the crayfish with equal enthusiasm and both agreed that the small crustaceans were probably even more delicious than their home-grown variety.

After the meal, while Amanda propped herself on the pile of paperbark they had left stacked to one side of the fire, Will worked on a new lance to replace the one that had been broken the previous day, hardening the point and straightening the shaft in the hot coals.

Amanda sat silently watching him as he worked. Occasionally she turned her eyes to the rapidly vanishing day. For a time she could still see where the marshes wound into the surrounding forest like crazy patterns cut from a flat strip of gleaming metal.

Eventually more clouds drifting in from the coast brought with them a steady downpour of rain. Brighter sky to the west turned the shower into gleaming shades that drifted slowly past the cave. As the sky darkened the glow from the fire sealed the occupants behind a whispering curtain of sparkling drops.

Will glanced up and met Amanda's gaze. She looked so forlorn he gave her a quick smile of encouragement. But her eyes immediately filled with tears.

'What's wrong?' he asked.

At first she shook her head and did not reply. Then when she had recovered a little, she said, 'I'm frightened. I've been able to hold my fears at bay pretty well up until now, but now I'm so frightened I'm not sure I can stand it.'

'There's no need to be. I'm sure we're safe here. And we couldn't be more cosy.'

She said nothing for a while, and then, 'What I'm frightened of is that something might happen to you. You were very sick; you could have died. And earlier you were running around and getting wet. If you caught a chill and became sick again there mightn't be anything I could do.' Tears began to well in her eyes again. 'Or if the blacks, or a wild animal attacked you ...' A large tear spilled from one eye and began to track slowly down her cheek. 'I couldn't stand it if I was left alone.' She began to shake with silent sobs.

Will put down the lance and moved to sit beside her. 'I'm not about to leave you alone. And don't underestimate your own survival abilities.

Remember how you dealt with the dingo.'

When she had recovered a little she asked, 'What are you going to do when we reach Sydney?'

'I'm not sure. I hope to get a better idea of what's happening with transportees when we get closer. I'll make up my mind then.'

'Then you're not going to hand yourself over to the authorities?'

'Not necessarily. And certainly not immediately we arrive. You'll be able to give them all the details they'll need about the shipwreck and the castaways.'

'So you'll go looking for her?'

'Of course.'

'Tell me about her.'

So he did. And when he asked her to, she told him about her fiancé.

Locked away together in their cosy cocoon in the middle of the wilderness, it would not have been difficult for them to believe they were the only people alive on the planet. They were also footsore and weary, and despite the meal, they were undernourished. If anyone had overheard their quiet conversation, the eavesdropper would have been excused for assuming that they had been discussing casual acquaintances from a long distant past, rather than loved ones.

They eventually grew silent and sat for some time without speaking, their gazes resting within the glowing embers of the fire.

Finally, Will stood and moved across to the stack of paperbark. 'How would you prefer that we arrange this?' he asked. 'Should we make up two separate beds, or one composite one?'

Amanda dropped her gaze. 'What do you suggest?' This was the subject that had teased her ever since they collected the bark. It hovered at the back of her attention when they cooked and ate their meal and while she watched Will working on the lance. And it was there scratching away at the periphery of her consciousness while she listened to him talk of his Jessica and while she was listening to herself tell him about her Granville.

What occurred immediately after she killed the dingo could perhaps be excused as being the spontaneous consequence of the heady events that preceded it. But what they were now moving towards was premeditated. A decision by both of them to continue with their physical relationship, and to risk the consequences.

'Making up one wide bed with plenty of room for both of us would save breaking up the sheets into shorter sections and probably weakening them,' said Will, with commendable objectivity. 'I think they'll hold together better in larger sheets and be more comfortable.'

So they set about making their bed.

First they placed a high foundation of bracken on the floor of the shelter and then they carefully stacked the wide strips of bark on top, positioning each layer, alternately lengthwise and crosswise.

'This should be the top layer,' he said at last.
'There isn't enough for another.'

As they straightened she met his gaze. They were
silent for a moment and then he bobbed his head
towards the bed and smiled. 'Ladies first. See if it's
comfortable.'

She ducked her head to move past him and
climbing carefully on to the centre, turned around.

'How does it feel?'

'Comfortable.' She pressed the surface beside
her hip. 'Firm, but comfortable.'

'Lie down. Give it a decent test.'

She did as instructed.

'What do you think?'

'Good.' She had one hand lying flat below her
throat so that her crocked arm hid much of her
breasts.

'Take your hand away,' he said softly.

She hesitated for a moment and then placed it
at her side.

He reached down and put the tips of his fingers
first to her cheek and then to her lips. He then ran
them down to lightly brush over the shreds of her
camisole. 'It might be sensible to remove that,' he
said evenly. 'If you want what's left of it to last
until we reach Sydney.'

She met his gaze for a moment and, without replying, sat up and pulled it over her head.
She then took careful hold of the waist of her
shortened petticoat and rocking from one buttock
to the other slipped it off. She placed both

garments beside the bed and met his gaze.

He reached down and ran the back of his fingers across each of her nipples. 'You're a lovely lady, Amanda Dalrymple.' He raised his hand again and lifted a curling wisp of hair away from her cheek.

He then slipped off his trousers and sat down beside her. She turned and was about to speak as he leant forward and lightly pressed his lips against hers. No urgent embrace followed. No crush of mouths. Just a light brushing of flesh. A nose to an ear, a nipple trailing across biceps, lips moving to a shoulder, a thigh nudging a thigh.

Light from the fire pulsed fitfully over the rock walls and ceiling, and pale reflections moved in harmony over the naked bodies below.

When Will awoke the next morning he found Amanda was sleeping peacefully, lying curled on her side with her back to him and the palms of her hands pressed together and clamped between her thighs. He sat watching her for a time, his eyes tracing the gentle symmetry of her form. The early morning light bathed her in a honey glow, a golden sheen that softened the edges of the sun's recent broad brush strokes across her body. His eyes came to rest on her face and stayed there for an age.

He rose as quietly as their bed permitted, picked up one of the lances and moved out of the shelter. He made his way down the slope to the edge of the marsh. The rain had stopped sometime during the night and a breeze had blown away all remnants of cloud. The sun streamed low through the tall trees on the opposite bank. Steam rose from a profusion of tiny fires sparkling in the rain-drenched foliage. The surrounding rocks perspired.

He breathed in deeply as he looked about him. And then for a few moments he found himself trying to identify the cause of a mild concern stirring somewhere in the reaches of his mind. Conscience, he wondered. Probably, he conceded. Because of what was happening between him and Amanda? He pondered that one for a moment. No. He shook his head. Not for what was happening between them. Then why? For the sense of contentment, he suddenly realised, and folded his arms. He knew he had no right to feel this happy.

Had Gunroi and Nunderri not met the party of timber cutters as they topped the crest of a ridge with the wind in their faces, they would have given them a wide berth. As it was, both groups were suddenly standing within a few yards of each other with similar startled looks on their faces.

'Lookee here,' the man who was probably the leader of the group finally managed. 'A couple of wild young nigger boys out a'huntin' for food. We got any rum left there, fellas? These boys look a bit chilled standin' here in the bollicky. A couple o' drams'll put a bit of warmth into them.'

A ceramic bottle was uncorked and passed

forward. There were six of them. Solidly built men beneath their bandannas and broad-brimmed hats, and clothed in a variety of coarse cotton shirts, some with sleeves torn off at the shoulder, and thick woollen trousers pulled up high above their waists beneath broad leather belts. Some of them carried axes, others long crosscut saws.

'I wouldn't mind puttin' somethin' warm into the shorter one,' a tall man at the back muttered, his face creasing into a gap-toothed leer.

As the bottle was pressed towards them Gunroi shook his head and, as if to fend it off, raised his left hand in which he was carrying his woomera and his spare spears and moved on past them with Nunderri following close behind. When it appeared they would be allowed to depart without protest the tall man suddenly dropped whatever he was carrying and grabbed hold of Nunderri from behind.

'Gotcha, my little lovely,' he whispered harshly in his ear as the young man cried out in alarm. 'Now be a good boy and don't struggle.'

And so it began.

Almost in the same movement as turning, Gunroi swung his spear around and without releasing it drove it into the big man's throat. As the man, shrieking in pain and alarm, fell away from Nunderri with blood gushing from his wound, Nunderri turned and plunged his spear into the chest of the man standing directly behind his fallen comrade. As the two wounded men kicked and writhed in their gurgling death throes, coating the surrounding ground-cover in broad crimson stains, the others backed away from them, their faces masks of fear and horror.

'Gawd 'elp us,' one of them wailed, as both Gunroi and Nunderri fitted spears into their woomeras and moved to give themselves throwing room. One of the men was carrying a musket, but was so consumed by fear he completely forgot he was clutching it in his trembling hands.

Just when it appeared the two blacks would unleash their spears, on a signal from Gunroi, both turned and dashed into the bush. Only then did the leader of the group step forward and, snatching the musket from his companion, put it to his shoulder and fire it. But Gunroi and Nunderri by then had disappeared and the ball whistled harmlessly through the forest understorey and finally thumped into the trunk of a tree.

Unfortunately for the fugitives a detachment of soldiers from the Newcastle garrison was nearby, and hearing the report of the musket, came to investigate. They immediately set off in hot pursuit. When they failed to locate their quarry, they notified other troops who were returning from further up the valley, and soon the entire area was being swept for the fugitives.

To avoid running into the prowling bands of their red-coated pursuers, Gunroi and Nunderri were at first forced to back-track to the east, and then to head almost due north. Several times they were sent scurrying into the bush with musket balls ripping through the foliage close by.

Continually being forced to hide, even from fellow blacks, whom they feared would turn against them to protect themselves, they were unable to hunt as they would normally hunt. So they lived mainly off the few birds that Nunderri could snare close to where they camped each day, and the sparse supply of edible fruits they could forage from the local forest.

Occasionally they would come across a white man's dwelling or a forest camp of timber cutters from whom they could steal some food. But these were risky ventures and they were forced to kill on three more occasions in order to avoid capture or injury. Nunderri grieved on most nights over the death of the young white boy he struck with a stolen tomahawk when the boy surprised him taking meat from a smokehouse. Immediately afterwards Nunderri found himself trying to press the gaping flesh and bone back together on the side of the boy's fair head, before he finally turned away in horror and raced back empty-handed to where Gunroi was waiting, watching the boy's father erecting a fence with his musket close by his side.

So it was that they came to a ridge overlooking a northern tributary to the Hunter in a condition that might have caused an acquaintance to have trouble recognising them from a distance. They were leaner than they had been at any time since they had left on their journey to the coast, and they had a furtive, predatory look about the way they crouched in the underbrush with their heads cocked, listening for any sounds of pursuit.

As Will and Amanda continued their journey south they were forced to move away from the coast when a succession of barriers in the form of a series of tidal lakes blocked their path. As they moved inland seeking a way around a vast expanse of wetlands, choked with mangroves and teeming with birds, they encountered a river running generally due south, so they crossed it where they were able to do so and made their way along its western bank.

A number of times the river meandered through reed-choked swamps that for a time forced them even further west. It was after they left the swampy area and were travelling beside a flat expanse of water that was either a branch of the river or a tributary, that Will decided to test the depth of the topsoil on the gentle slope above the river flats.

'Look at that,' said he, glancing up at Amanda. 'It's over three feet deep. And rich.' He crumpled a handful of soil in his hand. 'This is prime farming land. As rich as any I've seen back home. And the river flats themselves are covered in deeper soil again.'

'Why are you interested?' she asked as they made their way back towards the river.

'Because once I was a farmer, and perhaps one day I'll be a farmer again.'

It was as they walked out on to the riverbank that they were distracted by a mysterious sound in the distance. Faint. Hollow. Rising and dying in perfect counter-phase to the rising and dying of the song of cicadas in the trees on the slope behind them. Amanda believed it could have been the cry of a bird. Will thought it was perhaps the ring of an axe.

He was surprised by this because he estimated from what Cotter had told him that they were probably still over one hundred miles north of Sydney. And he was right. But what he did not know was that the river they had been following was a tributary of the Hunter, and that they were only about twenty miles north of the new settlement of Newcastle.

Believing the sound may have come from the higher country to the west of them, they decided to rest for a while, hoping that the cicadas' song would diminish. A number of times they thought perhaps they heard the sound again but were uncertain. After a while Amanda stepped down on to a stony beach, and picking up a flat stone neatly skipped it across the surface of the water.

'That was impressive,' said Will, and moved on to the beach beside her.

He picked up another flat stone, and flipping it over in his hand a number of times, ran his eye over all its surfaces. 'What would the record be?'

'Record?'

'Skips. At Pike's Hole near Lowfoley it was over twenty.'

'Over twenty. That is impressive.'

'Where was it that you learnt to skip stones?'

'At Burton Mill. I don't remember that we had a record.'

'Well, we have the opportunity of setting the record on this waterway whatever it may be called. How many skips did your stone make?'

'I didn't count.'

'Well, we'll count from now on.'

And so for a while they took turns in skipping stones across the smooth surface of the stream.

Amanda never tired of watching Will in full flight. Each time he drew back his right hand and bounded towards the water like a javelin thrower, her gaze would follow every move of his body. The fingers of his left hand, outstretched and aligned, blade-like, cutting the air ahead of him for aim and balance. The rippling muscles of his shoulders and the bare sweep of his back. As he unleashed each stone, pitching it with a late snap of his wrist at the precise moment he checked his stride, she watched his buttocks jolt within the shredded material of his trousers as they had jolted during each previous throw, as hers must have surely jolted beneath his eyes each time she took her turn. A familiar comforting murmur began to stir within her.

On a low ridge to the south-west of them, two

natives were resting in dense brush with their weapons lying close by their side. The noise that Will and Amanda had heard in the distance had come from a spur that extended from that same ridge. Will was right. It was the ringing of an axe.

Gunroi and Nunderri sat stock-still for a time listening to the foreign sound before silently gathering up their weapons and creeping along the ridge towards the timber cutters' camp. They made their way warily, their every sense attuned to react instantly if they heard the roar of a musket, or perhaps the warning snap of a flintlock that would give them an extra heartbeat to dive into the underbrush.

But this time they both froze in mid-movement well before they reached their destination. For through the trees they caught the flash of the afternoon sunlight on red coats. And shortly afterwards they heard the bark of a soldier's command. The camp was host to a contingent of their pursuers.

They backed off quietly through the bush and when they were well clear they turned and hurried away. Eventually they moved off the ridge and out on to a wooded plain that bordered the river.

About two miles directly ahead of them, Will and Amanda were skipping stones across its smooth surface.

After they had tired of skipping stones, Will and Amanda spent some time bathing in the deeper water adjacent to the stony beach. They were making their way back towards the bank when Will turned towards Amanda just in time to see her stumble and recover, and then lift a hand uncertainly to her forehead.

He stepped quickly to her side, his stomach lurching in alarm. 'What's wrong?'

Her eyes were clamped shut and the hand she raised to the side of her face was trembling. 'I don't know,' she whispered. 'Suddenly my vision swam'. She took a number of deep breaths. 'Whew,' she whistled airily as she opened her eyes. 'I think it's passed. I think I'll be all right now.'

'Are you sure?'

'Yes, I'm sure. I feel fine now.'

They turned towards the bank.

And there facing them, no more than ten yards away, were two natives. Young, broad-shouldered and slim; their ribs were clearly visible beneath the gleam of perspiration that clung to their ebony bodies. What gave a disturbing bite to the collective shock suffered by the two whites was that each of the blacks had a spear and woomera propped on his shoulder, and had his feet spread and his legs braced for action.

Out of the corner of his eye Will could see their own two lances lying on the riverbank about five full strides away beside their discarded clothing.

'What should we do?' Amanda's voice was hollow.

'I don't think we have too many choices,' he replied quietly. 'And whatever we do, we do it slowly. If I can get to my trousers, I'll offer them a sovereign. It's worked every time up until now.'

'Be careful. These two have a different look about them. Wilder. More dangerous.'

'Even if it doesn't work I'll be happier to be up on the bank with a lance within easy reach. Keep close behind me. Hullo there!' he called out. 'I have something to show you.' He began to move towards the bank with Amanda following him closely.

The natives remained where they were. The only movement Will detected, other than a ruffle of their hair in the breeze, was a slow waver of the points of their spears. He reached the edge of the stream and paused to help Amanda move with him up on to the bank. He then pointed to his trousers. 'I have something in my clothes you may be interested in.'

The younger man muttered something to the other.

'Do you see his little axe?' Amanda whispered.

'I do now,' Will replied, his eyes resting for a moment on the iron-forged tomahawk slung from a hair belt around the younger man's waist. 'Suddenly I'm not so confident that showing them a sovereign will be sufficient. But here goes.'

So saying, he knelt down and felt for the small

cache of sovereigns in his trousers' pocket. His eyes momentarily rested on the shaft of his lance and he wondered if he should pick it up to show he was prepared to fight if he had to.

'What's he doing?' Nunderri asked.

'I don't know,' Gunroi replied. 'But if he reaches for that sharpened stick he probably calls a spear, the moment he does I'll show him what damage a real spear can do from this distance.'

Will extracted a sovereign and held it up. As it caught the light he reached out and picked up his lance.

Before he had a chance to come to his feet Gunroi immediately danced forward and swung back his throwing arm. But in that instant Amanda, with her back to the black man and completely oblivious of the danger, moved in front of him as she stooped to retrieve her clothing.

As Will rose he found himself looking across her shoulder directly into Gunroi's wild eyes and at a spear that must have been a heartbeat from being hurled at them.

'No!' he shouted and knocked Amanda aside. He leapt over her, grasped the shaft of his lance in both hands and thrust it out in front of him.

Almost three years before he had defended himself in a similar manner with the pole of a boat-hook. In vain.

'Stop!' he bellowed. 'We have done nothing to

you. Nothing.' His voice was like a thunderclap and reverberated off the rocks on the opposite hillside.

Amanda's movement had caught Gunroi by surprise and he managed to arrest the launch of his spear almost at the point of releasing it. Perhaps to regain a sense of balance or momentum he began to shake the spear and dance backwards and forwards, left and right.

Nunderri, with his own spear raised high, quickly picked up his brother's beat. 'Will I spear him?' he called out.

Gunroi was uncertain. *What does he think he's going to do with that child's plaything? Why is he pointing it at the sky? Why isn't he pointing it at us?*

Behind Will, Amanda made to rise. He quickly pressed back against her. 'Stay down,' he snapped. 'Don't move. Stay where you are.'

Gunroi's eyes narrowed. *Of course! He's waiting for us to attack first. He's hoping he can knock our spears aside. If he manages that, then he'll attack. He's not as stupid as most whites. And he's protecting his woman.*

At that moment the sun came out from behind a cloud causing Will to squint into it as he tried to watch both men.

'I'll spear him first,' Nunderri yelled, moving further away from his brother. 'And then you spear him while I grab my second spear.'

Gunroi's eyes were on Will's hair.

'I'll do it now,' Nunderri called out, suddenly dancing forward.

'No!' Gunroi shouted.

Nunderri propped and backed away, confused.

Gunroi lowered his spear to his shoulder and stood still.

'What's wrong?' Nunderri glanced at his brother before he too stopped and lowered his spear.

'He's from Jessica's clan,' Gunroi replied.

Perhaps fortuitously, the black man's unfamiliar tongue partly concealed from Will the name he uttered.

'How do you know?' said Nunderri.

'I know,' Gunroi replied, and began to back away.

'What's happening?' Amanda asked as the younger man joined the other.

'I don't know,' said Will.

'Should you show them the sovereign?'

'Not if I have to chase after them to do it. I don't even know where it is.' He did not drop his gaze for an instant to see if he could spot it.

Suddenly the two blacks turned away and began to run at an easy lope up the slope towards where Will had earlier tested the depth of the soil.

Amanda came to her feet as they disappeared among the trees. 'I wonder what brought that on.'

Will stood watching the hillside in silence for a time, and then a rippling shudder passed through his shoulders.

'I don't know. But if I didn't know better, I'd have sworn the older one mentioned . . .'

'Mentioned what?'

He shook his head. 'No, forget it. It's stupid.' He bent down and picked up his trousers. 'That was definitely a modern axe the young one was carrying. And I'm now certain it was an axe we heard earlier.' He bobbed his head to the south-west. 'I'd like to reach that ridge by nightfall.'

They did. Barely. For by then Amanda had become ill and could hardly walk. By morning she was delirious and could not walk at all. So when Will heard the ringing of the axe again about an hour after sunrise, he was forced to carry her for the further four hours it took him to reach the timber cutters' camp.

The sergeant in charge of the patrol that was biv-ouacked at the camp was astute enough to arrange for both Will and Amanda to be escorted as quickly as possible to Newcastle. As soon as news of their arrival reached Dr Charles Throsby, the garrison Commandant, he took charge of Aman-da's welfare himself and organised for Will to be sent immediately to Sydney on a sloop to convey his news personally to the naval command.

'The *Lady Nelson* should still be in port. We have nothing here at the moment suitable to send on a rescue mission. And they will probably want you to accompany her.' He was right on all counts.

As Will took his leave of Amanda at the Commandant's residence, it was with a nurse in close attendance and Throsby himself and other officials hovering close by. When he moved to her bedside she ignored the nurse's caution and tried to sit up.

'Hullo,' she said softly, smiling at him as the nurse hurriedly rearranged pillows at her back.

'Hullo. You're looking a lot stronger.'

'Chicken broth. It can cure a wooden leg.'

He smiled and raised an eyebrow. 'I hear they have a few cures out here for that particular ailment.'

'I've heard that too.' Their eyes stayed on each other as she lifted a hand towards him.

When he took hold of it in his own, the nurse generated a soft uncomfortable noise somewhere at the back of her throat and cast an angry glance back at the open doorway. Perhaps in defiance, Will clasped his other hand over Amanda's. 'They're sending me to Sydney. The boat's waiting.'

'Yes, I heard.'

'They'll probably take me with them. To point out any landmarks I recognise.'

Her face suddenly collapsed into a grimace and tears sprang to her eyes. 'I pray you'll find them safe. All of them.'

He released one of his hands and held it against her cheek. 'When we get back—all of us, including your uncle—make sure you're on the wharf to meet us, hale and hearty and strong enough to kill wild animals with your bare hands.' She tried to smile and immediately pressed her cheek firmly against his palm. She made several attempts to speak but each time was forced to bite down hard on her bottom lip to try to stop it from trembling uncontrollably.

'I must go,' Will said, and leant forward and kissed her lightly on the forehead.

As he released her hand, leaving it still lifted towards him, she said, 'Keep safe.'

'You too.' He reached back and lightly gripped the tips of her outstretched fingers before turning and walking from the room to join those standing in the passageway.

TWENTY-ONE

The desk was a magnificent expanse of Australian red cedar. The man sitting behind the desk would be best remembered for having some eighteen years before lost his ship to mutineers. He was William Bligh, former commander of HMS *Bounty* and present Governor of New South Wales.

It would be difficult to separate whether the man sitting on his right would be best remembered for his drinking prowess, or for his being sentenced a little over one year after this day to seven years' imprisonment for perjury by rebellious members of the Rum Corps. He was William Gore, the Provost-Marshal of New South Wales, who served some four months in the coal mines at Newcastle before the sentence was overturned.

The man sitting on Bligh's left was his own secretary, Edmund Griffin. His most commendable claim to fame was that he constantly weathered such verbal abuse from his master as being called an 'incompetent scoundrel' for misdemeanours rarely more scurrilous than leaving open a window that caused a piece of paper to be blown from a desk. He presently had a stack of papers in front of him and was shuffling them rapidly in response to directions from Bligh, and either passing them across to him or reading aloud from whichever one was uppermost.

They were interrupted by a knock at the door. On a command from Bligh, the door opened slightly, a head appeared and an orderly announced, 'Mr Noling has arrived, Your Excellency.'

'Bring him in.'

'Mr Noling,' said Bligh, after introducing himself and the others to Will and bidding him to sit down, 'I've been hearing things about you for some time now.' He held out his hand and Griffin handed him two sheets of paper.

'Some time ago I received this letter from a sin bos'n in the navy, the Reverend Alexander Scott.' He peered closely at the top sheet. 'Don't know the blighter from Adam, but I read his letter anyway. Turns out he was chaplain to the late Horatio Nelson himself, no less.' Then, lifting that sheet aside and holding up the second, 'With a postscript from Captain Thomas Masterman Hardy. Now that's somebody I do know. Tom Hardy, I hear, is headed for a top spot overlooking St James's.'

He handed the letter back to Griffin. 'They say

in short that Mr William Noling is somebody that should be looked after. That he was dealt a rum deal. But all I could say when I received this letter was, "Who in the bright blue blazes is William Noling?"' He looked across at Griffin who confirmed this with a serious nod. ' "Could be on the *Tynemouth*," says somebody. "That's where he is," we concluded. On the *Tynemouth*, God save him! Along with all those other poor wretches, includin' Janette Randall and her lovely little twin girls. "Merciful Heavens!" we prayed, "Don't let Janette and the children be lyin' dead at the bottom of the ocean." You've met her husband, Jamie. He wanted to search for them. Of course he did. He was nearly mad with worry. "But where?" said I. "They could be anywhere between here and Cape Town. Anywhere."'

'Anywhere,' William Gore endorsed.

Bligh shook his head and looked from one to the other and ran a finger close below one eye in a gesture that may or may not have been wiping a tear from the corner. 'And to think that not only are they alive, but I'm assured that, with plenty of rest and healthy food, they'll be hale and hearty again in no time. Hale and hearty! In no time!' He threw up his hands and beamed at Will who at that point half expected him to shout a hurrah. 'Along with most of the others who were washed up on that rock. All thanks to you, accordin' to the ship's surgeon on the *Lady Nelson*. The supplies they managed to scrounge from the wreck wouldn't have lasted another week. If you hadn't brought the news to Newcastle, God knows how many would have been lost.'

'God knows!' confirmed Gore.

'And Miss Dalrymple, I believe, is recovering from her ordeal?'

'Yes, sir. She's still somewhat weak from the sickness she contracted but is now starting to get out and about almost every day.'

'Good! Good!' Bligh glanced momentarily at the others before fixing his gaze back on Will. 'Well, son, there's every chance you've earned yourself a full pardon for what you've done. So be very careful with your answers to the questions I'm now going to put to you.'

Griffin placed some papers on the desk in front of Bligh who leant forward and looked down at them before continuing.

'You were convicted of attempting to murder a man. Is that correct?'

'Aye, sir.'

'Did you attempt to murder him?'

'No, sir.'

'You're certain of that?'

'Yes, sir.'

Bligh waved his hand back at the other stack of papers sitting in front of Griffin. 'What your friends in the *Victory* say about you suggests I should believe you. Can I believe you?'

'Yes, sir.'

'Why?'

'I had every chance to kill him if that was my intent.'

Bligh leant forward and looked at him closely before dropping his gaze back to the papers in front of him.

'What was your grievance with him?'

'He paid to have me pressed into the navy.'

'Why did he do that?'

'He had his eye on my fiancée, sir.'

'Did he just?' Bligh glanced momentarily at Gore before looking for something among the papers in front of him.

With his eyes still down he said, 'Your fiancée is this Jessica Glider you've been making enquiries about?'

'Yes, sir.'

'Who was wrongly accused by this same man, according to you.'

'Yes, sir.'

'Who was he to you?'

'He was my local squire.'

Bligh looked up abruptly. 'Local squire! I don't like the sound of that, son. This isn't the result of some unnatural grievance you have with the gentry, is it?'

'No, sir.'

'Were you at the Nore, son? Were you at the mutiny?'

'No, sir. I was pressed in o-three.'

'Might have been lucky for you, you weren't there. You have a way about you suggests they'd have picked you for a delegate. And you know what happened to the delegates?'

'Aye.'

'Well, enough of that. I have cause not to hold much truck with mutiny. But I'm not in full agreement with what happened after that one.'

He dropped his gaze again and then apparently unable to find what he was looking for, began to shuffle angrily through the stack of papers. 'And what's his name, this local squire of yours?'

Griffin leant over and pointed to the middle of the top sheet.

'Fitzparsons,' said Bligh, reading aloud. 'Sir Rory Fitzparsons.'

'Yes, sir.'

Bligh suddenly recoiled from the papers as if they had burst into flames. 'Rory Fitzparsons!' His face erupted in a purple flush. 'Rory Fitzparsons!'

They waited as he lowered his head to read on. 'Lowfoley, Hampshire. That's him. Fitzparsons. I know him, the filthy miserable scab-sucking carrion. Knew him in the navy, the lecherous swine. No one's wife or sweetheart was safe. Nor their sons and daughters from what I've heard. The sod-rotten scoundrel.

'Knew him when I pursed the *Bounty*. He tried to rob me same as he's been robbin' the Victualling Board ever since he was kicked out. The thievin' rat-sellin' shit-crawler! He's the one had you pressed? God save us! Fitzparsons! Brought charges down on your sweetheart's head? Of course he did. Of course he did.'

He gripped Will with a ferocious gaze. 'You've got your pardon, son. Unconditional. Effective immediately. And for saving those lives you've also got yourself a grant of two hundred acres of land of your choosing. You've also earned yourself a note for fifty pounds, redeemable in goods from the store.' He watched him for a moment before adding, 'So what do you think about that?'

Will shook his head.

'He's speechless,' said Gore with a chuckle. 'That's what he thinks about that.'

'We're very grateful to you, son. All of us with friends and relatives on the *Tynemouth*. Pardons and grants of land have been handed out in this place for far less than your contribution.'

When Will had recovered sufficiently he said, 'The land, sir. Could I choose an area I saw to the north of Newcastle?'

'On the Hunter?'

'I'm not sure. It's on the northern arm of the junction the garrison call First Branch.'

Bligh turned to Griffin. 'What do we know of this? Has that area been surveyed?'

'Not formally, sir. Leastways not upstream from that first branch. And I believe there's some conjecture which is the main stream. At that point the northern branch is said to be the more substantial, but rumour has it that the western branch drains the bigger portion of the valley.'

'Based on accurate information, I'll wager,' Gore offered. 'Despite settlement being forbidden until an accurate survey can be made, from what I hear the former commandant turned a blind eye on his cronies staking themselves out parcels of prime land deep into the valley so they'll have the edge on others when it is finally released.'

'Well, make no mistake, I'm going to put paid to the antics of that collection of pig-swilling carrion if it's the last thing I do,' snarled Bligh. 'The first chance I get I'll rip all of their illegal holdings out from beneath them—whether they be to the north, south, east or west of here—and I'll herd every lofty-nosed man jack of them into the sea if need be. You see if I don't.'

He turned and gripped Will with an unsettling glare. 'Did I say two hundred acres? If you're choosing land that far from here I'll make it two thousand. Two hundred was assuming you'd select something local.' His face relaxed into what might have been a smile as he observed Will's obvious astonishment. 'Land is one commodity we have no shortage of in New South Wales, Mr Noling. Which is why some people have the impression they can take possession of any piece of it they fancy whenever they fancy. So my advice is for you to stake out your land and occupy it as soon as you can, and before any of those greedy bastards takes a shine to it. Lodge your application with Mr Griffin here and I'll see to it that it's surveyed as soon as practicable and the title formally registered.

'Don't, whatever you do, try to go through normal channels. Deal only with Mr Griffin. And don't trust any of those slimy red-coated wolves any further than you kick the bastards. And to be on the safe side on that score, I'll have both your pardon and your land grant, along with some similar matters of import, ratified back home in England by the Secretary of State, Lord Castlereagh, himself. Just in case one or other of these mangy curs that are lurking in the shadows gets himself appointed to a position after I'm gone where he believes he can have them rescinded.' His smile broadened. 'Castlereagh's a prick relative of Janette Randall and the twins, so there'll be no problems on that score.' He waved a hand over the papers. 'I'll also provide him with the details of these other matters from your time in the navy.'

'What of Jessica Glider, sir?' said Will. 'In light of what you know of Rory Fitzparsons, would it be possible for her also to receive a pardon?'

'It would, son. It would. In fact I'll get Mr Griffin to draw up the papers at the same time as he does yours. But I'm afraid it's all somewhat late as far as she's concerned.'

'How do you mean?' Will's voice was steady, belying the sudden swirl of concern deep within him.

'Mr Gore will explain.'

Gore gave a start as if perhaps he had been dozing.

'Tell our friend what you know of Jessica Glider.'

'She escaped, is what,' said Gore. 'On the . . . on the . . .'

'On the *Cobscook Bay*,' said Griffin, reading from a sheet of paper in front of him.

'Aye,' confirmed Gore. 'On the *Cobscook Bay*. An American schooner, I believe.'

'She escaped?' Surprises were coming at Will at a greater speed than he had prepared for. His head began to pound. 'When?'

'Last year,' Gore replied.

'Over two years ago,' Griffin corrected. 'Saturday, October twenty-seven, eighteen o-four.'

'Two years ago!' Will shook his head.

'Tell him, Mr Gore.'

'She's dead, son. Drown'ded.'

'What?'

'Drown'ded. They were wrecked same as you were on the coast north of here.'

'Somewhere further north of where you came to grief, we believe, son,' said Bligh. 'I'm terribly sorry. Her pardon will have to be posthumous.'

'How . . . How do you know she drowned?'

Gore looked across at Griffin. 'What's her name?'

'Crowling. Elizabeth Crowling.'

'The woman who escaped with her survived and was living with natives,' said Gore. 'She was recaptured earlier this year. She reported seeing her drown.'

'Maybe she lied.' Will glanced from one to the other. 'Maybe she's still out there somewhere.'

Bligh shook his head. 'Then why wasn't she with this other woman? Wreckage was found some months before. The vessel was torn apart. It was a miracle anyone survived.'

'It was discovered by the schooner *Francis*,' said Griffin, again reading. 'The captain reported that the timbers could not have been more damaged if they had been blown apart by a mighty explosion.'

'It must have hit a reef and disintegrated,' said Bligh. 'And God knows we have enough uncharted reefs along this coast. It's one of the wonders of the world that we don't lose more ships. Accept it, son. She's gone.'

'I'd like to talk to this woman.'

'What woman?'

'The one who reported her death.'

Bligh turned to Griffin. 'Where is she now?'

'Elizabeth Crowling,' said Griffin, eyes down. 'Upon release from the female factory at Parramatta she was assigned to ... Garth Barlester.'

'Barlester?' Bligh turned his head to the side. 'Where have I seen that name?'

'Somewhere or other,' Griffin replied, beginning again to flip through the papers.

'He's one of them,' said Gore. 'Macarthur's crowd. Ex-corps. And he's a flogger. We heard he had a triangle so I sent a constable around, but there was no sign of it. Tipped off by one of his cronies, I'll wager.'

'Garth Barlester,' said Griffin with his finger beneath the item. 'Jessica Glider was in his charge when she escaped.'

'Now there's a rum one for ye,' said Gore. 'Makes up for the loss of one by takin' charge of her accomplice. From what I've heard, shouldn't wonder he's been givin' this one some hurry-up for her involvement in the affair.'

'If he has, I'll have the bastard's balls on a platter,' said Bligh. 'You'd best send a constable around and see how she's farin'. King was far too weak on this devilish beatin' of women that's been goin' on. And the forced concubinin' of the poor wretches. Despite his proclamations on the matter.'

'Can I talk to her?' said Will.

'I can't see why not. But only if you accompany William's constable when he calls on Barlester. From the sound of the bastard, I wouldn't trust the likes of what he might do if he were to take a sudden dislike t' you. Some of these people think they're a law unto themselves.'

Jessica's ploy of calling herself Elizabeth Crowling had its desired effect for a time, in that when she was first brought back to Sydney, Garth Barlester remained unaware that she had survived. It was therefore unfortunate that she could not also have avoided the consequences of his thirst for revenge.

When he heard that the woman who organised Jessica's escape was about to be released from the female factory at Parramatta, he decided to call on an acquaintance who happened to be at that time the acting commandant.

Fortunately for Jessica, it was night-time when she and some others were paraded for the perusal of a small group of interested onlookers, and she had no idea who was standing in the shadows. Had she seen the look that crossed Barlester's face when he became aware of her deception she may well have sought a more conclusive avenue of escape than her previous one.

A few days before she was due to be released she was surprised to be shackled hand and foot, bundled into the back of a dray and covered by a heavy sheet of sailcloth. Perhaps this too was fortuitous, for after the bone-jarring journey that she was then subjected to, it was not until she was hauled from the dray and her eyes had become accustomed to the glare that she realised where she was and who was standing over her.

During the journey the possibility that this was her destination flitted fitfully through the far reaches of her mind; fleeting harbingers of a nightmare too terrible to focus on. Had she known for sure where she was heading, she may well have striven with every ounce of strength she could muster to break out from beneath her shroud and fling herself head first on to the roadway.

As her eyes fought the glare and Barlester's gloating visage came slowly into focus, she felt her entire body cringe, as if every fibre within her was contracting in sympathy with the narrowing of her pupils.

It suited Barlester to honour the deception that she was Elizabeth Crowling. Towards the end of his stewardship of the colony, Governor King was making examples of a number of members of the corps who flouted his regulations concerning the treatment of convicts in their charge. And being aware of his own reputation in this regard, Barlester concluded that had it been known he had taken into his charge the woman who had once fled the settlement to get away from him, he would risk losing her again. Particularly if some damned government official demanded to interview her.

He also had to be careful how he took it upon himself to exact retribution for the way she had defied him by escaping. A timely warning allowed him to dispose of the iron triangle before a constable arrived and began snooping around. But even if it had still remained, he could no longer risk beating her within sight of anyone. For the entire New South Wales community was being swept by a damnable undercurrent of defiance bordering on insurrection. No one could be trusted. No servant. No soldier. The lower orders were assuming rights and privileges for themselves and their fellows that threatened the very foundations of the colony.

How there could be order when a servant questions his place was anyone's guess; where an underling could no longer be relied upon to serve his master unswervingly, unquestionably; where the most lowly wretch believes his betters do not have the right to strike him down if he dares so much as to look them in the eye as if he were their equal. In this hell hole of Sydney Town, New South bloody Wales, Jack Arse-out-of-his-pants has the audacity to believe he's as good as his master. And his master doesn't even dare let Jack or Jill Arse-out-of-their-pants see him beat the living daylights out of someone who has openly defied him. Treated him as a fool. God rot this damnable country!

There were ways, of course. To redress wrongs. Limited ways. Nuisance ways. Behind closed doors. A rope. A gag. But even with these, care had to be taken to avoid too much bruising. But there was always time. Applying selective discomfort over an extended time could take its toll and be reasonably satisfying. Slow. But satisfying. Given time a discomfort can become an irritation, can become a pain. And with time even a mild pain can become an excruciating pain. Apparently. A suitable reminder of the folly of past defiances. Affronts. A suitable counter to any temptation to re-offend.

When Barlester suddenly entered her room on that day and ordered her to lie face down on the bed, Jessica's first thoughts were that he was about to subject her to some base indignity. Particularly when he bound her hands behind her back and gagged her. She felt certain he was going to take out some grievance on her. Assuage the appetite of one of his many devils.

But when he also bound her feet, spikes of uncertainty began to prick away at the surface of the anaesthetising shroud she was already beginning to wrap around her consciousness. And by the time he left the room and bolted the door behind him, she was fully alert again and examining possibilities. Had he forgotten something? Was this a reprieve or simply a delay?

Her bindings were secure but they were not biting into her and cutting off her circulation. Nor was the gag choking her. They were meant to hold, not to punish. But why?

Had something untoward occurred that involved her? Had someone arrived he wanted to keep her from seeing? From being seen by that someone? Will? Had Will arrived? Impossible! An absurd proposition! She admonished herself for even toying for a moment with such a ridiculous notion. But at the same time she was struggling to roll over so that she could place her feet on the floor. If she could get to the window, she could perhaps hear if someone had arrived.

'You wanted to see her. Here she is,' Barlester growled, ushering Molly Clinger in front of him to the balustrade that bordered that portion of the western verandah.

579

Two men stood on the gravel pathway that was a good three feet below the level of the verandah. One was a constable, this being defined more by the stout truncheon he was carrying than by his manner of dress, which was not remarkably dissimilar to that of the other man. The other man was taller, slimmer and younger. Will Noling was at that moment desperately trying to come to terms with the fact that the last time he saw the man standing on the verandah, that man was sitting on a chaise-cart beside Sir Rory Fitzparsons, with his gaze locked tenaciously on Jessica Glider.

'Elizabeth Crowling?' said the constable.

'Aye,' Molly replied softly.

'Will you step down 'ere please, Miss.'

'No, she will not,' snapped Barlester. 'You can see her well enough where she's standin' now.'

'I can't see 'er clearly. I'm tellin' you I'm 'ere to see that she hasn't received no mistreatment while she's been in your charge. And to do that I need to see her clearer. If you won't let 'er come down so's I can give 'er a good once over, I'll come up there.'

'Like hell you will! 'Tis enough that you dare come on to my property and try t' tell me anything at all! 'Tis enough that I've taken the time t' stand here and listen to your cheek.' Barlester aimed a finger down at the man as if it were a pistol. 'But if you think I'll dance to your tune you can think again. This woman is not moving

580

off the verandah. And if you make one move to step on to it, I'll knock you down and loose my hounds on to you. D'you hear me?'

'I warn you, sir,' stammered the constable, 'I'm here representin' the Crown.' Despite his effort to retain some composure, his face was flushed and his eyes bulged from the sheer impact of Barlester's attack.

Jessica in the meantime had managed to shuffle to the window of her room. By pressing her face against it she found she could see through a narrow vertical gap between the shutters to where a black rooster was pecking at the ground close to the hooves of two horses that were tethered to a post at the back of the house. Shortly afterwards she heard Barlester's raised voice. He sounded as if he was somewhere towards the southern end of the western verandah. But regardless of how she positioned her head she could not widen her angle of view.

She then noticed a narrow crease of light horizontally bisecting her body at the waist. So she pressed firmly against the window sill and allowed herself to slip down until her knees were braced against a narrow skirting board and her eye was aligned with a hairline crack beneath the shutters. She could then make out someone standing at the edge of the verandah. Perhaps two people. Molly? Was that Molly she could see? Why on earth would Molly be there? She turned her ear to the opening when again she heard Barlester's voice, and possibly another, but the sounds were indistinct and except for an occasional word she could not make out what was being said.

'I'd like to ask Miss Crowling a question,' said Will.

Barlester wrenched his gaze away from the other man and stared down at him.

'And who the hell are you?'

'I'm Will Noling.'

'I've heard of you, Will Noling. You're a cut-throat felon.'

'Miss Crowling,' said Will, ignoring the remark, 'I believe you were with Jessica Glider when you were shipwrecked.'

Molly glanced up at Barlester and waited for his response. He finally turned away from Will and nodded to her.

'Aye,' she said softly.

'What happened to her?'

Molly again looked at Barlester. When he made no response, she said in a voice that was little more than a whisper, 'Drown'ded.'

'What did you say?'

'She said she was drown'ded. Are you deaf, man?'

'Did you actually see her drown?'

Molly nodded.

'Were you shipwrecked at night or during the day?'

'What does it matter when the hell she was shipwrecked?'

'Was it day or night?'

Molly bit her lip and again glanced up at her master.

'It was at night,' said he. And turning to Molly repeated, 'It was at night. You told me it was at night.'

'If it was at night, how did you see her drown?'

'She didn't say she saw her drown at night. She said they were shipwrecked at night.'

'She didn't,' said Will.

'What?'

'You did. If you don't mind, I'd like Miss Crowling to answer my questions herself.'

'Oh would you?' snarled Barlester. 'Well I do mind. I mind having to stand here and be insulted in my own home. And I'm not going to put up with it for a moment longer. Go on, get out of my sight, both of you.'

'Sir, I protest,' said the constable. 'You have no right to flout the orders of the Crown in this way.'

'Well, what are you going to do about it? Arrest me? It will take more than some jumped-up yokel armed with nothing more than a bent stick to arrest Garth Barlester, I can tell you that. If you want to arrest me you'll need a contingent of marines, and then you might have to be lucky. And I doubt very much you'll be able to talk anyone into going to that kind of trouble for whatever piddlin' misdemeanour you suspect me of. Go on, get out of here, or I'll give you both a dose of bird-shot.' He grabbed hold of Molly by the arm and propelled her towards a door. 'Inside, you.'

'I need to ask her more questions,' protested the constable.

'So do I,' said Will.

Barlester gave them both a savage look, but it was Will he leaned towards, again aiming a finger as he would a pistol. 'Listen, you scoundrel, you're a convicted criminal. You have no rights whatsoever.'

'I'm no longer a convicted criminal. I've been fully pardoned.'

'What?' Barlester moved closer to the edge of the verandah and peered down at Will with his face a mask of incredulity. 'You've been pardoned?'

From her cramped vantage point Jessica caught a sudden glimpse of what might have been red hair. But the involuntary movement she made at that instant caused her cramped knees to slip from the skirting board and thud painfully on to the floor.

'Unconditionally.'

'Bligh pardoned you?' The black wings of Barlester's eyebrows beat slowly up and down as he glared at the man in front of him. He straightened as he recovered and ran the back of his hand across his high forehead. 'Well, don't for a moment think that fish-head's pardon means a damn thing to me. Get out of here now or I'll still blow a hole in you big enough to stick a bucket in. And that goes for if I ever see you around here again. D'you hear me? Get out of here, both of you.'

'Come on, Mr Noling,' said the constable. 'There's no sense in staying any longer.' He took hold of Will's arm and began to direct him back towards the rear of the house. 'Don't think you've heard the last of this, Barlester,' he called out over his shoulder in a parting display of resentment that was smothered by a gust of wind in nearby trees.

Bound as she was, it took Jessica some time before she managed to struggle back to where she could peer beneath the shutters. Nothing. There was no more movement on the verandah. She fought her way back to where she could see through the vertical crack.

Two horsemen were making their way back along the road between the blacksmith's shop and the dairy. But both riders were immersed in a deep shadow thrown from the stand of bamboo and she could not see them clearly. By the time they re-entered the light they were obscured by ornamental trees closer to the house.

Barlester came into the room before she managed to get back on to the bed. He did not utter a word but the strength of his breathing gave her the warning to brace herself for the blow. It knocked her to the floor. Without speaking he bent over and roughly checked the security of her bindings. Then still without speaking he left the room and re-bolted the door.

She lay on the floor sipping occasionally on the blood that welled inside the rims of both lips. One of her shoulders was partly trapped beneath the bed and it was some time before she could muster the strength to release it and move into a more comfortable position.

She found herself pondering over a change that had occurred within her. Something was different. Missing. But she was having trouble identifying what it was. For a time her frustration mounted. Surprisingly, when she finally did identify what it was, her discovery was accompanied more by a sense of curiosity than relief.

What was missing, she realised, as she continued to sip absently on her bloodied lips, was the stifling sense of dread that had draped her like a leaden cloak ever since she found herself back at this house. It was gone. Vanished. Completely. A great weight had been whisked away from her head and shoulders as if by some huge passing bird.

Later, she pondered whether this was because she now believed Will would save her. No, she decided. She was way past salvation. It was simply because she now believed he was alive and was nearby. Alive! The very thought of the possibility swept her with a tingling sense of comfort. Alive! And close!

Later still, after Molly was sent to release her,

she tried to press the older woman for details of what had happened. But Molly refused to discuss the subject. When Jessica asked her if one of the visitors was a young man with red hair, her friend's frightened eyes dissuaded her from pursuing the subject further. But now she believed she had no need. The core of her body purred.

She was brought down with a jolt shortly afterwards, however, when Molly whispered to her that Barlester had decided to bring forward a planned visit to his newly established property on the Hunter River.

'Where's the Hunter River?'

''Ow would I know? All I knows is, it's where the blacks is bad. And God help me but I've been prayin' he don't decide to take me along. He's takin' near everyone else, includin' you, lass.'

'Me? Why me?'

'You're the reason he's takin' off early. He don't want you to be hereabouts for a moment longer than it takes 'im to round up his supplies and the extra men he'll need to clear his land.'

On the eastern outskirts of Sydney a large stone house overlooked the harbour at Woolloomooloo Bay. In many ways the house and its surrounds resembled Garth Barlester's residence. The main building was of a similar size and style; the stone from which it was constructed also came from a quarry at the rear of the site and had weathered to the same cream hue; the landscaping and

gardens were equally immature, and the outbuildings were constructed from a similar range of local
timber and stringybark sheeting.

Had an observer been noting such comparisons
on this day, his interest may have quickened had
he known that the visitor walking down the red-
gravelled driveway to the house had only the
previous day visited Barlester.

As the newcomer approached the main door, a
middle-aged man and woman were departing and
were being farewelled by the housekeeper, who
remained standing at the open door. The departing
couple smiled and exchanged reserved good-days
with the newcomer as they passed him, and as he
walked on towards the waiting housekeeper they
turned, still smiling, to watch him for a moment.

'Mr Noling, how are you today?' The housekeeper was a slim, handsome woman in her early
forties.

Her name was Margaret Wilson, who some ten
years previously had been transported for receiving stolen goods, namely fifteen hundredweight of
tea. She was innocent, but the drunken importer,
who was both her husband and the guilty party,
died of a stroke before the charges against both of
them could be heard.

If this had not happened he almost certainly
would have been found guilty and she would have
been discharged. But having provided the money
to get the business started, her prudent measure of
insisting that it be registered in both their names

was the prime cause of her undoing. Denied the opportunity of incarcerating the true culprit, the Crown appeased the loss by transporting his widow. This was seen by some of those with an interest in the case as being a salient lesson to this daughter of a parson for having married below her station.

She gave a wave to the couple who had just departed and turning back to Will lifted her eyes momentarily to the heavens as she ushered him into the hallway. 'The Jenkins. They mean well, but few people would be strong enough to endure more than about ten minutes of their boring gossip. And Sir Peter is still supposed to be convalescing. No, no. He's well enough to see you any time.' She nudged him with her elbow. 'Your visits are good for him.'

'Is Amanda in?'

She gave him a look that was meant to convey something. Exasperation perhaps. 'No. Granville insisted on taking her for a drive again. Despite his promises, he always keeps her out for most of the day and she comes back exhausted. I'm not sure if that young man is as well equipped with the necessities of life as others might think. Common sense, for one.'

'My mother says it's not,' said Will.

'What's not?'

'Sense.'

'Not common?' She suddenly laughed and clamped the tips of the fingers of one hand to her lips. As she removed her hand she nudged him again with her elbow before taking his arm and escorting him down the hallway. 'Your mother's right.'

It was rumoured that Margaret Wilson was Sir Peter Dalrymple's mistress. As in later days, most of the colony's rumours of this nature were ill-founded, fed by jealousies and the power-playing antics of little people attempting to claw their way higher on the heap by trampling on others. But in this instance it was true. Only Margaret's refusal to give ammunition to Sir Peter's enemies prevented her from accepting his oft-repeated proposal that she become his wife.

Sir Peter made to rise from his chair as the two of them entered the sunroom, but Margaret moved quickly across to him and motioned for him to sit down.

'How are you today, sir?' asked Will, moving to shake the extended hand. Although Will had seen him a number of times since the *Lady Nelson* returned with the survivors from the after end of the *Tynemouth*, he was again struck by how much thinner he appeared than when he had seen him sitting beside Amanda on the quarterdeck of the ill-fated vessel.

'Well enough, boy. Well enough. But I'd be mending at a much faster rate if I were allowed to get up and about more. Have you ever noticed that women are never more in their element than when they have the upper hand over an ailing male?'

'As a matter of fact I have,' said Will, grateful at that moment that Amanda was not within earshot.

Margaret tut-tutted at the overt patronising as she positioned a cushion behind Sir Peter's back. 'I'm sure that neither of you would be referring to anyone that lives under this roof.' Straightening, she cast a glance at each of them. 'I'll have Cook prepare a pot of tea.'

They spoke for a time about Will's intentions with regard to his land grant. Sir Peter again suggested Will should allow him to help finance the development of the property. But on this occasion, to avoid offending the young man, he circumspectly framed his offer in terms that he was definitely offering a loan, rather than a gift or any form of payment for Will's role in his and Amanda's rescue.

So as not to offend the man by refusing him outright, Will remained non-committal, and as soon as he was able to do so, changed the subject.

When Margaret returned and served them tea, she asked how he was faring in his enquiries concerning Jessica. He told them of the frustrating encounter with Barlester and Elizabeth Crowling, and of having seen Barlester with Rory Fitzparsons back in Lowfoley. Sir Peter knew something of Barlester and offered to make enquiries of his own as soon as he was able.

'I'm not sure there's any sense in pursuing the

matter,' said Will. 'This woman Crowling wasn't very forthcoming. Probably because Barlester was there, but I don't think she would be much help anyway. Seemed to be a bit slow to me.'

'That's surprising,' said Sir Peter. 'From all accounts she organised their escape. Simeon Lord, to whom she was once assigned, dropped in to see me the other day. When I mentioned that you were intending to seek her out, he described her as something of a lively temptress.'

'A lively temptress!' Will exclaimed.

Margaret chuckled. 'We weren't sure we'd see you again after your trip to talk to her.'

'I find both "temptress" and "lively" hard to associate with the woman I spoke to.'

'They're the words Simeon used,' said Sir Peter. 'Apparently she was the one who picked out the *Cobscook Bay* as being their best chance of getting away from the colony. And then recruited a couple of young American crewmen to assist her. He says that Barlester is welcome to her.'

'Well, I don't believe he'd call her a "lively temptress" if he saw her now,' said Will.

They spoke for a time on various matters including local politics and the difficult task confronting Bligh in trying to keep Macarthur and the corps in check. Only when it appeared that Amanda and Granville would not be joining them did the conversation turn to them. By then Margaret had left to attend to other matters.

'Amanda will not thank me for saying so,' said

Sir Peter, 'but she's quite taken by you.'

Will smiled. 'I suppose that was mainly because she didn't have much of a choice in travelling companions.' He looked up and matched the other man's gaze. 'I was quite taken by her as well.'

'Would that be because you also didn't have much choice?'

Still smiling, Will shook his head. 'Not really.'

'I wouldn't be able to tell from the amount of time you two have spent together since I've returned.' His expression was for the moment somewhat sterner than before.

'I'm afraid that's not entirely of my doing. Once she was back on her feet, she's been out and about with Granville almost every day.'

'When I was a young man, I would have looked upon that as a minor inconvenience.'

'Granville's her fiancé. That's hardly a minor inconvenience. After all, she has agreed to marry him.'

'Young women who have lived a sheltered existence are sometimes inclined to make inappropriate decisions in that regard. I have the feeling now that she's a little older and a lot wiser.'

'Are you telling me I should attempt to come between them?'

'I'm not telling you what you should do, I'm just pointing out a few facts to you. She has a high opinion of you. That's a fact. You have a similar opinion of her. That's another fact. Her fiancé's a fool. And that's the most definite fact of all.'

Will shook his head. 'I can't just walk up and try to take her away from him. That choice has to be hers.'

'I agree. But she may not make that choice if she doesn't believe you're interested in her.' Then reflectively, 'Perhaps I should tell her.'

'Don't you dare.'

Sir Peter smiled, 'Then perhaps you should tell her.'

Margaret returned shortly afterwards and Sir Peter did not raise the subject again. But a number of times Will caught his eye and the older man's unspoken query could not have been more definitely pronounced.

As Will was leaving, Amanda and Granville were arriving.

Lieutenant Granville Meregreen, formerly of Petworth, Sussex, and now assistant quartermaster to the New South Wales Corps, was not quite the fool that some people were quick to call him. The fourth son of a fourth son of a minor baronet, he joined the corps after an evening at his club when someone at his table in the games room predicted that the war with France was about to restart and someone else suggested that fortunes were to be made in New South Wales. These two snippets of conversation coming hard on the heels of each other seemed too portentous to ignore. At the time he was looking down at the worst cards he had held in an evening memorable only for the number of useless hands that had been dealt to him.

When his research the following day indicated that there were few British possessions further from France than New South Wales, he immediately made preparations to enlist. His one regret in this matter was that he had already spent considerable time, energy and resources in courting Amanda Dalrymple, the most eligible belle within a day's ride in any direction of Petworth.

When he told Amanda of his plans, bracing himself for the outburst that would surely terminate their relationship, he was pleasantly surprised when she approved of his decision. And in support of the proposition that there was indeed a God, she told him of how her Uncle Peter had prospered in the colony and that he would be able to provide him with introductions, advice and cautions that would undoubtedly ensure his prosperity.

Now as he stepped down from his chaise-cart and helped Amanda to alight at Sir Peter's residence, he turned to see the one person who could threaten the advancement of his good fortune. Will Noling was standing in the doorway beside the old man's whore. He had hoped that by now the upstart bastard would have departed.

'Noling, how good to see you, old son. Just leaving? Pity. Would have enjoyed a good chinwag with someone who understands the blighters we have to deal with each day. Blank page to me. Can't tell by lookin' into their scrawny faces whether they're hatchin' to kiss me or kill me.'

He snorted when he suddenly became aware of his own unconscious wit and slapped the gloves he was carrying into the palm of his hand. 'Probably both, eh what? Many of them bein' former tars. You could tell us something about that. Not here though. Not in front of these lovely ladies. Not that either of you would know what he was talkin' about, eh, Mrs Wilson? And specially not you, Mandy, m'little rose petal. What's that look for? Only being silly old me. Only trying to cheer you up, lass. Good heavens, Noling, this little woman has some funny little ways, hasn't she? Should compare notes on her funny little ways some day. All right, all right, I know I'm being silly.'

He moved closer to Will and shrugged. 'It's the plaguey poor quality brandy we're forced to put in our flasks turns me into a bit of a silly bugger.' As he pulled a small hip-flask from his jacket he belched silently and Will caught a sharp blast of heat from his breath. Granville pulled out the stopper, and up-ending the flask, winked at Will. 'It gets a bit chilly out there on the headland. Been?'

Will shook his head.

'Great sight. But the wind goes straight through you. What you've got to take is some pleasant company to wrap around the outside of you, and some of what was in here . . .' He shook the flask and a few drops spilled out. 'But preferably of better quality, to slosh around the inside of you.'

'Amanda shouldn't be travelling as far as the headland,' said Margaret coldly, moving out and feeling Amanda's hands. 'What would happen if she caught a chill?'

Amanda turned to Will. 'Did you see the woman?'

'Aye.'

'And?'

'She wasn't much help. Barlester . . .' He glanced at Granville.

'Yes?' Amanda prompted.

'You'd better go in. It's getting cold.'

She detached her hand from Margaret's and moved closer to him. 'Come and see me tomorrow,' she said quietly. 'I'll be here.'

He did not go and see her the following day. That was the day he left for Newcastle. His decision may have been prompted by his running into the captain of the vessel he had approached earlier in the week to enquire about passage, and being offered a berth the following day. Or it may have been influenced by the hint on Amanda's breath, when she stepped close to him, of the same sharp smell of liquor that was on Granville's.

He was not averse to young ladies drinking alcoholic beverages from hip-flasks on a chilly day, or for that matter from any other appropriate container on chilly or pleasant days. So whether or not this incident was high on his list of reasons for leaving would be difficult to gauge.

A week after Will arrived in Newcastle, another vessel tied up in the river early in the morning and, with the accompaniment of endless relays of shrieking gulls, spent most of the forenoon discharging a cargo of people, and numerous crates, barrels and bales of assorted merchandise, into a small flotilla of longboats. Six horses, four of them heavy half-draught animals and the others leaner hacks, were also lowered over the side of the vessel and allowed to swim ashore where they were quickly rounded up by a group of men waiting for that purpose at the water's edge.

While some of the human cargo then assisted a small detachment of convicts to load the merchandise into two of three waiting drays, the remainder gathered in a ragged cluster beside the third.

A group of natives wandered across from a nearby campfire to watch. Their attention seemed to be mainly directed at the tall broad-shouldered man dressed in a high hat and frock-coat who was directing proceedings. When a thin black boy who stood no higher than the man's waist approached him and tugged on his coat, he stopped shouting orders and waving his arms about to look down at the intruder.

'Baccy?' cried the boy in a high-pitched voice that pulled the corners of his mouth back into a beaming smile that would have warmed the hearts of most people it was aimed at and obliterated the image of his spindly legs and bloated stomach. 'You got baccy, Master?'

'Get!' shouted the man, and knocked the youngster flying with a wild backhand swipe of his huge hand.

In the same instant the man's hat blew off and spiralled along the beach. The boy immediately sprang back to his feet and took off after it. The man stood watching him with his mane of white hair whipping around his face. The boy managed to grab the hat a moment before it would have skimmed out on to the water, and raced back across the sand to return it to its owner. The man snatched it from him and stood holding it by the brim.

'Baccy?' repeated the boy, holding out an upturned palm. Drops from a thin web of blood clinging to his chin fell to the sand between his feet.

All those who had witnessed these events paused to watch. Even the gulls chose that moment to stop their shrieking.

The man lowered his face towards the boy. With his mane pressed back around his ears and his aquiline visage finely slicing the wind, he could have been a giant osprey bending to tear the flesh from a fish clutched in its talons.

'Get out of here, you heathen brat,' he spat with a venom that stung the eyes of all who looked on. 'Get out of here before I kick your black arse clear across the fucking river.'

By the time he mounted one of the hacks that had been saddled for him, and he and those in his charge finally departed—some on horseback and the remainder in the third dray—most of the blacks had drifted away. Of the few who stayed, a woman, taller than the others and of more striking appearance, remained watching until the drays were out of sight. Then, gathering up a few possessions that were scattered around the campfire, she hurried after them, moving close to the edge of the road and scampering into the undergrowth whenever she believed she was in danger of being seen.

That evening she sat huddled in dense brush a good way from where the newcomers had camped. Throughout the night her entire body was racked by irregular waves of violent trembling and her mind was filled with a confusion of shouts and screams and dancing devils. Only immediately following periods when she lay sprawled on the ground dry-retching did she experience some relief.

When the sun finally rose, she sat for a long time fighting an almost overwhelming urge to return to more comfortable surrounds. But a distant shout from the man she had seen the previous day brought her to her feet, and when she began to move again, it was to continue her cautious pursuit.

Later that morning she managed to run down and kill a red-bellied black snake that the warmth of the sun had not by then given the speed to avoid her. She ate its flesh raw while crouching in the undergrowth overlooking a creek and waiting for the drays to crawl up the sharp incline on the other side.

Twice during the following days she turned away and retraced her steps. But each time she travelled no more than a short walk before she turned back again and hurried after her quarry for fear that they might somehow elude her. This was unlikely. Although there was no clearly defined road, where the terrain was flat or sloped only gently, the dray wheels cut grooves into the soft earth. And along most of the steeper and more stony slopes, a deep furrow had been cut to guide the high-side wheels and prevent the drays from toppling.

The whites were fortunate, she decided, that the local clans had been regularly firing the forest. The trees were well spaced and allowed ample room for the drays to pass between them. Only on few occasions did she hear the sound of an axe. But several times she heard the thunder of a gun and once she saw black hunters scurrying for cover through the nearby undergrowth.

The whites were finally forced to abandon the drays on the eastern bank of a wide stream that cut their path from the south. She then followed the travellers for a further ten days while they continued their journey on foot. If she had been asked why she was trailing them she would probably have had difficulty replying with any certainty, other than to acknowledge that she was Coranga, wife of Gunroi, and that the two truths which had confronted her on the waterside at the white men's camp were beyond dispute. They were in fact so remarkable they could have been nothing less than a message to her from Biamie Himself.

The first was that the woman with the crown of fiery red hair, who stumbled across the sand with her hands and feet locked in the white man's chains, was Jessica. The second was that the moment her own eyes took in Garth Barlester's fierce countenance, with his shock of white hair blowing straight back from his high-domed forehead and his piercing eyes astride the long hooked prominence of his nose, she knew she was looking at Gunroi's great white eagle. Of this she was certain. Many times she had shaken a trembling Gunroi awake when he was in the grip of one of his nightmares. And whether or not the creature he described had anything to do with Jessica's capture, it was certainly the one that now held her firmly and viciously within its grasp.

So, when they finally reached their destination, Coranga remained for several days observing the dwelling where the creature had deposited Jessica. Along with lesser buildings, it nestled beneath a heavily timbered spur that stretched out towards the coast from the great hills on the north-western horizon. All the dwellings had the pleasant smell of freshly sliced timber, aromas that on the day she arrived wakened within her some of her more comforting memories of the white men's camp. For a time her head was turned to the south-east.

When she was convinced that the newcomers were intending to stay, she took careful note of the rock formations that topped the highest nearby ridges and then set out along the steep spur that climbed away to the north-west. She had no doubt that these were the same hills that Gunroi spoke of when he decided to return to their homeland.

TWENTY-TWO

Margaret Wilson looked up from her book as the door opened and Amanda Dalrymple entered the room. Margaret glanced across at the large marble-encased clock on the mantelpiece. 'I thought I heard a carriage. Did the dinner finish early?'

'I'm not sure the dinner has finished,' Amanda replied, stripping off her gloves as she walked across the room and flopped into a vacant easy-chair beside where her uncle was sleeping in another with a copy of the *Sydney Gazette* news-sheet spread across his lap. 'But I am sure that Granville and I are finished. Finished, finally!'

'What?' Sir Peter awoke with a jolt. His paper slipped to the floor.

'What happened?' Margaret asked. 'What's he done now?'

Amanda allowed her shoulders to rise high and flop back down in a gesture that, despite its theatrical appearance, was charged with genuine exasperation. 'Nothing much different from what he's been doing ever since I arrived. I can't believe he was like this back home. If he was, I must have been blind or stupid. Probably both.'

'What's going on?' Sir Peter demanded. 'What's happened?'

'I've broken off my engagement.'

'You have?'

'I told him I never wanted to see him again. And I told him I wouldn't marry him if he were the last person on earth.'

Sir Peter cleared his throat. 'Well, he could accuse you of not being particularly original, m'dear, but he could hardly accuse you of beating about the bush. What did the blighter do? Don't tell me I have to polish up my pistols, or sharpen my sabre?'

Amanda shook her head and smiled weakly. 'Of course not. He hasn't done much more than be his boorish self.' She raised a trembling hand to her cheek. 'How could I have been so stupid?'

Margaret came out of her chair. 'You poor dear. I'll pour you a brandy.' She moved towards a cedar cabinet at the end of the room.

'And that's not all,' said Amanda. 'It doesn't even come close to the most important thing that occurred this evening.'

'What on earth could be more important than breaking off your engagement?' Sir Peter leaned towards her. Margaret turned back from the cabinet.

605

'I overheard Granville and some others laughing and chortling and acting absolutely beastly over something one of their acquaintances was doing. When I had the chance, I asked him what was amusing everybody and he told me that when this man's convicts were due to be released and he wanted to retain them, he would haul them before a magistrate on false charges and have them punished so their rights to a ticket of leave for good behaviour would be rescinded. By continuing to do this he could keep them for as long as he wanted. Can you believe that? He'd have them flogged when they were completely innocent of any wrongdoing, just so he could prevent them from being released.'

Her face creased in disgust and she shuddered. 'Granville then went on to say that this was how the man intended to keep his current favourite, a pretty red-haired woman whom he had assigned to him.'

'Barlester?' said Sir Peter. 'You're talking about Garth Barlester, aren't you?'

'Yes, Garth Barlester.'

'But that couldn't be the same woman Will saw,' said Margaret. 'Not from how he described her.'

'No,' Amanda agreed, 'but on a whim or ...' she shook her head. '... a moment of stupidity perhaps—considering the implications—I asked Granville if the woman was the one who escaped and was later shipwrecked and recaptured. And he said it was.' She raised both hands and placed the tips of her fingers against her cheeks, and in little more than a whisper, repeated, 'It was.'

'So Barlester tricked Will,' said Margaret, walking back empty-handed from the cabinet. 'According to him, the woman he saw certainly wasn't a red-haired beauty. So she couldn't have been Elizabeth Crowling.'

Sir Peter ran a spread thumb and forefinger down his jaw. 'What do you mean when you said, "a moment of stupidity, considering the implications"?'

Now Amanda leaned towards him. 'Why would Barlester hide the real Elizabeth Crowling from Will?'

Margaret cocked her head on one side. 'Because the real Elizabeth Crowling might have told him something Barlester didn't want him to know? Is that what you're saying?'

'Perhaps. But if Barlester could force one woman to tell Will what he wanted her to say, why couldn't he have forced the real Elizabeth Crowling to do the same?'

'Because she refused to comply,' offered Sir Peter.

Amanda shook her head. 'Not from what I gather this Barlester is capable of.'

'So what are you saying?' he asked.

'Perhaps he didn't want Will to see her because he would have known immediately who she really was, and was not Elizabeth Crowling.'

'Not Elizabeth Crowling? I thought we'd just

agreed she was, and the woman Will saw was the impostor.' Sir Peter shook his head. 'Are you saying we have two impostors?'

'Yes.'

'I'm becoming very confused. Why would he know who this one really was?'

'Because this one is really his sweetheart,' said Margaret in a rush, her eyes wide and her mouth remaining open for a moment in astonishment. 'Oh my God!'

'Yes,' Amanda nodded and showed her teeth in what might have been a painful grimace. 'The description fits. And I can think of no other explanation.'

'No other explanation!' Sir Peter threw both hands up in exasperation. 'There must be a thousand other explanations. Really, you women can be so ... so ... fanciful.'

'Name one other explanation,' demanded Margaret.

'I can't look into the mind of someone like Bar-lester. Perhaps this woman was bruised or injured, and he didn't want the constable to see her.'

'That's a possibility,' Amanda conceded. 'So I'm going out there to see if I can find out for certain. I'm going to ask to speak to Elizabeth Crowling.'

'You can't do that,' said Margaret. 'You can't go near that fiend.'

'Actually, he's not there,' said Sir Peter.

Both women looked at him.

'He left for his property on the Hunter River a

608

month ago.' He smiled at his niece. 'I've been making enquiries of my own. And he took Elizabeth Crowling—or whoever she is—with him.'

'Then it will be safe to go out to his place,' said Amanda 'Someone there should have some answers.'

'Perhaps,' said he. 'If anyone's prepared to talk.'

'They might be more prepared now than when he's around.'

'I'd wager that's true. But you can't go unless you take a constable with you.'

'And me,' said Margaret. She turned and stared down Sir Peter's frown. 'The more strength in numbers we have the better. And you know you're still not well enough to go yourself. Besides, I wouldn't miss this for anything.'

Shortly afterwards Margaret returned to the cabinet and poured three brandies. When she brought them back Amanda told them that it was while she was watching Granville's giggling endorsement of what Barlester was doing she realised she could never marry him.

Sir Peter then looked at her closely and said, 'And from what you said, you obviously know that if you're right about all of this, having just broken off your engagement to one man, you're now taking steps that could lose you another? You're timing isn't very good, m'dear.'

Again she showed her teeth in what might have been a sign of pain. 'Haven't I already lost him? He's been gone for nearly six weeks.' A tear threatened to spill from one eye and she quickly tried to brush it aside before the others noticed. 'But I have to follow this up. I owe him that.' She reflected on this for a moment. 'I owe him more.'

'We all owe him,' said Margaret.

'Amen to that,' endorsed Sir Peter.

Will saw them coming half an hour before they arrived. He was laying hardwood shingles on the roof of his partly constructed homestead when he noticed the sun flash on something moving on a ridge to the south. Shortly afterwards he saw three riders crossing a distant clearing close to the river.

He climbed down a ladder from the roof and picking out two heavy pick-handles from a collection of implements stacked beneath a broad sheet of stringybark, he carried them to where two men were constructing a stone chimney at one end of the building. Placing the handles close by, he spoke to the men briefly and then walked back and picked up a musket that was propped near a doorway leading off a partially completed verandah. After checking the priming of the weapon, he placed it out of sight behind an upright near the base of the ladder. The three of them then resumed what they had been doing before the interruption.

When the three riders emerged from a copse of casuarinas bordering the river and made their way up the slope towards the homestead, Will again descended from the roof and remained standing beside the upright behind which the musket was propped, even though by then it was obvious that two of the newcomers were soldiers.

He was pondering what was different about the third rider when he suddenly realised that not only was he looking at a woman, but that woman was Amanda Dalrymple.

The soldiers declined Will's invitation to shelter for the evening, the corporal in charge stating that his orders were simply to escort Miss Dalrymple to the homestead, and once he was satisfied she was in safe hands they were to return to Newcastle. A chisel-faced northerner from the outskirts of that other Newcastle, he gripped Will with what was obviously a well-practised scowl and cautioned that Miss Dalrymple had better be in safe hands. 'Because if I hears different, I'll come back and have a chat with ye that ye might take some time recoverin' from. D'ye catch me drift, lad?'

Will assured him he did and declared that Miss Dalrymple could not have been in safer hands. Amanda supported this, telling the man that her welfare had recently been entrusted to Will for an extended period and that his conduct then had been nothing short of exemplary.

Although the term 'exemplary' was not in this Geordie's vocabulary, he was reasonably satisfied he could leave with a clear conscience. This may not have been the case had he noticed that the look Amanda directed at Will was not quite in keeping with the solemnity of her assurance.

After they all shared a pot of tea, the soldiers departed and the two workmen returned to their rock-laying. Will led Amanda's horse to a make-shift barn that stood beside an area of about three acres enclosed by split-rail fencing. A number of domestic fowls scurried out of their way as they crossed to the yard. Two other horses, one a part-draught animal, watched them as they approached.

'Are those men convicts?' she asked as he unsaddled her horse.

'No, they're both ticket-of-leave men. I pay them in provisions from the garrison store. Why?'

'Just curious. Is that a cow I can see down by the river?'

'There should be three cows with calves down there somewhere. Milkers. I do like a drop of milk in my tea.'

'You're looking after yourself very well, considering the short time you've been here. Cows, hens, horses. The makings of a vegetable garden. How long is it now that you've been here?'

'About two months.'

'Two months,' she repeated in a tone that some may have believed was neutral, but which caused Will to cast her a suspicious glance. 'It seems shorter.'

When he would not rise to what he suspected was a bait, she added, 'Some said you left abruptly. Surprised them. No word that you were going.'

'The berth came up suddenly.'

'I see you have no pigs. Thought you would have pigs.'

'No. No pigs. As much as I like a piece of bacon now and then, I don't like it enough to put up with the smell of pigs.'

He released her horse within the fenced area and placed the saddle and bridle in the barn. The other horses came closer and all three spent some time warily checking each other over, until Amanda's horse suddenly bared its teeth at the part-draught animal and the three of them then pranced around for a time with their ears flattened and their necks bowed in a mainly theatrical display that soon abated.

As the animals lowered their heads and began to graze, Amanda turned to Will. 'I have something important to tell you.'

He held up a flattened hand. 'Tell me later. It's too pleasant out here at the moment for matters of import. First let me show you around.'

He directed her back to the building where he collected his musket. 'We might see a kangaroo,' he explained as he led her down the slope towards the river. 'You know where we are, of course?'

'Of course.' As she followed him her gaze made a complete sweep of their surroundings, pausing as it alighted on familiar features.

He was right. It was a pleasant day. The river could have been a marble path, a smooth mosaic of mottled blues and pinks and gleaming patches of white. The afternoon sun streaming through the trees on the opposite ridge and further along the slope beside them carved contrasting lumps, bundles and undulations in the foliage; deep greens and greys, with the divisions emphasised in places as if an artist had outlined them with a delicate edging of charcoal here, a broader sweep there, a smudge, a dappled shadow. In places the outer foliage of the trees was highlighted in a sheen that when touched by the breeze rippled like the beating of wings of swarms of silver moths. The air was clean, spiked by the gentlest hint of eucalyptus.

They walked out on to the riverbank. Will pointed to a distant rocky beach. 'Down there is where we skipped stones. And over here, beyond that grassy area, is where we encountered the blacks.'

They moved to where a driftwood log was partly buried in the bank and he rested the musket against it. The breeze was mainly absent here and on the occasions it did brush over them, its breath was warm.

He sat on the log and Amanda leant back against where part of it arched away from the ground.

She pulled a handkerchief from her sleeve and patted her neck. 'Suddenly I feel very overdressed.' She reached down and shook the folds of her heavily pleated riding dress to trap air beneath it. 'Ridiculously overdressed on a day like this.' There was more anger in her tone than complaint. 'This frock is crushing me.'

'That's your body reminding you that you were more suitably dressed last time you were here. Why don't you take your dress off?'

'Don't be silly.' She glanced back towards the house.

'They can't see us from back there,' said he.

'I don't care if they can or not. I'm not taking off my dress.'

'But you would like to. Otherwise why would you check to see if they could see?'

'I didn't.'

'Yes you did. Involuntarily perhaps. Your body taking charge again. It knows more about what you really want than you care to admit.'

'Splosh!'

'Splosh?'

'You don't know what you're talking about!'

'I think I do.' He rose and stepped towards her. 'For instance, I'm thinking that the only reason you're hesitating from removing your dress is because we haven't seen each other for a while and you're feeling a bit shy. I also think that after your journey you could probably think of nothing better than having a nice refreshing swim to rejuvenate you. Am I right?'

'No.'

'Here, perhaps this will help to relax you.' He stepped closer still, and placing a hand gently against her cheek, leaned forward and kissed her.

'Am I right?' he repeated as he drew back.

Her expression softened as he watched her,

reflecting a discernible easing of tension throughout her entire frame. 'I have something very important to tell you,' she said softly.

'Later,' said he, kissing her again. 'Your dress is killing you. Take it off.'

She matched his gaze for a moment and then sighed deeply and glanced back up the slope. 'Are you sure they can't see?'

'They can't see.'

She loosened some ties at her waist and pulled the dress over her head. He helped her fold it over a branch that projected from the log.'

'Doesn't that feel better?'

'It does. I must admit. It feels a lot better.'

He nodded to her camisole and petticoat. 'If we're going for a swim you'd better take those off as well.'

She looked at him steadily. 'You're a rogue, Will Noling.'

'No I'm not. I've been pardoned.'

'Not by me.'

He stepped close to her and kissed her again. She kissed him back. He took her in his arms then and lowered her to the turf.

'Will, we can't,' she whispered as he released the fabric that covered one of her breasts and lowered his head to kiss the nipple. 'We can't,' she repeated with more vigour as his hand slipped between her thighs. 'I must tell you why I'm here.' He silenced her with his lips.

When his fingers invaded her, she suddenly

struggled and broke her lips away from his. 'Jessica's alive, Will. She's alive.'

He pulled away. 'What?'

'She's alive. She didn't die in the shipwreck.' Extracting herself from beneath him, she sat up and closed the gaps in her underclothing.

He, too, sat up, his eyes wide. 'Tell me.'

So she told him; first of how her suspicions were raised and then how she and Margaret had spoken to the woman who had pretended to be Elizabeth Crowling.

'For a time she wouldn't tell us anything. And then she would only admit that she was not the real Elizabeth Crowling. But when Margaret asked her if Barlester had taken the real Jessica with him to the Hunter—Margaret actually called her "Jessica" not "Elizabeth"—the woman said, "Yes". As soon as we pointed out what she had just admitted to, she tried to cover up, but then broke down and told us everything. She was frightened of what the constable might do to her.'

'Where on the Hunter?'

'North-west of here. I have a crude map back in my things.'

'Why didn't you tell me all this when you arrived?'

'I couldn't just blurt it out in front of everyone. Particularly not the soldiers. They might know Barlester. And then when I tried to tell you, you wouldn't let me.'

'I thought you'd come to tell me that the date

of your wedding had been fixed. I suspected you were looking for me to give you some kind of absolution. Before you said anything I wanted the chance to persuade you that you were making a mistake.'

'Is that what this was all about?' She waved a hand between them. 'Persuading me I was making a mistake. What were you going to offer in return, Will Noling? Were you going to offer to make an honest woman of me?'

'Yes, I was.'

'And now?'

They watched each other. He reached out and placed the palm of his hand against her cheek and for a moment it appeared he was going to kiss her again. Instead, he withdrew his hand and turned his gaze to the north-west. 'Now I know she's alive, I must go to her.' He stood up. 'Immediately.'

'It's too late in the day to set off. We wouldn't get three miles before it was too dark to travel. We should have a good night's rest here and go first thing in the morning.'

'Yes,' he agreed absently, looking across at the sun. 'You're right.' And then realising all she had said, turned back and looked down at her. 'What do you mean we? You can't come. It's far too dangerous. You don't know this man. He's a devil.'

'I didn't come all this way to go back now. Of course I'm coming.'

'You're not.'

'I am if you want to see that map.'

'Map? I didn't know the upper valley had been surveyed.'

'It hasn't been. Leastways not officially, according to the commandant. It's a sketch he made from some charts drawn up by officers from the garrison that show outlying farms and timber camps. You'll certainly need it if you don't want to get lost.'

'If you don't give it to me I'll search your things and find it.'

She stood up and matched his gaze with a fierce glare. 'Then I'll charge you with theft.'

'I could take that hack you borrowed from the commandant with me.'

'Then I'll walk.'

On the first day that Gunroi and Nunderri moved close enough to Barlester's homestead to observe its occupants, they were given a comprehensive introduction to the man himself. A number of times they watched him striding purposefully to or from one of the outbuildings with his shoulders thrown back, his white hair whipping behind him and his aquiline features thrust forward threateningly.

Early in the day they saw him as he inspected a group of men armed with axes. Afterwards, on the slopes directly adjacent to the river, they watched him overseeing these men felling trees. Later in the day they watched him berating another group of men who were digging a large trench close to the homestead and several times they saw him slash at one man or another with a whip when the offender was apparently not doing as he had been directed.

Although Gunroi was not completely aware of the significance of all these activities he had no doubt whatsoever that here was his eagle and it was a creature that cut as fearful a swathe through its world as he had ever imagined it would.

It was not until dusk that they first saw Jessica. With Barlester watching from the verandah, they saw her emerge from the back of the house carrying a wooden bucket and walk down to the bank of the river where she sat for a time bathing her feet. When she had finished she filled the bucket with water and made her way back to the house.

When they returned to their camp on the hillside behind the homestead, they told Coranga of what they had seen. The following evening they watched for Jessica again. As on the previous day, just before dusk, and with Barlester again watching from the verandah, she emerged from the house and returned to the stream to bathe. That night they sharpened and oiled their spears.

Before dawn the following day, armed with a woomera and two spears each, they made their way to the river directly beneath the house and hid themselves in a dense clump of young casuarinas.

That evening they watched Jessica emerge from the house as on the previous occasions and walk down the hill towards them. When Barlester moved out on to the verandah behind her they ducked low and pressed their bodies against where the soft turf and clumps of marsh grasses were interlaced with the tangled roots of the trees.

She sat down on the bank opposite them and, placing her bucket beside her, hoisted up her skirts and placed her feet into the stream.

Only then did Gunroi raise his head again. 'Over here,' he whispered. 'Over here.'

She turned her head to one side, suspecting that either the stream or the undulating song of the cicadas on the hillside opposite was playing tricks with her hearing.

'Over here,' he called out again and raised his head a little higher. When he saw that he was completely hidden from Barlester's view by the casuarinas immediately in front of him, he came to his knees.

She saw him then and her mouth dropped open in a frozen gasp. She was looking at a ghost. A phantom. She had seen him killed!

He beckoned her with an outstretched hand. 'Quickly, come across the river.'

'Gunroi?' she whispered, still not trusting her eyes. Then she saw Nunderri rise to his knees behind his brother. 'Oh my God!' she whispered, and raised a hand to her mouth.

'Come on,' Gunroi urged, leaning towards her.

'No, don't,' she warned him in a mix of English and frantic hand language. She glanced back over her shoulder. 'He'll kill you. Oh my God!'

Barlester had walked to the end of the verandah and was moving his head slowly from side to side as he strained to see what was happening. 'I think he can see you. Get back. Get out of here.' She began to tremble. 'Please. Please. Don't come any closer. He will see you. Oh no!'

Instead of retreating, Gunroi stood up and was moving away from the bushes. She again glanced back over her shoulder and saw Barlester disappearing into the house.

She spun around and screamed, 'Gunroi! Quickly! Run! He's gone for a gun. He'll kill you. Run!'

Gunroi now broke completely from cover and stepping into the stream strode towards her. She turned to see Barlester re-emerge from the house wielding a musket in one hand and what must have been his twin-barrelled horse pistol in the other. As she watched, he dashed down the steps and ran towards them.

'Stay where you are,' he shouted. 'Don't move or I'll shoot.'

Gunroi slipped a spear into his woomera and danced to one side, trying to see past her. But she moved to stay between him and Barlester.

'You're in the way,' Gunroi shouted, waving his spear up and down in frustration.

Barlester was less than twenty paces away when

Nunderri stepped out from cover and hurled his spear.

Jessica ducked as it whistled past her shoulder and struck something with a solid thump behind her. She turned to see Barlester slump to the ground with the spear embedded high in one thigh.

Nunderri then leapt into the stream and, slipping a second spear into his woomera, splashed through the shallow water and clambered on to the bank beside her. Gunroi leapt out of the stream on the other side of her as Barlester's pistol thundered.

Jessica gasped as the ball slammed into Nunderri's chest and knocked him back into the water. She turned to see Barlester drop the pistol and raise his musket as Gunroi raced past her and hurled his spear.

Her scream was lost in the roar of the musket. The ball struck Gunroi's woomera, punching the weapon back into his shoulder and knocking him to the ground. The ball gouged a sliver of wood from the weapon and nicked the flesh at the base of Gunroi's neck before thumping into the opposite bank. His spear struck Barlester in the groin.

Shouting with pain and rage, Barlester grabbed his pistol from the ground beside him and tried to level it on Gunroi as the black man rolled from side to side while trying to fit a second spear into his damaged woomera.

Jessica screamed again and, snatching up the

heavy wooden bucket from the bank beside her, raced at Barlester. As his finger tightened on the trigger she knocked the pistol out of his hand with one wild swipe of the bucket and then brought it back again in another swinging arc that connected with the side of his head and knocked him back on to the ground. Gunroi in the meantime had abandoned his woomera and lurched to his feet with the support of the spear. He brushed past Jessica and plunged the blade deep into Barlester's chest.

Barlester was not done. Grasping the blade with both hands he released a succession of mighty roars as he tried to pull it out. Blood streamed from his palms as they were pierced by the barbs. Gunroi and Jessica drew away from him, not so much in fear perhaps as to avoid his wildly threshing legs.

But there was certainly fear in both of their startled faces when, with a supreme effort, he rose slowly to his feet. Then, releasing his mightiest roar yet, he wrenched the blade free and stood swaying in front of them. Then, with a triumphant leer he grasped the shaft of the spear and turned the blade around to bear on them.

With two spears still embedded in his groin, his trousers gleaming crimson from his crotch to his leggings and blood running freely from his hands and dripping from every splintered barb of the spear he aimed at them, he could have been the manifestation of some terrible nightmare: a relentless, indestructible, slavering beast hell-bent on their destruction.

But as they backed further away from him, the expression on his face froze as if his flesh was slowly turning to marble. Then, like a great tree beginning to topple, he fell backwards and struck the turf with a resounding thud.

Gunroi swung away from him and leapt into the stream to gather Nunderri in his arms.

On the hillside behind the house, Coranga was making her way cautiously down the slope carrying a bundle of spears when she heard Gunroi's wild cry as he crushed the lifeless body of his brother against his chest. Only once before had she heard a release of such frustrated anger and despair. And that had been Nunderri's own cry over the body of Mori. Whimpering with anxiety she quickened her pace.

Jessica helped Gunroi carry his brother from the stream and place him on the bank. Gunroi then checked to make sure that Barlester was dead. He was. But even so, the black man was not satisfied. Shouting in anger and grief he retrieved his spear and thrust it back into the dead man's chest. He then grabbed Nunderri's second spear and plunged it into his enemy's belly.

None of Barlester's convicts or servants was witness to these final events. They had believed they were under attack from an entire tribe of blacks and by then they were streaming to the south-east in scattered groups, most of them whimpering in fear. From well before Barlester's guns had grown silent and they heard him shouting in his death throes, they had abandoned the homestead and the surrounding buildings and had run for their lives. None of them was prepared to risk returning to assist him.

By the time Coranga reached the homestead and crept out of the shadows to join Jessica, Gunroi had already embarked on a grief-fired rampage. Entering each of the buildings in turn he scattered burning coals into piles of bedding, furniture and bundles of straw. In a short time all the structures were converted into roaring furnaces that painted a ferocious red glow against the backdrop of the mountains.

Armed with garbled reports from the escaping stragglers of what had happened, Will and Amanda expected the worst when they reached the homestead the following day. They found that the entire area including the neighbouring hills had been devastated by the fire. Bundles of smoke still hung about the river, and the smouldering remains of logs and tree trunks hissed and spat at them as they passed by.

The raucous clamour of a flock of crows led them to Barlester's body. 'Yes, it's him,' Will called out to confirm the discovery to Amanda, who stayed some distance away holding the horses.

Will stood up and released his breath as his gaze

scoured the nearby banks of the river. 'And no sign of anyone else, thank God,' he whispered. Suddenly he doubled over and a rush of vomit speared from his throat.

When he rejoined Amanda some minutes later she gave him a sympathetic grimace, 'Pretty terrible, I suppose?'

'Pretty terrible,' he confirmed. He did not try to explain that it wasn't the sight of Barlester's body that had caused his reaction. It was the overwhelming sense of relief that Jessica was not the one lying there, with empty eye-sockets staring at the circling crows.

He released one hand from the musket he was carrying and flexed his cramped fingers. Too tight, the twinges told him. Relax. Breathe deeply. You must remain alert.

'Look!' Amanda cried out, raising her arm shoulder-high and pointing beyond the charred remains of one of the outbuildings.

On a distant hillside, three small figures could be seen moving up the slope in single file. Two of them were almost as dark as their surrounds. But the third was pale, contrasting with the blackened spur like a flickering beacon against a darkened sky.

Will and Amanda caught up with the others shortly after they passed out of the fire-scorched area. As they rode their horses over a low rise that sloped away to a shallow stream, they saw the three of them waiting on the opposite bank. The man stood with his feet spread and braced for action resting a spear and woomera on his shoulder. Two women stood on either side and a little behind him. One was black, the other white.

Will turned and spoke to Amanda and then urged his horse to move down the slope towards them. When he realised she was still following closely he reined to a halt and turned to her again.

'Please, Amanda. Stay back.'

'I didn't come this far to stay back.'

'For God's sake, I don't know what might happen here.'

'Well, for my sake let's find out before I or this poor horse drops dead from exhaustion.'

He shook his head resignedly and then the two of them rode on down towards the creek.

He must know I'm injured, Gunroi decided as he watched Will approach and wondered if he should change his spear to his other hand. Sometimes he had tested his throwing skill with his left hand, but never with much success, and never while hunting. Certainly never in a situation as dangerous as this one. The white man was not aiming his musket at him at the moment but he had no doubt that he might do so in an instant. Curiously, he realised, he felt no apprehension that this man would kill him. His only concern was that he might try to take Jessica away and he wondered if this was Biamie's intention. The man was clearly from her clan as he had suspected when he had first seen him some months before. And his presence here now confirmed this. He could be her husband. Perhaps even her brother.

The Great God works in mysterious ways. This he conceded. And perhaps his own role in these happenings had concluded with his killing of the eagle. Perhaps that was Biamie's intention from the start. To have him kill this terrible creature or be killed by him. And during the journey that brought them to this final confrontation, to show him wondrous things that revealed the folly of his disbelief. Namulami, the birth stone. And the Namulami bora ground. So sacred his chest cramped at the thought of them and what had happened there. Places so sacred he was unable to discuss them with anyone other than old Gaidimi himself and only two of the elders.

He rolled his wrist from side to side and lifted his spear to ease the tension in his hand and the cramping of his injured shoulder.

You gave me the most wondrous gift of all, Great Biamie, he declared silently. To ensure I did not become lost you gave me this god-woman with the golden hair. To show me the sacred places and bring the eagle to me. For the sins of my earlier disbelief she was taken from me for a time. And Nunderri paid with his life. But please, Biamie, he prayed, don't let her be taken from me again. My grief is too great now to bear another loss. My stomach is already tied in knots. Forgive me if it is your desire that she be taken away again, but I will fight to keep her. And I will try to kill this man if I must. If this means I will die, then so be it. But I can't let him take her without trying to stop him. I couldn't bear losing her again.

The man and the woman were now less than twenty paces away.

'Hullo, Jessica,' Will called out as his horse lowered its head and pulled its way to where it could drink from the cool stream. Beside him Amanda's horse did the same. Diverging waves streamed away from their crinkled muzzles.

Jessica had watched him approach but now as he sat there so close to her, she could not bring herself to meet his gaze. Instead she stood looking past his shoulder at the skyline behind him.

She was leaner than he remembered, Will decided, which was understandable. And although she was smeared with dust and soot, bathed as she was in the afternoon sun, she presented a magnificent spectacle. With her feet spread wide and planted firmly in the dust and her golden-red mane brushing the nape of her neck, she glowed with a beauty that caused his breath to catch in his throat.

She was completely naked and someone had painted a vertical stripe down each of her cheeks and across her breasts to her lower abdomen, one yellow one red. Was it her finger, or this man's that had put them there, he wondered. A hollow discomfort affirmed its presence in the pit of his stomach.

'Jessica, I've come to take you back with me. Back where you'll be safe.'

Still she did not move or make any sign she had heard him.

Gunroi and Coranga exchanged some words and Will looked across at the tall black man. 'Please tell this man I have no quarrel with him and that I mean him no harm. I know him and he knows me. We met where I'm now building my house.'

Jessica turned and looked at Will as Coranga again spoke to Gunroi. Jessica turned to Coranga and exchanged some words with her. When the black woman spoke to Gunroi again, he seemed to relax a little but did not lower his spear from his shoulder.

'You must come back with me, Jessie,' said Will.

Her gaze returned to him. 'You're building a house?'

'Yes.'

'Here, in this country?'

'Yes. Not all that far from where we are now.'

She remained looking at him without speaking for a time. 'I'm so pleased you're alive, Will,' she said at last. 'I'm so pleased the French didn't kill you.'

'I'm pleased you're alive too, Jessie. They told me you were dead.'

'I was.' She looked at Gunroi for a moment. When she turned back she said, 'I can't go back with you.'

'You can. You have nothing to fear back there any more. You've been pardoned.'

'Pardoned?'

'Yes. The governor knows Fitzparsons for the liar that he is.'

'I can't go back. Not back there. Not ever.'

'But you can. The Governor's given you your freedom.'

She turned away and for some time stared at the hills in the distance. His gaze touched the scars on her ankles and wrists and the white ridges across her back.

He's given you your freedom, he thought, but he can't give you back the years that were stolen from you. Or your missing flesh. And he can't give you back whatever has been taken that I can't see.

As if she perhaps had read his mind, she said, 'He can't give me back my self-respect. He can't give me back what that devil stole time and time again.'

'Jessie!' Tears suddenly sprang to his eyes and as they threatened to spill he pushed them away roughly with abrupt sweeps of the palm of one hand. 'Jessie, your wounds will heal in time. You must come back with me.'

'I can't.' She again glanced at Gunroi. 'I . . .' She shook her head and stared back at the distant hills. 'I can't.'

'Tell me this isn't your final decision. Tell me you'll consider what I'm asking.'

'It is. It is my final decision.'

He, too, then looked away abruptly. When he turned back he said, 'Please promise me if you ever need me, you'll send word. He knows where I'll be. Tell him it's where we met near Newcastle. Will you do that?'

Coranga then spoke and Jessica turned and exchanged some more words with her.

'Does she understand what I'm saying?'

'Some of it, apparently.' She spoke to Coranga again. 'Yes. She understands you are building a house where you saw Gunroi.'

'Tell them that if you ever fall sick, or ever decide to leave, he must bring you there.'

'I won't. Fall sick, I mean. Or decide to leave.'

'You might. I won't let you go until you promise.'

She smiled. 'I promise.'

They watched each other.

'Can I come over there and hold you for a moment?'

For a time she made no sign that she had heard. Then she said, 'Perhaps it's best that you don't.'

'You'll be cold,' he said at last. 'At times. Too cold.'

'I'll have been colder. Many times.'

'And at times you'll be lonely.'

'I'll have been lonelier.'

'Jessie, Jessie.' He shook his head. And then recovering, 'Can I trust him to take care of you?'

'Yes.'

'As well as I would?'

She bit her bottom lip as she watched him, and nodded, but did not risk trying to speak. After some time she turned her gaze to Amanda. 'Who is this?' she asked softly.

'This is Amanda.'

'Is she a close friend?'

Will glanced at Amanda for a moment and then turned back. 'Yes, a close friend. When I thought you were dead, it was Amanda who discovered you weren't and told me where I could find you.'

'Will you take care of him, Amanda?'

Amanda smiled. 'If he'll let me.'

'As well as I would?'

'If he'll let me.'

Will looked across at Gunroi. 'What did you call your friend before?'

'Gunroi.'

'You take good care of her, Gunroi. Or I'll come and take her away from you.' He looked back at her. 'Tell him that. And tell him I mean it.'

She smiled. 'I'll tell him. When I can.' Her gaze stayed with him again for a time. Then she said, 'We must go.' She began to turn away. Then, as if on impulse, she turned back and waded across the stream towards him. Clucking softly to steady his horse as it lifted its head to watch her warily, she took hold of the bridle with one hand and motioned to him with the other. 'Lean down,' she said softly. And as he did, she reached up and placed the palm of her hand firmly against his jaw.

He in turn reached down and cupped his hand against her cheek.

'Come back, Jessie,' he whispered.

'Maybe one day,' she replied, and then turned away and re-crossed the stream. As she continued to walk up the slope away from them, Coranga turned and followed her. Gunroi walked backwards for a few strides, his gaze still locked on Will, before he too turned and moved quickly after the others.

Will and Amanda stayed watching until well after the others had entered the forest. From time to time they both believed they caught sight of Jessica's pale form moving between the trees. But afterwards they were unsure if what they had been watching was not merely the irregular beat of the bush itself. A bird alighting here. A butterfly rising there. The breeze trying to escape from a bundle of leaves. A white moth spiralling at the end of a strand of a spider's web.

When a flock of gaily coloured parrots exploded like fireworks from the dark understorey and hurtled past them to disappear beyond the ridge, they were suddenly gripped by an intoxicating sense that there was no clear division here—or perhaps anywhere else—between what was real and what was illusion: of where substance ended and the dream began.